MISCHIEF AT MARSDEN MANOR

PIPPA DARLING MYSTERIES
BOOK 6

JENNA BENNETT

England, September 1926

An engagement party at venerable Marsden Manor serves up annoyances big and small for Bright Young Thing Philippa Darling and her cousins, Christopher and Francis Astley.

There's the scheming Lady Laetitia Marsden, now engaged to Christopher's and Francis's cousin (and Pippa's personal nemesis) Crispin, Viscount St George.

There's Laetitia's brother, the handsy Lord Geoffrey, and his proclivity for trying to seduce anything in a skirt—by force, if necessary.

There's the general feeling of ill-will towards Pippa's and Christopher's new friend the *Graf von und zu* Natterdorff—including the tension between the *Graf* and Francis, left over from the war Francis fought against the Germans.

There's the handful of Crispin's old flames who have received invitations, one of whom is expecting a child, and who is close-mouthed about exactly whose child it is.

And then, of course, there is the murder, and the other murder, and the attempted murder, and the other attempted murder...

All in all, it's anything but a relaxing weekend in the country for Pippa and company. And that's before the bombshell ending turns everything on its head.

"A continual atmosphere of hectic passion is very trying if you haven't got any of your own."

DOROTHY L. SAYERS

CHAPTER ONE

"NO," I said.

Christopher squinted at me across the tea table. "What do you mean, no?"

I scowled back. "I mean no, I am not going to spend a weekend at Marsden Manor watching Lady Laetitia flaunt the Sutherland diamonds. I'm also not keen to spend a weekend trying to dodge Geoffrey Marsden's wandering hands. The man simply will not take no for an answer. Nor will you, it seems."

Admittedly, that was unfair of me. Christopher has absolutely nothing in common with Lord Geoffrey Marsden. I was getting frustrated, however. It wasn't the first time I had given him this answer to this question, and I was getting tired of repeating myself. The question being, did I plan to attend the engagement celebration at Marsden Manor in Dorset, for Christopher's cousin Crispin, Viscount St George, and his intended, Lady Laetitia Marsden?

And the answer was, as it had been every time he'd asked, no. I intended to do no such thing.

"Do not compare me to Geoffrey Marsden," Christopher said severely. "I would never squeeze a young lady into a corner of the sofa and try to kiss her against her will."

Of course he wouldn't. For one thing, he's too much of a gentleman, and for another, he prefers young men to young ladies, although he wouldn't force himself on one of them, either.

"That's not what I meant," I told him, "and you know it."

"As for Laetitia and the Sutherland diamonds, that was your own fault."

"Was not!"

"Was, too. If you hadn't lost your temper with St George and told him to go ahead and propose because he and Laetitia deserve each other..."

I grimaced. "I didn't imagine that he would actually do it. Although I maintain that they do deserve one another. She's a cow, and he—"

"—is going to be unhappy," Christopher said. "I thought you cared about his happiness, Pippa. Or aren't you the one who has been telling him for months not to succumb to Uncle Harold's pressure?"

"I was angry," I said. "And I'm not going to apologize for it. He said horrible things to me."

"I know," Christopher said sympathetically. "You had every right to be upset with him. He was unkind. He should have kept his mouth shut, or rather, should have kept himself from spilling his prejudices onto the stationary in front of him. He should certainly have refrained from sending it to you once he'd written it. Although in justice to him—"

"Don't you dare defend him, Christopher!"

"He was upset, too," Christopher said, going right ahead with the defense in spite of my protestation. "We did just fight a war against Germany, remember? One in which his cousin died? It's understandable that we might all have a problem with you getting close to the enemy."

"I know that," I said. "Robbie was my cousin, too. Nobody's sorrier than I am, believe me."

Not that any of it was my fault, but my father had been conscripted on the German side, and had been in the trenches, and might have killed Cousin Robert. Not that I thought he had done, but the possibility did occasionally torment me during sleepless nights.

"You seem to be forgetting," I added, "that I'm the enemy, too."

Christopher scoffed, and I added, "No, seriously, Christopher. It's not all that long ago that the Countess Marsden told Aunt Roz what a pity it is that my mother ran away and married a German. And St George was there for that conversation. He ought to have remembered that when he disparaged Wolfgang's heritage, he disparaged mine, as well."

"So he ought to have done," Christopher agreed. "It wouldn't be the first time he's gotten caught up in his own spite. You know he didn't mean it."

"I know no such thing," I said, offended. "If he didn't mean it, he should have sent an apology, and—"

"You told him not to write again."

"Well, I—"

I stopped myself before I could say that I hadn't meant it, because I had, in fact, meant every word. I hadn't wanted to hear from St George again, at least not right away. I was upset and angry and yes, hurt. Christopher's cousin Crispin and I had been getting along better lately, after more than a decade of being at one another's throats, and I hadn't expected him to throw the land of my birth in my face via letter. I had wanted time to process my feelings before I had to deal with him again, and yes, maybe I had wanted to hurt him back, too, at least a little bit.

It was no more than he deserved, after all.

So while I had, as Christopher had so kindly pointed out, told St George to go ahead and propose to Lady Laetitia Marsden because they deserved one another, I hadn't actually thought he would do it. I had assumed that he would take a couple of days to get over his anger while I did the same, and then we would figure out a way to get back on an even keel again.

As even as the keel ever is between two people who heartily despise one another and never let a chance go by to let the other know how they feel.

"Well, you're going to have to deal with them both next weekend," Christopher said, lifting the heavy piece of stationary that had precipitated this conversation. "She invited Natterdorff."

I blinked at him. "Laetitia Marsden? Invited Wolfgang to her engagement party? Why?"

If her fiancé despised the man enough to propose to her—a woman he didn't love—because I lost my temper with him over his disparagement of someone who claimed to be my cousin—why on earth would Laetitia invite him to her and Crispin's engagement bash?

"It's obvious," Christopher said, "isn't it?"

Was it?

"She's either trying to do you a good turn, after taking Crispin away from you—"

I made a face, and he nodded. "Yes, I know. But she doesn't. She wants him, so she thinks everyone else does, too."

"Or?"

"Or she's trying to make her new fiancé squirm."

That seemed like a valid guess. Wolfgang's presence would

definitely make Crispin squirm, although why Laetitia would want that, I couldn't tell you. I was in favor of the sentiment on a general level, though. I never pass up an opportunity to make Crispin squirm, but of course I'm not marrying him. "How does she even know that Wolfgang exists?"

"I imagine Crispin had himself a proper rant," Christopher said. "I can't imagine that he wouldn't have told everyone he knows about Natterdorff's existence."

"Surely not. Why would he tell his intended about another man? Especially one he clearly dislikes?" And one who, furthermore, was not only better-looking, but also higher up the aristocratic scale?

That was in German aristocracy, mind you, which is worth less than the paper it's written on in Germany these days, since the Weimar Republic did away with their nobility in 1919, but which still counts for something in England. It counted with Crispin, I was fairly certain.

"Because he's upset," Christopher said, "and when Crispin's upset, he spews bile to anyone who'll listen. Laetitia listens to him. That's part of the problem."

I grimaced. "Well, if Crispin told her, that's no more than I asked him to do, I suppose." Go cry on Laetitia's shoulder, and propose while he was at it. "He probably regurgitated it all. Including how much he despises Wolfgang. Which doesn't seem like a good reason for Laetitia to include him in their engagement celebration..."

"But which makes perfect sense if you consider the people involved in this farce," Christopher said. "At any rate, I wouldn't let Lord Geoffrey behave as he did at the Dower House. Nor would Natterdorff. Or, for that matter, Francis. And as for Crispin—"

"Laetitia will have him on a short leash," I said. "He'll be lucky if she lets him say boo to any of us."

Or to me, at least. She hadn't liked me before this, and she surely liked me less now. I highly doubted Christopher's assertion that she was trying to do me a good turn by including Wolfgang in the festivities.

Unless my having essentially thrown St George at her had disposed her more kindly towards me, of course. She had gotten what she had been working towards for months, after all. The Sutherland diamonds, and Crispin's hand—and title, and fortune—in marriage.

And all because I lost my temper and told him to kindly go self-destruct, and he had chosen to listen.

"She'll certainly keep him far away from you," Christopher agreed. "And that's where Natterdorff comes in, I expect. Him and Geoffrey. You'll be beating them both off with sticks."

"All the more reason to stay home." I eyed the piece of stationary in his hand. "Who wrote?"

He glanced at it, as if he didn't already know what it said. "Natterdorff. To let you know that he'd be coming. Evans handed it to me downstairs."

"And you decided to open it?"

"I assumed you'd eventually share the contents with me anyway," Christopher said with a shrug and handed the single piece of paper to me. I ran my eyes over it. The Savoy Hotel logo was in the corner, and then a few lines of German *Kurrentschrift*, of which I had seen enough in the past few weeks that it was easier to decipher than it used to be.

"Of course I would share it with you," I told him, "but that's no reason to read other people's correspondence."

"I wanted to know whether it was another invitation to supper."

Wolfgang Ulrich Albrecht, *Graf von und zu* Natterdorff, was a young German nobleman whose acquaintance we had made a few weeks earlier at the Savoy Hotel. Or rather, I had made his acquaintance at five years old or so, it seemed, in Heidelberg. He and his parents had come to visit me and mine. I couldn't remember the occasion, but Wolfgang said he did. We were some sort of cousins once or twice removed—I had never asked, nor been told about, the specifics—and he had recognized me, so he said, eighteen years later, across the Savoy tearoom.

Since then, we had gone out to supper a few times, and he had contributed to saving my life in that incident that had precipitated the correspondence with St George that had culminated in me telling him to propose to Lady Laetitia Marsden. And now Laetitia had invited Wolfgang to her and Crispin's engagement do.

"You simply must attend," Christopher said. "You can't leave Natterdorff alone with all the women of the Bright Young Set. With Crispin off the marital mart, and Francis engaged as well, and me not exactly in the market for a liaison with a Bright Young Thing—unless it's Cecil Beaton, I suppose..."

"Never mind that," I told him. "Beaton's all about Stephen Tennant these days, as you very well know. And you're all about Tom Gardiner."

Christopher muttered something, a blush staining his cheeks, and I added, "Although you do have a point. Wolfgang will be swarmed by eager young ladies, and so will you, since Laetitia won't let anyone flutter around St George..."

"Precisely why we have to be there," Christopher said. "If you don't look out, someone else will turn Natterdorff's head and end up with the *Schloss* in Bavaria."

I rolled my eyes. "I don't want a *Schloss* in Bavaria, Christopher. The situation in Germany is still much too fraught for me to feel comfortable with the idea of going back there. In my opinion, that madman *Herr* Hitler bears watching. I can't believe that they let him out of prison only two years after an attempted political coup."

Christopher nodded. "Yes, Pippa. We know."

"It's a valid concern," I said irritably, "whether you agree with me or not. The Germans started one war. There's no reason to think they won't start another."

"There's every reason to think they won't," Christopher answered. "With all the sanctions, they're only now getting back to normal, and it's eight years later."

"All the more reason for them to be upset." I waved it aside, since it was, after all, not germane to what we were discussing. "Aside from all that, I feel very English. More so than I do German."

I had spent my first eleven years in Germany. When the Great War broke out and my father was conscripted, my mother sent me to her sister in England for my safety. By now, they were both dead, and I was thoroughly acclimated to England.

"So if His Grace proposes..." Christopher said.

"Wolfgang? He's here in England too, at the moment. I suppose I would simply do my best to convince him to stay here. If I decided to marry him at all, that is. I don't know that I would."

"Well," Christopher said, "unless you go to Crispin's engagement party and keep all the other women off him—off Natterdorff, I mean; not off Crispin, Laetitia will see to that— you may never get the chance."

And that might be a bit of all right. The *Graf* von Natterdorff was handsome, titled, and presumably wealthy, but aside from being German—which was a bit hypocritical, I'll admit, but it was still a consideration—he was also my cousin. And while it's legal to marry one's cousin, that didn't mean I thought it would be a good idea to do so. One only has to look at

Tutankhamen for a lesson in what might happen to people whose parents marry their close relatives.

"So it's settled," Christopher said. "We'll go to Dorset next weekend."

I made a face. "If you insist."

"I do, Pippa. The least you can do is face the havoc you wreaked in person."

"It's not my fault that your cousin was stupid enough to propose to a woman he doesn't love while he's in love with someone else," I said crossly. "Yes, perhaps I shouldn't have said what I did; I'll admit that—"

"Finally!"

"—but I'm not responsible for St George's actions. He has been threatening to propose to Laetitia for three months now. He brings it up every time I see him so that I can talk him out of it. If me talking him out of it repeatedly was the only reason he didn't do it before now, then he must truly want to marry her. Or at least he doesn't want to marry anyone else enough not to buckle under his father's pressure."

"You hit him harder than you realize, Pippa," Christopher said, but I shook my head.

"I'll go to the engagement party. If I don't, I'm sure someone—St George or Laetitia, or perhaps someone else—will think it means something. But I'll need a new evening frock. Laetitia hasn't seen the beaded salmon, but both St George and Wolfgang have. I need at least one new evening frock for a weekend away."

"Selfridges, then?"

"Selfridges will do," I agreed.

Christopher rubbed his hands together. "Tomorrow?"

"We may as well. Who knows how long it will take to find something suitable?"

"Black, I suppose? For mourning?"

I snorted. "I'll leave that to Lady Laetitia."

Christopher tilted his head consideringly. "Surely, for her own engagement party, she'll pull something else out of the wardrobe? After all, she has just achieved everything she's ever wanted. Red or purple or something else indecently triumphant..."

"I have never seen her wear anything but black," I said, "joyous occasion or not. But I'll pay you five quid if her frock is a different color."

"You're on." He stuck out his hand, and we shook on it.

AND SO IT was that a week and a bit later, Christopher and I took the train from Waterloo Station to Salisbury in Wiltshire, where we were picked up by cousin Francis in the Astley family's Bentley. From there, we motored to Beckwith Place, where we spent the evening with Francis and Constance, and with Uncle Herbert and Aunt Roz, who were no happier about their nephew's engagement than Christopher and I were.

"Impetuous fool," Uncle Herbert grumbled over pudding. "There's no way out for him now unless the young lady decides to release him from his obligation, and having met her, I don't think that's at all likely."

"It would take something truly unforgiveable," I agreed, "and given the circumstances, I can't imagine what that might be."

If Laetitia had accepted him despite knowing that he was in love with someone else, I had no idea what he could do that would be worse in her eyes. Surely even bedding someone else wouldn't do it. She may even expect infidelity, and might have gone into the engagement prepared to forgive and forget if it happened.

"It boggles the mind," Aunt Roz said, twisting the stem of her glass between her fingers, eyes on the dessert wine inside while she spoke, "why a young woman like that would willingly put herself in a situation in which her future husband will most likely end up being unfaithful, not to mention end up resenting her. Has she no sense of self-preservation?"

"Or pride?" I muttered.

"Most of the time she has plenty of both," Constance answered in her usual soft way. She's Laetitia's cousin, and thus must be expected to know the answers to questions like that. "I don't know what it is about Lord St George that makes her behave like a fool."

"Must be the money and title," Francis said, "since it can't be his lovely personality."

He winked at me across the table. I smirked back. "No, surely not."

"Unless she knows something about him that the rest of us don't," Francis added, referring, of course, to the fact that Laetitia had dragged Crispin into bed at one point earlier this year, and might, indeed, know something about him that the rest of us didn't.

"Francis!" Aunt Roz said, shocked, and Constance blushed. Francis chuckled.

"Sorry, Mum. But there must be something, mustn't there? For a girl like that to accept him, even under the circumstances?"

There was a moment's pause, and then Christopher said, "There has to be something we can do to derail things. We all agree that we don't want Laetitia Marsden in the family, don't we?"

There was a general murmur of agreement from around the table. Even Constance nodded.

"What do you suggest?" I wanted to know.

He glanced at me. "Perhaps we could get him drunk and into bed with Beaton and Tennant? And then make it public. That might be shocking enough to get rid of her."

"That's dreadful," Uncle Herbert said. "You would destroy your cousin's reputation? And risk his health and future happiness? Just to get him away from Laetitia Marsden?"

"If I thought it would work," I said, "I would do it. Unfortunately, Uncle Harold would probably thrash St George to within an inch of his life if he thought Crispin was queer."

Better that he end up married to Lady Laetitia than dead. Marginally better, at any rate.

"Then I'm not certain what to suggest," Christopher said. "If adultery won't do it, of the male or female persuasion, I don't know what else I could come up with, honestly."

"I'm appalled that you came up with *that*," Aunt Roz told him. "Homosexuality is one thing, Christopher. Orgies are quite another."

"That's why it might work," Christopher said unrepentantly. "If there were photographs..."

"The tabloids wouldn't print them, surely?"

"Of course not!" Aunt Roz said, looking shocked.

"Then I don't see how that would work," Francis said. "Besides, is compromising Crispin likely to make her let go? If it were, surely he wouldn't be in the position he's in now, would he?"

None of us answered, and he added, "What we have to do, is find something we can use to blackmail her, not embarrass him. Surely she must have done something questionable herself at some point, that we can hold over her head. Connie?"

"Nothing she has confided in me," Constance said serenely, "unless you consider the fact that she lost her virtue to Lord St

George before becoming engaged to him. It's not unheard of, of course—"

No, not at all. And given that it had been her idea and not his, I was pretty sure her virtue had been non-existent at the time, anyway.

"—and at this point," Constance continued, "it's a non-issue, of course. He has agreed to make an honest woman of her."

After a second she added, "Although I suppose, while we're at Marsden this weekend, I could find the time to have a gossip with some of the maids. If anyone knows what's going on with the family, it's a maid."

"It's a shame that he has always refused to declare himself to this girl he claims to be in love with," I said. Francis and Constance exchanged a glance, but didn't say anything. So did Aunt Roz and Christopher, ditto.

I added, "We don't know her, of course. She could be worse than Laetitia. But if he loves her, at least he'd be happier than he would be with Laetitia, and we're going to be dealing with a shrew either way."

No one said anything, and I concluded, "If we could find her, and convince her to talk to him, perhaps he would throw Laetitia over."

"The Marsdens would bring a breach-of-promise suit," Uncle Herbert said, "and Harold would force Crispin to go through with the marriage after all."

"Besides," Aunt Roz added, with a glance at Christopher and one at Francis, "if he hasn't told her himself yet, it isn't our place to interfere."

"He's a grown man," Uncle Herbert added, "and I assume he knows his own mind—"

I snorted, because how could he, if he'd rather marry a woman he didn't love than risk being rejected by one he did?

"Perhaps if you talked to him, Pipsqueak," Francis began, and I shook my head.

"I'm the last person he wants a lecture from right now. Besides, it's not as if I haven't spoken to him about this before now. Every time we've had this conversation, I've told him that living in squalor on the Continent might not be so bad. My mother seemed to enjoy it."

It hadn't been squalor, of course. Not the Parisian garret with no heat or running water that Crispin imagined. We had lived in a small flat in Heidelberg, and it had been neat and clean, and we had had everything we needed. It wasn't a *Schloss* in Bavaria, of course, or for that matter a manor house in Wiltshire, but there was no reason why Crispin and his lady-love couldn't do the same and be perfectly comfortable.

Aunt Roz's expression softened. "I know, Pippa. Annabelle was happy with your father."

"And there's no reason why St George couldn't do the same." As long as someone found the girl and convinced her to cooperate. I narrowed my eyes. "Christopher..."

"No," Christopher said.

"What do you mean, no?"

"I mean no," Christopher said. "He told me in confidence, and I won't go behind his back. If he wants to confess his feelings, he'll do so. Or not, now." He made a face. "But either way, no. He made it clear what would happen if I said anything to anyone. Especially you."

Oh, especially me, was it?

"And what was it that would happen, Kit?" Francis wanted to know, eyes twinkling.

Christopher sighed. "Disembowelment featured largely. So did defenestration."

"Before or after the disembowelment?"

"Who knows?" Christopher said. "Does it matter, really? Whether I have my intestines removed before or after I'm thrown out the window makes very little difference to me."

He shook his head. "I promised him I wouldn't talk about it. The rest of you can speculate all you want, and I don't doubt that most of you could make an accurate guess, but we're not going to do it out loud. And as for you, Pippa—"

He pinned me with a stare, "—if he had wanted you to know, he would have told you himself."

He had certainly had plenty of opportunity to do so. If he hadn't done, then Christopher was most likely right and Crispin didn't want me to know. Afraid I would mock him, no doubt. Or worse, interfere.

"Fine." I folded my arms over my chest and stuck my bottom lip out.

"Thank you, Pippa."

"But if you do know who she is, you might just whisper a suggestion in her ear that St George is carrying a torch, and perhaps—"

"No," Christopher said. "Disembowelment and defenestration, remember?"

"Lady Laetitia Marsden," I shot back. "A life sentence."

"One he signed himself up for." He shook his head. "Sorry, Pippa. But he is a fully functioning adult who made up his own mind to do this. I know you feel like it was your fault—"

I made a face.

"—but you're not responsible for Crispin. He's old enough to make his own decisions."

"Kit's right, Pipsqueak," Francis added. "You've been trying to talk the brat out of proposing to the harpy for months now. If he did it anyway, it's not your fault."

"I was unkind to him. I oughtn't have been."

"He's been unkind to you for twelve years," Francis said bluntly. "If he's getting some of that returned, it won't hurt him. And if he can't handle it, that's his problem."

I supposed so. Francis was right, after all. Crispin wasn't my responsibility. It was hard to escape the guilt I felt over the situation, but my family deserved better than to have to listen to me moan about it repeatedly. So I forced a smile and nodded. "You're right. I suppose we'll just have to get used to the idea of facing Lady Laetitia Marsden across the Christmas goose from now on."

"We won't be invited back to Sutherland Hall if she's lady of the manor," Christopher said, and Francis nodded.

"Laetitia, Viscountess St George, won't want the likes of us cluttering up her dining room. Which is fine by me." He stretched. "If I never see that brother of hers again, it won't be too soon."

I felt the same way, although I recognized the fact that we were talking about Constance's cousins, and I didn't want to say anything too harsh. Bad enough that Francis wasn't holding back.

"I'm sure Geoffrey will have his own family by the time Laetitia becomes Duchess of Sutherland," I said instead. "He has his own succession to worry about, after all. Just like St George, I'm sure he'll be required to marry and carry on the Marsden name sooner rather than later."

"I pity the poor woman who has to marry Geoffrey," Constance said, so perhaps I had been more considerate than was necessary earlier. "I'm sure Lord St George will at least be discreet with his dalliances. Geoffrey is either too stupid or too venal to care what anyone thinks."

"And this is the gentleman—" Uncle Herbert's face twisted, "I use the word in its titular form only—who squeezed our Pippa into a corner of the sofa at the Dower House in May?"

Everyone nodded.

"That won't happen this time," Christopher said, and Francis nodded.

"We'll keep you safe, Pipsqueak."

"Thank you, Francis," I said, and that was the end of that conversation.

CHAPTER TWO

____

"YOU OWE ME FIVE POUNDS," Christopher said the following afternoon, as we entered the small ballroom at Marsden Manor.

We had left Wiltshire after breakfast, the four of us in Constance's burgundy Crossley with Francis behind the wheel. Aunt Roz and Uncle Herbert were following tomorrow in the Bentley, for the big sit-down dinner in honor of the happy couple, but they hadn't wanted to deal with all the Bright Young Things that were sure to be crawling all over the manor until then. Tonight was for the young set, while the older generation—aunts, uncles, and grandparents—would be arriving tomorrow.

After a leisurely drive through the lower half of Wiltshire and into Dorset, with a stop at a local pub for luncheon, we had arrived in Marsden-on-Crane in time for afternoon tea. The clicking of cups and clinking of spoons and forks was audible from the other end of the vast entrance hall as we were admitted into Marsden Manor by the Marsdens' butler, a spindly specimen of advanced age with a mostly bald pate and a bulbous nose.

"Good afternoon, Miss Constance," he intoned, inclining his head a perfectly appropriate amount. "It is nice to see you back in Marsden, if I may say so. And this must be your intended. Good afternoon, Mr. Astley."

"Hello, Perkins," Constance smiled. "Yes, this is Francis. And his brother Christopher, and Miss Philippa Darling. She and I went to Godolphin together."

Perkins ran an experienced eye over the two men, before coming to me. It felt as if he examined me a bit more intently than the other two, although it might have been my imagination. On the other hand, it might be that he had heard about me from Laetitia or her mother, too. Geoffrey might pursue me when I'm available, but I'm certain he wouldn't spare me a thought when I'm out of sight, and Maurice, Earl of Marsden, would have had no reason to bring me up to his butler.

Laetitia, on the other hand, or Lady Euphemia, might well have given Perkins instructions on how to handle me. I wondered whether I'd end up stuck in the servant wing as if I were someone's companion and not an invited guest in my own right.

"You will be staying on the first floor," Perkins told Constance, as he gestured to the wide staircase. "Leave the luggage. Bert will bring it upstairs."

A footman stepped forward out of the shadows as we were ushered up to the next level and to the left down the hallway. "Miss Constance—" Perkins indicated a door, "you'll be in the Primrose room."

Constance nodded, looking pleased.

"Miss Darling—" Perkins flicked a glance at me. "Your room is up one level, in Wisteria."

"Thank you." I looked at Constance's door. There was a small plate on it with the name of the room painted on porcelain. Presumably it was the same upstairs.

"Perhaps the Misters Astley wouldn't mind sharing a bedchamber? We have a full house this weekend, and some of the other guests are unaccompanied and unrelated."

In other words, it was all right to ask Christopher and Francis to share a room, because they had arrived together, from the same place, and were brothers. Much harder to ask, for instance, the *Graf* von Natterdorff to bunk up with the Viscount St George, and quite impossible to expect him to share a room with Francis.

For the first time it occurred to me to wonder how that whole situation was going to play out once Wolfgang got here. (Or he might be here already. I hadn't heard his voice in the buzz down in the entrance hall, and he has a distinctive accent, but he might have been there and simply been quiet.)

Christopher and I hadn't mentioned Wolfgang's existence to Francis, or for that matter to anyone else in the family. Crispin knew, of course. Christopher, for reasons known only unto himself, had decided to let his cousin know about Wolfgang's existence as soon as the latter introduced himself over tea at the Savoy last month.

Or not quite as soon as, but it was only a few hours later that he went out of his way to find a call box and ring up St George at Sutherland Hall. And then, of course, Crispin had hared off to London at the first opportunity to get a look at Wolfgang himself.

We hadn't told anyone else, however. Crispin might have done, but St George's relationship with his father was already fraught, and I didn't think His Grace, Uncle Harold, would have been receptive to his son's complaining. Besides, if

Crispin had told his father that I was being courted—or so it seemed—by a German nobleman, I couldn't imagine that the news wouldn't have made its way from Uncle Harold to Uncle Herbert and Aunt Roz. And neither of them had said a word about it in the past twenty-four hours. So chances were they didn't know, nor did Francis.

And that begged the question of how he was going to react once he found out.

As it turned out, I didn't have all that long to wait. But before we got to that point, I told Perkins that if bedchambers were a problem, I would be happy to share with Constance. We had done so before, at the Dower House. It wouldn't hurt me to spend another two nights in the same room as my cousin's fiancée.

But no, Perkins said that if the young gentlemen would just consent to bunking together, that would solve the problem, and then Christopher and Francis followed Perkins down the hallway for a look at their shared room, while Constance and I went into Primrose.

It had pale green walls and ivory bed hangings, with a sunny yellow counterpane. I looked around and nodded approvingly. "Very nice."

"I've always liked Primrose," Constance agreed, sitting down on the bed and folding her hands in her lap, "although Wisteria is lovely, too. Gray and lilac, with touches of green. The rooms on the second floor are all smaller than this."

I nodded. It was the same at Beckwith Place, so nothing new about that at all.

"There's something I have to tell you," I said, and Constance looked up at me with bright, brown eyes.

She's a small girl, a bit on the plump side, with soft, brown hair and a round face. If I wanted to be unkind, I could say that she looked like the human equivalent of a brown sparrow, but that's only a derogatory statement if you don't like sparrows. I would personally rather one of them than a peacock or parrot or anything of that nature.

Constance isn't the loud and flashy sort, is what I mean. She isn't shy, but she has always been quiet and thoughtful instead of forward. Not the type to draw attention to herself. We hadn't been close at Godolphin—I always found her a bit too meek for my taste—but I have grown to appreciate her over the past few months. It helps that Francis adores her, of course, and she him, but she's also a bit more sly and sarcastic than I remember. She might have grown into it as she has gotten older, or perhaps she had simply hid it better back in our boarding school days.

"A few weeks ago," I began, "I met this man. We were having tea at the Savoy, Christopher and I, and he came up to the table and introduced himself..."

"So that is why Lord St George suddenly decided to propose to Laetitia," Constance said when I had finished the tale, adding two and two together with admirable speed.

I nodded. "We argued back and forth by letter, and he was rude and dismissive of Wolfgang, which obviously extends to me, as I have the same faults as Wolfgang does. I told him to go cry on Laetitia's shoulder, and propose while he was at it, since they deserve one another."

"That was remarkably unkind of you," Constance said placidly.

I made a face. "I didn't think that he would actually do it. If I had done..."

I trailed off, and started over. "At any rate, Laetitia has seen fit to invite Wolfgang to the party this weekend."

"Oh, dear," Constance said.

I nodded. "I don't know what she was thinking. Crispin despises him, so for his sake alone, she ought to have left it alone. And Francis is here, and perhaps a few other men, too, who served in the trenches during the War. And you know that your Aunt Euphemia has no love for Germans—she made that very clear when she met me at Beckwith Place two months ago—"

"In justice to Aunt Effie," Constance said, with a twitch of her lips, "I think that may have been influenced by the way you greeted Lord St George on that occasion."

Well, yes. Perhaps so. He had been sharing a chair with Laetitia when Christopher and I walked into the drawing room, and I had ignored her presence to pass on love from a neighbor in London. Florence Schlomsky—or the woman we'd thought of as Flossie Schlomsky—had had a bad habit of pushing St George into the corner of the lift in the Essex House Mansions and snogging him, so I knew very well what passing on love from Flossie was supposed to look like.

Not that I did that. Of course not. Crispin and I are not on kissing terms. But I did put my hand on his cheek and stared deeply into his eyes for long enough that he might have expected something more than he ended up getting, and neither Lady Laetitia nor her mother had appreciated it. Nor had Crispin, for that matter.

I drew myself up. "Be that as it may, your aunt isn't a fan. Nor is Crispin, nor will Francis be, once he finds out. So I need your help with keeping Wolfgang and Francis away from each other."

"That won't be easy if the man is courting you," Constance pointed out.

I made a face. No, it wouldn't. Perhaps I should have stuck with my initial plan, and refused to be here this weekend.

Christopher had been right, though: if I didn't turn up, the ladies of the Bright Young Set would swarm Wolfgang, and then one of them might turn his head.

Being courted for a weekend wouldn't be too painful, I supposed. He was handsome, certainly—aside from Lord Geoffrey Marsden (and the late, great Rudolph Valentino, may he rest in peace), he was probably the best-looking man I had ever seen. And besides, it was likely to annoy St George to distraction, which is always enjoyable when I can manage it. Being monopolized by Wolfgang might also help to keep Lord Geoffrey away from me, which was all to the good.

Constance nodded when I said as much. "My cousin is horrible. Yours is too, of course, but at least he's engaged to Laetitia now. But this weekend is just the sort of occasion Geoffrey lives for. Lots of young women, and wedding bells in the air."

A rather unpleasant thought, that. "Do you know who's expected?"

Constance rattled off a string of names and titles. Interestingly, they included several Bright Young Persons whose names I knew. Lady Violet Cummings and the Honorable Cecily Fletcher had both received invitations, and in addition to being friends of Laetitia's—or so I assumed—they were also prior dalliances of Crispin's.

"Why on earth would Laetitia want to invite her new fiancé's former conquests to their engagement party?" I inquired, baffled.

"I imagine she wants to gloat," Constance answered. "She's the one who managed to tie him down, after all. I'm sure the others must have tried, or at least hoped for that outcome. Small wonder if she wants to rub it in their faces that she succeeded where they failed."

Well, yes. Getting herself permanently stuck to the future Duke of Sutherland was reason enough to gloat, I supposed, and it did sound like something Laetitia would do. Still, it seemed stupid. Why go out of her way to remind Crispin of that which he could no longer have now that he was engaged to her?

Although perhaps she hadn't considered that angle. Perhaps rubbing her good fortune in her friends' faces had been enough of an incentive, and she hadn't reasoned past it.

"Did either of them dally with Geoffrey?" I wanted to know, and Constance made a face.

"I don't know, Pippa. I never spent much time in those circles, and Geoffrey, believe it or not, doesn't brag about his conquests. At least not to me. You're probably more likely to know the answer to that than I am."

"I never spent much time with them, either," I said. "Most of what I know is because of Crispin's involvement." And that only because of Grimsby the valet's blackmail dossier. Crispin doesn't brag, either. Or at least he doesn't to me, nor do I think to Christopher.

"I suppose we'll see before supper," Constance said and got to her feet. "Will you help me with my toilette, Pippa? Otherwise, Francis might look at the other women and change his mind about marrying me."

"Don't be ridiculous," I told her. "Francis isn't shallow. He loves you. And he won't care what anyone else looks like. All he'll see is you."

The weekend party at the Dower House when they had first fallen in love was proof positive of that. Lady Laetitia had been there, and so had Lady Peckham's ward, an absolutely stunning Dutch beauty by the name of Johanna de Vos, and Francis hadn't had eyes for anyone but Constance. That wasn't likely to have changed.

"Fine," Constance said. "Perhaps I just want to look good enough that nobody will wonder why he's marrying me."

"No one who knows either of you wonders about that. But I'll be happy to help you dress. Although—" I glanced around, taking in the walls of the Primrose Room and beyond them, the rest of Marsden Manor, "aren't there maids here that'll do that?"

"Aunt Effie has a maid," Constance nodded, "as does Laetitia, of course. I'm sure either of them would be happy to help. But I'd rather have you."

"I'd be happy to help you get ready," I assured her. "And if you'd like, we can have Christopher do your face. He's better with makeup than I am."

Constance opened her mouth, presumably to decline, and I added, "I plan to have him do my face. The competition will be fierce this weekend. Both Violet Cummings and Cecily Fletcher are lovely, and so is Laetitia, and I'm not about to look like the poor country cousin by comparison. And if he's doing my face, he might as well do yours, too."

Constance thought about it and closed her mouth, and so it was that when we entered the Marsden Manor ballroom an hour and a half later—Constance on Francis's arm, and I on Christopher's—we both looked as good as we ever had.

Constance was in her rose-colored frock, which brought out that British roses-and-cream complexion and the flush in her cheeks, while Christopher had talked me into an ivory silk crepe gown on our shopping expedition the week before. It was deceptively simple, with beaded embroidery along the square neckline and at the dropped waist, and a fluttery handkerchief hem that danced around my knees when I walked. Francis took one look at me and let out a whoop of laughter.

"What?" I sniffed.

His lips twitched. "You're determined to kill him, aren't you?"

"I beg your pardon? Christopher talked me into this frock, I'll have you know."

"Of course he did." Francis turned to his brother. "He's going to murder you, Kit. You know that, don't you?"

Christopher hummed, but didn't respond beyond that. Nor did he look at either of us, just kept his attention fixed on the ceiling.

"Who's going to murder Christopher?" I wanted to know, glancing from one to the other of them. "And for what reason?"

"St George," Francis said.

I scoffed. "Don't be ridiculous. St George adores Christopher. He'd never hurt him. And what's wrong with my frock, pray tell?"

"Nothing at all," Francis said, giving it another once-over. "You look lovely, Pipsqueak. Just like a bride on her wedding day." His lips twitched again.

I rolled my eyes. "It's only to the wedding itself that one is not supposed to wear white, Francis. This is an engagement party, and white—or ivory; this is ivory, I'll have you know—ivory is fair game. The bride-to-be will likely be wearing black."

Constance made a face. "Surely not for her own engagement party?"

"We have a bet," I told her. "I have to pay Christopher five pounds if her gown is black. I suppose we'll see when we get downstairs."

At the reminder, Francis clicked his heels together and presented his elbow. Constance took it and they turned towards the stairs. I stuck my hand through Christopher's arm and followed.

"She does look marvelous in black," Constance said over her shoulder.

I nodded. "But a bit much for the occasion, don't you think?

Surely she won't want to look like she's in deep mourning for the second most joyous occasion of her life?"

Or perhaps the third most joyous. Or fourth. Engagement, wedding, birth of their first child. And surely the day when Uncle Harold kicked the bucket and Crispin ascended to the dukedom (and brought Laetitia with him) would rank high, as well.

"I'm with Kit," Francis said. "The gown will be black."

"Five pounds?"

He smiled indulgently. "Why not? More importantly, I think we need to discuss Pippa's wedding frock and what will come of walking in there wearing it."

"Nothing will come of me wearing it," I said. "And it's not a wedding frock."

Francis gave it another look over his shoulder. "It might as well be."

"Well, it's not. It's just an ivory frock. Although with the way you're carrying on, now I wish I had gone with the seafoam green with bronze beads instead."

"I don't," Christopher said. "You look lovely, Pippa. And you'll make a nice contrast with Laetitia once we get down there."

"If she's wearing black."

"She will be," Christopher said and shifted his grip to my elbow as we started to descend the stairs.

MARSDEN MANOR WAS in possession of an actual ballroom, and that's where tonight's gathering took place. When we walked through the open doors, the happy couple was standing in front of the fireplace directly opposite, each of them with a glass of champagne. Laetitia had Crispin in a death grip with her other hand, of course—it was almost as if she were afraid he would try to get away if she didn't hang onto him—and yes, she was wearing head-to-toe black.

Christopher turned to me, and I nodded, resigned. "I'll get it to you later."

"I'll hold you to that." He squeezed my hand. "In justice to her, she does carry it off."

And how. I made a face but didn't respond. There was nothing I could say, at least not without sounding green-eyed with envy, which I didn't want to do.

Laetitia Marsden is a year or two older than Crispin, and for that matter than Christopher, Constance, and myself. She's twenty-four or perhaps twenty-five, and she's remarkably beautiful. Tall, almost as tall as Crispin in her T-strap heels, and willowy. The current slinky fashions look marvelous on her. Her hair is cut in a sharp Dutch boy bob, most likely with the help of a ruler, and it's jet black and shiny, framing her face like a cap of satin.

The gown was amazing. A net overdress shimmered with black sequins and blue beads in the shape of peonies. It topped a black underdress of satin or crepe, and the whole thing ended in a row of beaded fringe that danced around Laetitia's calves every time she shifted her weight. It was beyond sophisticated, probably *haute couture* direct from Paris, and while I knew I looked good in my ivory silk crepe, I felt like a little girl in a pinafore next to a grown woman.

"Chin up," Christopher murmured as we made our way across the floor towards them, trailing Constance and Francis. There was something of the feeling of approaching royalty. The people on either side of us, chatting in groups of two and three with glasses of champagne in their hands, drew away from us as we crossed the floor, giving us what felt like furtive looks out of the corners of their eyes.

In some cases, the looks were less than furtive. One young

woman—I'm fairly certain she was Lady Violet Cummings, based on the peroxide blond shingled bob—looked Christopher up and down, and leaned towards her companion's ear with a titter and whisper. The companion—perhaps the Honorable Cecily Fletcher?—took one look at him, and one at me, before shooting an agonized look at her friend, and then looking away.

"Stiff upper lip," Christopher admonished, brushing past them without a glance.

"I don't know that I have it in me to congratulate her," I muttered, giving the two young ladies my back in favor of focusing on Laetitia. "She looks so indecently triumphant, doesn't she?"

"Then congratulate *him*," Christopher said.

I made a face. "That's even worse. At least she scored a future duke. All he got was a shrew with an eye to his title and fortune."

"I think perhaps you're being a little unfair," Christopher said gently. "She does seem to want him for himself, too."

"God only knows why."

"I imagine she knows him in ways you don't," Christopher said just as Constance and Francis came to a stop in front of the happy couple.

I flicked him an annoyed look. "Well, I know *that*, Christopher. It was discussed over dinner last night, remember? Do you really think now is the time to remind me?"

"No time like the present," Christopher said. "At least you've got some color in your cheeks now."

I sniffed. "There was color in my cheeks before, too. You put it there yourself, upstairs in Constance's room." Along with rice powder, mascara, and lipstick.

"You know what I mean," Christopher said and plastered a benign expression on his face. "Don't let her see that she gets to you. Turn that frown upside down."

I scowled at him as, in front of us, Constance went up on tiptoes to kiss Laetitia's cheek.

"Felicitations, old chap," Francis said and slapped Crispin on the shoulder. The latter staggered. Constance murmured something no doubt appropriate to her cousin along with the kiss, and then they stepped out of the way, and it was our turn.

Christopher squeezed my hand and took a step forward. I, perforce, followed.

CHAPTER THREE

THIS WAS my first time seeing Crispin since the engagement was announced in the *London Times*. Christopher, I was fairly certain, had spoken to his cousin on the exchange in the couple of weeks since then, but he hadn't told me anything about the conversation they may have had. I had no idea, at this point, whether Crispin was regretful of what he had done, or whether he was happy to have done it, and how he felt about my part in any or all of it.

He looked like a gentleman should at his engagement, resplendent in white tie with mother-of-pearl studs and cuff-links, and a platinum watch fob dangling from his waistcoat pocket. His hair was slicked back from his face into its usual sleek coiffure, a few degrees darker than the platinum shade it is naturally, and his eyes were the cool gray of metal. Steel, or perhaps chromium. Something hard and impenetrable. Something I hadn't seen in a while. Not since we had managed to bury the hatchet we had been carrying since we were children —not in each other's backs—and become something almost like friends.

"Darling." He showed teeth. There's really no other word for it. Although the smile became a touch more genuine when he turned to Christopher. His voice warmed, too. "Kit."

"Crispin." Christopher leaned in, one hand on Crispin's shoulder, and I could see his lips move as he murmured something in Crispin's ear. The latter closed his eyes for a moment, and leaned into the comfort, before he nodded.

"Miss Darling," Laetitia's voice cut through my preoccupation like the shrill sound of a police constable's whistle, and when I turned to her, she was showing teeth, as well. "How thoughtful of you to stop by to wish us well."

She's an inch or so taller than me, so she could quite literally look down on me, something I did not appreciate. Her tone wasn't very pleasant, either.

"It seemed the least I could do," I answered, with a show of teeth of my own, no more sincere than hers. "We were delighted to hear that St George had found someone worthy of him."

Meaning, of course, that they were both base individuals who belonged together. Next to Laetitia, Crispin tensed, although it might have been because of something Christopher said, not anything to do with me, or more likely, with his fiancée.

Laetitia's eyes narrowed. They're blue, surrounded by long, thick, mascaraed lashes, and they matched the flowers on her evening gown. After a moment, and an up-and-down look, she told me, condescendingly, "What a charming frock. Although I'm frankly surprised you left off the orange blossoms."

"Don't be ridiculous," I said, with a toss of my head. Until Francis said something upstairs, it hadn't crossed my mind that anyone would think I was making a statement by showing up in white, but now I was determined that no one should get the wrong idea. Least of all Laetitia; she might believe I was jealous, and that was the last thing I wanted. "I'm hardly likely to tell Crispin to propose to you and then show up to your engagement party in a wedding frock, am I?"

Her expression flickered a bit over that, so perhaps he hadn't mentioned my involvement in the proposal.

There was no reason why he would, of course, although I might have expected some sort of acknowledgement for my suggestion, seeing as it had worked out so well for the both of them.

"Trade places," Christopher murmured in my ear. A second later, he had tugged me over to his right and taken my place in front of Laetitia.

He's charm incarnate when he wants to be, and when he congratulated Laetitia on her betrothal, he sounded warm and sincere. I could see her practically melt under his regard. She clearly couldn't tell, as I could, that he was putting it on with a trowel, and was no happier about the engagement than I was.

Crispin cleared his throat, and I turned back to him. "St George."

"Darling." He gave me an up-and-down look of his own. "Is that for me?"

"The frock?" I looked down at it and back up. "You can have it if you'd like. But it's not precisely your color, and I expect it would be a bit short on you. Besides, your fiancée might not approve, you know."

"The mourning," Crispin said.

"Mourning?" I flicked a glance at Laetitia. "Isn't your fiancée the one in mourning?"

"Laetitia has no reason to mourn," Crispin said. "She's got me. You don't."

I rolled my eyes. "I didn't want you, you realize. If I had done, I wouldn't have told you to propose to someone else."

He shrugged. "So why the mourning?"

"I'm not in mourning. Who mourns in white?"

"The Chinese," Crispin said.

"Do I look Chinese to you?"

He didn't answer, because of course I don't, and I added, "Christopher chose the dress. I thought it was a bit bland, but he insisted." And at least Crispin couldn't tell me that I looked like an apple, or a banana, or—most recently—a stalk of rhubarb in it.

"Of course." He gave me—or the dress—another look before turning his attention back to my face. "What are you waiting for?"

"I don't know," I said. "I wasn't aware I was waiting for anything."

An apology would be nice, I suppose, but I wasn't foolish enough to think I would get one. Nor did I have any plans of apologizing myself, either. I may have felt guilty, but not that guilty.

"Aren't you going to congratulate me?"

"Of course." I smiled toothily. "My very best wishes for your happiness, St George, and for a long—" I said it again for good measure, "*long* life together. Your grandfather was almost ninety when he passed, wasn't he?"

Of course he had been. We all knew that.

"And that wasn't even natural causes," I added, helpfully. "Just think: the two of you could be looking at the next seventy years side by side. Or more. You could live to be a hundred, St George, just to spite the rest of us. I wouldn't put it past you. And through all of it, you'll be side by side with Laetitia, and—"

"Yes, yes." He interrupted before I could wax poetic about the twelve children and twenty-seven grandchildren he'd have by then, not to mention the fidelity Laetitia would surely expect in exchange for it all. "I get the point, Darling."

"I'm sure you do," I said. "After making such a well-reasoned and deliberate choice, not rash at all, not at all emotionally motivated, I wouldn't want your marriage to be cut tragically short. Not before you've had the chance to truly appreciate your decision. To wallow in it. Decade upon decade upon decade of it—"

"Yes," Crispin interrupted. "Thank you, Darling. Without you, I wouldn't be here now, looking at such a glorious future."

No, he wouldn't. "I was delighted to be of assistance," I said, "and I can't wait to see you put on the old ball and chain. December, wasn't it? Not very long at all."

He looked like he might have winced at the reminder, and I twisted the knife, "I don't mean to be indelicate, but that's quite a quick denouement, isn't it? Is there something I should know?"

For a second he looked at me, his face blank, before a flush stained the tops of his cheekbones. "Are you asking me whether my fiancée is in the pudding club, Darling?"

"I'm simply suggesting that it seems fast," I said. "Francis and Constance got engaged before you, and they're waiting until next summer. Of course, if you know that you love one another, there's no need to wait..."

"No." The syllable sounded like it had been wrung from him by force.

I arched a brow. "No?"

"No," Crispin said, through gritted teeth. "You, of all people, know why I proposed, and it wasn't because I had to. We are not..." He looked nauseated, "expecting."

I patted his arm. "That's good to know. I knew, of course, that that might have been an issue after what happened in January," when he had brought Laetitia to Sutherland House and spent the night with her, "but I didn't know whether it had happened again since then."

He gave me a look. It could have flayed fish. "We are not expecting."

"Just eager to tie the knot." I smiled sweetly. "I understand."

And I did, of course. Laetitia wanted to close the deal before he could change his mind. Not that he could do that at this point. Not without being subject to that breach of promise suit we had discussed over dinner last night. But even so, it was hard to blame her for wanting to make sure that the marriage—and Crispin—was in the bag before anything could happen to change anything.

His nostrils flared, and I opened my mouth, but before I could comment on Laetitia's indecent hurry to tie him down, his eyes fixed on something over my shoulder. "What's *he* doing here?"

I assumed it was Wolfgang, of course, so I preened a little. "Your fiancée invited him."

He flicked me a look, but it was more distracted than I would have expected under the circumstances. "How do you know that?"

"He wrote to me," I said, and watched Crispin's eyebrow arch.

"Dear me, Darling. I didn't realize that you and Dom were on such friendly terms."

"Dom—?" I swung on my heel to gaze in the same direction that he was. "No, of course we're not."

That was Dominic Rivers in the flesh, though, standing just inside the door to the ballroom, side by side with another young gentleman of the bright and young variety. To my knowledge, I had never seen him before, and now didn't seem like the time to ask for elucidation.

"That's what I thought," Crispin said. "So who...?"

And then the shilling dropped, and his lip curled. "Let me guess. Wolfie's coming?"

"Don't call him that," I said. "And don't look at me like that, either. I wasn't the one who invited him. That responsibility lies with your fiancée."

"My..." It sounded as if he lost his breath for a moment. "Laetitia invited His Highness?"

"Got it in one."

He stared at me, eyes wide. "Why?"

"Something you'll have to take up with her," I said. "I just plan to enjoy the weekend. Between Wolfgang and Mr. Rivers, not to mention Lord Geoffrey, there's no lack of eligible young gentlemen, is there? Your removal from the marriage mart will hardly be noticed at all."

I smiled sweetly. "My felicitations, St George, to you and your betrothed. I'll get out of the way for Mr. Rivers and his companion."

I stepped into Christopher, who took me by the arm and tugged me away.

It was a few steps later that we came face to face with Dominic and his companion crossing the floor in the opposite direction. I smiled blandly as we stopped in front of them. "Mr. Rivers."

He inclined his head. "Miss Darling. Mr. Astley. May I present the Honorable Reginald Fish?"

The Honorable Mr. Fish was a washed-out dirty blond, who couldn't have been a starker contrast to Dominic Rivers's smoldering Latin looks if he'd tried.

"Fish," Christopher murmured, while I dimpled.

"A pleasure, Mr. Fish."

"Call me Reggie," Mr. Fish said. "Long time, no see, Astley. You're here to wish your cousin well?"

Christopher nodded and glanced at me. "This is my other cousin, on my mother's side. Miss Philippa Darling."

"Miss Darling." Reggie bowed.

"Call me Pippa," I told him, "please. If you're Reggie, I'm Pippa."

Reggie nodded. "A pleasure."

I waited for him to say something else, but when he didn't, Christopher said, "A pleasure to see you both. We'll get out of your way. Let you go and congratulate the happy couple."

He shot a look over his shoulder to where Crispin and Laetitia were waiting. I shot one across Reggie's, to where Lady Violet Cummings and the girl I thought was the Honorable Cecily Fletcher were standing. They had been joined by a third young woman I didn't know, a darker-haired brunette— darker than the maybe-Cecily, whose hair was a fluffy medium brown, not unlike my own—and all three of them were watching us. When they caught me looking, the new girl and Lady Violet turned away to whisper to one another across Cecily's body. The latter ignored them in favor of continuing to watch; us, or perhaps it was Crispin and Laetitia beyond us that she was watching. She looked somewhat pale and hollow-eyed, although that may have been the color of her frock. Not everyone can pull off that particular shade of green.

For a second I could hear St George's voice in the back of my head, "—like a stalk of celery, Darling," and then I shook it off. I wasn't the one in the green dress, and Laetitia surely wouldn't let him say anything like that to Cecily. Saying it to me was one thing; saying it to someone else came dangerously close to flirtation.

Dominic Rivers and Reggie Fish moved on towards the fireplace and the engaged couple, and Christopher pulled me in the direction of Francis and Constance, who had visited the bar cart and were now holding glasses of bourbon or brandy and some sort of cocktail and perhaps sherry. When we got close enough, Constance handed off the two cocktails to me and Christopher, and took the glass of sherry back from Francis, who gave it to her with a little bow before he lifted his own glass in a toast. "To the happy couple, and to none of us strangling the bride."

"Or groom," I said, and took a sip of what turned out to be some form of gin drink, with Crème de Menthe and bitters.

Francis eyed me over the top of the glass. "Were you tempted to kill him and not her?"

"I'm always tempted to kill him," I said.

Of course, I was usually tempted to kill her too, but this calamity was firmly on his shoulders. What happened wasn't Laetitia's fault; she had simply snatched at the opportunity she had been waiting for when it was presented to her.

"He's a fool," Francis grunted.

"No argument here."

In front of the fireplace, Dominic Rivers and the Honorable Reggie were in the middle of their obsequies. Laetitia looked gracious, while Crispin eyed the Honorable Reggie with amused disdain and Rivers with something more like calculation.

They got along well enough, from what I knew. Crispin had occasionally made use of Rivers's services in the past, although the last time I had seen them together, he had been trying to lure Rivers into a trap, one that Rivers had noticed and managed to avoid.

If there was bad blood between them at this point, it wasn't evident, however. Crispin responded graciously to Rivers's greeting and—I assumed—his felicitations, while Rivers seemed to extend them in all seriousness.

I turned my back to them, in time to see the door to the hallway open again, and Lord Geoffrey Marsden slip through.

He is, like his sister, extremely good-looking, with the same glossy, black hair and vivid blue eyes that she has. The little clique of girls tittered as he approached them, and Lady Violet went weak in the knees for a moment in what was either an abbreviated curtsey, or simply a response to such ostentatious male beauty. "Lord Geoffrey."

The brunette—not the Honorable Cecily, the other one—fluttered her eyelashes and simpered up at him. "How simply marvy to see you, Geoffrey!"

I applied my elbow to Christopher's ribs. When he glanced at me, I inquired, "Who's that?"

He glanced in the direction I indicated. "You know Violet Cummings, don't you? The blonde? And Cecily Fletcher is the one who looks a bit like you."

I nodded. "I meant the brunette."

"The one in blue? That's Olivia Barnsley."

"Lady Olivia Barnsley? The Honorable Olivia Barnsley?"

"The latter," Christopher said, "I think."

"Another of Crispin's conquests?"

Francis suppressed a snort, not very successfully, and Christopher shook his head. "Not as far as I know. Or if she is, not exclusively."

Clearly. Right now she was giving the impression of someone working overtime to keep Geoffrey's attention on her, and away from... was it Cecily or Violet? Her eyelashes fluttered, her dimple quivered, and her bosom heaved. Lady Violet looked amused as she watched the display—a mere Honorable can't compete with a Lady in the matrimonial stakes, and I'm sure they both knew it—while Cecily simply looked blank.

"Any idea what's wrong with Cecily Fletcher?" I asked.

The other three looked at her and then, as a man, shook their heads. "She looks doped," Francis opined, which was certainly something he ought to recognize. "Downers, not uppers."

"Sedatives, do you mean?"

He nodded. "Veronal or valium or something like that. She looks out of it."

She did. Olivia Barnsley's attempted flirtation with Lord Geoffrey got no reaction, nor did Lady Violet's response to it. Cecily merely blinked at them both, slowly, as if her eyelids were too heavy to move easily.

Violet put her hand on Geoffrey's arm and as he turned towards her, Olivia shot her friend a look of concern. Cecily didn't seem to notice that either, but simply sank back below the surface of her thoughts, her eyes vacant.

Olivia watched her for a second before turning her attention to the group in front of the fireplace. I twisted my head in that direction and saw Reggie Fish and Dominic Rivers expanding under Lady Laetitia's regard, while Crispin watched, two steps removed. He looked indulgent, as an impending husband ought, although to someone who knows him well, the coolness in his eyes told its own story.

When I turned back to the other small group, Geoffrey was in the process of kissing Violet's hand. That done, he kissed Olivia's. When Cecily made no move to present him with her hand for kissing, Geoffrey looked blank for a moment before he gave a sort of mental shrug and moved on.

"Incoming," Francis murmured.

I nodded. "I see him."

"Who?" Constance made to turn her head, but was too late.

"Cousin Connie." Geoffrey stopped beside her and leaned in to peck her cheek. Constance flinched, but by the time he straightened, she had managed to paste a polite smile on her face.

"Cousin Geoffrey."

She might as well not have bothered, because Geoffrey didn't look at her again. She wasn't available to him—probably wouldn't have been even if she hadn't been engaged to marry Francis—and so he couldn't care less about her presence. He nodded to Francis—"Astley," and to Christopher—"Astley," before turning to me, with what he undoubtedly thought was a seductive smile.

"Miss Darling."

His eyes smoldered under lowered lids—bedroom eyes— and the smirk that played around his mouth was suggestive and practiced.

"Lord Geoffrey," I told him, coolly. When he reached for my hand, I contemplated moving it behind my back and out of his way, but decided that it would be too rude a reaction to a man whose house I was standing in. So I let him bring it to his lips, and let him breathe on it, moistly, for several seconds longer than necessary, before he gave it back to me. I wiped it surreptitiously against my skirt before I told him, sweetly, "Congratulations."

He blinked. While he's brilliantly handsome, and much too well aware of it, he's as thick as a stack of bricks. "What for?"

"Your sister's engagement," I reminded him. "The reason we're all here."

He looked around, and I could see the thoughts chasing one another, with the speed of snails, across his countenance. Eventually, his face cleared and he chuckled. "Yes, St George is quite a catch."

"Quite so," I agreed pleasantly. From beside me, I could hear Christopher smother a laugh.

By now, the Honorable Reggie Fish and his less than honorable companion had moved on, and Crispin and Laetitia were standing alone in front of the fireplace. But instead of smiling fatuously at his fiancée, the way she was gazing at him, heart in her eyes, Crispin was scowling in our direction. When I caught his eyes and smirked, his brows lowered further. I turned back to Geoffrey. "You must be so pleased."

Geoffrey stuck his chest out. "Of course. Couldn't ask for better, really."

"Not really. He's one of a kind." I smirked into my gin. Francis turned a bark of laughter into a cough, and addressed his future cousin-in-law.

"Welcome to the family, Marsden."

"Same, Astley," Geoffrey said jovially. "Although you were there already, weren't you?"

He flicked a glance at Constance, and of course he was absolutely correct. We were a fairly incestuous bunch, between Geoffrey's cousin being engaged to marry Francis, and Francis's cousin being engaged to marry Geoffrey's sister. All we needed to tie it all together was for me to marry Geoffrey, but that was entirely out of the question, of course. I didn't think that marriage was likely to change his proclivities—it would simply give him more opportunity to philander—and I was certainly not going to get involved with it.

Not that he was interested in me for marriage, anyway. Whoever he married would have to come with a title and preferably a fortune of her own. Someone like, I assumed, Lady Violet Cummings or, in a pinch, the Honorable Cecily Fletcher or Olivia Barnsley, whatever her title was. Not a nobody from the Continent, whose only claim to nobility was that she was the Duke of Sutherland's younger brother's wife's niece, with no money or standing of my own.

And that, of course, was when the door to the drawing room opened again, and someone new entered.

I only knew about it because Crispin's eyes, already narrowed, now turned to slits, while something that felt very much like an electrical current ran around the rest of the room.

Laetitia straightened, and so did the three young ladies who had heretofore been dividing their attention between Dominic Rivers and the Honorable Reggie. The latter's mouth shaped words that I would have been willing to bet were, "I say!" while Dom Rivers's jaw clenched.

Francis's eyes narrowed, too, and just as I was about to turn around to see what all the excitement was about, a presence stepped up beside me. A voice I recognized said, warmly, "Philippa."

Francis growled, and I saw his knuckles turn white around the brandy glass he was holding. For a second, I worried that he would squeeze so hard that the glass broke and cut him, but then Constance's hand landed on his arm and I stopped worrying.

"Natterdorff," Christopher said blandly, and I turned on my heel with a blinding smile.

"Wolfgang. How lovely to see you."

CHAPTER FOUR

"YOU KNOW THIS KRAUT?"

Francis's voice was dark and threatening, barely more than a growl.

"Don't be rude, Francis," I admonished, while Christopher told him, "The *Graf von und zu* Natterdorff is Pippa's cousin."

Francis looked at me with betrayal in his eyes. "Pipsqueak?"

"Once or twice removed," I said apologetically, "or something of that nature. On my father's side. I'm not certain how the relationship works."

Nor was I to blame for it, really, although I didn't think that argument would really hold water with Francis right now.

He didn't respond to it, just turned his attention back onto Wolfgang. They stared at one another. Everyone else stared, too, while whispers spread throughout the drawing room, starting low and slowly building to a buzz. The girls' attention was avid, probably because Wolfgang is exceptionally handsome, at least aside from that Mensur scar bisecting his cheek.

Not that there's anything at all wrong with the way Francis

looks, or for that matter the other Astleys. They're all good-looking young men of the British type, with their fair hair and fair skin. Wolfgang, though, it must be said, is stunning.

After a moment's contemplation of Francis, he turned to me and arched a brow. "Another one?"

Another Astley, I assumed. He had met Christopher and Crispin before, and they look enough alike to be twins, aside from a slight difference in coloring. Francis looks enough like them both to be a brother to both of them.

The latter's eyes narrowed into slits. "Yes," he growled. "There are three of us."

Constance put a hand on his arm, clearly trying to calm him down, but instead of responding favorably, Francis merely took a step closer to Wolfgang and leaned into his face. He was a bit shorter, but it didn't stop him from looking like he would be capable of breaking Wolfgang into little pieces should he decide to do so. Francis's face was livid, and his voice shook with anger when he added, "There used to be four. But our brother never made it home from the Continent in 1918."

Wolfgang's eyes flashed with something—it might have been contempt or compassion, there was no way to tell—but it was gone again in an instant. He opened his mouth, but then his eyes flicked to me, and the sight must have made him think better of whatever he had planned to say, because he closed his mouth again without utterance.

Francis straightened, but not before he had poked the index finger of his free hand into Wolfgang's chest—hard. "Stay away from my family."

"That will be hard to do—" Wolfgang began, but then a hand landed on his shoulder and squeezed, and he shut up.

One might have expected it to be Christopher, who had been standing silently next to me during the whole exchange, but no. It was Crispin who had walked the couple of yards from the fireplace—leaving his fiancée standing there alone—to interfere.

Francis looked at him for a moment, before flicking a glance at me, and then another at Wolfgang, before he sneered and stepped back. Constance pulled him away from the fray, and the whispers that had quieted at Crispin's arrival picked up again.

"My fiancée invited you here," Crispin told Wolfgang, his voice as cold as ice. "It wouldn't have been my choice, but this is her home, not mine. But if you think for a moment that your presence here—"

He would have gone on, of course, but Wolfgang twitched his shoulder out of Crispin's grasp and turned to him. "I am well aware of your feelings, Lord St George."

He practically sneered Crispin's title, and Crispin's lips tightened. Wolfgang, being a *Graf*, is a slight step up the aristocratic ladder from a Viscount, and they both knew it.

Of course, once Uncle Harold pops off and Crispin comes into the title, the Sutherland dukedom beats Wolfgang's earlhood, but until then, Wolfgang delights in trying to make Crispin feel young, short, and inferior. He continued, silkily, "But as you say, your fiancée invited me. Please allow me to congratulate you on your spectacular fortune. She's lovely."

He clicked his heels and made a perfectly executed bow, just on the edge of insolent.

Crispin pried his teeth apart. "Thank you."

"Perhaps you would be so kind as to introduce me, so I may extend my congratulations?"

There wasn't anything Crispin could say to that, of course, so the two of them took off for Laetitia, who was still standing in front of the fireplace, one foot tapping and arms folded across her chest. She managed to hide the latter feature somewhat by virtue of clutching a glass of champagne in one hand, while the other had come up to support the opposite elbow, but it was still, clearly, a petulant crossing of her arms.

I had once seen her slap Crispin's cheek with her fan when he hadn't obeyed her summons quickly enough. There was no fan this time, but I watched anyway, curious as to what form her displeasure would take. He had abandoned her there, in front of the fireplace, after all. Surely she must want revenge. With any luck, perhaps I would get to see her throw the dregs of her champagne in his face.

But alas, no. She flicked her fiancé an absolutely fulminating glare when he got close enough to be blasted by it, but it turned to one of simpering welcome when he presented the *Graf von und zu* Natterdorff. Wolfgang bent over her hand, and Laetitia sent me a triumphant smirk over his bowed head. I rolled my eyes and turned away.

"That was unfortunate," Christopher commented, as he watched Constance pull Francis to the edge of the room, amidst looks and whispers.

I nodded. "But surely you knew that would be coming? As soon as we knew that Wolfgang was invited, you must have realized that putting him and Francis in the same room would turn out to be a problem."

"I thought it would be best not to upset the apple cart prematurely," Christopher said, with another glance at his brother. "If we had told him about Wolfgang yesterday, we would have been exposed to twenty-four hours of nothing else. But in retrospect, it might perhaps have been kinder to let Francis know what to expect ahead of time."

Francis and Constance had ended up by the wall on the opposite side of the room. He had his head bowed attentively towards her, and she was talking quickly, her hand on his arm and her eyes on his face. They were big and brown and beseeching. Francis's complexion was still flushed and his eyes were angry, but he was nodding along with what she was saying.

"The War seems far away for us," Christopher added, eyes still on them. "We didn't fight, and we've already lived a third of our lives since it ended. But you know Francis is still struggling with it all."

"Of course. Although I don't think Wolfgang took part in the War, you know. Like you and me," and Constance and Crispin, "he's too young."

"He's still German," Christopher said, and of course there was nothing I could say to that. Other than to, perhaps, remind him that so was I, but it didn't seem like an opportune moment for that.

Things went downhill after that, not that the reason for this party hadn't already been a downer. More people showed up, some I recognized, some I didn't. A supper buffet was served, which we all ate standing up, balancing tiny plates and cocktail glasses, and then a gramophone started playing and the dancing commenced while the drinking continued. Laetitia circled the room in Crispin's arms, tulle floating behind her, while the gaudy Sutherland engagement ring sparkled on his shoulder. More than once, a beam of reflected light caught me directly in the eye and made me squint. Laetitia's expression was caught somewhere between indecent triumph and petulance, the latter because Crispin looked mostly bored, at least until she caught his eye and glared at him, and then he dragged a smile onto his face and gave her a spin. It only lasted until she looked away, and then his mask dropped off into weariness again.

"The poor sod looks miserable," Christopher muttered. He and I were taking a turn around the floor too, and he kept twisting me around to keep them in sight.

I nodded. "And this is just the engagement party. Just

imagine what he's going to look like in December. Not to mention five years from now."

Christopher looked at me. "That's a bit callous, Pippa, isn't it?"

"Is it? He made his own bed—quite literally. Perhaps it'll be good for him to lie in it."

Christopher hummed. A moment passed while he eyed me, and while I avoided looking at him. "How bad do you feel, really?" he wanted to know.

"Lousy," I admitted, since I regretted my own part in this farce rather deeply. "Although I don't know why I should, Christopher. When I spoke to him earlier, he was as unpleasant as ever."

"That's just his way," Christopher said. "He hides everything. It doesn't mean he isn't upset."

"Well, I don't see what I can do about it. I didn't want him to propose to Laetitia. I was just lashing out because he'd been a prat. But now that it's done, I don't know how I can fix it. We discussed this last night, and short of killing her, I don't know what anyone can do to help."

"Me either," Christopher admitted, and gave me another twirl. "Getting rid of Laetitia Marsden would probably not be worth the trouble of going to prison for the rest of my life."

"It wouldn't," I agreed. "If you were the one marrying her, or I was—not that that's a possibility—I could have made a case for it. I'm not consigning either of us to a life of misery. But I'm not risking my freedom for St George. Especially not when he isn't kicking up more of a fuss than he's currently doing."

We eyed them both in silence for a moment. Laetitia floated around the floor like everything was perfect in her world, and Crispin looked like he wanted to sink right through it.

"I suppose we'll just keep the idea of murder in reserve,"

Christopher said, "unless he brings it up himself. If he does, I might consider it. And meanwhile, we can hope that something happens so murder won't be necessary."

I couldn't imagine what that might be, and told him so. But since there was nothing else we could do, we left the conversation there. Elsewhere in the room, Lady Violet Cummings was floating in Lord Geoffrey Marsden's arms, smiling beatifically up at him while his hand rested low on her back. A bit lower than I would have been comfortable with, honestly, but perhaps Geoffrey Marsden was next in line for Violet's affections now that Crispin was off the market. Olivia Barnsley was waltzing with the Honorable Reggie Fish, and she looked pleased, as well. So did he, as a matter of fact. Cecily Fletcher, meanwhile, was dancing with Dominic Rivers, but she appeared no happier about the situation than he did. Neither of them even looked at the other.

Over by the wall, Francis was throwing back a glass of something clear that probably wasn't water, while Constance watched, her expression worried. And behind Christopher, a hand came out of nowhere and landed on his shoulder.

"May I cut in?" a lightly accented male voice asked.

There is no way to say no, of course. Etiquette dictates that when a rival asks to cut into a dance, the polite young gentleman steps back. (The young lady gets no say in the matter, but has to accept, with a smile, being passed from one young man to the other like a package.)

In this case, it was Wolfgang who wanted to cut in, and I had no problem dancing with him. Christopher had no problem letting me, it seemed, because he bowed. "I'll go check on Francis," he told me.

I nodded, and watched him step back before Wolfgang took his place and swept me into a smooth Foxtrot. As we traversed the floor, Wolfgang smiled down at me. "Philippa."

"Wolfgang," I smiled back, while the faint echo of Crispin's derisive 'Wolfie,' sounded in the back of my head. "I'm pleased to see you."

"Likewise, *mein Schatz*." The arm around my waist squeezed a little tighter. I simpered. Out of the corner of my eye I could see that Crispin had come out of his stupor and was scowling at us over Laetitia's shoulder, while Francis was doing the same from over by the wall. Constance looked downcast, which was understandable. Francis can be difficult when he's in a sulk—or for that matter in his cups.

I saw Christopher reach the duo by the wall, and then Wolfgang turned me and I was looking at Cecily Fletcher and Dominic Rivers again. They were talking now: anger, or perhaps distress, had broken through Cecily's mask of ennui, while Rivers simply looked bothered. Behind them, Violet Cummings was beaming fatuously at Geoffrey Marsden.

And that was all I saw, before another couple ran into us— or rather, into Wolfgang. The impact knocked him forward a step. I, perforce, had to take a step back, and thus ended up knocking into someone else, and so it went.

"Pardon me," a man's voice sneered, with no apology whatsoever, followed by a woman's titter. I peered over Wolfgang's shoulder, into the self-satisfied face of a man—I wouldn't want to call him a gentleman, although his mother undoubtedly did —with carrot red hair and a rabbity chin. The young lady in his arms was another bottle blonde of the young and bright variety, with perpetually plucked eyebrows that gave her a surprised look, over heavily mascaraed eyes.

Behind me, the gentleman I had backed into—Crispin, as it turned out—set me upright. "Careful, Bilge," he told the redhead tightly. "This is supposed to be a celebration. We don't want any injuries tonight."

Bilge—five years older or so, and an inch or two taller—

sneered down at him. But of course Crispin was Laetitia's fiancé, and we were in Laetitia's home, and Bilge—what sort of name was Bilge?—must have thought better of condescending to the man of the hour.

"Are you all right, Darling?" Crispin added when Bilge didn't say anything, and I nodded.

"Thank you, St George. Sorry for stepping on your toes."

"It's hardly the first time, Darling, is it? What about you, Wolfie?"

Wolfgang's eyes, a stunning midnight blue, narrowed at the familiarity. "As well as can be expected, my lord."

Crispin smirked. "No need to be so formal, *Graf*. We don't stand on ceremony here. Do we, Bilge? We're all rich and titled, aren't we?"

Bilge muttered something uncomplimentary before he swung his partner back into motion. Crispin grinned and turned back to me. "As you were, Darling."

"Same to you, St George," I told him, and let Wolfgang sweep me back into his arms and into another Foxtrot. Like Bilge, he was muttering under his breath, and I grinned, too. "My apologies for the rudeness, Wolfgang. Some people have no manners."

"Your cousin is an impudent monkey," Wolfgang growled.

Crispin? I had been referring to the acrimonious Bilge, but if he wanted to see Crispin as the problem, I supposed he could. "He's right, you know. We really don't stand on ceremony much. Everyone here is from a good family, half the people have titles and money, and the rest are connected to the first half."

Like me. And like Christopher and Francis and Constance. The children of younger sons and daughters and assorted hangers-on.

Wolfgang grunted, and I added, "Aside from Dominic

Rivers, I suppose. He knows everyone, and everyone knows him, but according to St George, he grew up in Southwark. But when you're peddling something everyone wants, I guess your background doesn't much matter."

"Pardon me?"

"Dominic Rivers. Over there, the young man with the black hair and olive skin."

Wolfgang eyed him.

"He's a dope merchant. From what I know, he supplies the entire Bright Young Set with dope. Someone must have asked him to bring something, I suppose, and he's here to deliver."

Crispin had made it clear with his reaction that he hadn't invited Rivers, so perhaps Laetitia was the culprit. Although I couldn't imagine what reason she might have had to want to get high. She was already on cloud nine over the engagement, and wouldn't be looking to forget anything.

No, it was more likely that one of the other guests had contacted Rivers with a request for some sort of dope, and Rivers had arranged to meet him or her here. That was how it usually worked: you didn't go to Rivers, he came to you.

My eyes flicked to Francis, who was still standing by the wall, sullenly clutching a glass. It was more than half full, so it had been refilled since the last time I had seen him toss the contents back. Constance stood on one side of him, teeth sunk into her bottom lip and eyes worried, while Christopher stood on the other. From his expression, and the way his hands flew, he was doing his best to reason with his brother, but from Francis's face—brows lowered and jaw clenched—Christopher wasn't making much headway.

Did Francis know who Dominic Rivers was, I wondered?

Francis has spent most of the eight years since the War blunting the shellshock with any kind of dope he can get his hands on. I've seen him strung out on opium and practically catatonic from high levels of Veronal. I didn't think his supplier had ever been Dominic Rivers—Francis is thirty, and deals with a rougher, more adult crowd—but if Dom was here, and had what Francis wanted, I wouldn't put it past Francis to make use of that opportunity. Not in his current state of mind, at any rate. I hoped Christopher had realized the danger and was taking steps to prevent it.

"Nice company your cousin keeps," Wolfgang remarked snidely, and I returned my attention to him.

"St George? He's not my cousin. And he wasn't the one who invited Rivers here. I don't know who did, but he made it clear that he hadn't."

"Hmm." Wolfgang eyed the dope dealer. He had switched from dancing with the Honorable Cecily Fletcher to dancing with Lady Violet Cummings now, and Cecily was the one in Geoffrey's arms. She looked stiff and uncomfortable, as if he were attempting to grasp her more closely than she wanted to be held. It was certainly something he would do, I thought, even if I had never had the displeasure of being forced to dance with him myself. At any rate, Cecily looked as if she were making an effort to keep her body at a distance from his.

Although he wasn't slobbering all over her, at least. Instead, he was pointedly ignoring her in favor of watching something, or perhaps someone, on the other side of the room. I twisted my head in that direction, but saw nothing interesting. Francis, Christopher, and Constance were still holding up the wall. A maid in a neat gray uniform was approaching them with a cup of tea that she handed off to Constance, who I guessed must have had her fill of sherry already. Not much of a party animal, my future cousin-in-law. Although in justice to her, with the way Francis was knocking back the heavy liquor, perhaps she thought that one of them had better stay sober, and perhaps she was right. Francis would become more and more of a cross to bear the more he drank, I imagined.

Then Wolfgang turned me around again, and I was looking at Crispin and Laetitia, still revolving around the floor together. Being newly engaged, they probably weren't expected to dance with anyone else tonight, or perhaps it was simply a choice on Laetitia's part, to not let Crispin out of her grasp.

"They make for a handsome couple," Wolfgang commented, and I made a face.

"I suppose."

My tendency, since I dislike them both, is to disregard that particular fact. Or rather, I'm well aware that Laetitia is lovely. I just don't like to acknowledge it. As for Crispin... he looks practically identical to Christopher, and Christopher is quite cute, so of course I'm aware, on a purely esthetic level, that Crispin is good-looking. It's not something I usually think about, however. You won't find me gawking at him with stars in my eyes the way Laetitia was doing.

Wolfgang smirked. "They'll make beautiful babies."

"Ugh," I said.

He chuckled and spun me around. "Not ready for that step?"

"Not ready for them to take it, certainly. Nor are they, I imagine."

Or at least Crispin wasn't. Aunt Roz had dumped a baby in his arms a few months ago—a baby that looked enough like him to be his own, and a baby that everyone had, in fact, believed to be his—and he had looked like a rabbit in the headlamps of an oncoming motorcar.

No, definitely not ready for fatherhood.

"I saw in the *Times* that the wedding is to take place in December," Wolfgang remarked. "In German society, that would be cause for gossip."

Yes, no doubt it was cause for gossip here, too. Crispin had assured me that Laetitia wasn't in the family way—if she had been, it wouldn't have taken my involvement to make Crispin propose; between Uncle Harold and Laetitia herself, they would have forced him to do the right thing—but there was no question that people would be, and probably already were, talking.

"She's just eager," I said. "Not expecting."

He squinted at me. "You're certain of this?"

"As certain as I can be. St George said so. And as far as I know, the last time they shared a bed was in January."

"He told you this?" Wolfgang sounded shocked.

"Not in so many words." I had learned it from Grimsby the valet's dossier of misdemeanors. "Although he has never bothered to deny it."

Wolfgang muttered something in German. It was uncomplimentary. I could tell from the tone, even if the words themselves were new to me.

"Don't worry about it," I told him. "It's all moot now anyway."

He scowled. "He shouldn't be speaking to you about such things."

Perhaps not. It was a tad inappropriate, perhaps, when we weren't related and weren't romantically involved. "He doesn't, mostly. And from now on, I'm sure Laetitia will stop him from speaking to me about anything at all."

"Good," Wolfgang said decisively and twirled me around so the skirt of my—virginal, white—frock fluttered.

CHAPTER FIVE

"TELL ME WHAT TO DO, PIPPA," Constance said.

The party was over, at least for the two of us. There were a few stragglers still downstairs, but they were slowly making their way up, too. We could hear them on the staircase, and out in the hall, and above our heads. I ought to be up there myself, given the late hour, but after Christopher and I had dragged a legless Francis up the stairs and into Bluebell—I'm taller than Constance by several inches, so it made more sense for me to take Francis's other side while his distraught fiancée ran ahead, wringing her hands, to open the door—she had pulled me into Primrose and shoved me onto the divan.

"I don't think there's anything you can do," I said, folding my hands primly in my lap and getting comfortable. "He was going to backslide sooner or later. He did in July, after Abigail and the baby showed up at Beckwith Place. Now it's September. Honestly, I don't think two month intervals are terrible."

Constance didn't say anything, and I added, "And all he's doing is drinking too much. Christopher will make sure he doesn't get into anything else. Not that there's likely to be anything to get into. Francis doesn't travel with Veronal anymore..."

"You told me about Mr. Rivers," Constance said tonelessly. "He'll have whatever Francis requires."

"Christopher won't let that happen." And besides, I doubted that Dominic Rivers traveled with a suitcase full of pharmacology, just on the off-chance that someone might ask him for something he could provide. If someone had invited him here for an exchange of goods for money, Dom would have brought the requested substance with him. That was how it worked. But he probably hadn't come prepared for a bustling evening of business. Certainly not of anything Francis might want to indulge in. He's not much for party dope, my cousin. When he uses, it's with the purpose of dulling the senses, not enhancing them.

Constance looked doubtful, and I reassured her. "I promise. Christopher will take care of him. He's a light sleeper. If Francis tries to get up in the middle of the night, Christopher will wake up and go with him. He won't let Francis do anything stupid. And honestly, with as much as he has had to drink tonight, the only place he's likely to go, is the lavatory."

Constance bit her lip, and I added, "Just be prepared that he'll be a bear tomorrow morning. Give him lots of coffee and water. Make sure he eats something. And keep him away from Wolfgang for the rest of the weekend."

Constance looked wretched. "Are you angry with him, Pippa?"

"Of course not," I said. How could I be? "Francis spent two years in the trenches, being shot at by people who sound like Wolfgang. Robbie died in the War. So did a lot of other people Francis knew and presumably cared for. Of course he's upset."

Constance nodded.

"But it wasn't Wolfgang's fault. He wasn't there. He was too young to be conscripted, and he didn't volunteer. Francis oughtn't take it out on him."

"I imagine it's not that easy," Constance murmured. I was about to respond, but before I could, there was a knock on the door. "Come in."

I had expected Francis, in case he had gotten a second wind between the time we had left him in Christopher's care and now, or perhaps Christopher himself, to let us know that Francis was settled and asleep, and for Constance not to worry.

In a pinch, I suppose it might have been Laetitia Marsden, looking for a heart-to-heart with her cousin. Not that they'd ever been on those terms, but miracles do happen, even if Laetitia was far more likely, in my opinion, to have her heart-to-hearts with one of the Bright Young Things.

As it happened, it was neither of the above. Instead, the young maid I had noticed in the ballroom earlier, the one who had brought Constance the cup of tea, stood in the doorway. "Would you like help before bed, Miss Constance?"

"No, thank you, Nellie," Constance said gently. Nellie looked younger than the both of us, a fresh-faced twenty-one or so, and quite pretty, in that perfect English rose way, with big, blue eyes and soft brown hair trimmed in a tidy French bob under a little frilled cap.

She turned to me. "Miss Darling? Do you require help with your toilette?"

I shook my head. "That's not necessary, thank you, Nellie. I'm used to dressing myself."

Nellie nodded. She made no move towards the door, however, and after a moment, I added, "Some of the other young ladies might appreciate it. I don't get the impression that Laetitia or that cow who was dancing with the insufferable Bilge handle their own toilette."

Nellie looked like she wanted to smile but didn't quite dare to. Constance had no such compunction. "The cow is Bilge's wife, Lady Serena Fortescue," she told me with a giggle. "And no, she's definitely not used to handling her own toilette. Nor is Laetitia. But she has her own lady's maid. So does my aunt. Nellie is just stepping up for the occasion."

"That's kind of you, Nellie," I said. "I'm sorry we have no need for your help."

"That's quite all right, Miss Darling." She took a backwards step towards the door. "Perhaps I'll go see if Lady Serena is in need of assistance."

"Or Violet," I said. "Or Cecily. Or Olivia Barnsley."

"Lady Violet is in the garden with Lord Geoffrey," Nellie said, "and Miss Fletcher is in her room with Mr. Rivers."

Was she really? The two of them hadn't looked like they were flirting earlier, but perhaps I had misunderstood something. Or perhaps Cecily was the reason Dom Rivers was here. If so, her appearance earlier—pale and tired, with dark circles under her eyes—was certainly no advertisement for his services.

It was none of my concern, however, so I merely said, "Crispin is with Laetitia, I suppose?"

"No, Miss Darling," Nellie said. "Lord St George excused himself to his room."

Oh, had he? I exchanged a glance with Constance, who rolled her eyes. "That can't have made Laetitia happy."

"No, Miss Constance," Nellie agreed. "Miss Laetitia tried to talk Lord St George into coming in with her, but he pleaded a headache."

Of course he did, the coward. Trying to put off the inevitable, no doubt. I snorted.

"Don't be unkind, Pippa," Constance admonished. "I'm sure this is an adjustment for both of them."

"I'm sure it is. I just find it funny that after proposing and being accepted, now he's doing everything in his power to stay clear of her." As if that was going to be an option after December.

Constance gave me a jaundiced look before turning back to Nellie. "How long have you been here at the manor, Nellie?"

She herself had lived across the valley at the Dower House until early May, so Nellie must have arrived since that time, I assumed, or Constance would already know the answer.

And indeed, Nellie explained that she was new to the manor; she had only been in the Marsdens' employ for a month.

"Has anyone bothered to warn you about Geoffrey?" I wanted to know, since Constance had told me all about the speed with which Lord Geoffrey moves through the female staff. Nellie would be particularly exposed, I figured, being both quite young and quite pretty.

"Yes, Miss Darling." She looked a bit uncomfortable to be asked, although she answered the question readily enough. "Mrs. Frobisher—"

"The housekeeper," Constance interjected.

Nellie nodded. "—told me that Jane—"

"The previous chambermaid."

"—was let go because of Lord Geoffrey, so if I value my job, I should keep my distance."

I snorted. Well, that was typical, wasn't it? "It's easier said than done to keep your distance, when someone isn't inclined to give you space to keep yourself to yourself."

Nellie didn't answer, and I added, persuasively, "You can tell us, you know. Miss Constance can talk to Mrs. Frobisher and make sure that she knows it isn't your fault and that Geoffrey's being a bother."

I had no idea whether the housekeeper would believe that —likely not—or what she could do about it if she did, but at the moment I was really just saying whatever I thought I had to, to put Nellie at ease so she would feel comfortable enough to be honest with us.

She looked a bit discomfited, but she shook her head. "That won't be necessary, Miss Darling. No one is bothering me. Although Miss Laetitia warned me to stay away from her new fiancé last week, too."

"It's the curse of being young and pretty," I told her. "Although you don't have to worry about Lord St George. He has his faults, but seducing the staff isn't one of them."

"No, Miss Darling."

"Although Laetitia isn't likely to be understanding, so it's probably best if you keep a wide berth there, too. Just to avoid upsetting her." She was liable to be more of a problem than Crispin, as far as Nellie was concerned.

The maid nodded. "Yes, Miss Darling." She flicked a glance at the door, outside which there was the sound of footsteps and a soft laugh. Over our heads, the ceiling squeaked as someone crossed their bedroom floor.

"You may go, Nellie," Constance said. "Miss Darling and I can manage on our own tonight."

"Yes, Miss Constance." Nellie withdrew. The door shut behind her with nary a snick of the lock.

We sat in silence for a moment before Constance sighed. "I never know whether to warn them or not. It always makes me feel guilty, whether I do it or I don't."

And quite understandably so, too.

"He's your cousin," I said. "I'm sure you love him. But he can't be allowed to carry on the way he does. It's one thing when he tries to push me into the corner of the sofa and paw me. I can take care of myself, and I have people around me who'll come to my rescue. It's altogether different when he does it to the maids. They can't really say no. Not if they aren't willing to risk their livelihood in the process."

Constance nodded. "And Nellie's so young. And also so very pretty. I'm honestly surprised that Geoffrey hasn't already begun his offensive, but you know it's just a matter of time."

Indeed. "At least she knows now that it's coming, and she can decide for herself what she wants to do about it when it does."

"It's an automatic dismissal either way if Aunt Effie finds out," Constance said. "You know she wouldn't keep a maid on after she'd dallied with Geoffrey, so it's a case of damned if you do, damned if you don't, really."

Yes, of course it was. No good options at all.

"I thought about asking her about Lydia Morrison," I said, "and whether anyone has heard from her, but if Nellie's only been here a month, she wouldn't know Lydia Morrison to look at, would she?"

Constance shook her head. "Morrison was before her time. I suppose one of us shall have to inquire of Mrs. Frobisher tomorrow."

I supposed so. The whole convoluted mess was getting on my nerves, and the fact that no one knew where Lydia Morrison was, was frustrating.

Up until recently, Morrison had been the late Lady Peckham's maid at the Dower House, while Margaret Hughes had been her counterpart at Sutherland Hall. Before that, though, while Crispin and Constance (and Christopher and I) had been babies, it had been the opposite. Back then, Morrison worked for Aunt Charlotte, while Hughes worked for Constance's mother. The two gentlewomen had been old friends, and at some point while their children were infants, they had decided to switch maids. Morrison had ended up at the Dower House with Constance's mother and Hughes had come to Sutherland to work for Aunt Charlotte. And so it had been for more than twenty years.

Until that awful weekend at Sutherland Hall this past April, when Morrison had received a phone call from persons unknown. The next morning she had been gone. No one had seen or heard from her since. And now Hughes was dead—the victim of a botched mugging in a Bristol alley—and Morrison was still nowhere to be found, and I was beginning to be irritated. A grown woman of fifty-odd shouldn't be able to just vanish into the ether like that.

"Of course not," Constance agreed, "but short of asking Mrs. Frobisher, I don't know what to do about it. Why don't we start there? Tomorrow?"

I nodded. It certainly seemed like a good enough place to start.

"You should have let Francis know about your German friend before this evening, Pippa," Constance said. There was nothing particularly accusing in her voice, but I squirmed guiltily anyway.

"I understand why you would say that, Constance. And I agree that what happened downstairs was not ideal..."

"Hardly," Constance said.

"But if we had told him—and everyone else—about Wolfgang last night, Francis would have spent last night and all of today fretting about it. He would have driven you mad, and you know it."

"Don't you mean that he would have driven *you* mad?" Constance wanted to know. She flicked a glance at me from where she was sitting on the edge of the bed, hands tidily folded in her lap.

I made a face. "That too, certainly. Although to be honest, I thought there was a chance you already knew."

Christopher had rung up Crispin the same evening Wolfgang had appeared in our lives. It wouldn't have been surprising if he had let his parents in on the news, too.

"No," Constance answered when I said as much. "No one has said a word to us about your German suitor. Not Christopher, nor Lord St George, nor his father."

I arched my brows. "He's not my suitor, you know. Just a friend, or more accurately, a distant relative."

"So Christopher said," Constance nodded. "Does that mean you're German nobility, too?"

I shook my head. "Lord, no. My mother shocked everyone when she ran off to the Continent and married a commoner. My father was nobody. If I'm related to Wolfgang at all, it's on the distaff side of the family, and several times removed."

Constance made a little humming noise. "So Lord St George..." Her voice tilted up at the end, making it a question.

"You're practically married to Francis," I told her crossly. "You're soon to be Crispin's cousin by marriage. On both sides of the family, since you're Laetitia's cousin, too. You can call him by his given name."

She gave me a look. "So can you, but I don't see you doing it."

"That's different. And he has known about Wolfgang since the day we met him. Christopher wasted no time in ringing him up; God knows why."

Constance muttered something, but I ignored it. "It was when he insulted Wolfgang—and by extension, me—that I suggested he should propose to Laetitia. I thought he might have whinged to his father about it, and that Uncle Harold may have included it in the happy news when he called his brother and sister-in-law to let them know that Crispin is engaged."

"No," Constance said. "If His Grace mentioned anything about the *Graf* von Natterdorff to Roslyn and Herbert, neither of them said anything to Francis or me about it."

I nodded. "Well, you're right. Considering what happened downstairs, it would undoubtedly have been better to prepare him. But we thought—Christopher and I—that it would be easier if he didn't know. At least he wouldn't have time to stew."

In retrospect, stewing might have been better than what happened. Then again, there was no reason to think that stewing would have prevented it, either.

"He'll be all right," I added, optimistically. "He'll sleep it off tonight, and as long as you and Christopher keep him away from Wolfgang tomorrow, I don't think there'll be a problem. Aunt Roz and Uncle Herbert will be here then, too, and they'll help."

Constance nodded.

"And in the worst case scenario, he can take the Crossley and drive back to Beckwith Place. Crispin will understand."

She opened her mouth, and I added, "You can stay or go with him. It's your Crossley, and by now you have suffered through the first part of the engagement weekend anyway. It's understandable if you want to leave before the second half. Especially if your fiancé is going."

"You can go, too," Constance pointed out.

"I could, although I don't think Christopher would approve of that. He'll want to be here to support Crispin. And I enjoy watching him squirm, you know. Besides, there's Wolfgang. Now that I'm here, I don't think I ought to leave him to the wolves."

Constance nodded, and I added, "Aunt Roz and Uncle Herbert will be coming down in the Bentley tomorrow. We can return to Beckwith Place with them."

"I suppose we shall have to wait and see how things look tomorrow morning, then," Constance said. "Who knows, Francis may be feeling better after a good sleep."

He might. And if not, he could always leave early, before Aunt Roz and Uncle Herbert made it here. That was if the hangover didn't keep him in bed until the late hours of the morning, of course.

"I should turn in," I said and pushed to my feet. "Will you be able to sleep, or should I ask someone for something?"

"I'll be fine, Pippa." She gave me a warm smile. "What about you?"

"Oh, I sleep like a log." I headed for the door. "I'll see you in the morning, Constance. For... a shooting party, wasn't it?"

Constance wrinkled her nose. "It was."

"I'll sit that one out," I said. "So will Christopher. He doesn't like to shoot at things." Much to Uncle Herbert's chagrin.

"Francis doesn't anymore, either," Constance said.

No, of course not. "They can both keep us company, then."

"And your German friend?"

I had no idea how Wolfgang felt about hunting, but I would guess, based on the Mensur scar on his cheek, that he wasn't opposed to blood sports. "I would assume he'd hunt, but I have no idea whether that's true or just my own perception of his character. He didn't volunteer for the war effort, at any rate. I suppose we'll find out."

I pulled the door open and stepped through and into the hallway. "Sleep well, Constance. I'll see you for breakfast."

"Good night, Pippa. Be careful walking through the house."

Of course. Although if the handsy Geoffrey was in the garden with Lady Violet, or perhaps holed up in his room with her now, he wasn't lurking in the shadows looking for me, and I doubted I was in danger from any of the other gentlemen present. Even so, I kept a sharp eye out as I wandered down the hallway towards the back stairs.

Lady Euphemia and Lord Maurice had the suite on the

eastern end of the manor house, Constance had told me, and Laetitia was next door to her mother. I assumed that would have been the Countess's decision, and not Laetitia's own, since I couldn't imagine the latter wanting the former to cramp her style at this point in her life. There was no light trickling out from below the doors of either Laetitia's room, or those of her parents.

The light was likewise out in the room that Christopher and Francis shared. I sidled up to the door and put my ear to the crack for a moment as I passed by, and could hear loud breaths from Francis—I wouldn't go so far as to say that he was snoring, but it was something like it—and I also heard rustling as someone turned over in bed. It might have been Francis himself, or perhaps Christopher was unable to sleep with the noise, and was trying to get comfortable.

For a moment I thought about knocking, to see whether my best friend was awake and wanted to talk—we hadn't had a chance to converse privately after the scene in the ballroom— but then I thought better of it. I didn't want to risk waking Francis and having him go off on me again—or worse, go off looking for Wolfgang, or for more to drink—and besides, if Christopher really was asleep and was simply moving rest- lessly, I didn't want to wake him. We'd have plenty of time to talk on the morrow, when everyone else was out shooting pheasants.

Crispin's room was next door to his cousins, and the light was out there too. He must be asleep already, because when I sidled up to the door—not for long; I didn't want Laetitia to suddenly come into the hallway and find me listening at the door to her fiancé's room—there were no sounds whatsoever from within.

The room on the other side of the staircase was a different matter. There was flickering light coming from under the door

—romantic candlelight as opposed to the glare of electricity—and the sound of laughter and of murmured voices wafted out from within. I didn't recognize them, and furthermore had no idea who was staying there. Judging from what I did know, it might have been Geoffrey's room, and he was in there with Lady Violet, or perhaps the room belonged to Bilge Fortescue and his wife.

The room across the hall was similarly dark—Geoffrey's, if the couple was the Fortescues, or perhaps the Fortescues' if the giggler was Lady Violet—and beyond that was another suite of two bedrooms on the far end of the house, all dark and, as far as I knew, empty. I assumed Uncle Harold would be bunking in one of them tomorrow, and that Uncle Herbert and Aunt Roz would end up in the other.

The staircase was around the corner from what was either Geoffrey's or the Fortescues' room, and I scurried up and into what was clearly the servants wing upstairs. Three small bedrooms and a lavatory were crammed together in one corner of the house. At this point, the reason for Geoffrey's chosen room was obvious: he hadn't been attempting to get away from his parents—or rather, that was of secondary benefit. What he had really wanted, was easy access to where the maids slept. All he had to do was step across the hallway downstairs and creep up the stairs, and here he was, with his pick of maids.

I wrinkled my nose and pushed the green baize door open. And there was my bedroom, at the end of the hall and on the left.

There were six bedrooms up here, in addition to the maids' quarters, and two washrooms. I hadn't been surprised to find my own tiny bedroom squeezed into the corner beyond one of the lavatories: that was certainly Laetitia's doing. Violet, Cecily, and Olivia had the three bedrooms across the hall, and then there was Wolfgang on the other side of the lavatory from me, and the duo of Reginald Fish and Dominic Rivers, who seemed to be bunking together.

The lights had been turned down low in the upper hallway, which I took to mean that everyone was where they were supposed to be at this point, or if not that, at least where they wanted to be. Two of the girls' bedrooms were dark, so two of them were either asleep or—in Violet's case—still out with Geoffrey. In the third, the light was on, and I could hear the murmur of voices as I tiptoed past. One male and one female, but too soft to make out words, or even whether they belonged to anyone I knew. I wouldn't be able to tell Cecily Fletcher's voice from Lady Violet's, of course, but I'd probably be able to tell Dominic Rivers's voice from, for instance, Geoffrey's.

I was in front of my own door, and had my hand out to grab the handle, when there was the slight scrape of a doorknob somewhere on this level. I stopped where I was, torn between ducking inside my room quickly so I wouldn't be seen, and wanting to discover who else was sneaking around after everyone else was in bed. That latter impulse won out, and I turned and peered down the hall for who was stirring.

There was a soft *click* as one of the doors across the hall opened, and a figure came out. The moon glimmered for a moment on fair hair, and my stomach dropped.

CHAPTER SIX

I SUPPOSE I SHOULD HAVE—OR could have, at least—pretended that I hadn't recognized him instantly. To myself, if to no one else. There were other men here with fair hair, after all. Christopher and Francis, Wolfgang, even the Honorable Reggie. I could have made a case for it being someone else.

Although Francis wasn't going to come out of some unknown young lady's bedchamber in the middle of the night, nor was Christopher. I certainly hoped that Wolfgang wouldn't do. And at any rate, I had known who he was as soon as he slipped through the door, long before the light had had any chance to find his head.

He must have known I was there, too—or that someone was—because his shoulders braced before he turned to face the hallway. His eyes flickered for a second before they landed on me. I suppose I was more visible than I'd thought I was. Even tucked into the dark corner of the hallway, my ivory frock must have stood out like a beacon, much like Crispin's head of platinum hair.

He breathed out. Relief, perhaps. "Philippa."

He sauntered my way, and if he had been nervous earlier, there was no sign of it now.

"St George," I retorted. Severely. Under no circumstances would I let him soften me up with my rarely-used given name.

Besides, it wasn't as if I had any doubts as to what he had been up to. I'm not stupid. There was only one reason why the newly-engaged Viscount St George, notorious cad and philanderer, would have been in... was it Olivia Barnsley's room? Most likely, if Lady Violet was in the garden with Geoffrey and Cecily Fletcher was entertaining Dominic Rivers—in the middle of the night.

Still, it was sobering to see the results with my own eyes. His hair was ruffled, as if someone had had her hands in it. He hadn't bothered to do up the buttons of his shirt all the way, so there was a V of pale skin visible at the bottom of his throat where the ends of the bowtie dangled. And his neck sported what could only be a bruise. From someone's teeth, no doubt.

I narrowed my eyes on it. "You had better do something about that before Laetitia sees it."

He sighed. "Darling..."

"You're vile," I told him. My voice shook, and I hoped he knew that it was from anger and disgust, not anything else. "You're... you're..."

"Vile." He nodded tiredly. "I know."

"Betrothed!" I hissed the word at him. I was careful not to raise my voice, though. While I loathed both him and his behavior, I didn't want to draw any more attention to his presence here than I had to. "You have a fiancée, St George. You have no business visiting other women's bedchambers at night."

"Laetitia's under no illusions about this being a love match, Darling."

"That's beside the point! You committed yourself to her; you shouldn't be coming out of Miss Barnsley's room in the—"

"Miss Fletcher's room," Crispin corrected.

Miss Fletcher? But she had been entertaining Dominic Rivers, hadn't she?

Unless Nellie had got it wrong, of course, but I couldn't imagine how anyone could have mistaken Dom Rivers for Crispin or vice versa. They looked nothing alike. They didn't even sound the same. Rivers's accent was a lot less elegant than Crispin's Eton-educated vowels. Besides, Nellie ought to be able to tell the fiancé of the daughter of the house from a random party guest who looked nothing like him.

Perhaps Cecily had entertained them both.

"Ugh," I said, wrinkling my nose. "Rekindling an old flame on the eve of your engagement party, St George? Lovely behavior."

"It's not what you think, Darling."

"Of course not," I said. "If I'm wrong, why do you look like that?"

He smirked. "Like what, Darling?"

I made a face. "Like you've had a close encounter with a vampire. One who decided to run her fingers through your hair before she sucked your blood."

He shook his head. "No vampire. And no one else has had her fingers in my hair."

He sounded sincere about it, so I tilted my head and gave him another look. "Why would you do that to yourself?"

"Cecily is with child," Crispin said.

He pronounced it so matter-of-factly that it took a second for the words to properly register. Then my jaw dropped, but before I could say anything, Crispin stiffened like a Pointer. The next second, he had wrapped his hand around the door handle and shoved my bedroom door open. A second after that, he had backed me into the room and pulled the door shut behind us.

"What on earth—" I began.

He flicked me a look. "Shhh."

I stuck my hands on my hips. "Why should I? You have no business coming into my room. Besides, I thought you told me that you didn't care if Laetitia found out that you were up here?"

"It's not Laetitia I'm worried about. Now be quiet, Darling."

It wasn't? "Who—?"

But he put a finger to his mouth and closed his eyes, the better to hear what was happening outside. Unless he just really didn't want to look at me. At this point I had caught on, anyway, and I could hear what he had heard: rapid footsteps jogging up the stairs towards our level.

"Did you see who it is?" I wanted to know, although I kept my voice low. At this point I was no more keen on being found with him in my room than he was on being found with me.

Crispin shook his head. "I got us out of sight before whoever that is could see us. I didn't get a chance to see him."

"Him?"

"It sounds more like a man than a woman."

I took a moment to listen, and decided that he was most likely right. The steps had entered the hallway, each one a decisive thump against the carpet runner. Not quick and light the way a woman's steps would have been.

"It isn't your fiancée," I pointed out. "We don't have to hide."

He arched a brow. "Is that something you want, Darling? For someone else to see me come out of your room, looking like I've just been shagged?"

Probably not. I was grateful for the relative darkness, as it covered the flush in my cheeks. "Definitely not."

"Then just wait until whoever is out there has gone into his room. Or into someone else's."

There was a moment of silence. The footsteps had stopped, but I hadn't yet heard a knock.

"Maybe Cecily is entertaining someone else," I said sourly.

Crispin shrugged. "I wouldn't be surprised. It certainly isn't my child she's carrying."

"Do you know that for a fact?"

He slanted me a look. "Yes, Darling. I haven't laid a finger on her since February. She'd look like a zeppelin if it were mine."

And she certainly hadn't done earlier. The current tubular fashions are kind to any slight affluence around the middle, but if Cecily had sported anything more than a slight stomach bulge, it would have been visible.

"Why talk to you, then?"

"Why not? She spoke to everyone else."

I supposed she had done, now that he mentioned it. Or to anyone who could possibly be involved, anyway. She had danced with most of the men in the ballroom earlier—save for Crispin, who'd been busy with Laetitia, and Francis, who'd been sulking, and Wolfgang, who was German and new to this crowd, and so, I presumed, no candidate for the father of Cecily's baby. But I had seen her dance with Dominic Rivers and with the Honorable Reggie, and even with Christopher once, when he had been taken away from Francis and pressed into service. The odious Bilge had even abandoned his wife to take Cecily for a turn around the floor, while the lovely Serena had simpered at Dominic Rivers.

"Do you think one of them is the father?"

"Who knows?" Crispin said, and sounded like it didn't much matter to him. And why would it, as long as he wasn't on the hook? "I asked, but she wouldn't tell me. Just said, when I told her she looked like a wilted tulip, that she was expecting and would I kindly keep my opinions to myself."

Good for her. "I think I might like Cecily," I said.

"You'd like anyone who gave me a hard time," Crispin answered, which was certainly true. He reached for the door-knob. "It's quiet out there. He must have gone inside his room."

Or inside someone else's. But either way—

"I'm sure it's safe to leave. Go get some sleep, St George. Tomorrow's going to be another long day of playing the happy fiancé. Better make sure you're rested."

He nodded. "What are you doing out and about at this hour anyway?" He looked me up and down, and his lip curled. "Coming from your own late-night rendezvous, are you?"

"It's certainly none of your affair if I am," I said, "seeing whose room you just came out of. But for your information, I sat with Constance for a while after we came upstairs. She's upset about Francis."

He sniggered. "Drunk off his arse, is he?"

"Yes. And so would you be, I believe, if you had spent two years in a foxhole and you suddenly came face to face with a German."

"Wolfie affects me that way even without the two years in the foxhole," Crispin said. "I'm just glad that someone else in the family shares my opinion of the bastard. The way you and Christopher fawn over him is appalling."

"Wolfgang," I corrected, "and I don't fawn. Christopher doesn't, either. He just thinks Wolfgang is handsome. Which he is."

Crispin sneered. "That's why you spent the rest of the evening making cow eyes at him, I suppose."

"Of course. And after the way you and Francis behaved, I had to make sure that he wasn't uncomfortable."

"Oh, I'm sure you made him very comfortable indeed,"

Crispin said. The sneer had taken up permanent residence now.

There was nothing I would have liked more than to smack it off his face, but I took a breath and refrained. "With you leaving your fiancée downstairs in favor of visiting Cecily's bedchamber at one in the morning, it's not as if you have any room to talk, St George."

Crispin shrugged, but it was sulky.

"I'm going to bed," I said.

He gave me an up and down look. "I imagine you'd like me to leave?"

"If you don't mind. I'll share with Christopher, but not with you. Besides, you have a room of your own, don't you?"

Crispin's lip curled. "I do. Across the hall from Laetitia's."

"The better to keep an eye on you, I suppose? She warned the maid to stay away from you, you know."

He sneered. "As if I would ever have anything to do with the maids."

"Of course you wouldn't," I said. "I know that, even if Laetitia doesn't. Although I think she's probably asleep by now, so you can get downstairs undetected. At least she didn't stick her head out to look at me when I left Constance's room earlier."

He sighed. "I suppose I'd best go, then."

I nodded. "I wish you would, St George. Go get some sleep. Tomorrow's going to be another long day of shooting pheasant and playing the happy fiancé."

He rolled his eyes. "Hunting. What fun."

"You don't have to ride out if you don't want to," I pointed out. "Your father isn't here yet, to yell at you for deviating from the approved path. You can stay with us. I don't plan to ride out. Christopher won't, either. Or Constance. And I doubt

Francis is interested in pointing a weapon at anything anymore."

"Bilge Fortescue spent some time on the Front, too," Crispin said, "although I doubt it will keep him from shooting at birds."

"Bilge Fortescue can do whatever he wants. It's none of our concern. Go to bed, St George." I reached past him and turned the door handle. "Off you go. Sweet dreams and all that."

The door opened and Crispin backed out. Right into the arms of the man standing outside in the hallway.

For a moment, I was afraid it was going to be Wolfgang and that we'd have a shouting match in the upstairs hallway. But it wasn't, something which the next second made very clear. Just as no one would mistake Dominic Rivers for Crispin, no one—especially me—would mistake him for Wolfgang, either.

"Well, well," he said as he set Crispin upright, "what do we have here?"

He leered at Crispin, from his ruffled hair to his open shirt, before he turned to me, and inspected me up and down, as well. I gave him a stony look in return. My hair wasn't disheveled, my dress wasn't wrinkled, and my makeup wasn't smudged, so he could stare all he wanted to. And he did, until Crispin stepped in front of me. "What are you doing here, Dom?"

Rivers didn't answer, just gave Crispin another amused look. "I could ask you the same thing, old bean, couldn't I? The unlikeliest people popping out of rooms all over the place tonight."

"I'm having a conversation with my cousin," Crispin said, "if you must know."

Rivers flicked another look at me. "But she's not your cousin, is she? Isn't that what you told me a few months ago?"

"Close enough for jazz," Crispin told him. "Especially at two in the morning."

Rivers made a little humming noise and gave him another once-over before he said, "You might want to fix your hair before Laetitia sees it."

"Laetitia is asleep," Crispin said.

Rivers smirked. "Are you sure of that?"

"Unless you came from there, I'm fairly certain." Crispin eyed him. "Are you trying to blackmail me, Dom? Because if you are..."

"Would I do that?" Rivers wanted to know, spreading his hands innocently. Trying to look like someone who had nothing to hide, I guessed.

"Weren't you one of the men in Cecily Fletcher's room earlier this evening?" I wanted to know, and Rivers turned to me, brows rising. "Do you think you should be making threats?"

"Are you trying to insinuate something, Miss Darling?"

"Only that people who live in glass houses shouldn't throw stones, Mr. Rivers. You're not exactly free from controversy yourself, are you?"

He didn't respond to that, just turned back to Crispin, who told him, "Go to bed, Dom. There's nothing going on here, but I can't stop you from telling Laetitia that you saw me if you decide to. I don't think you'd be telling her anything she doesn't already know, though."

Rivers didn't say anything, just contemplated him for a moment with his lips pursed. Then he gave a short nod. "Good night, St George. Miss Darling."

I got a truncated bow before he headed off down the hallway. A few seconds later, I heard a door open and close. Crispin turned to me. "Sleep well, Darling."

"The same to you," I told him, and pulled my head inside the room and shut the door. If he turned around at the top of the stairs, the last thing I wanted was for him to see me standing there, watching him walk away. Knowing him, it would undoubtedly give him ideas.

Inside the room, I did my usual evening toilette: Pulled the dress over my head and hung it on a hanger to air out, rolled down my stockings, and shimmied out of my unmentionables and into my pyjamas. That done, I fetched my toiletries bag and wandered next door to the lavatory. The hallway was empty when I entered it, although there were rustling sounds to be heard from inside a few of the rooms. Dominic Rivers must be getting situated for bed, for I could hear someone moving around in his and Reginald's shared room, and there was also a murmur of voices from inside, so he must have woken the Honorable Reggie when he walked in. Likewise, there was the sound of movement from inside one of the rooms on the other side of the hall. Cecily's again, or perhaps Lady Violet's or Olivia Barnsley's.

But that was none of my concern, so I shut the door to the loo and went about the business of getting ready for bed. Cold-cream on my face to remove the makeup, toothpaste on the brush to clean my teeth. After it was all said and done, I opened the door to the hallway again, only to find myself face to face with the expectant mother herself.

"Oh." I took an involuntary step back. Cecily Fletcher took that as an invitation, and brushed past me into the lavatory, where she fell to her knees in front of the commode and proceeded to empty her stomach. Loudly.

I winced. I'll sit beside Christopher while he attempts to turn his guts inside out, but only because I love him. I had no love for Cecily Fletcher. The noises she made were obscene, and the smell was indescribable.

At the same time, I didn't feel as if I could simply walk away and leave her to suffer alone. I may be cold, but I'm not callous. And she was so clearly suffering. I had gotten a good look at her when she brushed past me—a look I hadn't achieved down in the ballroom earlier—and without the red lipstick and rouged cheeks, she was deathly pale, with dark rings under her eyes.

So I made a face, but the only decision I could live with. I left my toiletries bag on the side of the sink and went over to Cecily.

One good thing about the newly bobbed hairstyles is that there were no long braids to keep out of the way of the toilet. I did put my hand on her forehead, and it was clammy and cold. Her bangs were wispy and wet with sweat as they brushed the back of my hand.

She flinched when she felt me take hold of her, but she didn't protest, and then another bout of sickness made that impossible, anyway. I wrinkled my nose, but stuck with it.

Once the new spasm was over, I left her to lean drunkenly on the toilet bowl, whimpering, and went to the sink. She hadn't brought a flannel, and there were none sitting around, so I used my own. Once it was wet, I took it back over to Cecily and used it to wipe her forehead and cheeks and the back of her neck. She was trembling, and the hand that wasn't clutching the toilet bowl was lying across her stomach, fingers spread.

"How often does this happen?" I wanted to know. "I thought it was called 'morning sickness' for a reason."

She shot me a look. "Of course he told you."

"There's no reason why he wouldn't," I said. "Although I won't spread it around any further. It's none of my affair."

Not as long as Crispin—or Christopher or Francis—weren't involved.

She nodded. "For your information, this happens at any time of the day. It's usually worse when I get up from lying down, but sometimes it comes on for no reason, as well. I had a cup of peppermint tea earlier, but it didn't seem to help."

Clearly not. "Do you feel well enough for me to help you back to your room? Or is it likely to happen again so you want to stay here?"

She wasn't actively vomiting anymore, and a touch of color was coming back into her cheeks.

"I think I'm done for now." She gave the toilet bowl a scowl. "I'm not sure there's anything left to throw up. Not that that always means I won't."

"Why don't we see if you can stand?" I suggested, and held out a hand. Hers was ice cold and limp as a dead fish. I braced myself and hauled her to her feet. "I'll find some sort of container for you, and that way, if it happens again, you'll have something beside your bed."

She staggered as she gained her feet, and I reached out automatically to support her. I ended up half dragging, half carrying her into the hallway, with one arm around her waist. "Would you like for me to knock up Rivers or the Honorable Reggie," I asked, breathlessly, "so you don't have to suffer the indignity of me trying to drag you into your bedchamber? One of them would be able to carry you, no doubt."

She shuddered. "No, thank you. It's very kind of you to help."

Very well, then. If she wanted to be manhandled by me, I would simply carry on with the handling. We staggered across the landing and towards the door to her room. It was standing halfway open, but the room inside was dark. She must have been in bed and been woken up, or perhaps hadn't fallen asleep yet, but her eyes had been accustomed enough to the dark that she hadn't needed to turn on a lamp as she ran for the lavatory.

I staggered to a stop a few steps in, so as not to run into any of the furniture. Cecily, perforce, stopped too.

"The bed is this way." Her voice sounded strained, as if she were in pain, so when she moved to the left, I followed. A few seconds later, she reached the bed and collapsed down on the edge of it with a sound halfway between a groan and a grunt.

I tucked my hands behind my back, feeling awkward. "Is there anything else I can do?"

"You can keep this to yourself," Cecily said, and I could hear the rustling as she swung her legs up onto the mattress and pulled the covers over herself.

"Of course. It's not as if a pregnant woman puking is anything newsworthy." Nor was it as if Cecily's getting in the family way was anything I should be gossiping about. Unless— "St George did tell me the truth, didn't he? It's not his problem?"

"I haven't had anything to do with Crispin since last winter," Cecily confirmed. After a second's pause, she added, tiredly, "If you feel that way about him, why is he marrying Laetitia and not you?"

"I don't feel that way about him. He's family, that's all. The cousin of my cousin is my cousin, and all that. And he's marrying Laetitia because that's what he chose to do."

Aside from which, Uncle Harold would never approve of him marrying me. Nor would I ever, unlike Laetitia, agree to marry a man whom I knew was in love with someone else. Laetitia was welcome to him, or would have been, had I not actually cared about the fact that she was a horrible cow who would make him unhappy and he should have known better than to propose.

But it was neither here nor there. "Is there anything else I can do for you before I go?"

I glanced around, my eyes a bit more used to the dim light now, and spotted a chamber pot and matching slop jar tucked away in a corner. "Would you like me to...?"

"No," Cecily said with a shudder, "thank you. I think that would only make the experience worse. I'd rather run across to the loo again."

"Would you like me to stay with you? In case you need help?"

She shook her head. "That's not necessary. But thank you for offering."

Very well, then. "I'm across the hall and to the right of the lavatory if you need help. Feel free to knock on my door. And if you can't make it, yell loudly and I'm sure I'll hear you. I'm not a particularly heavy sleeper."

"Thank you, Miss Darling. You've been more than kind."

"Call me Pippa," I said. "And it seems the least I can do. I hope you get to sleep. I'll put this—" I lifted the teacup and saucer from the side table, "—outside the door. That way, perhaps the maids will leave you alone tomorrow morning and you can stay in bed a bit."

She nodded gratefully. "Thank you, Pippa."

"You're welcome," I said, "Cecily."

With nothing more said, I took myself and the empty teacup out the door, which I closed carefully behind me. There was still an inch or so of brown liquid at the bottom of the cup, smelling strongly of mint, although to me, it was more spearmint than the peppermint Cecily had mentioned.

I took it across the hallway to the bathroom, where I poured the dregs of the tea down the drain. No sense in leaving a half-full cup of tea on the floor for someone to kick, after all. That done, I gathered up my flannel and my toiletries bag, before finally heading back to my own room for some peace and quiet.

CHAPTER SEVEN

BREAKFAST WAS LAID on in the breakfast room the next morning, in a come-and-go fashion. By the time I made it down there, the room was practically empty. Bilge Fortescue and his wife were sitting across from one another enjoying a post-breakfast cigarette and cup of coffee, while Constance, Francis, and Christopher were grouped around a table at the other end of the room with their heads together. Other than that, the room was empty.

Francis looked faintly green, a similar shade to Cecily's pyjamas, while Christopher was gesticulating with one hand and waving a cigarette around with the other. Or gesticulating with both, while holding a fag. Francis must not have been able to stomach the idea of food, because the only thing in front of him was a cup of coffee. There was also a plate of buttered toast, but it was untouched, and pushed in front of the chair no one was sitting on.

I snagged a scoop of eggs and a rasher of bacon before they disappeared, and took the empty seat. "Thanks for the toast."

"Don't mind if you do, Pipsqueak," Francis said, with a

baleful eye towards my eggs. Constance, meanwhile, was nibbling on kippers, but that didn't seem to bother him much at all.

"Feeling poorly this morning?"

"Sick as a dog," Francis said succinctly.

I nodded. "Cecily Fletcher, as well. I ran into her coming out of the toilet last night—I was going out, she was coming in—and she didn't even wait for me to leave, just dropped to her knees in front of the commode and proceeded to empty her stomach."

"At least I wasn't in bad enough condition to have to worship the porcelain god," Francis commented, while Constance added, concernedly, "Is she all right?"

"Expectant," I said, with my mouth full of egg.

"Come again?"

I swallowed. "I don't want to say it again. I said I wouldn't talk about it. But I'm certain you heard me the first time."

They all eyed me in silence for a moment.

"It's not—?" Christopher began.

I shook my head. "They both said no."

"You saw Crispin last night?"

"As he left her room. He looked a bit like Francis does now." Pale and drawn, faintly green. "I thought I ought to ask what was wrong."

"But it's not..." Christopher hesitated, "his problem?"

"He said not. And so did she."

"Whose problem is it, then?" Francis wanted to know.

I stabbed my fork into the eggs. "I didn't want to ask. None of my affair, as long as it doesn't involve anyone I hold near or dear."

"And that includes Lord St George?" Constance inquired.

I eyed her. "Well... he's near, anyway. But one would hate

for anything to get in the way of the happy nuptials in December."

"Of course." She went back to her kippers.

I grabbed a piece of Francis's toast. It was cold by now, and the butter a bit too congealed, but I chewed and swallowed determinedly anyway. "I took her back to her bedchamber and put her to bed. I even asked if she wanted me to stay."

And I was fairly certain that I deserved a medal for that bit of empathy.

"And did she?"

I shook my head. "I told her to come find me if she needed help, or to yell loudly if she couldn't make it out of bed—"

"She looked bad enough for that?" Christopher asked.

I nodded. "She looked awful. Pale and shivery, with circles under her eyes. I had to practically carry her from the lavatory to her room. She must have been all right, though, because I didn't hear from her again."

I took another bite of egg and added, "Her door was shut this morning, but so was everyone else's, so I suppose she might have left already. I didn't knock, just in case she was still asleep."

The teacup had been gone, at any rate.

"I haven't seen her," Christopher said, with a look around the mostly empty room, "but we haven't been here long."

"Are the others getting ready to ride out?"

"Pheasants," Christopher said with a grimace. "What harm did they ever do to anyone?"

Francis snorted, but all he said was, "I'm staying here. The last thing I need is shots going off in my ears."

Yes, I couldn't imagine that being healthy for anyone suffering from shellshock. But Francis might be the only one here with that problem, unless Crispin was correct and Bilge Fortescue had served on the Front during the War. I shot a look in their direction. Bilge was making eyes at his wife across the breakfast table, and making no moves towards getting up, so perhaps they were staying put, as well.

"I suppose everyone else is riding out?" I asked.

"We're not," Christopher said, and Constance nodded. "Stay with us, Pippa. We'll watch from the terrasse."

"They'll be in the woods," I said, "won't they? Will there be anything to see?"

"I can't imagine there'll be much. But it's a nice day. We could set up a game of croquet on the lawn. I imagine there must be a croquet set somewhere."

Christopher glanced around, as if mallets and balls were likely to materialize in the breakfast room.

"We used to play when I was younger," Constance told him. "I'm sure there's something in the carriage house."

No doubt. "Just the four of us, then?"

"Ordinarily, Crispin might want to join," Christopher said, "although I don't think Laetitia will let him."

No, probably not. "But surely, if everyone else is riding out, it doesn't matter if he's here with us?"

"You'll be here," Francis said. "And I'm sure Cecily Fletcher won't be riding out, either."

Probably not, now that he mentioned it. What if she fell off her horse?

Unless she was trying pretend that everything was fine and she was not with child, of course. Then riding to hounds might be something she'd risk. But otherwise...

"Perhaps she'd like to play croquet with us," I said.

"It couldn't hurt to ask," Francis agreed. "You know, Pipsqueak, I could have sworn you didn't like Cecily Fletcher."

"I didn't know Cecily Fletcher," I said. "I still don't. A few minutes of helping her vomit and then dragging her back to her bed doesn't mean I know her. I suppose we must have met at some point—I recognized her in the drawing room yesterday evening, so I must have seen her before—but I don't think we've ever exchanged more than a few words."

Most of them had probably taken place at some point when I had had to remove her, forcibly, from Christopher. He's not good about fending off matrimonial young ladies, and the women of the Bright Young Set don't seem to have caught on to the fact that Christopher prefers their brothers to them, in a romantic sense.

Discovering that she was an old flame of Crispin's hadn't endeared her to me, either, of course, although that was beside the point.

"Croquet seems a nice, pleasant pastime for someone who's expecting," Christopher opined, just as Bilge and his wife got up from their table and headed for the door to the hallway. Bilge was dressed in full hunting kit: Tattersall shirt and checkered tweed suit, with breeks tucked into his Wellies and ducks in flight on his tie. And it appeared as if Lady Serena hunted, as well, because she was dressed similarly.

"Breeches," Constance murmured as they approached. I nodded.

"Must be nice."

"You can wear trousers if you'd like, Pippa," Christopher told me. "You wear pyjamas instead of a nightgown. Why not?"

I'm certain he meant it rhetorically, but I answered anyway. "I don't think society is quite ready for women in trousers, Christopher. We're allowed them to play sports, or to sleep, but not in polite company. Perhaps one of these days. They're much more comfortable than skirts for many things."

"Glad I'm not Scottish," Francis commented and gave a nod to Bilge as the latter reached the table. "Fortescue."

"Astley." Bilge nodded back. He gave the rest of us—well,

Christopher and me—a sneer, but he was polite to Francis. "Not riding out, old chap?"

"I had my fill of shooting things in France," Francis said blandly. "We're getting up a party for croquet on the lawn. Would you like to join us, Lady Serena?"

Serena's red lips curved in a smirk. "I'm riding out with my husband, Mr. Astley. But thank you."

"More coldblooded than I am," Bilge commented, with a look at his wife that was part proprietary, part indulgent, and part admiring. "And a crack shot, too. The Boche wouldn't have known what hit them."

"A shame we didn't have you with us on the Continent, Lady Serena." Francis managed a truncated bow from where he was sitting at the table. "Perhaps we could have made it home sooner."

And with fewer casualties. He didn't say it, but I'm sure we all heard it.

Serena simpered. "Enjoy your game." She tucked her hand through Bilge's arm and tugged him towards the door. We sat in silence until they had vanished, and then Christopher said, "Was it me, or was that condescending?"

"Bilge Fortescue has always been a prat," Francis said calmly. "We went to Eton together, you know. And then we went to France together. He was a form below me, and one above Robbie."

So nineteen, then, when conscription was instituted in January, 1916. The conscription that snagged both Francis at twenty, and Robbie, at eighteen, as well.

"Do you know his wife?"

"Just to look at," Francis said. "I heard that old Bilgy had married her. It must have been two or three years ago now. But we've never been close."

And two years ago, Francis hadn't been in any kind of

shape to celebrate a friend's nuptials anyway, even if he and Bilgy had been friendly.

"Out of curiosity," I said, "what sort of name is Bilge?"

Francis chuckled, and even Constance cracked a smile. "His name is William. We called him Billy, but it became Bilge after a while, since he had a tendency to talk a lot of rubbish."

"Such as?"

"Oh." Francis shrugged. "How special he was, how much money his family had, how the Boche would run had it been him on the Continent..."

He shook his head. "This was before we were conscripted, of course. I don't think he acquitted himself any better than anyone else in the trenches."

Likely not. He seemed like the kind of bloke who was all talk and very little action. All hat and no cattle, as Hiram Schlomsky would have said. Although his wife had seemed pleased enough with him, I supposed, considering the way she had chivvied him out of there.

"So..." I asked, "croquet?"

"Fine by me." Francis got to his feet and pulled out Constance's chair. "Kit?"

"I'm in." Christopher stood, too. "Do you want to go and ask Miss Fletcher if she wants to join us, Pippa?"

"I might as well," I said. "Would you like to come up with me, Constance?"

Constance nodded. "I have to go upstairs anyway. Don't want to ruin my new shoes on the lawn."

They were lovely, I have to say: a mix of patent leather and suede with a dainty Cuban heel that was sure to sink into the grass. The dew wouldn't do the suede any favors, either.

"You can put them back on later," I told her, as I got to my feet. "You'll be more comfortable in brogues once we get outside."

"We'll hunt up the mallets and wickets," Francis said. "Which part of the lawn should we use, my dear?"

Constance pointed him in the direction of the carriage house and the bit of lawn where the game of croquet usually took place, and then the men headed for the back door and the great outdoors while Constance and I took the main staircase up to the first floor.

I waited until we had gained the next story before I leaned towards Constance. "I didn't want to ask in front of Francis—"

Francis's fiancée gave me a jaundiced look out of the corner of her eye.

"—but have you seen Wolfgang this morning?"

His room was on the second floor, as far as I knew, somewhere in the vicinity of my own, but I hadn't wanted to go knocking on doors this morning. I didn't want the noise to disturb Cecily, for one thing—she could probably use all the rest she could get, both with her condition and after the disturbed night she had had—and for another, it's not proper for a young woman to knock on the bedroom door of a young man to whom she has no familiar or romantic ties. I didn't want to give anyone, including Wolfgang, the wrong idea.

We were cousins, strictly speaking, and I suppose I wasn't opposed to entertaining the idea of marrying him, should he decide to float a proposal, but there was a chance that that suggestion would include relocating to Germany, and I certainly wasn't open to that, or to anything else that would include my leaving Christopher behind and returning to the land of my birth.

At any rate, I had assumed that Wolfgang would be downstairs in the breakfast room and I would see him there, but it seemed as if he had either breakfasted in his room or had come and gone early.

Or done without food, I suppose.

"I saw him for a moment," Constance said. "He was in the breakfast room when we came down. But as soon as he saw Francis, he got up and left."

That was considerate of him. "I don't suppose you happened to notice what he was wearing?"

"Not tweed," Constance said.

"I don't think the Germans are as enamored with tweed as we are here." And then something occurred to me, and I shot her a look. "Surely he wasn't wearing short trousers?"

She gave me a look back. "Of course not."

"In Bavaria they do. Even the grown men." I remembered that much from my first decade of life. Men in *lederhosen* with suspenders and bare knees, with *Loden* jackets and hats with *Gamsbart* hair on top.

Constance shook her head. "He wasn't wearing anything out of the ordinary. Brown wool breeks, a gray and green jacket with silver buttons, and a hat with feathers in the band. And tall boots."

A German version of the traditional British hunting gear, then.

"He looked good," I said, "I assume?"

"Good enough that Laetitia deigned to flutter her eyelashes at him," Constance answered.

I snorted. "I can only imagine how St George responded to that."

"From the look of him, I would say that Lord St George would be only too happy to have the *Graf* von Natterdorff take his fiancée off his hands."

I could well imagine it. Or at least it would be my own inclination, had I been the one to ill-advisedly get myself shackled to Laetitia Marsden.

"Serves him right," I said.

Constance made a moue and pushed open the door to Primrose. Only to stop on the threshold. "Oh. Nellie."

"Miss Constance." Nellie made a quick curtsey.

"I was just going to change my shoes." Constance headed for the wardrobe. I stayed where I was, in the doorway, and watched as she unbuckled the strap-shoes, tucked them away in the bottom of the wardrobe, and pulled out a pair of brogues.

When she perched on the edge of the divan to tie the laces, I turned my attention back to Nellie. "Have you been upstairs yet, Nellie? Or is there another maid doing the rooms up there?"

"No, Miss Darling." Nellie ran her hands over the counterpane to smooth out the wrinkles. "I'll be doing the rooms upstairs once I'm done down here."

"You can leave mine alone," I said. "I made my own bed. And Miss Cecily Fletcher might still be in bed, when you get up there. She wasn't feeling well last night."

Nellie nodded. "Yes, Miss Darling. I'm sorry to hear that."

"Just be careful when you knock on her door. If she's still unwell, just leave her be."

"Yes, Miss Darling." Her hands were careful as they smoothed out Constance's counterpane.

"I'm ready," the latter said, getting to her feet.

I nodded. "We're going out on the lawn for a game of croquet, Nellie, if anyone asks."

"Yes, Miss Darling."

We headed out of the room and along the hallway to the small staircase, the way I had done last night. "Did you sleep well?" I inquired as we entered the stairwell and started up.

"Well enough," Constance said from behind me. "Nothing happened to me like what happened to you. I was worried that Francis was going to wake up screaming—he does that sometimes, when something happens that reminds him of the War—"

Like coming face to face with Wolfgang, I assumed. "But he didn't?"

Constance shook her head. "Or if he did, I didn't hear him. Christopher must have taken care of it if anything happened."

"You can call him Kit, you know. He'll be your cousin before too much longer."

"You don't," Constance said, as we emerged into the upstairs hallway.

I stopped to wait for her so we could walk side by side towards Cecily Fletcher's door. "I do sometimes. But when I first met him, on the docks at Southampton when I was eleven, he introduced himself as Christopher. I don't think he minds when people call him Kit—"

Tom Gardiner did, in addition to Francis and Crispin and of course his parents.

"—but I got in the habit of calling him Christopher because that's what he told me to call him, and I suppose I never got out of it."

Constance nodded and flicked a glance at my door. "How did you enjoy Wisteria?"

"It was lovely," I said, although between getting in late last night and having to drag myself downstairs after an uneasy night this morning, I hadn't paid it too much attention. "The bed was comfortable."

"Which is Miss Fletcher's room?"

I pointed. The little plaque, that I hadn't noticed in the middle of the night, said Honeysuckle.

"Pale pink, yellow and green," Constance said.

"Quite so. I didn't get a chance to see the décor in the middle of the night. She ran out of the room and left the lights off. And I was more concerned with getting her back into bed safely than with what the walls looked like."

Constance nodded. "I suppose we knock?"

"It seems indicated." I applied my knuckles to the wood and waited. When nothing happened, I did it again.

"She might have come down before Francis, Christopher and I," Constance suggested, looking around. "We hadn't been in the breakfast room very long when you arrived."

"Bilge and his wife were there. And you said you'd seen Wolfgang and Laetitia. Who else did you see?"

Constance surveyed the hallway as she thought about it. "Lord St George, as I mentioned. He came down with Laetitia. Or I suppose more accurately, she brought him down with her."

I nodded.

"The three of them left together when we came in. Lord St George—"

"Crispin," I said. "He's practically your cousin. There's no need to stand on ceremony."

"He looked like he wanted to stay with us, and let his fiancée leave with your friend, but she brought him to heel."

I made a face. "I wish you wouldn't say it like that."

"That's how it was," Constance said, and I gave her a look.

"You were a lot meeker at Godolphin."

"I was a lot more cowed as a child," Constance said, and continued, "Geoffrey came down, in full hunting kit. So did the other two gentlemen."

"Dominic Rivers and the Honorable Reggie?"

She nodded. I tried to picture Dom Rivers in houndstooth and Tattersall, and failed. He looked so extremely cosmopolitan that it was difficult to imagine him in anything other than evening kit, or at most, a nice afternoon suit. But tweed and plus-fours, no.

"The girls arrived eventually, too," Constance added. "Lady Violet and Olivia Barnsley."

"That's everyone, then. Isn't it?" I knocked on the door one more time and raised my voice for good measure. "Cecily? Are you in there?"

"Other than Aunt Effie and Uncle Maury," Constance agreed and reached for the doorknob. "The older generation relatives won't be arriving until this afternoon."

She twisted the knob and pushed the door in.

The first thing I saw was that the drapes were still drawn. That became obvious as soon as the door swung open. The room was dusky. Not as dark as it had been last night—sunshine crept in around the edges of the curtains—but dark enough that it was difficult to see.

"Cecily?" I took a step across the threshold, with Constance right behind me. "Are you awake?"

There was a lump under the covers, but it didn't move at the sound of my voice or my approach. She must still be exhausted from last night, I supposed.

We stopped at the edge of the bed and looked down at the part of Cecily we could see above the blankets. Her face was exposed, and twisted in a grimace of pain.

"Cecily?" I put my hand out and, after a moment of hesitation, rested it on her forehead. Her skin was cool under my palm, and a bit clammy.

"She's breathing," Constance said. It ought to have been a confident statement, although it sounded more like a question than anything else.

I nodded. "Yes." Cecily was indeed breathing. Shallowly and with some difficulty, but she was taking in air.

"Open the curtains," I said, and Constance scurried to obey. The curtain rings rattled along the drapery rod, and a flood of sunlight illuminated Cecily's pale face. "Thank you."

Constance came back to my side, wringing her hands. Her face was worried as she peered down. "What's wrong with her?"

"I don't know," I admitted. Something clearly was. No matter how tired—or how pregnant—she might be, our voices and my touch and the flood of light ought to have done something to wake her. "Cecily?"

I reached under the blankets and found her shoulder, and shook it. "Wake up."

Cecily's body moved with my action, but her eyes didn't open.

"This isn't good," Constance said.

I shook my head. "One of us should fetch Francis. He might know what to do."

He had had quite a lot of experience with dope of various sorts, after all. Overdoses and otherwise. And that was what this looked like. An overdose of something.

"I should try to find Dom Rivers, too," I added. "If he gave her something, it would be helpful to know what it was."

Constance nodded. "I'll stay with her. You go, and hurry."

I hurried, out into the hallway, down the back stairs to the first floor, down the hallway to the main staircase, and then down that and across the foyer to the hallway and the back door.

There were two of them, one beside the storerooms just outside the servants' wing on the west side of the house, and the other between the boot room and game room on the east side. This latter was the one I aimed for, and I saw no one until the moment I burst through the door onto the lawn and spotted Christopher and Francis in the distance, setting up the wickets for a friendly game of croquet.

"Francis!" I let the door slam behind me and started across

the grass at a run. Francis straightened from driving wickets into the lawn to peer at me. "I need you!"

Christopher straightened too, and started moving towards Francis, if at a more decorous pace than the one I was employing. In the distance, I could hear the sound of shots, and the beating of wings and of hooves.

"Francis," I panted as I skidded to a stop a few feet away, and then stumbled forward when my momentum carried on. "Oof! Francis, we need help."

Francis stiffened. "Constance?"

"There's nothing wrong with Constance. I left her in the room—"

And that was when another shot rang out from within the trees, close enough to us that I could hear the whistling sound the bullet made as it moved past me with but a few inches to spare and embedded itself in the gray stone wall of the manor with a *thwack*.

CHAPTER EIGHT

"DOWN!" Francis barked. He put a hand on the back of my neck and shoved me onto the grass, and followed me down, half on top of me. Christopher, meanwhile, had the sense to drop on his own.

"What—?"

"Bullet," Francis said grimly.

"You don't say?"

We were all expecting more bullets to follow, but none did. Nonetheless, Francis kept us close to the ground as he gave us instructions for what to do next.

"Get to cover. Inside the door, Kit. Stay low. Go!"

Christopher crawled as fast as he could across the grass towards the door I had just come out through. I winced at the thought of what the knees of his flannel bags would look like when he stood up.

"Now you," Francis said and gave me a shove. "Hurry."

I followed, scurrying on my hands and knees across the grass. In this position, any additional shots that came would catch me in the derriere, as I kept my head down as I went. By this point, though, no one else had tried to shoot at us, and all the shots we could hear were from farther away. I thought I could—perhaps—hear the sound of hooves moving away through the trees, but it might have been the blood beating in my ears, or alternatively, just the horses' hooves from the rest of the shoot.

Christopher reached up and opened the door, and vanished inside, still in a crouch. I put on a burst of speed and followed him into the manor. A few seconds later, Francis had come in behind me and slammed the door.

For a second or two, we all three just sat there on the floor, wide-eyed, breathing heavily and staring at one another in shock. Then—

"Someone shot at us," I said blankly.

"Someone shot at *you*," Christopher corrected.

"Me?"

"Well," he hesitated, looking from me to Francis and back, "one of you. The bullet went too wide to be intended for me."

"Unless someone's just a bad shot," Francis said and pushed to his feet. He took a moment to brush down the fronts of his flannels before extending a hand to me. "Come on, Pipsqueak. Up you go."

I took his hand and let him haul me to my feet, while Christopher got up on his own and brushed himself off, with a grimace at the state of his knees. Mine were bare but dirty, and currently hidden under my skirt, so I could get away with going into the lavatory and washing them later.

"We need you upstairs," I told Francis. "Constance—"

"What's wrong with Constance?"

"I already told you. Nothing is wrong with Constance. I left her with Cecily Fletcher, and something *is* wrong with her."

Francis headed towards the main staircase, and I scurried

after, with Christopher on my heels. "What's going on with her?" Francis threw back over his shoulder.

"The same thing that went on with Christopher in May. Or something like it." I hustled to keep up with his longer strides. "She won't wake up. She's breathing, but it's very shallow."

"Did you check her pupils?"

I shook my head, and then answered verbally, when it occurred to me that he didn't have eyes in the back of his head. "No. Her eyes were closed, and I didn't try to open them. I wouldn't know what to look for."

Francis nodded, and started up the main staircase two steps at a time. I hurried after, double-time, since I had to step on every step instead of every other. Behind me, Christopher started up, as well.

"She's on the top floor," I said, a bit breathlessly, as we gained the first floor hallway. "The staircase is at the end of the hall."

We headed that way, and half a minute later, found ourselves in the upstairs hallway. There was still no one else around, although the door to the Fortescues' room on the first floor had stood ajar and I thought I had heard Nellie's humming from behind it.

"Down there," I pointed. "The door in the middle."

Francis headed that way, and gave a peremptory knock but without stopping to wait for permission. Christopher and I crowded in behind him as he pushed the door open and stalked inside.

Nothing much had changed in the minutes—and had it truly only been a few minutes?—since I had left. In my absence, Constance had sat down, perched on the embroidered chair beside the bed. Her eyes were fastened on Cecily and her hands were gripping each other tightly in her lap, so hard that her knuckles were white. When she looked up and saw us, the worry in her eyes flickered for a moment, as if she were happy not to be alone with the sick girl, but then clouded over again when she noticed our dishevelment.

"What happened?"

"Stray shot," Francis said blandly, as if the bullet hadn't come within a few inches of his head. "Someone has bad aim."

Constance's eyes widened. But before she could say anything—

"We're fine," I reassured her. "Someone's gun must have misfired in our direction. It didn't hit either of us. We just dropped to the grass in case there were more shots."

Constance bit her lip, but when neither of us made the incident out to be any more than that, she seemed to accept that it wasn't a big thing that had happened. I fully intended to get to the bottom of it at some point, but right now, we had more important matters to concern ourselves with. "How is she?"

"The same as earlier," Constance said with a glance at the still figure in the bed. "She hasn't moved."

I nodded, as Francis bent over the bed for a closer look. We watched as he peeled one of Cecily's eyelids back to peer at her pupil, before putting his hand against the pulse in her throat. That done, he straightened, and took hold of the blankets to pull them down.

I made a forward movement, and then checked it. It wasn't as if Cecily was unclothed under the blankets—I had put her to bed myself and knew she was wearing pyjamas—and after the first moment it didn't matter anyway. Constance gasped and Christopher winced. Francis cursed.

I stared in appalled silence for a moment before I blurted, "We need a doctor. Or perhaps a midwife would be better."

"I doubt there's much a doctor could do," Francis said, eyeing the considerable amount of blood under Cecily's pelvis. It had soaked into the bedding and mattress—the latter must be utterly ruined—and the celery satin of the pyjamas looked obscene. "And it's certainly much too late for a midwife."

"Dear Lord," Constance said faintly, hand over her mouth. She was almost as pale as Cecily, and looked as if she were midway between fainting and vomiting.

"Was she—" Christopher cleared his throat. He looked as bad as Constance, and faintly green. "She wasn't like this when you saw her last night, Pippa, was she?"

"Of course not," I said automatically. And gave it a moment's thought before I added, "No, I'm certain she wasn't. The light was on in the lavatory, so I would have spotted copious amounts of fresh blood. She was fine then."

Or perhaps not fine—violently ill to her stomach, pale and trembling—but not bleeding. I would never have left her alone if she had been.

"Tell me again what was wrong with her last night?" Francis asked.

I shot a glance at Cecily. "Shouldn't we ring for a doctor instead of standing here and discussing it?"

"I'll go," Constance said and ducked around me and out of the room with the air of someone escaping a torturous situation. That might have been why none of us tried to stop her: she looked so obviously relieved to have a reason to get away. The look Christopher sent her indicated that he would have liked the opportunity to escape, too.

Francis watched until Constance was out of the room and we could hear her brogues hurry towards the end of the hall and the staircase before he turned back to me. "A doctor won't be able to do anything for her, Pippa. Although I suppose it can't hurt to have one come by to take a look. The certificate of death will probably require an autopsy before it can be signed, anyway. The doctor will have to order that."

"You mean—"

I stopped myself before I could say anything further, and started over once I had reconsidered what I wanted to ask, or more specifically the way I wanted to ask it. More carefully, for one thing. First of all was the implication that he expected her to die, and he said it as if there was no question whatsoever about it coming true and like there was nothing we could do to prevent it. But in addition to that, there was the suggestion that an autopsy would have to be performed. And for that to be *de rigueur*... "Are you suggesting that someone tried to kill her?"

Francis looked surprised. "I wasn't. Do you have reason to think someone did?"

I didn't, of course. Only... "What did you mean, then? Why would there be an autopsy if there wasn't a question about the cause of death?"

"There can be questions about cause of death without it being murder," Francis said. "This doesn't look like a natural death to me. Especially not with what you told me was going on last night. She was sick, you said?"

"Violently. And clammy and pale and unsteady on her feet. She wasn't bleeding, though. I would have noticed that. But she was sick to her stomach and in pain."

Although that wasn't necessarily anything out of the ordinary for someone *enceinte*, was it?

"No," Francis agreed, "although this is more than that, isn't it?"

He waited a second for the thought to sink in, before he added, "Perhaps she took something she thought would eliminate her problem. Or the problem she did have, I suppose. It won't be a problem any longer. Nor will anything else."

"You mean—"

"Yes," Francis said. "She fed herself an abortifacient, and in the process, it killed her."

I looked away from the blood, up to Cecily's face and to her chest, which was moving almost imperceptibly. "She isn't dead yet."

"She will be," Francis said. "I've seen enough death to recognize it."

"But surely there's something we can do? We can't just stand here and watch her die."

Christopher made a small sound of agreement. "I'm with Pippa."

"So am I," Francis said. "Believe me, the last thing I want, is to watch someone else die. But I don't know what to do to help. She rid herself of whatever was left in her stomach last night, so inducing vomiting at this point would do no good. Whatever it is, is already in her bloodstream and affecting her."

He glanced at me. "The tea smelled like spearmint, you said?"

I nodded. "Pennyroyal, I suppose. I wish I would have realized it then, although I suppose it was already too late at that point."

"If it had already made her ill," Francis nodded, "then yes. Most likely it was already too late. There's no antidote for pennyroyal that I know of."

"So we just stand here and watch?" Christopher's voice was higher than usual. "Shouldn't we let someone know, at least? One of her friends? Or the Earl and Countess of Marsden, if no one else?"

"Or the housekeeper," I said, since Mrs. Frobisher might be more help with this than Lady Euphemia would be.

Francis lifted a shoulder. "We can do. Perhaps we ought to. Perhaps her friends who are here would like to say goodbye while she's still alive. She won't know they're here, but it might make them feel better."

Ugh. "I'm sure Constance will tell her aunt and uncle, at least," I said.

Francis nodded. "Other than that, there's nothing anyone can do at this point. I don't know how long it'll be, but she won't last until the doctor gets here. She's already fading. Look at her lips."

I did. They were turning blue. "Why—?"

"Not enough oxygen," Francis said.

"Perhaps if we helped her breathe...?"

"We'd only prolong the inevitable. There isn't anything anyone can do to keep her alive beyond a certain point. Her inner organs will shut down—liver and kidneys and heart—and then she'll be gone."

"How do you know so much about this?" Christopher wanted to know. He sounded ill, and looked it, too, with both arms crossed tightly over his stomach.

Francis glanced at him, but continued without answering the question. "If this was pennyroyal, and it sounds as if it was, then chances are that she was attempting to do something about the pregnancy, not about herself. If she had wanted to escape the embarrassment, arsenic or foxglove or a bullet to the head are simpler and easier ways out."

And there was the answer I hadn't wanted to hear: that Francis had at one point looked into ways to kill himself. The fact that he hadn't taken any of them helped a little, but I still didn't like to contemplate it.

"Pennyroyal has been used as an abortifacient for centuries," I said distantly. "She might not have realized that too much of it could kill her."

I hadn't realized that myself, until now. I knew about the plant and its uses, of course. What I hadn't known, was that I would have to worry about an overdose if I ever tried to use it. It had never been anything I had had to worry about personally.

Christopher gave me a sideways look. "Do I want to know how you know that?"

"It came up," I said. "Girl-talk at Oxford, or perhaps at Godolphin."

"That's what you girls sit around and talk about when there aren't men present?"

"Among other things," I said. "Just as I'm sure you men discuss how not to find yourselves in a position where you have to marry some damsel because you had too much fun one night."

He made a face. "I won't deny that that conversation has taken place."

"You'd better not, or I'd call you a liar." I waited a second before I added, "I don't suppose you'd know the answer to this —either of you—but is pennyroyal the sort of thing someone could ask Dominic Rivers for?"

There was a moment's pause, and then— "The dope deal-er?" Francis said. He sounded intrigued.

I nodded. "He's here this weekend. Didn't you see him last night?"

"We're not acquainted," Francis said.

"Well, he's here. The darkhaired chap who arrived after you had your scene with Wolfgang and retreated to the wall in the drawing room."

His face darkened at the reminder, but he didn't say anything, so I continued, "Someone invited him, and it must have been to some purpose. It's hard to imagine that either Laetitia or Crispin would require stimulants at this happiest of occasions."

Christopher snorted. "I wouldn't put it past Crispin, honestly, but I heard his reaction when he saw Rivers. I don't think it was him. Do you suppose it was Cecily who asked him to meet her here, then?"

"I don't know," I said. "She might have done. Mightn't she?

"Or she might have picked the pennyroyal herself. It grows wild, doesn't it?"

"Of course it does." It was a weed of sorts, wasn't it? Or a wildflower or something like that. I added, "Although I don't know whether it grows around here. I'm sure it doesn't in London. What's more likely is that she contacted Rivers and he gave it to her as an oil or something like that, and she mixed it with the tea to make it easier to drink."

"Or used the tea as a chaser," Francis said, "after she downed the oil."

"And you think she would have done this here?" Christopher asked. "Now?"

And that was a point, wasn't it? Cecily had a home, or so I had to assume. She might have a flat in London, the way Christopher and I do, or she might be living with her family somewhere, the way Crispin, and Francis and Constance, still did. Either way, she had somewhere to go, where there was more or less privacy. Why would she come to someone else's house—and someone else's engagement party—to take something to rid herself of an unwanted pregnancy? Surely something like that would be better achieved behind closed doors at home?

I meant to say something about it, but before I could, there was a gurgle from the bed. For a moment, caught up in the discussion, I had almost forgotten that Cecily was lying there, and now I turned back to her in chagrin. How could I have been so callous as to discuss this with her lying just a few feet away? What if she had heard us, and been distressed by it?

But when I faced the bed, it was to see Cecily's body seize, and arch up from the mattress like something out of a horror story. A rattling gasp came from her throat, and her eyes were wide-open and staring at the ceiling.

For a second she held there, body bowed, before the tension

broke and she flopped back down onto the bed in a heap, quite as if someone had cut the strings of a puppet. I waited for her chest to rise in another shallow inhalation—

And waited—

And waited—

"She's gone," Francis said. His voice sounded peculiar, although it could have been my ears and not him. There was a buzzing I recognized as a precursor to feeling faint. Next to me, Christopher stared, eyes wide and horrified.

I turned to him and wrapped my arms around his waist, as much for support for myself as to support him. After a second, he returned the favor: wrapped both arms around me and buried his face against my shoulder. He's a couple of inches taller, but not so much that my shoulder is inconvenient.

"Excuse me," Francis said distantly. I raised my head to watch him walk out, but he didn't turn to look at me.

"We should go after him," I said into Christopher's tweed-covered shoulder. "I don't think he should be alone."

"I don't think I want to be alone, either."

I nodded, cheek rubbing against the tweed. "I know you don't. Nor do I. But I'm sure this must bring back bad memories for Francis. How many men do you suppose he saw die in the trenches?"

A shudder passed through Christopher, from shoulders to feet. "A lot."

I unwrapped my arms. "Go after him. I'll stay here and wait for Constance to come back. And then the doctor. You go and make sure your brother is all right."

He stepped back and nodded. "What about you, Pippa?"

"I'll be fine," I said steadily. Beginning with Christopher's late grandfather, Duke Henry, in April, and ending with poor Flossie Schlomsky a month ago, I had seen more than my fair share of dead bodies in the past few months. Nothing like

Francis and the War, of course, but for peacetime, more than enough of them. And this couldn't in any way compare to that nightmarish trip through London in June, in the back of Crispin's Hispano-Suiza, with Freddie Montrose's dead head in my lap, his blood soaking through the towel and into my clothes. "At least I only have to sit beside the bed and wait this time."

Christopher nodded. "If it becomes too much, shut the door behind you and wait in the hall. Or in your own room."

"I'll be fine," I said and gave him a nudge towards the door. "Go. Be with Francis."

"I'm sure he would rather have Constance."

"And he can have her, just as soon as she comes back here and tells me what's going on. I'll send her down to you. But in the meantime, you go and sit with him. He'll probably want a drink." And someone to drink with.

"I wouldn't mind one myself," Christopher said, with a final glance at the bed. He headed for the door. "We still have to talk about what happened earlier."

"Outside, do you mean?"

He nodded.

Yes, we most certainly did.

"Come and find us when you're finished up here."

I promised I would do, and then I settled onto the needle-pointed chair and waited for Constance to come back, with or without her Aunt Effie, and with or without the butler or housekeeper, to tell me whether or not the doctor was on his way.

THE HUNTERS RETURNED in the early afternoon, red-cheeked and hungry from their ordeal. By then, the doctor and local police had made their way from Marsden-on-Crane up to the manor, and the van from the local mortuary was parked at the bottom of the steps, back doors gaping open.

We saw the others come back through the window in the library, where we had settled with our drinks while we waited for luncheon to be served. The local police was upstairs processing Cecily's room for evidence—evidence of what, I didn't know—and the doctor was instructing the two bowler-hatted blokes from the morgue on what to do with the body.

I recognized the doctor—a small man with a bald head and a luxurious mustache—from the murder at the Dower House in May. I also recognized several of the local constables, including one named Collins, who had helped Tom Gardiner back then. Blokes in black suits and bowler hats look the same everywhere, but I wouldn't have been surprised if they, too, were the same pair who had attended to the late Johanna de Vos.

Crispin took one look at them all, including the covered stretcher coming through the door and down the stairs and into the back of the mortuary van, and turned deathly pale.

So, in justice to her, did Lady Laetitia. Geoffrey had been out with the hunting party, of course, so she knew that he was intact, but I could see fear on her face as she ran up the steps calling for her mother and father.

Lord Maurice was in the study next door to the library, as it happened, conferring with the constable in charge, and we could hear him respond to his daughter's call through the wall.

Crispin had more hostages to fortune here than anyone, between Christopher and Francis, Constance and myself, and all the many girls he had at one point dallied with and—I assumed—still had fond feelings for. Olivia Barnsley and Lady Violet Cummings were making their way towards the house, arm in arm, as we watched, but there were still the four of us, and of course there was Cecily. Uncle Harold, Uncle Herbert, and Aunt Roz were also expected today, and for all Crispin knew, might have arrived already.

He took the steps into the house two at a time, and raised his voice as soon as he entered the outer hall. "Kit! Where are you?"

Christopher looked at me, God knows why.

"Go on, then," I told him. "Put him out of his misery."

"Don't think I don't realize how that sounds, Pippa." But he pushed his chair back and strode towards the door. "In here, Crispin!"

There were rapid steps outside in the hallway, and then Christopher stepped back to let Crispin into the room. The Viscount St George stopped just across the threshold and looked around, frantically. His eyes lingered for a second on each of our faces—not just making sure we were upright and breathing, but assessing all of us for state of mind as well as general health.

When he looked up and met my eyes, I began, "I'm sorry to be the bearer of bad news," and watched the color drain out of his cheeks before I could get any further.

Francis nudged me. "Enough, Pipsqueak. You'll make the boy faint."

Crispin shot him a look of dislike. "It's hardly as bad as all that. I even shot at a bird or two this morning. My father would be proud."

When none of us responded to that—the idea that Uncle Harold had made his only son feel bad for not being blood-thirsty enough, didn't endear His Grace to me further—Crispin added, "There was a mortuary van outside."

"Not for any of us," I said.

"Clearly." He glanced around the room. "Who, then?"

"As I said, I'm sorry to be the bearer of bad news—"

"Cecily Fletcher," Christopher interrupted, and took Crispin's elbow when the latter swayed. "Come and sit down."

He shoved Crispin into his own chair and put his own glass of sherry in his hand. Crispin gave it a look of disgust before he tossed it back. After a moment, a little color leaked back into his cheeks. "Bloody hell."

"I'm sorry," Christopher said with a look at me. "But Pippa leading up to it only made it sound worse than it was. Better to rip the plaster off all at once."

"Says you."

Crispin glanced around the table, at Francis's brandy—the latter gave him an arched brow and a distinct if tacit warning against trying to take it away—and Constance's tea before landing on my sherry. I handed it over with a grimace. "Laetitia won't like it if you get bladdered before luncheon even kicks off."

"I won't get bladdered from two glasses of sherry, Darling." But he didn't toss it back the way he had done the first one, just took a healthy swig and handed it back to me. And then he took a breath and let it out. "Cecily, you said?"

I nodded. "After you left my room last night—"

The others eyed each other after I said this, so perhaps I hadn't been specific enough about it earlier, although now certainly wasn't the right time to clarify anything, "—I ran into Cecily in the loo. She was sick to her stomach, the poor thing."

Crispin nodded. "That's fairly normal for someone *enceinte*, of course."

I nodded. "That's why I didn't think anything of it. But when she didn't come down to breakfast this morning, Constance and I went up to her room to check on her."

"And she was dead?"

"Not yet," I said, and he winced. "She was unconscious, however—"

"Comatose," Francis shot in, with a swallow of brandy.

"Constance ran downstairs to ring the doctor and let her aunt know what was going on. Your future mother-in-law."

Crispin winced again. Under different circumstances I would have tweaked him about it, but at the moment it seemed better to let it go.

"Miss Fletcher died while Christopher, Pippa, and I were with her," Francis said. "She never woke up."

"She didn't say anything?"

I shook my head. "She was in no condition to do that."

After a second I added, "Out of curiosity, what did you think she might say?"

She had already assured him he wasn't the father of her baby, so it couldn't be that.

He eyed me. "The thing dead people in books always say. The name of the murderer."

CHAPTER NINE

"MURDERER?" Christopher echoed.

Crispin nodded. And turned to me. "Isn't that right, Darling? People in books say the name of the murderer with their last breath? And write it in the dust with their fingertip and such?"

"In books," I said. "But she wasn't in any kind of condition to communicate. Besides, what makes you think anyone murdered her?"

He looked nonplussed. "Well, she certainly didn't kill herself."

I exchanged a look with Francis and one with Christopher. "We assumed this was accidental, as a result of taking steps to deal with her..." I hesitated, "problem."

He looked at me. "You mean, she took an abortifacient."

I nodded.

"Not on purpose," Crispin said.

"How do you know? The tea—what was left of it—smelled of spearmint, so we thought..."

"Pennyroyal." He nodded. "She wouldn't."

"Did she tell you that?"

It was Christopher who asked this time, not me. Crispin turned to him and shook his head. "But if she wanted to, don't you think she would have done it before now? She was several months along. And don't you think she would have done it somewhere else? Not here, during my engagement party?"

"Unless she was making a statement," Francis said, and Crispin's eyebrows arched.

"What is that supposed to mean? What sort of statement would that be?"

Francis arched his own brow back. "There's one reason why she might want to do it here, in front of you and your new fiancée, isn't there?"

If the baby had been Crispin's, I assumed he meant.

Crispin shook his head. "Her situation wasn't my doing."

"Does your fiancée know that?"

"We haven't discussed it," Crispin said coolly. After a second he added, "I don't know whether Laetitia knew that Cecily was expecting. She didn't hear it from me, if so."

"If it was yours," I said, "Cecily would have made certain that Laetitia knew, wouldn't she have? And not relied on you to do it?"

He turned to me. "*Et tu, Brute?*"

I shook my head. "You misunderstood me. I believed you last night, you know. You're many things, St George, but you're not someone who would leave a pregnant woman to fend for herself and your child."

He grimaced. "Thank you. I suppose."

"Besides, we all know that you don't love Laetitia enough to kill Cecily to stay with her. Although does Laetitia know that?"

"I have no idea what Laetitia knows," Crispin said, and leaned back in his—or rather, Christopher's—chair. The latter was perched on the arm of it. "And I'll thank you to keep your voice down, Darling."

I eyed him. "Why on earth should I? You told me yourself that she's under no illusions about it being a love match."

"That's no reason to rub it in," Crispin said, and pushed to his feet. "Excuse me. I should find my fiancée and see what I might do to help."

"Before you go…" Christopher said, and Crispin turned to him with an expectant sort of expression. "When you were out there, stalking quail…"

Crispin grimaced, but nodded.

"Did you happen to notice anyone shooting in this direction?"

"Shooting in—" He stopped. I got the impression that he lost his breath, and it took him a moment to find it again. Then he turned back to the table, and those stormy gray eyes ran the circle of faces again, from Christopher to Francis, to Constance and to me, before going back to Christopher. He braced himself, visibly, before asking, "What happened?"

"Pippa came to find us," Christopher said, and Crispin shot me a look. "Or Francis more so than me. Someone to look at Cecily and perhaps be able to tell what was wrong with her. When I was taken ill, back in May—"

"You weren't taken ill, Kit. You were poisoned."

Christopher nodded. "When that happened, Francis was the one who figured out what was wrong. And you, of course, but you were out with the shooting party."

"Get to the point, Kit. What happened?"

"Someone shot at us," Francis said. He was tilting the almost empty brandy glass in his hand, watching the little bit of liquid at the bottom slosh around. "It's been a while since I was in that position."

No wonder he was so out of sorts. That must have brought

back bad memories, too, that he had suppressed to be able to help me with Cecily.

It hadn't been that long for me, sadly. I still had the scar on my upper arm from late April, when a bullet had graced me. It was covered by my blouse at the moment, but I didn't miss Crispin's flicker of a glance at it. "Who?"

"If we knew that," I said, "do you suppose we would be asking you?"

He lifted his upper lip in a sneer, but it was half-hearted. "I'm sure I don't know, Darling. It was all rather unorganized out there in the woods. I know that Laetitia stuck pretty close to me. I don't know about everyone else."

"The Kraut?" Francis said.

I turned to him with my mouth open, ready to take umbrage, but he gave me a stern look. "We know nothing about him, Pipsqueak. Everyone else is a known entity—"

"I don't know half the people who are here this weekend!"

Bilge and Serena Fortescue, the Honorable Reggie Fish, and Olivia Barnsley were all total unknowns to me. And it wasn't as if I knew Dominic Rivers well enough to think that he wouldn't turn a gun on anyone. He was a dope peddler, so anything was possible. It was less likely that Violet Cummings would do, I supposed, but I didn't know her well enough to be certain of her idiosyncracies, either.

"You may not," Francis said, "but someone does. No one knows him."

"I know him!" I said. "And he wouldn't shoot at me. Why should he?"

"Perhaps he wasn't shooting at you," Christopher suggested. "Perhaps he was shooting at Francis, because of the way Francis reacted to him last night."

Well... perhaps. Although— "That seems like a rather poor motive for murder."

"We don't know what someone else thinks is a reasonable motive for murder," Christopher said, "and it might not have been attempted murder. Perhaps he shot to miss."

"Why would he do that?"

"To scare?" Christopher suggested, with a glance at Francis. The latter was staring morosely at his brandy. "To upset someone who would get flashbacks by something like that?"

Francis grimaced.

"Or perhaps someone thought they were shooting at Cecily Fletcher," Constance said. She had been quiet so far, so her voice came as a surprise. So did the suggestion. Crispin's eyebrows flew up. I opened my mouth to protest, but she had already gone on. "You do look a bit alike, you know. Similar bob and hair color. From a distance, someone could mistake you for her, or vice versa."

Crispin glanced at me and then away, his cheeks turning pink. I rolled my eyes. So he had once bedded someone who looked a bit like me. He had bedded plenty of women who didn't look like me, as well. More of them, probably. Laetitia and I had nothing in common, for one, nor did I and Lady Violet Cummings, so it wasn't as if it were a requirement.

"Would that be someone else trying to kill her," Christopher ventured, oblivious to or at least purposefully ignoring his cousin's reaction, "or the same person, not realizing that she was upstairs breathing her last?"

I shrugged. "If that's what happened, I don't see how it could have been Wolfgang, at any rate. He'd have had no reason to want Cecily dead."

Crispin snorted. "I'm sure Wolfie is as innocent as the day is long."

I bristled, but before I could say anything, he added, "At least I have an alibi. I'm sure that would be your next suggestion."

"If you wanted to shoot anyone," I said coldly, "I'm sure you would have potted Wolfgang in the back instead of me, St George."

He flushed angrily. "Are you calling me a coward, Darling?"

Well, yes. I was. Not because I thought he was one—he was a well-brought-up Englishman with all the usual Anglo-Saxon morals; he would never shoot an opponent in the back—but because I knew that it would anger him. Before I could double down, however, Francis had spoken up. "Enough, Pippa. So you have no idea who might have taken a potshot at the house while you were out in the woods?"

Crispin shook his head. "Sorry, old chap. We were spread out and there were trees. It could have been anyone."

After a second, he added, "Anyone except me. And I believe Laetitia. I had her in my sights for most of it."

"That's too bad," I said with a toss of my hair. "I wouldn't have put it past her."

Crispin scowled. "I'm sure you wouldn't, Darling. If you could, you'd probably pin Cecily's death on her, too."

I scowled back. "What do you mean, if I could? I can, quite easily." I raised a finger. "Number one, Dominic Rivers peddles dope. Number two, someone invited him here, and for a reason. That reason might have been to get their hands on something that could kill Cecily. It wasn't you. It's Laetitia's family's house, and Laetitia's engagement party, so she—and of course Geoffrey—are the most likely culprits."

I waited for him to tell me that I was wrong. When he didn't, I administered the *coup de grace*. "If she thought you were responsible for Cecily's condition, and that you might have to throw her over to make an honest woman out of Cecily, she had every reason to want Cecily as well as her baby out of the way."

"Well-reasoned, Pipsqueak," Francis said. "Is she your number one suspect, then?"

"She's always my number one suspect." I had, after all, suspected her of Johanna de Vos's murder in May and of Abigail Dole's murder in July, as well. If she had been in London last month, I would have probably suspected her of Flossie Schlomsky's kidnapping, too.

"It's good to be self-aware," Christopher told me, with a twitch of his lips.

I rolled my eyes. "I can't help it that she always has a motive whenever anyone associated with St George is murdered." Or kidnapped.

"I was not associated with Abigail Dole," Crispin said, "and I'll thank you to remember it."

"Of course not." I gave him a condescending smirk.

He sneered, but before he could respond, there was the sound of Laetitia's voice from the hallway. "Crispin, love! Where are you?"

Crispin's face took on an expression of pure panic, and I sniggered. "Better go, St George, before she comes in here and finds you fraternizing with the enemy."

I could see his attention flick to the door in the side wall, the one leading into the study next door. But of course there was no way around it, and in credit to him, he stood his ground as Laetitia appeared in the doorway.

"There you are."

She glided into the room, elegant even in jodhpurs and knee-high boots. Both boots and jacket were black, of course. Trailing on her heels was Wolfgang, decked out as Constance had described to me earlier, and looking better than any man has the right to. The slate gray of his jacket managed to set off both the midnight blue of his eyes and the golden blond of his hair, ruffled from the hat he was holding in one hand, and the time outside and on horseback had brought roses to his cheeks.

Francis growled and pushed his chair back. I shot him a look, but to be honest, I was too busy gazing admiringly at Wolfgang to pay him much mind.

"Philippa." Wolfgang snatched up my hand in his free one, and bent over it.

"Wolfgang." I gave him my best smile as, beside me, Laetitia leaned in to peck Crispin on the cheek. I suppose she might have planned to catch his lips, but either she miscalculated or he turned his head away at the last moment.

I ignored them, of course. It was none of my business. Instead, I enjoyed the pressure of Wolfgang's warm lips on the back of my hand as I told him, "I missed you at breakfast this morning. I'm glad you found something to occupy you in my absence."

He raised his head, but held onto my hand for a little longer than was necessary. "It was an enjoyable time."

"Like shooting at things, do you?" Francis asked disagreeably, and Wolfgang finally let go of my hand in order to turn to him. His eyebrows lifted.

"Pardon me?"

Francis's brows lowered in response. "I asked if you like to shoot at things."

"I heard the question," Wolfgang said. "What I don't understand, was what you meant by it. It sounds as if you are implying something."

"I'm asking," Francis said, "whether we have you to thank for being almost killed earlier."

"Killed?" Wolfgang looked from him to me to Christopher, and then back to me again. "Someone shot at you?"

"I'm sure it was just an accident," I said diplomatically, while Francis snorted.

"That wasn't what you said earlier, Pipsqueak."

"Well, I also said I knew that it wasn't Wolfgang, so you can't get me that way, Francis."

There was a beat of silence, and then Laetitia threw herself into the fray. "Connie," she addressed her cousin, "why don't you and Francis sit with Crispin and myself for luncheon?"

There was a question mark at the end of the sentence, but it was clearly an order, or if not quite that, a strong suggestion. "I haven't had the chance to get to know your fiancé," she added, with a glance at Francis.

That was partly her own fault, honestly, since every time they had been together, Crispin had been there too, and she had focused on him. But be that as it may, there was nothing Francis or Constance could do at this point, except to agree. So Laetitia latched onto Francis's arm, leaving Crispin, perforce, to escort Constance.

Neither of them looked thrilled about that. I think Constance is a little bit afraid of Crispin, or at least she's not as comfortable with him as she is with me or Christopher. Considering how sharp his tongue can be, it's hard to blame her.

Not that he'd use it on Constance, of course. She's a dainty, lovely, soft-spoken young woman, the kind you treat gently. Nonetheless, she threw me a look of abject despair over her shoulder as he tugged her away.

"Chin up, Constance," I called after her. "If he bites you, bite back."

Crispin curled his lip in a sneer, but didn't rise to the bait. They passed through the door and into the hallway and left the three of us alone.

"What is this about someone shooting at you?" Wolfgang wanted to know, sternly, and I turned my attention from the now-empty doorway back to him.

"I'm certain it was nothing. A stray shot from someone in

the woods that just happened to pass within a few inches of my head." And Francis's.

Wolfgang paled. "That close?"

"Well... within a foot, at least. But we're all just fine now." I smiled reassuringly. After a moment he smiled back.

"I understand one of the young women from last night has passed on?"

"Cecily Fletcher," Christopher said. "You may have noticed her yesterday. Looked a bit like Pippa. Same brown hair. Green dress."

"Of course." Wolfgang turned back to me. "Did someone shoot at you in the belief that it was her?"

I smiled, pleased that he had come to this conclusion without me having to spell it out for him. "The thought crossed our minds."

"Did you communicate with Miss Fletcher at all last night?" Christopher wanted to know, fetching up next to us after a leisurely wander across the floor.

Wolfgang shook his head. "I spent my time with Philippa." After a second's hesitation he added, "I noticed the young lady, of course. A pretty girl in a celery green dress, although she looked tired, or perhaps ill."

"Both, I imagine," I said, while Christopher added, "She was with child."

"Ah." Wolfgang looked enlightened.

"Your room is on the top floor," I said, "isn't it?"

He nodded. "Beside the two young puppies."

Dominic Rivers and the Honorable Reggie, I assumed. "Did they bother you?"

"Not in the way you mean," Wolfgang said. "Nothing was said. They kept me up with their coming and going, but not by anything they said."

Nothing personal, then. Good. It was bad enough that

Francis, and of course Bilge Fortescue and his wife, had been blatantly rude.

"I'm up there, too," I said, "and I didn't notice anyone walking around."

"He probably means you," Christopher told me. "You came in late. And then you entertained Crispin for a while. And then you dealt with Cecily."

"I didn't *entertain* St George." Certainly not in that tone and with that inflection.

"That's not what he said," Christopher said with a smirk, one that made him look uncomfortably like his cousin.

"He's a dirty, rotten liar, then. He was only in my room for a few minutes, and only because someone came up the stairs that he didn't want to see him there. Then St George went downstairs and I went to the lavatory and Cecily came in and I held her hair and then put her to bed."

"Clear as mud," Christopher said politely. "Sounds like entertainment to me."

In retelling it, I could see why. It sounded a bit like a French farce, didn't it? People coming and going into and out of other people's rooms all night long.

"Sorry," I told Wolfgang sincerely. "I didn't mean to keep you up."

He clicked his heels together. "You didn't, *mein Schatz*. It was the others."

"I don't suppose you noticed who, other than St George, spent time in Cecily's room?"

He hesitated for a moment. "The young dark-haired man—Rivers?—walked her upstairs at the end of the dancing. He went into his room for a moment, and then into hers for a bit longer, albeit not much more than a few minutes."

A dope delivery, perhaps. I could picture them coming up the stairs together, and Rivers asking Cecily to wait a moment while he ducked into his room to pick up whatever it was she had asked him to bring her, before crossing the hall and passing it to her.

That put Cecily on the hook for her own death, though, and while that was certainly a possibility—accidentally, I assumed—it wasn't a thought I liked.

Then again, the idea that someone had killed her on purpose didn't appeal, either. Nor did the idea that someone had tried to induce a miscarriage—someone other than Cecily, for their own reasons—and that it had ended up being fatal.

Truly, there was no palatable option in this whole mess. And I suppose that was the way it had to be, when a vibrant, young woman (and her unborn child) was dead.

"Anyone else?" Christopher inquired.

"Your cousin," Wolfgang told him, with a flicker of a glance my way. "I heard a woman's voice at one point. And I can't swear to it that none of the other gentlemen visited, either."

He hesitated for a second before he added, "There was a lot of traffic on the landing."

Yes, there had been, and no, I couldn't swear to it, either. The Honorable Reggie would have had the opportunity to stop by while Dominic Rivers was downstairs. Geoffrey Marsden had been with Lady Violet, if Nellie the maid was to be believed, but I didn't know how long that might have lasted. Geoffrey might have walked Violet to her door and then turned around and knocked on Cecily's on his way down. As for the woman's voice Wolfgang had heard, that could have been me, or it could have been practically anyone else. Violet, after Geoffrey dropped her off. Laetitia, since Crispin hadn't been with her. Olivia Barnsley, after the Honorable Reggie had gone to bed. Or Nellie, delivering the cup of tea Cecily had asked for—if she had done, and someone else hadn't brought it to Cecily.

It might even have been the Countess Euphemia or Lady

Serena Fortescue. Just because it seemed unlikely that either of them would bother to visit Cecily in her room, didn't mean it was impossible that they had done.

Or perhaps Cecily had simply been talking to herself. That would be the simplest explanation.

I felt pretty certain that it wouldn't have been Constance, anyway. Of everyone here, she had the weakest motive for wanting Cecily out of the way. There was no possibility that Francis had got Cecily in the family way, and no way he would have killed her if he had. And if he hadn't, then Constance had no motive, either.

"Is there a reason to think it wasn't an accident?" Christopher wanted to know. "I know Crispin said otherwise, but he might be wrong."

"I have no idea," I admitted. "I didn't get the impression, when I saw her yesterday, that it was something she had done to herself. She didn't mention having taken anything on purpose. But I suppose it's possible. It's not something she necessarily would have mentioned to me. We weren't friends, and she might have been concerned about the way I would react."

"She might have done it and not realized how bad it would be," Christopher said.

Perhaps. Although it still seemed to me that it was something a woman would do at home, not in someone else's house during an engagement party.

Christopher nodded. "Unless, as discussed earlier, she was doing it to make a point."

"What point would that be, though? St George said he hadn't had relations with her since February. It couldn't have been his child."

Wolfgang was looking from Christopher to me and back,

watching as we batted ideas back and forth between us like two people who are used to discussing things rapid-fire.

"Perhaps I wasn't talking about St George," Christopher said.

Oh, really? "Who, then? Geoffrey?"

"He does have a way of getting around," Christopher said apologetically.

Yes, of course he did. "He spent yesterday evening tangled up with Lady Violet Cummings. Do you think Cecily would have stood for that if she were carrying Geoffrey's child?"

Christopher made a face. "Depends on how she felt about him, I suppose. Personally, I would have been happy to have someone take Geoffrey off my hands."

So would I, now that he mentioned it.

"How do you know that Geoffrey was exercising his wiles on Lady Violet last night?" Christopher added.

"Nellie told me," I said. "The maid. She said Geoffrey was in the garden with Lady Violet, and Olivia Barnsley was somewhere with the Honorable Reggie. Cecily was in her bedchamber with Dominic Rivers."

"Which is a bit suspicious, don't you think?"

That Cecily had had a private meeting with a known dope dealer just before she ended up dead from a suspected overdose? Yes, I would have to say so. "It might have been innocent. Perhaps he's the baby's father. Or perhaps she wanted a vial of bismuth."

"If she wanted bismuth," Christopher said, "she could have gone to any corner chemist. Bismuth isn't controlled."

No. But pennyroyal isn't, either. In fact, pennyroyal grows wild all over the place. Anyone with access to an AGA cooker can make a pot of pennyroyal tea, as long as they know where to find the leaves.

I tried to imagine Geoffrey, stalk in hand, wandering into

the Marsden Manor kitchen to brew up a dose of lethal poison to feed to Cecily Fletcher, and drew a blank. Someone would have seen him, surely. The staff would have said something to someone, and the news would have been all over the manor by now if Geoffrey had been messing about in the kitchen.

Could he have asked someone to do it for him? Handed them a handful of leaves and asked them to turn it into tea?

That made more sense. Or did it? Someone would have mentioned that, too, wouldn't they? Unless he had sworn someone to secrecy, of course, but if Cecily had been murdered, that someone wasn't likely to keep it to themselves forever. People don't tend to keep things to themselves when murder is concerned. Not unless they're on the hook for it themselves.

Or perhaps Crispin was simply wrong, and Cecily had done this to herself. Having a child out of wedlock isn't something a well-bred young lady should aspire to, not even in our modern day and age. Perhaps the gentleman had rejected her, or wasn't someone she could see herself being married to.

If the gentleman in question was Lord Geoffrey Marsden, that would explain—or would at least go some way towards explaining—why this had happened here at Marsden Manor, and not in the privacy of Cecily's own flat. And it certainly made sense that she wouldn't want to marry him, since he would undoubtedly keep on bedding anything that moved even after he was married. Especially if the marriage was forced on him by an unexpected pregnancy.

No, that all made an unfortunate amount of sense. But then the pennyroyal had turned out to be too strong, and Cecily had died instead of simply ridding herself of the unwanted pregnancy.

It was a terrible outcome, of course, but it explained everything. And all I had to do to square it in my head, was disregard Crispin's assertion that Cecily wouldn't.

But then again, what did Crispin know? Until last night, by his own admission, he hadn't had anything to do with her in months.

"I think you ought to leave the detecting to the constabulary, Philippa," Wolfgang said, and I blinked and looked up at him. He smiled, and added, persuasively, "What's more likely, after all? That it was an accident, or that it was murder? That someone shot at you deliberately, or that someone had a misfire?"

It was much likelier that someone had a misfire, I supposed. There was no reason why anyone would shoot at me, after all. More likely that someone would have shot at Cecily. But that only made sense if the pennyroyal poisoning had been deliberate. If that had been an accident, the shooting was no doubt accidental, as well. And Wolfgang seemed to want my attention, so I shoved all the questions and all the speculation into the back of my head and smiled up at him. "Luncheon must be ready by now. Shall we go and partake?"

He smiled back. "Let us do so."

Christopher headed for the door, and left Wolfgang with the job of offering me his arm and escorting me out of the room and down the hall towards the formal dining room.

CHAPTER TEN

THE ATMOSPHERE in the dining room was subdued. There was a lot of chatter, but most if it took place privately. Constance and Francis had their heads together and were conversing in low tones over the roast beef. Francis glanced our way occasionally, at me sitting next to Wolfgang, and scowled, so I thought I could guess what their discussion was about.

Laetitia was whispering sweet nothings in Crispin's ear—or whispering something, at any rate, whether it was sweet or not. From his expression, I would guess not. At one point he looked across the table and saw me staring, and crossed his eyes in my direction. He stopped short of sticking his tongue out, but I thought he might have wanted to. Then Laetitia noticed my looking, and shot me a glare that could have dropped me dead where I sat, before she turned back to Crispin and hissed more intensely, directly into his ear. He winced.

I rolled my eyes and turned my attention to the rest of the table.

After last night, one might have expected to see Lady Violet Cummings pressing her advantage with Lord Geoffrey, and Olivia Barnsley likewise with the Honorable Reggie Fish. Such was not the case. Geoffrey flirted expertly with Lady Serena while her husband watched sourly, and Violet and Olivia were engaged in what looked like a tense conversation of their own, that involved a lot of sideways glances at the rest of the table—or more specifically, at the men present. If I had to guess, I would say that they were discussing Cecily, and perhaps who might have been responsible for her predicament.

Reggie, meanwhile, kept his attention on his plate, and didn't say a word to anyone. So did Dominic Rivers, who—it must be said—looked a bit the worse for wear this morning. One might even use the word 'hunted,' if one were so inclined. He was wan under the olive skin, and when he caught me looking his way, his eyes got wide and he shied like a spooked horse.

Beside me, Christopher gave a snort. "That's a sign of a guilty conscience if I ever saw one."

I nodded. "Chances are the pennyroyal came from him originally, whether Cecily bought it herself or someone else did. I'm sure he's worried that someone will figure it out."

Christopher tilted his face to give Rivers another contemplative look. "I wonder whether he would be inclined to share that knowledge?"

I shook my head. "Not likely. It's a crime, isn't it? Not on par with actually using it on someone else, but still a crime. And he's avoided getting caught in one of those so far."

Not for lack of trying on Tom's part.

After a second, I added, "Besides, I don't get the impression that the local constabulary is terribly interested in investigating this as a homicide."

So far, they hadn't asked any of us any questions beyond the very obvious, and nothing they had asked had led me to

believe they thought Cecily's death was anything but a tragic—
if self-induced—accident.

"Hard to blame them for that," Christopher said fairly. "I'm
sure murders don't come along very often here."

No, of course they didn't. It was rather surprising that there
had already been another one, actually, so soon after the events
at the Dower House the first weekend in May.

Back then, there had been no question at all that what had
happened had been a murder. Johanna de Vos had been found
in the Dowager Lady Peckham's bed with her tongue sticking
out and a scarf wrapped around her throat. This was much
more ambiguous.

And besides, back then, a representative for Scotland Yard
had been right there to take charge. Such was not the case this
time.

And speak of the devil—

"I wish Tom were here," Christopher muttered.

I nodded. So did I. And not only because it would be
uncommonly nice to have a professional on site again, one who
can recognize a homicide when he sees one, but because I like
Tom, and so does Christopher.

Thomas Gardiner is a Detective Sergeant with Scotland
Yard in London. Back in May, we had just discovered Johanna's
dead body when Tom arrived from Sutherland Hall to inform
the Peckhams—Constance and her brother Gilbert—that their
mother had died. She had been at Sutherland visiting Duke
Harold for her late friend, Duchess Charlotte's, funeral, and
had succumbed in her sleep. (That turned out to be a murder,
too, but of course we didn't know that at the time.)

Tom, bless him, had volunteered to make the drive from
Little Sutherland in Wiltshire to Marsden-on-Crane in Dorset
to deliver the news of Lady Peckham's death personally. He's
rather fond of Christopher, too, which was partly why he had

done it, I thought. I'm not entirely sure whether that fondness is romantic in nature, the way Christopher is sweet on Tom, or whether it's simply because Tom was Robbie's best friend at Eton, and Christopher is Robbie's little brother. But in either case, he had made his way to the Dower House, and when he had, he had taken charge of the investigation into Johanna's death.

He was not here this time. Had it been up to Crispin, I wouldn't have been surprised to see him—they were friendly, if not as friendly as Tom and Christopher; Crispin, it must be said, is not as loveable as Christopher is, nor is he Robbie's brother—but I was sure Laetitia would have put her foot down on any suggestion of inviting a policeman to her home and her engagement party.

"We could ring him up and ask him to come?"

Christopher sighed. "We've been over this, Pippa. One cannot simply ring up Scotland Yard and tell them they're needed. Only the Chief Constable can do that."

I glanced around the table. "Surely the senior Marsdens must be friendly with the local Chief Constable? Could we perhaps prevail on them to intercede?"

"Not if they believe Cecily's death was an accident," Christopher said, "and everyone here has incentive to believe that."

Yes, of course they did. If it had been an accident, no one was guilty of murder, or even criminal negligence.

I should have questioned Crispin more closely on why he believed that Cecily wouldn't have done this to herself, I realized, but of course I hadn't had the opportunity right then. And —I glanced in the direction of Laetitia and St George—there was no possible way I could question him now. Not without the entire table hearing me.

Although... would that be so bad? It would certainly get the conversation going, and if people were thrown off balance and talking impulsively, perhaps someone might let something slip.

"St George."

He looked up and over, harassment clear in his expression.

"When you were in Cecily's room last night—"

Laetitia's eyes narrowed. Someone gasped. Crispin sighed. "Yes, Darling. Was it really necessary to say it like that?"

"It's nothing to be ashamed of," I told him sweetly. "You weren't the only one, after all."

"No, I'm sure I wasn't."

Every other conversation had stopped dead now, while everyone was watching us. Laetitia leaned away from Crispin but kept her eyes on me. The expression in them could have peeled the skin from my bones.

I ignored her in favor of her fiancé. "Was she drinking tea, by any chance, when you were in there?"

He eyed me silently for a moment. "As a matter of fact she was."

"Did you bring it to her?"

He shook his head.

"Do you know who did?"

"No," Crispin said. "I didn't see it arrive, and she didn't mention it."

That was too bad. I had hoped she might have said something at a point when she would have had no reason to lie, and no inkling that something was wrong with the tea.

"Would anyone else like to confess?"

There was the sound of a collective intake of breath and an almost visible stiffening of spines that spread around the table, and suddenly everyone was talking, all over one another.

Laetitia raised her voice. "Quiet!"

The voices cut off as if by a knife. Laetitia turned to me. "Miss Darling."

"Lady Laetitia."

She scowled at me. "Why are you asking about the tea?"

"That should be obvious, shouldn't it?" I flicked a glance at Crispin, who made a face. "If this didn't happen on its own, someone made it happen. And the tea is a likely vehicle."

There was a moment of appalled silence. Then—

"That's an awful suggestion, young woman," Bilge Fortescue said roughly. "I'll have you know that it's a lot more common than you might think."

'It' being a spontaneous miscarriage, I assumed. His wife made a pained sound, and he looked immediately guilty, before reaching out and putting a paw on her shoulder. "Sorry, Serena. But you know—"

Serena bit her lip, eyes on the table, while she blinked rapidly. Not just a loss, it seemed, but a recent one.

"I'm sorry to have brought up a difficult subject," I said, since I certainly hadn't been going for this kind of reaction. "It wasn't my intention to make anyone uncomfortable."

Or not this kind of uncomfortable, at any rate. Guilty and afraid, yes, in the event that they had murdered Cecily. But upset because they had lost a baby of their own, certainly not.

"I'm so sorry, Serena," Lady Violet said, patting Serena's hand, not without a vicious glance my way, while Francis muttered, "Sorry, Bilge, old chap."

Bilge nodded, and kept patting his wife's shoulder, even as he scowled at me. I was about to apologize again, but before I could, a voice intoned my name from the doorway behind me. "Miss Darling?"

I turned on my chair. "Oh. Constable Collins. How good to see you again."

Collins looked uncomfortable. "If I could have a word with you, Miss Darling?"

"Of course," I said, and made to push my chair back. Wolfgang got there first, and pulled it out for me. I gave him a smile. "Thank you."

He clicked his heels and smoldered. As Constable Collins shut the door behind me, I could hear the voices start up in the dining room again.

I smiled. "What can I do for you, Constable?"

Collins shifted from one foot to the other, looking awkward. He's a young man, even younger than me, and he was clearly feeling out of sorts. "It's about what you said in there, Miss Darling."

I nodded encouragingly.

"About the young lady being dead…"

"Yes, Constable." I took pity on him. "As I'm sure you noticed, the consensus seems to lean towards natural causes."

"But you don't think so?"

"I'd like to," I said. "Nobody likes to contemplate murder, do they?"

Except for those of us who enjoy a good detective novel, of course.

"Then why—?"

"The teacup in her room last night smelled of spearmint," I said.

Collins eyed me. "Pennyroyal."

"That was the assumption I made."

"We assumed she would have done it to herself," Collins said. "Many girls do, when they find themselves in the family way."

He sounded practically blasé about it. I didn't think it happened that often, but perhaps I was traveling in the wrong circles.

Or perhaps the women in my circles—like the Hon Cecily —had other ways of dealing with the matter when it happened.

"Lord St George didn't believe she would have done it

herself. We talked about it this morning, after we learned what had happened. He spoke to her last night, in her room, after the party. I don't know what she said to give him that impression; you'd have to ask him."

Collins nodded. He had pulled out his little notebook, and was scribbling in it with the ubiquitous pencil stub that every policeman seems to carry in his pocket. "And how did Lord St George seem?"

I could see the trap clearly, so it was easy to step aside and avoid it. "He was shocked, I suppose. Or surprised, at least. A bit pale, if I'm honest."

"Aside from that?"

"He told me that it was none of his concern. He hadn't been intimate with Miss Fletcher in a long time."

Constable Collins blushed, and so did I. He cleared his throat. "What happened then?"

"We heard steps on the staircase from downstairs," I said, "and we didn't want to be seen talking together— This is his engagement party, you know. His fiancée is the jealous sort."

Collins eyed me. "Is that so? What did you do?"

"We stepped into my room and finished our conversation. When we opened the door to the hallway a few minutes later, Dominic Rivers was standing out there."

"I'm not familiar with Mr. Rivers," Collins said.

Of course not. That had been a different murder case. "Dark-haired gentleman. A bit swarthy. A dope peddler from London down for the festivities."

Collins's eyebrows rose. "A dope dealer?"

I nodded. "Scotland Yard is aware. You remember Detective Sergeant Gardiner, don't you?"

"Of course." Collins glanced around vaguely. "He's not here, is he?"

"I'm afraid not. But he knows about Rivers. If they had

enough evidence against him, I'm sure he'd be in Wormwood Scrubs by now."

Collins nodded. "So you opened the door and Mr. Rivers was there. Was anything said?"

"Nothing pertaining to her death," I said. "He tried to give Lord St George a hard time. I reminded him that Lord St George wasn't the only one to have had a conversation with Miss Fletcher last night—the maid told me that Mr. Rivers had been in there, too—and then he withdrew to his room, and Crispin went downstairs, and I went to bed."

Collins scribbled it all down. "You mentioned a teacup?"

"It was in her room," I said. "She said she asked for peppermint tea for an upset stomach, but it smelled more like spearmint to me. Do you know for certain what killed her?"

"Doctor will have to do the autopsy first," Collins said, "but pennyroyal's as good a guess as any. Do you know what happened to the cup?"

"I dumped the dregs down the drain and put the cup and saucer on the floor outside her door. It was gone the next morning. I'm sure by now it's been washed and put away."

"Just so." Collins looked at his notebook for a moment. "Anything else you can tell me?"

"She came into the lavatory when I was brushing my teeth," I said. "She was already unwell then. She vomited. I had to help her back to her room and into bed."

"Did you talk?"

"Not about the tea. She did confirm that Lord St George is not—*was* not—the father of the child."

"And you think she told you the truth?"

"She had no reason to lie," I said steadily.

Collins nodded. "Who does that leave?"

"Of the men here, I suppose you mean?"

"If someone killed her," Collins said, "as you seem to think someone did, it's likely to be connected to the situation, don't you think?"

It was, rather. Although— "I didn't imply that anyone killed her deliberately, you know. Pennyroyal—if it was penny-royal—is fatal in large doses. But someone might have just tried to induce a miscarriage, not kill her. The murder might have been an accident."

"It's still murder," Collins said coolly. "And in case you're unaware, just procuring the means to induce an abortion is a crime, too."

Yes, of course it was. "I wasn't quarreling," I said blandly. "As for who is here, you already know a lot of us. Lord Geoffrey Marsden is local, of course."

Collins made a face, one he tried to smooth out a moment later, a bit too late.

"He gets around," I added, "as I'm sure you know. I don't think anyone would be surprised if it turned out to be his baby."

Collins shook his head.

"You probably know him better than I do—I've only met him a few times—so you might know better than I would whether dosing someone with pennyroyal is something he'd do if he found himself in this position."

Collins's eyes were distant, as he undoubtedly thought about whether Geoffrey was capable of such a thing or not.

"You met Christopher and Francis Astley, me and Lord St George at the Dower House in May. I can assure you that neither Christopher nor Francis was responsible for what happened. Francis is engaged to Constance Peckham now, so in that sense he might have had motive, but he didn't know Cecily Fletcher."

Collins nodded.

"And Christopher is... well, you've met Christopher. Miss Fletcher wasn't his type."

Collins's lips twitched, but he didn't say anything.

"She absolved Lord St George of involvement," I added. "He told me that he hasn't had anything of that nature to do with her for six months, and she confirmed it. She showed no outward sign of being pregnant, so whenever this happened, it was less than half a year ago."

Collins nodded.

"Dominic Rivers is here, as I told you. He's well known to this group, and provides them all with dope. I don't know whether that includes things like pennyroyal, or if he sticks with cocaine and opium and the like, but it would be worth asking him about it. I also don't know who invited him here. Lord St George said he hadn't done, and I know that Christopher or I didn't. I don't think Francis or Constance knew who he was. He arrived with the Honorable Reginald Fish, so it might have been him."

Collins scribbled it down. I took a breath and continued. "I know nothing about the Honorable Reggie. We met for the first time yesterday. He looked and sounded like the typical young man about town, and I have no reason to think he isn't. He danced a dance with Cecily last evening, so I know they know one another, but beyond that I can't tell you what their relationship might have been like."

"But it's possible he was the father of the child?"

"It's possible from where I'm standing. It's also possible that it was Dominic Rivers or Lord Geoffrey Marsden."

Collins nodded. "Who else is here? There was another young gentleman, wasn't there?"

"There were two," I said. "The blond is the *Graf von und zu* Natterdorff—"

"German."

There had been no emotion in Collins's voice, but I bristled nonetheless. "My cousin, as it happens. Or so he says."

Collins didn't comment, just waited with his pencil stub poised over the page of the notebook. When he didn't say anything else, I continued grudgingly. "As far as I know, he's never met Cecily before. As far as I know, he's never met anyone here, except for me, Christopher, and Crispin."

"Did Lord St George invite him?"

"I think Laetitia did," I said. "I can't imagine any world in which Crispin would have wanted Wolfgang here. They don't get along."

"But you can imagine why Miss Laetitia would have wanted that?"

I couldn't, honestly. In her position, I would have done it to irritate Crispin, but there was no reason why Laetitia would have wanted to irritate her new fiancé, and it wasn't as if she would have done it to do me any favors, either, since she and I don't get along.

Besides, his being here was upsetting Francis, and apparently also Bilge Fortescue, so inviting him at all was a thorn in a lot of people's sides.

"You'll have to ask her," I told Collins. "But that's Wolfgang. The last gentleman in attendance—other than the Earl of Marsden—is Bilge Fortescue."

Collins's eyebrows rose as he wrote it down.

"William," I corrected myself. "William Fortescue and his wife, Lady Serena. Apparently he's nicknamed Bilge because he talks a lot of rubbish."

"What information do you have about Mr. Fortescue?"

"Not much beyond what I've already told you. He and Francis went to Eton together. And then to France. He married Lady Serena a few years ago. My cousin didn't go to the wedding, and I don't imagine he has seen Bilge Fortescue in years. Mr. Fortescue was rude to Wolfgang when he and his wife first arrived, but so was Francis, so I can't really complain about that, I suppose."

"It's natural," Collins said absently, still writing, "for someone who served in the War."

"I suppose. At any rate, that's the whole group. Or the male half of it, anyway."

"What about the female half?"

"There's Constance Peckham and Laetitia Marsden. You know both of them. There's me. There's Bilge's wife, Lady Serena. There *was* Cecily Fletcher. And there's Lady Violet Cummings and the—apparently—Honorable Olivia Barnsley. I've seen Violet Cummings before—I recognized her face in the ballroom yesterday—but I've never met Olivia Barnsley."

"Can you tell me anything about either of them?"

"Olivia spent the evening with the Honorable Reggie," I said, "or so Nellie told me. Lady Violet seems to be making up to Geoffrey Marsden."

Collins made a face. "Nellie told you this?"

"The maid, yes. I assume you know Nellie?"

"We've met," Collins said. "She has been here for a few weeks now."

The tips of his ears were red, from which I deduced that he might think Nellie was pretty.

He was a nice young man, however, so I decided not to twit him about it. I wouldn't have extended Christopher or Crispin the same courtesy, for the record. Not that either would have reacted with red ears to a pretty girl: Christopher because he doesn't swing that way, and Crispin because he has far too much experience with women to blush simply because someone's pretty.

"As for what else I know about them," I said instead, "it's not much. Like Cecily Fletcher, Lady Violet at one time had a fling with St George. Olivia Barnsley might have done, as well."

"Gets around, doesn't he?"

And then Collins blushed, as if he hadn't intended to say anything, but the words had simply slipped out. I smirked. "You're not wrong. Although from now on, Laetitia will keep him on a much shorter leash, I'm sure."

Collins muttered something. He was bent over his notes, and the back of his neck was red.

"Before I go back to the dining room," I added, "I ought to let you know that someone shot at me earlier. Or at us, I suppose I should say. It might have been Christopher or Francis who was the intended victim and not me."

He raised his eyes from the notebook to look at me. "Why would anyone want to shoot at any of you?"

"I have no idea," I said. "The suggestion was made that I look a bit like Cecily Fletcher from a distance. Perhaps the murderer—if there was one—thought the pennyroyal had failed to kill her and decided to take a more active role."

"Poisoning is active enough," Collins said. "When and where did this take place?"

I gave him the details, and added, "The bullet should still be in the wall outside. Or on the grass below the wall. We didn't stop to pick it up."

"Would you show me?"

"I'd be delighted." I gestured him down the hallway towards the boot room and the exit to the outside. A minute later we were standing there in the warm sunshine, at the back of the house, and I had to fight back the shiver that ran down my spine as I recalled the sound of the bullet whistling past my ear and embedding itself in the wall.

"We were standing there." I pointed to a spot a few feet out from the wall and to my right. "I had come out through this door. It was just after Constance and I had found Cecily. She was still alive, but not doing well. I ran downstairs to find Francis. He and Christopher were setting up wickets for a game of croquet for those of us who didn't want to shoot partridge. Over there, see?"

I pointed out the already-standing wickets, and the ones that had been tossed to the grass when the two men had dropped everything to come towards me.

"The shot came from the trees. I'm not certain where. But the bullet ended up in the wall... somewhere over there." I waved vaguely to the gray stone. "It passed within a foot of my head, and not much farther from Francis's."

Collins gave me a look on his way past, as he headed for the wall to look for the bullet. "What happened next?"

"We dropped to the ground and crawled to the door," I said. "It was quite undignified. But there were no more shots. And it might have been an accident. Someone in the woods being careless."

Collins hummed something that might have been agreement or its complete opposite. "Here we are," he said. I wandered closer, and saw where a chip of stone had been taken out of the wall, sometime recently. The wound was lighter in color than the rest of the stone around it.

Collins squatted down and began looking around for the bullet. "You may go back to the dining room, Miss Darling," he told me. "Would you tell your cousin I would like a word with him?"

"Of course. Which cousin do you want to see?"

"The younger Mr. Astley," Collins said. "Ah. There we are."

He eyed with satisfaction a piece of ground just to the left of his knee. I peered at it, too, and saw a glint of metal.

"Is that the bullet?"

He nodded. "Go fetch your cousin, Miss Darling. In the meantime, may I borrow a handkerchief?"

"Of course." I pulled it out of my sleeve and gave it to him. "I'll be right back."

"Just your cousin, Miss Darling. You know how this goes. Separate statements."

I made a face. "Of course, Constable."

I headed for the door to the house, leaving him squatting there on the grass like a gnome, handkerchief in hand.

CHAPTER ELEVEN

IT FELT as if I had been away from the dining room for a long time. However, when I came back through the door, everything was as it had been. Francis was whispering to Constance, Laetitia was hissing into Crispin's ear, and Lady Violet and the Honorable Olivia had their heads together in a low-voiced and tense conversation. Crispin's expression was one of resigned suffering. The chair between Christopher and Wolfgang was still empty, and I pulled it out. "Your turn."

"Excuse me?"

They both turned startled blue eyes on me, one pair of cornflower and the other a dark shade of navy.

"Not you," I told Wolfgang with a smile. To Christopher I added, "Constable Collins wants to see you. He's outside with the bullet."

Christopher's brow wrinkled. "What am I supposed to tell him that you haven't already?"

"Nothing. He wants you to confirm what I told him." I took my seat and shook out the napkin I had placed on the table earlier. "I'm sure you have nothing to worry about."

I picked up my knife and fork as Christopher muttered an apology and walked away. Crispin shot a look at his back and then one at me, question in his eyes. I shook my head and he rolled his eyes and turned back to Laetitia. I directed my attention, and a warm smile, Wolfgang's way. "Did anything happen while I was away?"

"Most of the guests wondered what you might be sharing with the police," Wolfgang said. He had finished his luncheon in my absence, and now he was fiddling with his napkin ring, turning it over in his fingers.

I arched my brows. "What secrets did they think I was sharing?"

"They don't know," Wolfgang said. "Although someone mentioned that the person who finds the body is always a suspect."

Yes, of course someone had mentioned that. I shook my head. "Not this time, I'm afraid. None of us even knew Cecily Fletcher before this weekend. We certainly didn't know that she was expecting. Whoever procured the pennyroyal and did away with her would have had to have known that ahead of time."

I let my eyes linger of Dominic Rivers for a moment. If he noticed, he gave no sign of it. He was either so deeply into his own thoughts that he didn't notice—and hardly surprising, if he had brought the pennyroyal here—or he knew, but refused to give me the satisfaction of showing me a reaction.

"No one did away with her, Miss Darling," Laetitia said coldly. "It was an unfortunate accident, that's all."

I smirked. "Of course, Lady Laetitia. If you say so."

"I do say so." She was sitting down, and it's hard to stomp your foot under those circumstances, but she appeared as if she wanted to.

"Darling," Crispin said.

I turned my attention to him. "Yes, St George?"

"Let's not speak of it, if you don't mind. It's inappropriate conversation for the luncheon table, and frankly, it's making me feel quite ill."

"I've never known you to care about something like that before," I said. He certainly doesn't have a weak stomach, and it wasn't as if he had been the one to watch Cecily breathe her last.

"I know, Darling. But believe it or not, I rather liked her."

Laetitia twitched in her seat, and he shot her a look before turning back to me. "She was a nice girl, and she didn't deserve this."

Violet shook her head aggressively. "No, she didn't."

No, of course not. No one deserves to be foully murdered, or to die from an accidental overdose of pennyroyal, even. I eyed Violet. "You were friends."

She nodded. "The best."

"She must have confided in you, then."

"Oh." She blinked, and her eyes flickered for a second back to... was it Crispin? Or the Honorable Reggie, or perhaps Dominic Rivers?

"No," Violet said finally, turning her eyes—and attention—back to me. "She didn't tell me anything."

"She was your best friend, but she didn't tell you who she had been sharing her bed with?"

Violet shook her head.

Well, that was interesting, wasn't it? "Perhaps you weren't as close as you thought?"

"What a horrible thing to say," Olivia Barnsley uttered, scowling at me down the length of the table.

I smiled sweetly back. "I'm so sorry you feel that way. Did she confide in you, perhaps?"

"No," Olivia said mulishly. "It was none of my affair."

I looked up and down the table. "So no one here knows whose child she was carrying?"

No one answered. Until— "Do you?" Laetitia asked.

I shook my head. "Of course not." She'd been in no condition to tell me much of anything last night, although I suppose I might have asked. It hadn't crossed my mind, honestly. And I refrained from saying any of it out loud. Someone would likely blame me for not realizing how bad things had been, and then I'd be told how I might have saved her if I'd done something other than put her to bed and hope for the best, and I already blamed myself enough that I didn't want to hear that from anyone else.

"I don't really know any of her boyfriends," I added. "With the exception of St George, of course."

Laetitia glanced at Crispin. He sighed. "Thanks ever so, Darling. And on that note, I think I've had enough." He tossed his napkin on the table and got to his feet. "Please excuse me."

I think he was probably addressing Laetitia, or perhaps more generally the rest of the table. Certainly not me. But no one said anything as he walked away from the table, so I took it upon myself to issue a final warning. "Be careful out there, St George. You never know who might be gunning for you."

He shot me a look. "I know exactly who's gunning for me, Darling. And I wish you'd stop."

He didn't wait for me to answer, just stalked out of the room. The corner of my mouth turned up and I had to hold back a snort. As parting shots go, it had been a good one, and one has to admire that.

I had meant the warning more literally, of course— someone had been out there with a rifle this morning, and we didn't know whether I, Francis, or Christopher had been the one in the crosshairs. If it had been Christopher, then Crispin was in danger, too. It wouldn't have been the first time someone had mistaken one of them for the other, especially at a distance.

Or more likely, Crispin had been the one in the crosshairs to begin with, and someone had mistaken Christopher for him, which made a lot more sense. Crispin is much more shootable than Christopher is. For instance, I have never been gripped by an overwhelming need to punch Christopher in the nose, and I deal with that feeling quite regularly as relates to Crispin.

"Was that really necessary, Pipsqueak?" Francis wanted to know when Crispin's footsteps had faded down the hallway.

I turned to him. "Was what necessary? I wasn't trying to give him a hard time. He already has enough on his mind, poor bloke."

Francis's lips twitched, but he didn't take the bait. "That's my point exactly, Pippa."

Laetitia sniffed indignantly, but she didn't say anything, either.

"He'll be fine," I said. "It sounded as if he was headed outside. Constable Collins is there, and he will talk to him. St George will explain that the last time he had relations with Cecily Fletcher was in February, and that'll be that. They're both capable of basic maths."

Nobody said anything to that, although Laetitia made a face. She had only herself to thank, however. When you accept the proposal of a known philanderer, reminders of his philandering are going to crop up whether you like it or not.

I pushed my chair back. "Mr. Rivers—"

Dominic looked up in startlement.

"—would you walk with me?"

He looked like he wanted to refuse, but after a moment, and a glance at Francis and then at Laetitia, he nodded. "Of course, Miss Darling."

"Thank you." I smiled at Wolfgang. "I'll see you later."

He nodded, halfway between agreement and a polite bow. "Of course."

"Mr. Rivers?" The latter presented his arm, and I tucked mine through it. We walked out of the dining room in polite silence. Once outside in the hallway he wasted no time twitching his sleeve out of my grip.

"What's this all about?"

"A few questions," I said, dropping my hand but continuing forward down the hallway towards the main foyer, away from the dining room door. Dominic Rivers, perforce, followed.

"I don't have to tell you anything," he told my back, petulantly.

I glanced at him over my shoulder. "No, of course you don't. Although it will look suspicious if you're deliberately unforthcoming, don't you think?"

He turned a shade paler, not a marvelous look for someone with his skin tone. He tried to brazen it out, however, and his sneer was almost—almost—as good as Crispin's, at least on a bad day. "To who?"

"Whom," I said, and waited for him to come up beside me before I continued to walk. "To me, and to everyone else I tell about it. Like Constable Collins."

He scoffed. That was a creditable effort, too, although Francis does it better. "A small town bobby investigating a crime that may not have happened? I'm shaking in my boots."

"A small town constable with the power to arrest anyone involved," I corrected, "whether you have any respect for him or not."

He didn't say anything to that, and I added, "Nobody's suggesting it's your fault, you know. I don't think *you* planned to kill her."

All the blood drained out of his cheeks and left them pasty, like day-old porridge. "I certainly did not. How dare you?"

"I just told you that I don't think that," I said irritably. "Stop behaving like such a damsel, Mr. Rivers. If you provided her with the pennyroyal, you still aren't responsible for whether or not she took it."

He muttered something, in which I was pretty certain I heard the words *Billy* and *Chang*. I stopped in the middle of the main foyer and put my hands on my hips. "Billy Chang was convicted of pushing cocaine, not medicinal herbs. And he wasn't even charged in Freda Kempton's death. It's not the same situation."

"It's close enough," Rivers grumbled. "There's a prison sentence on the books, you know. *Offences Against the Person Act.* Up to three years for the procurement of drugs to cause abortion."

"But surely that's less than for selling, say, cocaine or heroin?"

"You would think," Rivers said mulishly, "but you would be wrong."

Was that so? "Well, that's too bad, isn't it? You really should have known better, Mr. Rivers."

He made a face.

"All I want to know," I told him, "is whether or not it was Cecily Fletcher who invited you here and asked you to bring her pennyroyal."

He looked at me for a moment in silence, seemingly trying to determine whether or not he should, or had to, answer the question. Finally, he said, "No. It wasn't."

"But someone else did?"

He didn't answer, and I added, "Who was it?"

"I can't tell you that, I'm afraid." His tone was bland, businesslike. "That's confidential information. Professional courtesy, you understand."

His color was back to normal now, and he looked as if he

thought he had the upper hand. I decided to see if I could disabuse him of that notion.

"Or perhaps you just can't tell me because there wasn't anyone else," I said as I watched his face. "Perhaps no one asked you to procure pennyroyal for them. Perhaps you did it on your own, because you were the one who wanted the baby gone."

He didn't look particularly guilty, but I pushed forward anyway. "We both know that you spent some time in her room last night. If it wasn't to hand over the supply of dope she had requested you bring, perhaps it was so she could tell you that she was expecting?"

"Yes," Rivers said, clearly through gritted teeth.

"Was it your baby?"

"No." He turned a bit pale at that question.

"Can you prove it?"

"Of course not. But I have no reason to lie."

"You have every reason, if you killed her."

He shook his head. "Why would I kill her? As Astley said—Lord St George, I mean—she was a nice girl. I would have married her if the baby was mine and if she had wanted me to."

Well, of course he would have now that I thought about it. Cecily was, or had been, a Fletcher. The daughter of a younger son, and a mere Honorable, but a Fletcher. She would have been several steps up the societal ladder for someone like Dominic Rivers, who, as far as I knew, was a product of Southwark or some other equally depressed—or depressing—section of London.

"Perhaps she didn't want to marry you," I said, turning it over in my head and trying to get the pieces to fit in other ways. "Perhaps she didn't think you were suitable husband-material, and she turned you down."

I would have expected him to get angry over the slight to

his eligibility, but all he did was shake his head again. "If that were the case, I would have let her do whatever she wanted. I have no desire to get married, you know, even if I would have done the right thing had it been required of me. But I certainly wouldn't have taken the choice out of her hands by killing her."

That was a reasonable point, actually. "Fine," I said. "I never really thought you'd done it, anyway."

He shook his head. "I didn't. She was a client. I don't get romantically involved with clients."

He was smarter than Billy Chang in that, at least. Billy had bedded quite a few of the women who fetched and carried dope for him, or so I had heard. It hadn't helped him at all in his trial.

"At least you admit that she was a client," I said. "Would you like to tell me what she bought from you?"

But he shook his head. "I believe not, Miss Darling. My apologies."

He gave me a little bow. It might have been my own frustration that assigned mockery to it.

"All I'm trying to figure out," I said, "is whether or not she took something herself, not pennyroyal but something else, because she wanted to deal with the predicament she had found herself in, and it accidentally killed her, or whether someone else gave it to her deliberately, either to bring on a miscarriage or to get rid of Cecily altogether. That's all I want."

He didn't answer, and I added, "She's dead, Mr. Rivers. She can't be hurt by anything you tell me now. What's happened is already scandalous enough. Surely you can just tell me this one thing...?"

"I'm afraid not, Miss Darling. She might be beyond care, but other people are not."

"Yourself included," I said sourly. When he didn't answer—

because what could he say, other than that I was right?—I sighed. "Can you at least tell me who invited you here?"

He smirked. "Of course, Miss Darling. It was your cousin."

"My— Do you mean St George?"

"Who else?"

"I have quite a few cousins here this weekend," I told him. "And St George isn't one of them, as it happens, although it's an easy mistake to make. Did he ask you to bring him anything?"

"Of course not. Requiring gifts would be terribly uncouth. I'm sure he's above that."

"That wasn't what I meant," I said, "and you know it."

I waited a moment, but when he didn't seem willing to incriminate himself further—or at all—I added, "I suppose I'll just have to tell Constable Collins what you said and have him deal with it."

"I said that I didn't kill her, or provide her with drugs to cause an abortion, and that I wasn't the father of her child," Rivers said.

I nodded. "And I'll have to tell him that."

"Be my guest, Miss Darling." He sketched some sort of salute and glanced down the hallway in the direction of the back door. "They're outside on the lawn, you said?"

I nodded.

"In that case, I think I'll head up to my room. Enjoy the peace and quiet while Reggie's down here."

There was nothing I could do to stop him, nor did I feel the need, so I merely told him, "Enjoy your solitude," and watched as he climbed the staircase up to the first floor and turned down the hallway towards the back staircase up to the next level. Once he was out of sight, I turned on my own heel and headed down the hallway towards the boot room and the door to the backyard.

. . .

THE OTHERS WERE STILL on the lawn when I got out there, standing in a group in the middle of the grass, in roughly the spot where Francis, Christopher, and I had stood this morning when the bullet had whizzed by. I glanced at the wall on my way past, and saw that the bullet was now gone, and so was the chip of stone it had kicked loose.

The afternoon sun lit up Christopher's butter yellow hair, and Crispin's silver blond ditto, and brought out chestnut high-lights in Constable Collins's dark mop. They all three turned towards me when they heard the door shut.

"Darling," Crispin said after a moment, neutrally, at the same time as Christopher uttered a more welcoming, "Pippa."

"I just had a talk with Dominic Rivers," I said. "He said you're the one who invited him here this weekend."

Crispin glanced up at the top floor of the manor. I wondered whether he could see Rivers up there—my first instinct would have been to check the window, had I been Rivers and been told about the gathering on the lawn—but if he did, he didn't react in any way. After a moment, he turned his attention back to me. "Only in the sense that he rang up to congratulate me after the engagement notice ran in the *Times*, and I said something along the lines of 'the more, the merrier.'"

"So it wasn't a formal invitation?"

"Not from me. Laetitia may have followed up with some-thing written."

"You told her that you had invited him?"

"Of course I did." He sounded surprised that I'd ask. "It's more than my life is worth to get on the wrong side of my intended, Darling. You know that."

I made a face. "Of course."

Constable Collins had followed this exchange back and

forth impassively, but now he asked, "So Mr. Rivers did receive an invitation?"

"If he says he did, I'm sure he did," Crispin said. "I wouldn't have invited him if he hadn't phoned me—we're not close; more associates than friends—but perhaps Laetitia wanted to round out the numbers. Cecily was a friend. So are Violet, Olivia, and Serena. And of course there's Constance and Philippa who had to be invited."

"You could have told me to stay home," I said, stung.

He flicked me a glance. "I didn't mean it that way, Darling."

"How did you mean it, then?" Because he certainly made it sound as if my presence here, and Constance's as well, was a necessarily evil.

And in Constance's case, maybe that was true. She was Laetitia's cousin as well as Francis's fiancée; it would have been impossible to leave her out. Not that anyone would have wanted to. Constance is supremely unobjectionable. But for myself, I would have been happy to stay home had he indicated that I wasn't welcome.

"Don't be a prat, Crispin," Christopher said, and put an arm around my shoulders. "You know it wouldn't be the same without her."

Crispin looked at me down the length of his nose. It wasn't a fond look, and he managed to make it quite condescending in spite of being just a few inches taller than me. "I know my life would be a lot simpler if she didn't always stick her nose into it."

"For the last time," I said, "I am not taking responsibility for your bad decisions. Just because I told you that you deserved her, didn't mean that you had to propose. You could have sulked in silence for a day and gotten over it without doing something that has the potential to ruin the rest of your life."

He sniffed airily. "I don't know what you're talking about,

Darling."

"Of course you don't." I turned back to Constable Collins. "Rivers said he was invited. He didn't say by whom, nor whether it was a written invitation. But he's here as a guest and not merely to do business. At least according to himself."

Collins nodded. "Did he say anything else I ought to know?"

"He said that he had not given Cecily Fletcher pennyroyal tea. Nor pennyroyal on its own."

"So if she took pennyroyal," Collins said, "she got it from somewhere else."

"Or someone else. For all I know, it grows wild around here." I gazed around the admittedly pristine lawn. There wasn't a weed in sight.

"I wouldn't know what to look for," Crispin muttered, and I shook my head.

"Nor would I. Nor would Cecily, I expect. She's a city girl, isn't she?"

"Clan Fletcher is from the Scottish Highlands," Christopher said, and Crispin nodded.

"I think Ceci's family is from somewhere up north. Yorkshire or somewhere like that."

"Pennyroyal does grow around here," Constable Collins said. "Miss Constance and Miss Laetitia would both recognize it. So would Master Geoffrey, I assume."

And the Marsden parents and all of the Marsden servants, no doubt. Although anyone but that small group would have had a hard time distilling it into anything drinkable. It wasn't as if the guests could wander into and out of the kitchen at will.

Nor that the family would have a habit of doing so—this wasn't Beckwith Place, where Aunt Roz likes to spend time in the kitchen.

"What does it look like?" A walk in the pleasant afternoon

sun sounded good. And if I were walking, I might as well look around at the same time.

"A bit like thistle," Collins said, "but less prickly. Spiky with pale purplish flowers."

"We could take a stroll down the lane," Christopher suggested, "and see what we see."

I nodded. That was exactly what I wanted. The atmosphere inside wasn't conducive to my peace of mind. Not between Francis being angry at me over Wolfgang, and Laetitia giving me attitude over Crispin, and Crispin himself being upset with me over Laetitia... although he was out here with us, and might choose to come on the walk, too, so I might not necessarily get away from him by strolling down the lane.

"I'd come with you," he said, and I steeled myself, "but I suppose my fiancée is likely to be looking for me. I should go inside and do my duty vis-à-vis our guests."

I had, perversely, my mouth open to tell him that he didn't owe either the guests or Laetitia anything, but I shut it again when Christopher pinched me warningly. "That sounds like a good idea, old chap."

"We'll let you know if we come across anything that looks like it could be pennyroyal," I told Collins, who nodded.

"I'd better get started on my search of the guest rooms. If you wouldn't mind, Lord St George?"

He nodded towards the back door. Crispin glanced at Christopher, who gave him a reassuring nod—I have no idea what the reassurance was for, but they knew each other well enough to communicate wordlessly a lot of the time—and then they went off in one direction, into the back of the house, and we went off in the other, across the lawn and around the corner towards the lane.

CHAPTER TWELVE

"WHAT WAS THAT ABOUT?" I asked Christopher a few minutes later, after we had reached the lane and were ambling in the direction of the village, with Marsden Manor behind us and the Dower House, Constance's late mother's house, looming up ahead.

He shot me a glance. "What?"

"That look you gave each other. I thought you and I were adept at speaking telepathically, but so are you and St George."

"He's worried," Christopher said.

"Well, of course he is. If I had tied myself to Laetitia Marsden for the rest of my natural life, I'd be worried, too."

He snorted. "Not about that. About the murder."

"It might not have been a murder."

He glanced at me. "That isn't the impression you've been giving so far."

I shrugged, eyes on the ditch beside the road where I was trying to spot something that looked like a thistle but wasn't. "I have no idea what happened. But there are only so many scenarios that work. Murder is one of them."

"One," Christopher said, "she was pregnant and didn't want to be, so she took the pennyroyal herself to restart her flow, and it had unintended consequences."

I nodded. "Crispin told me that he didn't think she would do that, but he could be mistaken. She might have given him that impression deliberately, so he wouldn't do anything to stop her, or he might have simply misread her behavior. Or he could be lying, of course."

"He'd have no reason to lie unless he was involved," Christopher said, "and he can't have been. You said it yourself: if he hasn't been with her in six months..."

"He might have lied about the six months."

"That wouldn't change the fact that you already knew he'd had relations with her in the past. If he did it again, it's not as if it would change your opinion of him."

No, of course it wouldn't. I had known St George for the cad he was for a while now, and finding out that he had bedded Cecily Fletcher in the recent past as well as half a year ago, would have made no difference to my opinion of him whatsoever.

"That wouldn't be why he'd lie about it, though, Christopher. He doesn't care what I think of him. But if the baby was his..."

"It wasn't," Christopher said. "He would never kill the mother of his unborn child, nor do anything to harm the baby."

"He's engaged to Laetitia..." I began, and got a jaundiced look for my trouble.

"That's hardly his fault, is it?"

I sniffed. "It certainly is. Although I suppose I'll accept a small part of the blame, too."

Christopher nodded, satisfied, and moved on. "It would be different if he had proposed to Laetitia because he loves her. But he doesn't. Nor does he—or did he—love Cecily Fletcher.

But if that baby had been his, he would have done the right thing. And I don't think he would have cared one way or the other whether he ended up marrying Cecily or Laetitia. Laetitia Marsden isn't important enough to him that he'd commit murder over her. Certainly not the murder of his own heir."

"Fine," I said. "I didn't really think he'd done it, anyway."

Christopher snorted. "That's a first. You always think he's done it."

"Not this time. And I didn't think he'd bashed Abigail Dole over the head back in July, either. There are limits to what I think he's capable of." And killing pregnant women was certainly well over that line.

"Glad to hear it," Christopher said. "So option one is, she took the pennyroyal herself because she wanted to rid herself of the pregnancy, and she died as a result, by misfortune."

I nodded. "Option two is that someone else gave her the pennyroyal to force a miscarriage, and it backfired and killed her."

"That would be the father of the baby, then, I assume? Not Crispin, but someone else who didn't want to have to settle down and marry her?"

"Something of that nature," I agreed. "Or alternatively, someone else who wanted to prevent that from happening. I think that motive can probably be applied to several of the men present, as well as a few of the women."

"Most of them, I would think," Christopher nodded. "Although for many of us, it's also not a likely scenario. For instance, I wouldn't have wanted to marry her. But I also haven't put myself in a situation where I'd have to."

"No, of course not. I didn't include you on the suspect list. Nor did I include Francis or Constance. I don't think Francis knew of Cecily's existence until yesterday, and if he did, it was likely only from word of mouth because Crispin had dallied with her."

Christopher nodded. "We decided it wasn't Crispin."

We had. "I don't see how it can be Wolfgang," I said.

"We don't know enough about Wolfgang and who he might or might not know to say for certain," Christopher said fairly, "but I agree that it seems unlikely."

"That leaves Rivers and the Honorable Reggie, then, along with Bilge Fortescue and the Earl of Marsden—"

"Bah!" Christopher said.

"The Earl of Marsden, do you mean?" I sniggered. "I agree with you. I doubt he would lower himself to dally with one of his daughter's friends. I doubt Cecily would have wanted anything to do with him if he tried. And there's no way Lady Euphemia would have let him live if it had happened and she found out."

Laetitia and Geoffrey's mother was a scary woman. Lord Maurice, meanwhile, was a friendly and likeable dumpling of a man who certainly didn't have 'great seducer' written anywhere in his makeup.

"You asked Dominic Rivers," Christopher asked, "I suppose? It seems like something you would do. Ask a bloke you barely know straight out whether he'd begat an illegitimate child on a woman."

I nodded. "Of course I did. What's the point in being well-mannered about it?"

He didn't answer, and I added, "Besides, the fact that I barely know him, and really don't care what he thinks of me, makes it easier rather than harder to ask him invasive questions."

Christopher rolled his eyes. "What did he say?

"He said he would have married her if it had been his child, but it wasn't. And I believe him; marrying Cecily would have been marrying up, wouldn't it?"

"It would," Christopher agreed. "Probably not him, then. Unless you think he had a reason to lie?"

"I never underestimate the reasons people may have for lying. But I don't see how that particular lie would have helped."

"Unless it was his child and he didn't want to marry her, so he killed her," Christopher said.

"Yes, of course. I don't suppose we can write him off entirely. He did spend part of the evening with her. And he did have access to the dope."

"But you don't think it was him."

"I didn't get that impression," I said, "no."

"The Honorable Reggie, then?"

"I don't know anything about Reginald Fish. I'm not sure I've even heard his name before."

That might indicate that he was one of the more well-behaved members of the Bright Young Set, and not inclined to get up to trouble or to talk himself into Cecily Fletcher's bed. Then again, looks can be deceiving.

"He seemed like a nice enough chap for the few minutes that I saw him yesterday," I added, "but I hadn't the chance to spend much time with him."

"At least Lady Violet kept Geoffrey busy, so you didn't have to deal with him."

Yes, indeed. "Now, he's someone who—"

"Later," Christopher said, pointing to a stand of stalks up ahead. "Over there. Is that—?"

I squinted. It wasn't thistle, but it didn't look too dissimilar, either.

"It might be."

We made our way over, and then I waited on the road

while Christopher lowered himself into the ditch and waded over to it. "Ugh. I'm getting wet."

"Never mind that," I told him. "You'll be shifting into dancing shoes later."

He flicked me a look. "I doubt there'll be much dancing when the older generation gets here, Pippa. It'll be a stuffy sit-down dinner under the beady eye of Uncle Harold and my parents, and Crispin's future inlaws, and whatever eagle-eyed old ladies arrive from the Marsden side of the family. Laetitia has a grandmother, doesn't she?"

She might have. I had a vague memory of it being mentioned at some point or another. Not by Laetitia, but by Constance, who shared her.

"I'm certain there'll be dancing afterwards," I said. "Or if not, at least there will be card games or some other form of entertainment. Unless it's deemed too callous under the circumstances, I suppose."

"I thought about ringing up Beckwith Place," Christopher said, "and telling Mum and Dad to stay home. But nobody said anything about canceling the celebration."

He reached a hand towards a purple-flowered stalk and I snapped out, "Don't touch!"

"I thought I'd bring it back for Constable Collins to have a look at."

I scowled at him. "Not without gloves, Christopher! If the plant is toxic, I don't want you to touch it with your bare hands."

"I'll be careful," Christopher said, and before I could stop him, he had ripped off a stalk with four or five pale purple flowers and oval leaves. "There."

"I wish you wouldn't have done that," I grumbled, as I watched him scramble back onto the pavement. "We could have simply told Collins that they were here, and let him do his own gathering."

"I'll wash my hands when we get back to the house." He shoved the stalk towards me and I leaned back, out of its way.

"I'm not touching that."

He shook his head. "I don't expect you to. I'm going to keep it in this hand until we get back inside, and then I'll hand it off to Collins and visit the lav. That way, I won't be touching you, and I won't accidentally stick my thumb in my mouth..."

I rolled my eyes. "As if you still suck your thumb, you nitwit."

"I don't. But I do sometimes touch my face with my hands when I'm not thinking. I can't imagine it would do me any good to get it in my eye, either."

I shuddered. "No, I imagine not."

"Look at it, though. Do you believe it's pennyroyal?"

"It looks like what Constable Collins described," I said, leaning in a bit and drawing in a deep breath. "And I think it definitely smells like mint."

Christopher lifted the stalk to his own face and inhaled. "Spearmint, not peppermint."

"Precisely."

"I think we may have found it, then. And no more than a few minutes' walk from the manor."

I nodded, as we turned around and headed back towards the big, gray structure in the distance. "There are a couple of issues with this scenario, you know."

He glanced acrss at me. "And what are those?"

"Well, if someone picked the pennyroyal out of the ditch here... by the way, do you have any idea which part of the plant one uses for tea? Is it the flowers, or the leaves, or the stalk? Or all of it?"

"I have no clue," Christopher said and waved his free hand. "But carry on."

"Well, whoever picked it would have needed to turn it into tea somehow. Or turn it into something that could have been mixed with the tea. I wonder if simply steeping the leaves or petals in water would be enough to do it? Would the water have to be hot, do you suppose, or would cold water from the tap be enough?"

And for that matter, would pennyroyal tea be enough to kill someone? Or would it have to be something more concentrated than that?

"A question for Collins," Christopher said. "But what you're saying is that if someone picked the plant here, they would have had to have the supplies and the know-how to turn it into poison."

"Or something that works like poison, yes."

Christopher nodded. "I could see that being an issue for someone. Especially if it came down to actually brewing the tea themselves. The guests can't just wander into the kitchen and start using the AGA."

No, definitely not. "But on the other hand," I said, "if someone brought the pennyroyal liquid here already ready for use, that person must have known about the situation before coming here. It's not likely that someone would be traveling with an abortifacient just in case they came across a pregnant woman, you know."

"No," Christopher admitted, "I suppose it's not. She didn't even look pregnant, did she?"

"Not to me. I don't think she was more than a few months along. Not enough for it to be visible."

"Who knew about Cecily's condition before they arrived?"

"That's the problem," I said. "Not many people, it seems. We didn't. Crispin didn't seem to. She told him about it in her room last night, and he appeared shocked enough that I'm willing to stake money on the fact that he hadn't known beforehand."

Christopher nodded. "He's a passable liar when he's prepared. When he's faced with things without warning, he gets flustered easily."

I waved it away. "We've already decided it wasn't St George, whatever he knew or didn't know before yesterday. Lady Violet and Olivia both said that Cecily hadn't confided in them, and Violet claimed to be Cecily's best friend."

"Had she not told them who she had been spending her time with?"

"They said she hadn't. I don't know whether they were telling the truth or not."

"Hopefully whoever the murderer is believes them," Christopher said, as we turned into the driveway of Marsden Manor and made our way up towards the house. "Because if he doesn't, and if he truly killed Cecily rather than acknowledge her and the baby, he might decide to take out anyone else who knows who he is, as well."

I made a face. "I hadn't thought about that. I guess perhaps I did a good thing, bringing it out in the open like that at the luncheon table. At least he won't think, assuming he was there, that people know things that they don't."

"Why wouldn't he be there?" Christopher wanted to know. "The only person on the guest list who wasn't at the luncheon table was me, and surely you're not suggesting that I'm it?"

"Of course not." Geoffrey had been there, and Reggie, and Dominic Rivers, and of course Francis and Crispin and Bilge Fortescue, as well. Everyone except Christopher had heard Violet and Olivia claim not to know who the father of Cecily's baby was. Hopefully that would be enough to keep them both safe.

"At any rate," I said, "if the pennyroyal was brought here yesterday because Cecily was expecting, then someone knew about her condition before this weekend. It's still possible that it was Cecily herself who arranged it with Dominic Rivers, and that Rivers simply lied to me. But it could also be that the young man was someone she sees regularly, whom she had already told. Someone who also came down from London for the party. If he's part of the Bright Young Set, she would have seen him again before now, I assume. They get up to their shenanigans most weekends in Town, don't they?"

"One supposes," Christopher nodded, as he headed for the front door into the manor. "There's no point in going back to the croquet lawn, I imagine. Constable Collins won't be there anymore."

I shook my head. "He said he was going to start searching the rooms. He'll be somewhere on the first or second floor."

"On the other hand," Christopher said, picking up the conversation again, "there are surely a few members of the Bright Young Set that she would not see on a regular basis. Crispin has been staying in Wiltshire lately. The last few times he's been up to London, it was to see us."

I made a face. "To see Wolfgang, you mean."

"To assess Wolfgang," Christopher corrected, "yes. I think the last time he did any kind of heavy partying was for his birthday, and that was the first week in June."

"It was also with us," I pointed out, "although he was already sozzled by the time he arrived at the flat, so he must have spent time with someone else first. But that's three months ago, Christopher. If he bedded Cecily in June, and she conceived, surely she could have found a way to let him know about it sooner than this weekend? Sutherland Hall is on the exchange, and it's not as if the postman doesn't deliver. And she knows where Sutherland House is; she could always have gone to Mayfair and asked Rogers to pass on a missive."

"I suppose that's true," Christopher said, and pushed the front door open, only to come face to face with Perkins the butler. "Oh. Hullo, Perkins. You wouldn't happen to know where I could find Constable Collins, would you?"

Perkins looked from the weed in Christopher's hand, up to Christopher's face, and back to the weed in Christopher's hand again before he intoned, "The constable is on the upper floors, Mr. Astley."

"Thank you, Perkins," Christopher said. His cheekbones were pink, and I had to bite my lip to keep from laughing. "Would you happen to know what kind of flower this is, Perkins?"

"It's pudding grass, Mr. Astley," Perkins said.

"Is it really?" Christopher gave it a dubious look, and then shot me one out of the corner of his eye. My lips twitched. Christopher turned back to Perkins. "Thank you."

"Of course, sir."

Perkins took a step back. We proceeded across the marble floor and up the stairs. I managed to keep a straight face until we were out of sight down the first floor corridor before I burst into laughter. "Good grief, Christopher, did you see his face? He thinks you're bringing flowers for Constable Collins because you're sweet on him."

"Yes," Christopher grumbled, "thank you for pointing that out, Pippa." The tips of his ears were hot. "You don't think Collins will think that, do you?"

"Of course not," I reassured him. "And he'll also be able to tell us whether this is pennyroyal or whatever pudding grass is, if they're different. We just have to find him."

I looked around.

The first floor was quiet. All the bedroom doors were shut,

and there were no sounds of voices anywhere except behind the Fortescues' closed door. As a married couple whom no one could fault for wanting their private time, I suppose they had opted for a lie-down after luncheon and all the excitement of this morning.

"He must have started the search upstairs," I said. "There's simply no way he could have managed to go through all of these rooms already if he hadn't."

Christopher nodded. "And why not? Cecily's room is up there, and so are the most likely suspects."

I arched a brow at that, and he added, "Or at least most of them are. I suppose Geoffrey is down on this level, and so are Crispin, Francis, and I. Just because we know that none of the Astleys are involved, doesn't mean that Constable Collins believes that to be true."

Indubitably. Although I had done my best to convince him of it.

"He probably started in Cecily's room, in case there's something among her possessions that would shed some light on this situation. Perhaps even... a diary." He sounded optimistic when he added, "It's what I would have done."

"She was in no condition to update her diary last night," I said. "If it's there, it won't tell us who brought her a cup of tea to settle her stomach."

"Of course not," Christopher agreed. "But she might have mentioned which gentleman—I use the word advisedly—she has been spending her time with lately."

Yes, of course she might have done. She hadn't confided in anyone else, it seemed, but she might have told her diary. Even an initial would be helpful, since we had, here at Marsden, a rather finite suspect pool. And all of them with different initials, at least apart from the youngest Astley boys and Constance.

"We'll try there first," I said. "And if he's not in Cecily's room, I suppose we can yell for him."

"I'm sure we'll find him," Christopher said, and exited into the second floor hallway. It looked much the same as the first floor ditto, if a bit narrower and a bit less opulent. All the doors were shut except for the one into Cecily's room, from which we could hear rustling and the occasional mutter.

I expected there to be someone else inside, but no, when we reached the doorway, Constable Collins was on his own inside the room, and the muttering must be him talking to himself. By that time he had heard us approach, and had turned towards the open door.

"Oh," he said when he saw us, and his posture lost some of its stiffness, "it's you two."

"It's us. Christopher has something for you." I moved aside so Christopher could step into the room and present Collins with his weed.

There was a beat of silence.

"Really," Collins's voice said dryly, "you shouldn't have."

I bit back a snigger as Christopher's shoulders dropped. "It's the wrong kind, isn't it? Perkins called it a pudding plant."

"No," Collins said, eyeing it, "it's exactly the right kind. Where did you find it?"

"Just a quarter mile or so away from the manor," I told him, as I leaned my shoulder in the doorway. "In the ditch between here and the Dower House. Well within walking distance for anyone interested in picking some."

"What we don't know," Christopher added, "is what someone would do with it after they got it. It's possible to brew it into tea, of course, and it seems someone did that…"

He glanced at me, and I nodded, "but we're not sure who would have had that opportunity apart from the kitchen staff.

It's not likely that the staff would have allowed any of the guests to walk into the kitchen to use the cooker."

Collins nodded and put the stalk down carefully on top of the tallboy. "Cook or the kitchen maid would definitely be able to say whether anyone did that. But it's not likely that they'd allow it. It's more likely that they'd have taken the leaves off someone's hands and brewed the tea themselves."

"And if that's how it happened," I said, "they would know who it was."

Collins nodded. "I'll ask once I'm done up here."

"I assume," Christopher asked, "that the leaves would have to be boiled? Just steeping them in water from the tap wouldn't have the same effect?"

Collins and I looked at one another. "I honestly don't know," I said, when the constable had no answer. "Although I doubt she would have drunk it if it were cold." Unless she did it herself, of course, and then she might have forced it down for the effects she wanted.

"It looked like tea," I added. "Brown color, served in a cup with a saucer and a spoon. I imagine it was heated up before it was given to her. But if you're asking whether a pennyroyal draught can be made by soaking the leaves in cold water, I wouldn't be surprised if it could. I can't imagine it would taste very good, though."

"Nor would it be enough to kill anyone," Collins added. "People drink pennyroyal tea all the time. It's a common remedy for—" he flushed, "—female things."

"So it's only a problem when someone takes too much," Christopher said.

Collins nodded. "A few leaves in a pot of water isn't going to kill anyone. This was more than that."

So figuring out who had used the kitchen to brew the tea might not help at all.

"Is it possible," I said, and hesitated.

They both looked at me. "Yes?" Collins asked.

"Is it possible that there are two different people involved in this? Someone who gave Cecily the tea, and someone else who tried to kill her?" Perhaps Cecily gave herself the tea, and then someone else came along and gave her more? "Maybe this second person didn't even want to kill her, but the second dose on top of the first turned out to be too much?"

There was a pause while we all contemplated what that scenario would look like.

"I can't say that it wouldn't be possible," Collins said. "If she, say, picked the leaves herself, and asked Cook to brew the tea, and then she drank it to... um... restore her flows..."

He trailed off, flushing again.

"And then someone else came along—" I prompted.

He nodded gratefully. "And then someone else came along and gave her more of it. Or perhaps it's more likely that that happened the other way: she picked the pennyroyal leaves and gave them to Cook to turn into tea before bed. She went to dinner and then to drinks and dancing. Someone fed her a cocktail with pennyroyal in it."

That was certainly possible. I had seen for myself, at the Dower House in May, just how easy it is to poison someone with a doctored cocktail. And mint is a fairly common garnish; Cecily might not have noticed the taste at all.

"Then, after she retired to her room," I continued the story, "she called for the tea, and someone brought it up, and by the time I had finished speaking to St George and was doing my ablutions in the lavatory, she was vomiting."

"That works for me," Christopher said.

I nodded. It worked for me, too. Even though we now had to look for two different people who wished Cecily harm, unless Cecily herself had been one of them.

Constable Collins looked around the room with a sigh. "I expect I should go speak to Cook and the other servants. I can always come back to the searching later. It would be good to have this tea issue clarified one way or the other."

It would. And I would have offered to go and ask myself, but this was an official inquiry while I wasn't an official participant, so I had to let the constable do his job without my help.

But at least I could make suggestions. "You should talk to Dominic Rivers, too. He told me he didn't give Cecily any pennyroyal, and if she picked her own, then he told the truth. But he may have given some to someone else."

"I tried," Collins said. "I knocked on his door when I came upstairs after finishing my conversation with the two of you and Lord St George. There was no answer."

"Just because he told me he'd go upstairs for some peace and quiet, doesn't mean he did."

He might have lied about his intentions, or he may have been waylaid by someone on his way to his room.

I turned and glanced at the door to the room he shared with the Honorable Reggie. It was closed.

"He wasn't downstairs," Constable Collins said. "At least not anywhere where I saw him. He wasn't with the others in the dining room—"

I shook my head. "No, he escorted me out of there earlier. The last time I saw him, he was on his way up the stairs."

Collins nodded. "Perhaps he changed his mind and decided to take a walk, like you did."

Or perhaps he'd gone upstairs, tossed all his belongings into his bag, and high-tailed it down to the garage, before anyone more official than me could start asking him questions.

"You didn't notice a motorcar leaving the manor," I asked Christopher, "did you?"

He shook his head. "One didn't pass us, certainly. Do you think he did a bunk?"

"He seemed fairly spooked when I spoke to him about Cecily. There's a prison sentence for providing someone with an abortifacient, did you know that?"

"The question has never come up," Christopher said dryly. "I'll just try his door, shall I? If all his possessions are gone, then we'll know he's scarpered, and perhaps the London police can intercept him when he gets home."

He didn't wait for Collins to give him the go-ahead, just left the doorway of Cecily's room and started across the landing.

"That's Wolfgang's room," I told him, when he approached the door on the other side of the lavatory from mine. "Theirs is the next one."

Christopher nodded and applied his knuckles to the wood. "Rivers, old boy? Are you in there?"

There was no response, and he knocked again. When he reached for the doorknob, I told him, "Wait!"

He glanced at me. "Are you still worried about the sap from the pennyroyal?"

"Not this time. Although it wouldn't hurt for you to go into the lavatory and rinse it off. But mostly I don't want you to touch the doorknob."

Understanding crossed his countenance, and he took a step back. "I'll just do that, shall I? It's all yours, Constable Collins."

He exchanged glances with Collins, who had come into the doorway to see what was going on, and headed for the lavatory door. A few seconds later, I heard the water turn on and then splashing as Christopher washed his hands.

Collins, meanwhile, gave me a look before he moved past me with an murmured apology and approached the door to the young men's room.

A third knock on the door had no more effect than the first

two times Christopher had knocked—or for that matter the time when Collins himself had done it. The constable put his ear to the door. "Mr. Rivers? This is Constable Collins. If you're in there, can you call out?"

I didn't hear a response, and Collins mustn't have, either, because after a moment he took a step back and eyed the door. By now, Christopher had come out of the lavatory, too, shaking the last of the water off his now clean hands, and stopped beside me. "Nothing?"

"Doesn't seem so," I said grimly. Collins pulled a handkerchief out of the pocket of his uniform jacket and draped it over his hand.

"Mr. Rivers?" he called one last time. "I'm coming in."

He waited a second or two, and then reached out and grabbed the knob.

At this point, there were only two options, and we had all, surely, calculated them in our heads. One: Rivers had done a bunk, in which case the door would be unlocked and the room empty. Or two: he hadn't, he was still inside, alone or with someone else, and the door would most likely be locked.

The knob turned and the door opened. I braced myself for the outraged squealing of one of the female guests, but none came.

"He's likely gone, then," Christopher muttered beside me as Constable Collins pushed the door open and stepped into the doorway.

And stopped.

"What?" I asked, heart in my throat. Christopher's hand fumbled for mine, and I grasped it and gave it a reassuring squeeze.

Collins shook his head. "Don't come any closer."

I didn't listen, of course. Pulling Christopher behind me, I took the couple of steps up to the door and peered into the room over Collins's shoulder.

CHAPTER THIRTEEN

"GAH!"

Constable Collins flicked me a look over his shoulder. "I did tell you not to look."

Yes, of course he had done. But I had been too curious to listen, and now I was paying for it.

"Is he dead?" I asked, and while I did a passable job of keeping my voice steady, I could hear the emotion threading through it. Shock, mostly, with a bit of horror.

Collins nodded. "I imagine he would have to be. I can't think that anyone would have survived a blow to the head like that one."

No, I couldn't either. I turned on my heel and buried my face in Christopher's shoulder. He peered into the room over my head and made a gagging noise.

We had both seen broken skulls before. There had been Freddie Montrose in London in June and then Abigail Dole at Beckwith Place in July. (And when I put it like that, I realize that I make it sound like we deal with an awful lot of dead bodies. I suppose we do, or at least we have done in the past few months. I'm not sure how that happened, exactly.)

At any rate, Dominic Rivers's skull was clearly broken. There was an indentation on the back of his head, and quite a lot of blood, and then there were the shards of what had been a lovely art deco vase with an image of birds and flowers, that were scattered across his back and the carpet surrounding him.

I swallowed hard. "The vase came from the alcove over there." I waved vaguely in the direction of the staircase, but without lifting my head from Christopher's shoulder. "I noticed it yesterday." It had been full of peacock feathers, of all ostentatious things.

"Someone from downstairs, then." Christopher eyed the alcove from where we were standing. It was between Rivers's room—and my room, and Wolfgang's room, and for that matter Cecily's room—and the staircase.

I nodded. "It would have to be. When he—" my eyes flickered to the corpse on the floor and away again, "came upstairs, everyone else was in the dining room. Except for you two and St George, you were outside. There's only one staircase up to this level. Anyone who came this way, would have walked past the alcove and the vase."

"Weapon of opportunity?" Christopher suggested.

"Most likely. There are better things to hand—I have a lovely chamber pot and slop jar in my room, in heavy earthenware; there's even a handle to make swinging it easier—but someone would have to know that it was there in order to use it."

"Safer to use something from the common rooms," Christopher said. "That way it doesn't point the finger at anyone in particular."

I nodded. "Looks less premeditated, too. Here, they just grabbed the vase on their way past. If they had made a stop in one of the rooms to fetch the weapon, or brought it from downstairs, it would have been planned."

"It's still planned if the vase only came from here," Collins said without looking up. He was squatting next to the body with a hand on Rivers's wrist. "If it had been directly beside the door, maybe not. But someone picked it up and carried it to the door with them. That's premeditation. If only a few seconds' worth."

Yes, of course it was. "He's dead, I assume?"

"As a doornail," Collins said, and pushed to his feet, "I'm afraid."

"He turned his back to the door."

The dead man's feet were just inside the room, and he had fallen forward, towards the window.

Collins nodded. "Someone must have knocked, and he opened the door to them. Whoever it was, didn't seem to be a threat, so he turned away."

"He must have missed the vase," Christopher said. I don't think it was sarcasm, although sometimes he surprises me.

"It's a rather large thing to miss," I said, "isn't it? I think I would have noticed if someone showed up outside my door holding a vase. Or at least I would have done if they were holding an empty one; if there were flowers in it, that might be a different matter."

"No flowers in this one," Collins said. "No water, either."

I shook my head. "No, it was full of peacock feathers this morning. I noticed it when we came up to see whether Cecily wanted to play croquet."

There was a moment of silence.

"That's two murders in one day," Collins put word to it, finally. "Or at least this makes it less likely that Miss Fletcher's death was anything but a murder."

I nodded. "He must have known something he didn't know he knew. Or perhaps he knew it and just refused to tell me."

"He said that he hadn't provided Miss Fletcher with pennyroyal," Collins said as he got to his feet and brushed his hands off. There was nothing on them, nothing I could see, but I imagined that the feeling of Dominic Rivers's cold skin must be present.

"He did," I agreed. "He also said that he wouldn't tell me what he might have brought here for anyone else. Client confidentiality, he called it."

But it was pretty obvious after this that Cecily hadn't been the recipient of whatever substance Dom Rivers had brought to Dorset. She hadn't been in any condition to kill him. Someone else must have done that.

"A pity," Collins said succinctly. After a moment, he sighed. "I hadn't even started to interview the guests properly. Not aside from you two and Lord St George. Now I suppose I'll have to talk to them about this, as well."

"You know we're off the hook," I told him. "We were down the road picking pennyroyal. You saw us walk away."

He nodded. "The gathering in the dining room was breaking up when I came back into the house with Lord St George. He excused himself to find his fiancée, and I came upstairs to start searching the bedrooms. I decided to start with Miss Fletcher's chamber."

"So you were right across the hall when Mr. Rivers was killed," I said.

I don't know what I was thinking. The words simply fell out of my mouth. Christopher made a horrified little noise, although Constable Collins shook his head.

"I'm afraid not. It would have been easier had I been. But the door to Miss Fletcher's room stayed open while I was in there. I would have heard anyone coming up and knocking on

Mr. Rivers's door. I would certainly have heard the impact of someone breaking a vase over his head."

"Someone must have done it while we were still outside on the lawn, then," Christopher said. "After Pippa had her conversation with Rivers in the foyer, but before you and Crispin came back inside."

Collins nodded. "It'll be a case of interviewing everyone present, and then afterwards comparing the statements to see whether we can determine where everyone was during that time. A whole lot of conversations and a whole lot of information."

He sighed.

"It sounds boring," I said sympathetically. "Is there anything we can do to help?"

He shook his head. "I'm afraid not, Miss Darling. Except..." He glanced from me to Christopher and back, "perhaps the two of you wouldn't mind standing here in front of Mr. Rivers's door until I come back? I'll have to ring up the village again. I'm going to need help with this. I suppose I'll have to interrupt the post mortem, too, to let doctor know we have another victim."

"Of course we'll stay here until you come back. Not to worry."

Christopher nodded. Collins nodded back, and took himself off down the hallway towards the staircase. I could see him glance into the alcove on his way past. I hadn't noticed on our own way up—too focused on Cecily's open door—but I supposed the peacock feathers were now lying across the plinth where the vase had stood.

"How tall would you say someone would have to be," I asked Christopher as Constable Collins disappeared through the baize door and down the stairs, "to get enough power behind this vase to kill someone with it?"

He looked from me to the remnants of the vase, still scattered in shards across the floor and Rivers's back, and made a face. "I'm going to shut the door again."

"I don't mind if you do," I told him, since I would prefer not to see the corpse out of the corner of my eye for the entire time we were standing here, too. "Just be certain not to destroy any of Collins's fingerprints. The fingerprints on the doorknob that Constable Collins will want, I mean. Not his own. They oughtn't to be there."

"I know what you meant, Pippa." He took his own handkerchief out, draped it over the knob, and pulled the door shut by tugging on the ends of the cloth. "And if the killer was holding the vase—in both hands, one has to assume—and knocked on the door, and Rivers opened it, there wouldn't be the murderer's fingerprints on the doorknob anyway. There'd only be Rivers's, on the inside."

He pulled the knob until the door slotted neatly into the frame.

"Oh, well done," I told him. "You didn't even have to touch it."

"I have my uses." He shook the handkerchief out after the door latch had clicked, and stuffed it back into his pocket. "Now, to answer your question. Rivers was about my height, wouldn't you say? Not overly tall, but not short, either?"

"Shorter than Francis or Wolfgang," I said, "and for that matter shorter than Geoffrey and the Honorable Reggie."

Christopher nodded. "Shorter than Bilge Fortescue, too. Taller than all of the girls."

"Not much shorter than Laetitia, or for that matter Lady Serena. Or the countess, I suppose. Not that I think Lady Euphemia was the one who whacked him."

"Not even if he killed another guest in her home?" He didn't wait for me to answer, since the question was fairly ridiculous to begin with. If Lady Euphemia Marsden was going to kill someone, I thought it was more likely to be either myself or Wolfgang. Constance's Aunt Effie had made her disdain of Germans known in July at Beckwith Place. I was honestly surprised that she had allowed her daughter to invite us both.

"If we're counting the Marsdens," Christopher added, "Lord Maurice is too short."

I nodded. "So is Constance. I could have done it, most likely, depending on how heavy the vase was, although I was with you when it happened."

He didn't respond, and I added. "Lady Serena is also tall-ish. And she's suffered a miscarriage lately. Did I tell you? It came up over luncheon, while you were outside with Constable Collins."

"That's interesting," Christopher said, "isn't it?"

"Is it?"

"It doesn't have anything to do with Cecily. But if she blames Dominic Rivers for it? If she took something—something she got from him—and it had an adverse effect? Do you suppose she might blame him enough to kill him?"

That was certainly a possibility, and one I hadn't considered. "She'd be tall enough," I said, "although perhaps not strong enough."

"She rode out yesterday. She wouldn't have done that if she weren't recovered."

Likely not. "Her husband would definitely be both tall enough and strong enough. And they were in their room when we walked past, so at least halfway here."

Christopher nodded. "They definitely stay on the list, then. Who else is there?"

"Violet is about my height," I said. "Olivia Barnsley is a bit shorter, if not quite as short as Constance. I don't know whether she'd have been able to raise the vase high enough and bring it down with enough force to kill a man with it."

"I'm quite certain Constance didn't do," Christopher said. "Not only does she not have it in her, but I'm sure she was with Francis."

"And that gives him an alibi, too, hopefully. Not that he had a motive, either, but an alibi is an alibi." And always a better thing to have than no motive. Means and opportunity trumps motive each time.

"Not to mention," Christopher said, with the cynicism of someone who knows how it works, "that it is always possible to come up with a motive if you're looking for one. Francis is—or was—a dope addict, and Rivers is—or was—a dope dealer. That's motive enough."

"For some people. But I'm sure you're right, and Constance and Francis were together. Just as you and I were together, and Crispin and Laetitia were together."

"Bilge Fortescue was probably with his wife. I haven't seen them apart yet."

I hadn't either, although— "That doesn't mean that one of them couldn't have run up here and killed Rivers while the other stayed in their room downstairs, to make it sound as if they were both there."

"They'd be in it together, then?"

"They're married," I said. "It was both of their baby that they lost."

"Or so you assume."

Well, yes. I had done. "I can make a case for Serena giving Bilge an alibi while he kills Rivers, or vice versa. I can't make a case for one of them doing it with the other unaware. Not if they were both in their room when we came in thirty minutes later. There's a finite window of opportunity when this could have happened. After Rivers went upstairs, while I was out on the lawn with the three of you, and before Collins went upstairs."

"Not a long period of time at all," Christopher said.

I shook my head. "And neither of us knows who was left in the dining room at that point. All we can do is speculate."

"Collins will figure it out," Christopher said and put an arm around me. I leaned my head against his shoulder. "A good thing we have an alibi."

He nodded, chin rubbing against my hair. "A good thing Francis and Constance and Crispin do, too."

I waited a moment, but when he didn't say anything else, I said, "I notice you don't mention Laetitia."

"I don't care about Laetitia," Christopher said. "I might go so far as to say that it wouldn't bother me if she had killed them both. She would go to prison and Crispin could break the engagement with impunity."

That was a good point, and I told him so. "If we get lucky, perhaps she won't have an alibi. She was in the dining room when I left, but that doesn't mean she stayed there."

She might have excused herself a minute or two after I had asked Dominic Rivers to accompany me into the hallway. She might have heard Rivers and me talk, and then part company in the foyer, and she might have followed him upstairs. As for why

...

"If Cecily informed Laetitia that she was pregnant," I said, "or better yet, if someone else informed her, so that it looked like Cecily was keeping it from her—"

Christopher nodded. "She might well have concluded that it was Crispin's baby, and that Cecily was here to throw a spanner into the engagement works. And if she did do..."

"She might have decided that Cecily needed to lose the baby."

He flicked me a look. "You don't think she would have tried to kill her?"

"I don't see why she would have done," I said, thinking it

through, "when the miscarriage might be written off as an acci-dent, and would accomplish the goal more safely than murder. If Cecily remained pregnant, Crispin might be forced to marry her, but if there was no baby, there would be no need for anything to change. Cecily didn't have to die for that to happen."

Christopher nodded. "And as you say, why do something drastic when something less drastic is just as likely to work?"

"Precisely. After all, if she got caught and went to prison, she would lose him that way, too."

Christopher shook his head with a sigh. "I don't understand it, Pippa. We look enough alike to be twins, or so you've told me more than once."

"Crispin and you, do you mean?" I nodded. "I don't think you'd find anyone who would disagree with that. When you first started at Eton, you told me that people got you mixed up all the time."

Two young boys with the same surname and complimen-tary given names; was it any wonder that everyone thought they were brothers instead of cousins?

"I suppose as far as personality goes, we're a bit different," Christopher ventured.

"You're much nicer than St George," I agreed. "He's a spoiled brat. You're mostly all right. Although you have your moments, too."

"I'm not denying it. I just wonder why it is that women fall all over themselves to get Crispin's attention, but nobody seems to want me."

I slanted him a look. "I don't think it is that no one wants you, Christopher. I can remember quite a few times when I have had to take you away from some young lady or other hell-bent on wooing an Astley. I'm sure both Lady Violet and Olivia Barnsley would be happy to have you."

He made a face, and I added, "Yes, see? It's not as if you want them, is it?"

He sighed. "I suppose not. Although if there was any fairness in the world, shouldn't I have the same effect on men that Crispin has on women?"

"You seemed popular enough when we went to Rectors in June," I said.

Christopher arched his brows. "What do you mean, when *we* went to Rectors? *I* was at Rectors for a ball. You and Crispin crashed. There was no *we*."

I brushed the consideration aside. "You know what I mean. There were plenty of men there vying to dance with you."

"That's Kitty," Christopher said.

"You *are* Kitty, Christopher." Kitty Dupree, Christopher's alter ego when he goes to drag balls, is a raven-haired beauty not unlike Laetitia Marsden in appearance, whose wig, makeup, and wardrobe lives in my bedroom in London. In the event we have visitors, it wouldn't do to have anyone find any of those items in Christopher's room.

"That's different," Christopher said.

It didn't seem different to me, but I shrugged. "This seems a silly conversation to have with a murderer breathing down our necks. To get back to what we were talking about before this discussion about Crispin's appeal derailed us—"

He smirked. "Crispin's appeal, was it?"

I rolled my eyes. "You know what I mean. I'm not saying that *I* find him appealing; you're the one who said that everyone else does."

"And yet you'll admit that you think *I* am attractive," Christopher said.

"Of course you're attractive, Christopher. You both are. But never mind that now. We were talking about Laetitia, and whether or not she might have induced Cecily's miscarriage."

"She'd certainly know where to find the pennyroyal," Christopher said, "considering that it grows just a few minutes from her front door. And this is her house, so of everyone here, she would have had the easiest time getting the leaves brewed into tea."

"It would have been easy," I agreed. "Tell them that Cecily had asked for her help, and then, when Cecily died, they'd all keep mum because they thought it was an accident and they wouldn't want the daughter of the house to be implicated."

"That would be clever," Christopher agreed. "Is she clever enough for that?"

"She was clever enough to get her hands on the Sutherland engagement ring." Or clever enough to get the Sutherland engagement ring on her finger, rather.

"There was nothing clever about that, Pippa. It was your fault. Yours and Crispin's."

I shrugged, even as I stuck my bottom lip out. "It's an ugly ring. She can keep it."

"You don't mean that," Christopher said.

"Of course I do. It *is* ugly."

"If she keeps the ring, she keeps Crispin. Unless you think she ought to do that, too?"

"Unless she killed Cecily," I said, "she keeps him anyway."

"We'd best get busy trying to prove she killed Cecily, then."

I sighed. "When Constable Collins comes back upstairs and relieves us of duty, I suppose it couldn't hurt for us to go and talk to some people."

"Nellie, for instance?"

"We might as well start with Nellie," I agreed. If Laetitia had used the Marsden Manor kitchen to brew pennyroyal tea, Nellie might know something about it.

CHAPTER FOURTEEN

WHEN CONSTABLE COLLINS came to relieve us of duty, it wasn't with immediate effect, however. Before he allowed us to go, he insisted on having me there while he gave a quick look through my room, since he hadn't had a chance to do it so far.

"It's not because I suspect you of anything, Miss Darling," he assured me as he dug through my unmentionables; I think his complexion turned pink, but he had his back to me, so all I had to go by were the tips of his ears and what little skin I could see between his collar and the dark hair. "We all three know that the two of you were with me when it's likely that Mr. Rivers was killed. But in thoroughness, I ought to look."

"Of course you ought," I said, making myself comfortable on the edge of the bed while I waited. Christopher, meanwhile, leaned against the wall just inside the door. "I don't mind at all. There's nothing here that I'm worried about anyone seeing."

"Tell me, Collins," Christopher said as Collins withdrew his hands from my drawer and pushed it shut with a relieved breath, "what is happening downstairs?"

"Nothing much, Mr. Astley," Collins answered, and pulled

open the doors to the wardrobe. I had brought two evening frocks this weekend—the ivory from last night, plus an apple green that I adored, in spite of the fact that Crispin had informed me that it made me look like a Bramley. There was also a peachy-pink afternoon frock with a pleated skirt (it had been intended for today, but due to the excitement of this morning I was still wearing the skirt and blouse I had put on for breakfast), a pair of blue satin pyjamas, a matching dressing gown, and another blouse to exchange for the one I was currently wearing. They were all hanging where I had placed them, neatly side by side in the wardrobe. Below stood my two pairs of evening shoes and one pair of slippers—the footwear I had brought in addition to the brogues on my feet.

Collins made short process of sifting through it all before he shut the doors and turned back around to finish answering Christopher's question. "The drinking has started, although given what this day has brought so far—two deaths and a murder investigation—I'm not certain I can blame anyone for that. I can't imagine it's what Miss Laetitia had planned for her engagement party."

Probably not, and for a moment I felt almost sorry for her. But then I remembered whose ring was weighing down her finger, and how she might have killed Cecily to keep it, and I sniffed instead. "No more than she deserves, if you ask me."

Besides, there had been plenty of alcohol last night, so it wasn't at all certain that the drinking had anything at all to do with the tragedies.

"Now, now, Pippa," Christopher admonished, but his voice was uneven with suppressed laughter.

Collins glanced at me but didn't comment. "Your German friend appeared to be involved in an exchange with your cousin —" His eyes flickered to Christopher.

"Oh, dear," I said. "Francis, I suppose, not Crispin?"

"The elder cousin," Collins said. "Not Miss Laetitia's fiancé. And I think your parents may have arrived."

Christopher's brows rose. "My parents?"

"I don't know," Collins said. "I've never met them. But there was a middle-aged man with fair hair and a lady with a brown bob."

That definitely sounded like Uncle Herbert and Aunt Roz. "It's a shame they arrived in the middle of all this mess," I commented, and Christopher nodded.

"I imagine Uncle Harold isn't far behind, then, and he'll be the cherry on the cake."

I winced. He probably would be, at that.

"Your parents didn't behave badly," Collins said. "In fact, your mother took the German gentleman off somewhere to look for a plaster."

A plaster? "What did Francis do to him?"

"Nothing of note," Collins said. "A bit of fisticuffs. Scraped knuckles. It sounded more like an excuse than anything else."

Of course. Aunt Roz would want to know what was going on between Wolfgang and Francis, and since someone had undoubtedly brought me up—Crispin, at a guess—she would want to plumb those depths, too, and learn what the connection was.

"We should go downstairs and greet them," I told Christopher, who nodded.

"Are we done up here, Constable?"

"Go on, then," Collins told him. "I have to stay with the crime scene, but you two may feel free to move around. We'll get a signed statement from you at some point."

"We'll be here." I tugged Christopher after me into the hallway. "Come along, Christopher. Don't dawdle."

"Afraid of what your boyfriend is telling Mum?" Christopher wanted to know, but he tripped along behind me.

I flicked him a look over my shoulder. "He's not my boyfriend, Christopher. But yes, I admit that I am, a little bit."

I was also worried about Aunt Roz's and Uncle Herbert's reactions to the situation in general. They're less used to hobnobbing with dead bodies and murderers than Christopher and I.

"They had to deal with the trouble at Beckwith Place in July," Christopher reminded me as we started down the staircase to the first floor, "as well as at Sutherland Hall in late April."

"All the more reason for them not to have to worry this time."

"I don't see how we can keep them from worrying," Christopher said, "but if you have a plan, I'm all ears."

I didn't, more's the pity. "We should have headed them off while we had the chance."

"When did we have the chance?" Christopher wanted to know. "It didn't cross my mind to ring them up until well after Cecily had died, and by then, I assumed it was already too late to catch them at home."

I made a face. "You're probably right about that."

"Of course I'm right. Besides, I'm happy they're here. Constance can use someone's help with Francis. Someone who isn't you or me. We're both busy, and besides, neither of us is in Francis's good graces at the moment."

We clattered onto the first floor landing and rounded the corner of the staircase only to find ourselves stumbling into the Fortescues coming out of their room.

Or on a second look, it was only Lady Serena, not Bilge. If he had been there, he had either stayed behind, or headed down first. She shut the door behind her with a rather decisive click, so perhaps he was still inside and she wanted to make certain we wouldn't bother him. As if it had even crossed my mind to do such a thing.

"Pardon me." I skidded to a stop just before I literally ran into her.

Serena gave me a sneer worthy of Crispin, and a, "Watch where you're going," before she looked beyond me and graced Christopher with a warm smile. "Good afternoon, Mr. Astley."

"Lady Serena." Christopher managed a half-bow as he pulled himself up and did his best to look grown up and responsible.

"Are you going downstairs, by chance? Perhaps you wouldn't mind escorting me?"

I snorted, albeit softly. But really, did she need help navigating the single flight of stairs? She was only a few years older than we were, and not expecting, so it wasn't as if her center of gravity was upset.

Christopher, of course, said that he would be delighted. It's all you can do in that sort of situation. Saying no would have been unforgivably rude.

I took a step towards the staircase. "I'll leave you two to it, and run ahead."

Christopher nodded and presented his elbow for Lady Serena to latch onto. "Tell Mum and Dad I'm on my way."

"Of course." I scurried down the hall towards the main staircase, and towards the voices I could hear from downstairs. Behind me, I heard Lady Serena thank Christopher for the courtesy as she latched onto his arm and they followed me, at a much more sedate pace. Just as I reached the top of the staircase, I heard her voice again, inquiring about what had been going on upstairs to prompt Constable Collins's many comings and goings.

It sounded like a fishing expedition, a quest for information, and for a moment I considered whether I ought to stop Christopher from telling her anything. But then I reasoned that if she (or her husband) had killed Dominic Rivers, she already knew that he was dead. Telling her wouldn't give her information she didn't have already. And if she hadn't known, she'd find out as soon as the mortuary van came back and the other constables started swarming. There was no point in not letting her know the bare facts, so I left Christopher with the task of explaining.

I put on a burst of speed and exited the staircase on the ground floor just as the two of them entered it on the floor above. And then I was gone, down the hallway towards the drawing room and Aunt Roslyn's voice.

"Auntie!"

"Pippa, my dear." She caught me in an embrace that went on longer than it would have normally done, because once she was holding me, I found myself disinclined to pulling away. I had held myself together reasonably well so far today, I believed, through finding Cecily bleeding, to being shot at, and Cecily breathing her last, and sparring with Dominic Rivers, and walking with Christopher, and then finding Rivers's dead body... and now someone had taken some of my weight and I didn't want to let go and have to stand on my own.

Of course I had to eventually. There were stares and murmurs all around the room, and then Christopher entered, gallantly bowing to Lady Serena as she relinquished his arm, and as he came towards us, Aunt Roz softened the arms that had held me tightly, and allowed me to ease away as she turned toward her youngest son. "Christopher."

She gave him a quick up-and-down look, perhaps to see whether he was in the same state I was in.

"Hullo, Mother." He leaned in and gave her a peck on the cheek before turning his eyes to the rest of the room. "Where is Father? And I see you brought Uncle Harold."

I saw that, too, now that I took the time to look around. The

Duke of Sutherland was standing on the opposite side of the room, next to his son and heir, and I got the impression that he was reading him the riot act, because Crispin's bottom lip was protruding and he was scowling at the floor.

"What did he do now?" I wanted to know.

Aunt Roz shook her head. "Who knows? It seems to be a perpetual state with the two of them."

"And Uncle Herbert?" I asked, since Christopher was practically twitching to have his earlier question answered.

Aunt Roz waved a negligent hand. "Off somewhere with Francis. What on earth has been going on here to get him into such a state, Pippa?"

The real reason for the state, as far as I knew, was standing a few feet away. Wolfgang had been speaking to Aunt Roz when I came running through the door—or perhaps it had been vice versa—but he had removed himself to a polite distance when I had stumbled into my aunt's arms and stayed there. Now he cleared his throat, but didn't actually say anything.

I didn't, either. Not about that. "We've had two murders today," I told Aunt Roz instead, "and someone shot at us this morning."

Her eyebrows rose. "Again?"

Wolfgang arched his brows in surprise, and now that I thought about it, I realized that I hadn't mentioned that previous incident to him. It had been the least exciting part of that particular weekend, and to be honest, I had mostly forgotten about it. The scar on my arm was still there, but fading, and I really only thought about it when I was putting on a sleeveless gown and happened to glance in the mirror and notice it.

"I have no idea who they were trying to take out," I told Aunt Roz, "and that's if it wasn't just an accidental shot from someone going for a partridge in the woods. I'm sure they were warned not to shoot in the direction of the house—"

Wolfgang nodded.

"—but it's easy to lose a sense of direction in the woods. The bullet didn't hit any of us. But Constable Collins collected it and put it with the rest of the evidence. Just in case it turns out to be relevant."

Aunt Roz tilted her head. "Why would it have anything to do with the other matter?"

"Pippa looks a bit like Cecily Fletcher did," Christopher explained, and Aunt Roz's eyebrows rose. For some reason, she glanced over at Uncle Harold and Crispin. Uncle Harold had stopped haranguing his son, and was standing over him looking stern. Crispin still looked sulky, more like the thwarted eleven-year-old I remembered than a man ready to get married.

"We thought that someone might have believed the poison had failed," Christopher said, "and that person decided to take a more active approach in getting rid of her."

"But it wasn't her at all."

Christopher and I both shook our heads. "She was lying upstairs with Constance," I said, "and I was the one on the lawn. But I suppose, if someone was in the trees and not able to see very well, it might have been an easy mistake to make."

Aunt Roz nodded. "You're all right, at any rate—all four of you—and I'm certain the police will get to the bottom of it."

I hoped so. I didn't really think that anyone was out to get me—not this time—but the bullet had still come uncomfortably close. And you're just as dead either way, aren't you? Whether it's a case of mistaken identity or not, doesn't matter to the final outcome.

Wolfgang cleared his throat. "Are you all right, Philippa?"

"I'm fine," I told him. "Just another dead body."

He nodded. "The young *Polizist* came down and told us. It was the drug dealer, *nein?*"

"*Ja*," I said. "I mean, yes. It was. Dominic Rivers. Someone conked him over the head with a vase."

Wolfgang's face twitched. "Barbaric."

What had happened to Cecily was a lot more barbaric, but it wasn't a quarrel I wanted to have. They were both dead, and most likely by the same hand, so whoever had done it, was certainly a horrible person either way.

"You stayed in the dining room after I left," I said, and Wolfgang nodded.

"For a short time. The gathering broke up quickly."

Of course. First Christopher had gone to confer with Constable Collins, then Crispin had swept out in a fury, and then I had left and taken Dom Rivers with me. Any and all of those things would have been cause for curiosity, and I could well imagine how some people would have wanted to put their heads together to gossip, while others would have wanted to go off on their own to lick their wounds.

Case in point— "What happened to Laetitia?"

"Our hostess? She left shortly after you did."

Looking for Crispin, no doubt. I hadn't seen her while I'd been standing in the foyer with Rivers, so perhaps she had taken the servants' staircase up to the first floor—up to Crispin's bedchamber—and instead, he had been on the lawn with Christopher and Constable Collins.

Or perhaps she had waited out of sight until Rivers and I had parted ways, and then she had followed him up to his room and whacked him over the head because—

Well, no. That didn't make any sense. If Laetitia had poisoned Cecily with pennyroyal, she would have picked the pennyroyal herself. Christopher and I had proven that she could have done so. So she would have had no reason to murder Rivers.

Unless she had gotten the pennyroyal from Rivers, and someone else had picked the plant and made the tea.

And I probably ought to get over my propensity to see Laetitia in the role of any murderer in our vicinity. She hadn't been guilty either of the other times I had suspected her, so she probably wasn't guilty this time, either.

"Who else?" I asked.

Wolfgang made a show of thinking about it. "The married couple left next. Up to their room for some time alone, I suspect. They've been attached at the hip ever since they got here."

"Did you see them in the woods this morning? Bilge mentioned how good a shot his wife is."

"I saw them," Wolfgang said, "occasionally. But there were trees, and we were, none of us, in sight of the others at all times."

No, of course not. And if he had seen either of them shoot in the direction of the house, surely he would have mentioned it after hearing about what had happened earlier.

"The two young ladies left the dining room together," Wolfgang continued. "They looked very shaken. Lord Geoffrey suggested that those of us who were left have a brandy in the drawing room, but your cousin and his fiancée withdrew. So did the unattached young man. I suspect he ran after the two young ladies. He spent most of last night with one of them."

The Honorable Reggie, of course. He had spent the evening with Olivia Barnsley, I thought.

"And you and Geoffrey came in here," I said.

Wolfgang nodded. "We had a pleasant conversation about estate management. Although his father seems to be in good health, so he doesn't have to worry about taking the reins anytime soon."

He sounded wistful.

"And you do?" I asked.

He looked at me for a moment. "My father is gone. I'm my grandfather's heir, and he's an old man. The time will come, most likely sooner than I'd like, when I will have to stop living the bachelor life and do my duty."

"Of course." By duty, he no doubt meant what Uncle Harold had been pushing Crispin towards all this time: stop playing the field and find a wife. Beget an heir (and a spare) and settle down to married life. Titled landowners were the same in every country, it seemed.

Aunt Roz cleared her throat. "I would like to see Constance, Pippa. Would you help me find her?"

"Of course." I gave Wolfgang an apologetic smile. "Excuse me, please."

He clicked his heels together and bowed, to Aunt Roz first, and then me. "Will I see you later?"

"I imagine I'll be back down again before too long," I told him, and flicked another glance across the room. "Go say hello to your uncle, Christopher. St George looks like he could use an intervention."

Christopher nodded. "Be careful wandering around, you two. There's a murderer about."

"Nobody is interested in murdering *me*," Aunt Roz said stoutly and tucked her hand through my arm. "Come along, Pippa. Good afternoon, *Graf* von Natterdorff."

She gave Wolfgang a nicely calculated inclination of her head before drawing me away. I directed a last apologetic smile across my shoulder at him before allowing myself to be drawn.

.   .   .

I ASSUMED I was in for a talking to, of course, and I wasn't surprised at the direction it took. Aunt Roz waited until we were outside the drawing room, and in the relative privacy of the hallway, but then she said blandly, "Your German friend is charming, Pippa."

"Thank you," was the automatic rejoinder, but I didn't feel quite comfortable using it—it wasn't as if I could take any of the credit for it, after all—so I merely muttered something noncommittal.

"It might have been nice if you had mentioned his existence before now, however," my aunt continued pointedly. "Let alone the fact that he would be here this weekend."

"I'm sorry," I said, as humbly as I could manage. "Part of me thought you knew. Crispin certainly did, and I thought he might have mentioned something. Or Christopher, of course."

"No," Aunt Roz said ominously, and I felt rather bad for having thrown them both under the bus this way. They were in for a talking to of their own, I reckoned.

"I actually didn't plan to go," I said apologetically. "The last thing I want, is to watch Laetitia Marsden swanning about with the Sutherland diamond ring on her finger."

Aunt Roz nodded, with a bit more sympathy than was strictly necessary. It wasn't as if I was *that* put out.

"But then Wolfgang said he had been invited, and I didn't want him to have to be here on his own, and Christopher was going, and wanted me to go, and so I changed my mind and came along after all."

"And that's all understandable," Aunt Roz said, as we reached the bottom of the main staircase and started up, "but what I want to know, Pippa, is why we're the last to know of his existence?"

"We didn't want to mention it in front of Francis," I said. "We didn't think he would take it well."

Aunt Roz eyed me. "And you didn't think a prior warning might have been better than having him show up here and come face to face with the enemy?"

"He's not the enemy," I said irritably. "I'm sorry that Francis is upset. Truly. And I understand why he would be. But the War has been over for almost eight years now. And I'm a bit German myself. Francis doesn't seem to have a problem with that."

"You weren't in the trenches shooting at him," Aunt Roz said.

"Neither was Wolfgang. He's too young."

Aunt Roz gave me a beady look, and I repeated it, defensively. "He wasn't! I believe he's around twenty-six or so. Too young for conscription."

"That's not what I meant, Pippa," Aunt Roz said, "and you know it. You being half German, and your male friend being all the way German are two very different things. Besides, you know as well as I do that Francis loves you."

Of course I knew that, and very well, too. "I'm sorry," I said. "Perhaps we should have said something, and then Francis could have stayed home and not had to deal with Wolfgang. Although I don't know how that might have worked, honestly, since Constance is Laetitia's cousin and was expected to be here in her own right, not just as Francis's fiancée. I don't think St George would have minded if Francis hadn't shown up—he doesn't like Wolfgang, either; St George, I mean—"

"You don't say?" Aunt Roz said dryly, and I gave her a look, but decided to continue with my sentence instead of derailing myself to inquire what she had meant.

"—but I'm sure Laetitia would have been horribly offended had Constance not been here, and I can't imagine that Francis would have let Constance make the trip on her own, Germans or no Germans—"

"No, I can't imagine so," Aunt Roz agreed. "So Crispin doesn't like your friend, does he? I can't imagine why. He's quite well-mannered, and seems to go out of his way to be pleasant."

That had always been my impression, too. Of course, we were talking about Crispin here, who has no concept of going out of his way to be anything but horrible.

"They took against one another pretty thoroughly from the moment they met," I said. "One might have expected them to get along like a house on fire—two handsome, wealthy, titled, arrogant, young gentlemen; Crispin has plenty of friends just like that, and he doesn't seem to mind them at all—but they took one look at one another and started bristling like two tomcats in an alley..."

"Imagine that." Aunt Roz glanced around the first floor landing. I think she may have been attempting to hide a smile, although she couldn't quite manage. "Where is Constance's room?"

"Down there." I pointed. "Primrose."

"Lovely. We're in Columbine, down at the end." She started walking towards Primrose.

"I'm in Wisteria upstairs," I said. "Christopher and Francis share Bluebell." I indicated the door.

Aunt Roz glanced at it in passing. "Quaint."

"We just have Pippa's room and Christopher's room in the flat."

Aunt Roz nodded. "At home, as well. But of course you know that."

Of course I did. I had spent eleven years in a room at Beckwith Place. One with no name beyond Pippa's room.

Aunt Roz stopped outside the door to Primrose and applied her knuckles to the wood. "Constance? It's Roslyn, dear. Are you in there?"

CHAPTER FIFTEEN

FOR A SECOND, the déjà vu was stunning. It was as if a fist had reached into my chest and wrapped around my lungs, squeezing. I wasn't even aware that I had been worried. Not until now, when—for the third time today—I stood outside a bedroom door after knocking, and I remembered what had been waiting inside the room the other two times I had done the same thing.

But then there were noises from inside, and a moment later, the door opened and Constance's face peered out. "Oh!" She smiled. "Hullo, Roslyn. Pippa."

"Hello, Constance," I managed, and if my chest felt a bit tighter than it ought to, I think I was the only one who noticed.

Aunt Roz swept past Constance. I took a breath and followed, and Constance shut the door behind us, looking from Aunt Roz to me and back. "Is everything all right?"

"Everything is fine," Aunt Roz assured her, at the same time as I said, "Other than the two murders."

My aunt and I glanced at one another, before we both

seemingly decided that it was the better part of valor to simply let that statement lie.

"Yes," I turned back to Constance. "All is well. There's nothing new."

"Miss Fletcher was murdered? As well as Mr. Rivers? Constable Collins said he was dead when he came downstairs."

I nodded, after taking a moment to sort out the pronouns. "Someone cracked him over the head with a vase. There was no attempt at all to try to make it look like anything but a violent attack."

Unlike Cecily's death, which had been carefully designed to look like a natural occurrence, or at best an accidental overdose with death as the result.

Unless, of course, it had actually been an accidental overdose and nobody had tried to make it look like anything else.

Although with Rivers dead, it did make it more likely that whatever had happened to Cecily had at least been instigated by somebody, whether the goal had been to kill her or simply to make her body reject the pregnancy. If it hadn't been done on purpose, why kill the person who was the most likely purveyor of the pennyroyal?

"Pippa, dear," Aunt Roz's voice cut through the noise in my head, and I blinked and took another step into the room.

"I'm sorry." Aunt Roz had taken a seat on the edge of the bed, while Constance was standing halfway between me and her, with her hands twined anxiously together before her. "I was just thinking," I added, vaguely.

Aunt Roz's eyebrows rose. "I just arrived. Would one of you care to explain exactly what has been going on here this weekend?"

I exchanged a glance with Constance, who made a face, but waved at me to go ahead.

I drew breath. "From the beginning, then. Last night, when

I came up to bed, I ran into St George coming out of Cecily Fletcher's room..."

After going through the entire sordid story, up to and including walking in on Dominic Rivers's dead body, I closed my mouth and waited for Aunt Roz to give her verdict.

There was a moment's silence.

"In my day," she said, "there were Beecham's Pills."

I blinked. "There are still Beecham's Pills, aren't there?"

She nodded. "There were also Dr. Vandenburgh's Female Restorative Pills, and French Periodical Pills, and of course there was turpentine and diachylon and gin..."

"I don't think she drank turpentine," I said, while Constance made a face, "although there was probably some gin last night. A lot of the drinks were gin-based, as I recall."

Constance nodded agreement. "Turpentine has a very pungent smell, as I recall, and I can't imagine it being in either the drinks or the tea. Someone would have noticed, surely?"

Oh, surely. "What was left in the cup last night smelled like mint," I said. "I think I would have noticed had it smelled like turpentine."

"Pennyroyal is quite easy to find, as well" Aunt Roz said. "Easy to distill, too."

"We found a patch of it growing just a few hundred feet from the front door," I nodded, "so anyone who wanted to make their own wouldn't have had a problem."

"Laetitia, Geoffrey, and I are all familiar with the area," Constance said, and I turned to her.

"Nobody suspects *you*, Constance. You had no reason to want Cecily Fletcher dead. Or her baby gone, either. It certainly wasn't Francis who got her in trouble."

Aunt Roz shook her head firmly. "Of course not, Constance. That would be silly."

Constance didn't look reassured. "Do you think it was one of my cousins, then?"

"I think it could have been any number of people," I said. "I've been to the Dower House before, so I could theoretically have known that there was pennyroyal growing in the ditch. Crispin has been here before, so he might have known. If Laetitia has had her friends here to stay, they may have known. Violet, Olivia, Cecily herself, maybe even Lady Serena."

"Your aunt and uncle," Aunt Roz added, "I assume. And all of the servants."

There was another moment of silence.

"I don't think Aunt Effie would have done something like that," Constance said. "And I don't believe that Uncle Maury would have known what to look for."

"Of course not, my dear." Aunt Roz smiled reassuringly. "We're just talking, you know. No need to worry."

There was a moment's pause.

"If Laetitia thought it was Crispin's baby..." I ventured, and Constance made a face.

"I don't think she would have tried to kill Miss Fletcher, Pippa. She didn't appreciate being a suspect in Johanna's murder at all. Although she might have decided to add some pennyroyal to Miss Fletcher's drink just to see what would happen. She's not the most empathetic person in the world."

No, she certainly wasn't. On the other hand, Crispin had made it clear that the baby hadn't been his, and all she'd have had to do was ask him. Surely she would have checked with him first, before she started poisoning people? And if she had done, then she wouldn't have had any reason to go after Cecily.

"What about Geoffrey?" I asked, and watched Constance grimace again.

"He's not the most empathetic, either. And he's not at all interested in being tied down."

No, I imagined he wasn't. "Would he have done something about it?"

"Again," Constance said, "I don't think he would have killed her. He's self-absorbed, but not deliberately cruel."

"Stupid, though."

"Not the brightest bulb in the chandelier," Constance admitted, "but he knows that, believe it or not. And he had to deal with the murder investigation at the Dower House, too. I don't think he would have wanted to risk it."

"So what you're saying is that he might also have given her something to get rid of the baby, to get himself out of a sticky situation in which he might be expected to step up and do the right thing, but he wouldn't have committed murder."

Constance shook her head. "Not in my opinion."

I nodded. I shared her opinion, as it happened. Geoffrey was stupid, and sneaking pennyroyal into someone's tea to try to induce an accidental-looking miscarriage seemed like it was more cunning than he would be capable of. "This is all moot. Living down the road from where pennyroyal grows is one thing. It doesn't mean that he has ever had anything to do with Cecily Fletcher."

"I wouldn't be surprised if he has done," Constance said. "He's made his way through a lot of the young ladies of the Bright Young set. Although you're right, I know nothing about Miss Fletcher specifically."

"One of the other girls, perhaps?" Aunt Roz suggested. "Miss Fletcher's friend, trying to fix a problem Miss Fletcher couldn't bring herself to fix on her own? Or another girl after the man whose child Miss Fletcher was carrying, so she wanted Miss Fletcher out of the way, or at least wanted to eliminate the reason why the man she liked had to marry Miss Fletcher and not her?"

"Lady Violet spent last evening with Geoffrey," Constance murmured.

I nodded. "And Olivia Barnsley spent it with the Honorable Reggie." Who wasn't very honorable if he got Cecily with child and didn't offer to marry her.

"Perhaps I should have a chat with one or both of them," Aunt Roz said thoughtfully. "I'm sure they're both very upset about their friend's death. An older, maternal presence might do one or both of them good."

It had done me good, so I could hardly quibble with that.

"I can't imagine that Lady Euphemia will step up," I commented, and Constance shook her head.

"Aunt Effie isn't the maternal type. She'll worry about Laetitia and Geoffrey, but none of the others."

"I think perhaps I'll go and see if I can't be of service to the young ladies," Aunt Roz said and pushed to her feet. "Perhaps they would appreciate someone to talk to. Not just about their friend, but I can reassure them as to the investigation, as well. We did go through one of our own just a month or two ago."

"Let us know if they say anything interesting," I said, as I took Aunt Roz's place on the bed as she crossed the room to the door. "I'll let you tackle this on your own. My presence would only complicate things, I think."

The two young women were much more likely to be forthcoming with my aunt than with me.

She nodded. "Of course, dear. I'll see you both downstairs later."

We assured her that of course she would, and told her where to find Violet and Olivia—"Most likely upstairs in one of their bedchambers. I didn't see either of them downstairs earlier. Olivia is in Snowdrop and Violet in Lilac, I believe," and then Aunt Roz was gone and it was just Constance and me looking at one another.

"I can't believe this has happened again," she told me as she came over to sit next to me on the bed.

I nodded. "At least none of us are suspects this time."

Constance shuddered. "Thank the Lord. I barely even knew Cecily Fletcher. And Francis didn't know her at all."

"Nor did I. Enough to recognize her face downstairs last night, but nothing more."

After a moment's pause, I added, "I feel horrible, though. If I had realized last night how ill she was..."

"How could you have done?" Constance wanted to know. "You knew that she was expecting. It wasn't unreasonable that she would be sick. And it's not as if we go around expecting people to have been poisoned, even after the last few months."

No, I supposed not. "I'm not saying I could have known, or should have. I just feel bad that I didn't do more. But it simply didn't cross my mind that anything extraordinary was wrong. I knew she was expecting, so the vomiting made sense. She told me that she had had peppermint tea, and it smelled more like spearmint, but even that wasn't enough to make me wonder."

"No, of course not," Constance said. "Why would it? I would have thought it was a simple misnomer, as I'm sure you did."

I nodded. "Spearmint or peppermint seemed like a minor distinction then."

"It's a minor distinction now," Constance said. After a second's pause, she added, "I understand how you feel, Pippa. I felt the same way when Johanna was murdered. Not that you disliked Miss Fletcher the way I did Johanna. But I felt as if I should have prevented it somehow. As if there was something I could have done to make a difference."

"There wasn't," I said. "I was there, and there wasn't anything you could have done differently."

"Well, I don't think there was anything you could have

done differently, either. By the time you saw Cecily, she was already ill. The poison had already affected her, and I don't think there was anything anyone could have done after that. She was already trying to dispel it on her own, after all—or her body was—so even pumping her stomach at that point wouldn't have helped. Even if she had told you that something out of the ordinary was going on, I think it was too late by then."

We sat in silence a moment while I chewed on her words.

She was right, of course, but it had taken me until now to realize it.

The truth was, I hadn't liked Cecily much. Hadn't known her well, of course, but what little I did know, I didn't like. She had bothered Christopher in the past, and had gone to bed with Crispin; what was there to like?

But because I hadn't liked her, I had felt guilty over her death. As if there was something I should have done that I hadn't, out of dislike. But the truth was that after she had stumbled into the lavatory and dropped to her knees in front of the commode, she had simply been a sick young woman who needed help. I hadn't held anything in her past against her.

If I had had any inkling of what was going on, or had thought of anything I could have done differently, I would have done it. I felt bad that I hadn't caught on sooner, but Constance was right: the clues really hadn't been there. Saving her hadn't been in my power, and I hadn't failed.

"Thank you," I said.

She squeezed my hand once before letting go. "I should go and see if I can find Francis."

"Aunt Roz said Uncle Herbert took him off somewhere," I said.

Constance nodded. "He and your German friend almost came to blows. Your aunt and uncle arrived, and broke it up.

Herbert took Francis away, and Roslyn latched onto your friend. I came up here to wait for things to settle down, since everyone was staring at me."

"Christopher went to look for his father and brother when we arrived downstairs," I said, "so I think I'll just go up to my room for a few minutes and freshen up."

Constance got to her feet and smoothed her skirt down. "I'll see you downstairs later?"

"I'll get out of these clothes and into something else," I said, "and then I'll be down. Won't take me but a few minutes."

"Do you want me to come with you?"

I shook my head. "You go ahead and find Francis. If you see Christopher, tell him I'm on my way."

Constance said she would do, and then we parted ways: Constance down the main staircase to the ground floor and me up the smaller stairs to the second floor.

IN COMPLETE HONESTY, I should perhaps confess that I did have an ulterior motive for wanting to go upstairs. Yes, I had worn the same clothes since I got up this morning. I had crawled across the lawn in them after being shot at, and I had found two different dead bodies wearing this skirt and blouse, as well as walked down a dusty road and picked weeds in them. I did want to get out of them and into my afternoon dress.

That was not the only reason I wanted to go upstairs, however. I wanted to see what, if anything, Constable Collins might have discovered since the last time I had seen him, but more than that, I wanted a chance to listen in on the conversation Aunt Roz might be having with Lady Violet and the Honorable Olivia.

And since I did, and didn't see the sense in giving anyone

advanced notice that I was coming, I stopped at the foot of the stairs and kicked my shoes off. With them in my hand, I proceeded up the stairs silently, in my stocking feet.

The upstairs hallway looked the same as it had the last time I'd been here. I peered into the alcove on my way past, and saw that the peacock feathers were gone from the plinth. The door to Dom Rivers's room was closed, and that was fine by me. The gentlemen from the mortuary hadn't arrived yet to pick up the body, and I assumed Collins was trying to keep it from being gawked at by anyone else until then.

There were faint noises from within the room, the sounds of Collins investigating, I assumed. I didn't think any of the reinforcements from the village had arrived yet, either, so it was still only him working the case here at Marsden Manor. Perhaps he had thought it possible to get fingerprints off the peacock feathers, and he had taken them in there with him. It wasn't an outrageous idea: whoever had picked up the vase must have lifted the feathers out first, and laid them on the plinth, although if he—or she—had been wearing gloves, there'd be no fingerprints on any of it.

I didn't knock on the door. Instead, I edged down the other side of the hallway towards the rooms on the opposite side.

Cecily's room was the one in the middle. The door was still standing open. First on my right was Snowdrop, which I thought was Olivia's room. I sidled up to the door, crossing my fingers that the floor wouldn't creak, and held my breath.

There were no sounds from within. I could hear the rustling from across the hall, as well as the faint murmur of voices, but from further down.

Lady Violet's room it was, then.

I abandoned Olivia's door and skirted Cecily's—the room inside was empty, and the bed had been stripped; the sheets, I assumed, had been gathered as evidence—to wind up in front of Lilac, directly across from my own Wisteria.

"—cannot believe it," a voice said from within. I recognized the slightly adenoidal undertones as belonging to Violet. I don't think I had heard enough of Olivia's voice to recognize it, and it definitely didn't belong to Aunt Roz, who may or may not even be here. It could simply be that Violet and Olivia were having a conversation.

But no— "That she would take such a step?" Aunt Roz inquired. "Or that someone would do it to her?"

There was a pause. I imagined Violet and Olivia looking at one another. Then—

"Either," Olivia said. It had to be Olivia, since it wasn't Violet, nor was it anyone else whose voice I recognized. "Ceci wasn't the maudlin sort. She wouldn't have offed herself over something like a baby, even if the bloke wouldn't marry her. "

Violet seemed to agree, because she added, "If she wanted the baby, she would have kept it. If she didn't, she would have taken steps. There are ways for a girl to get out of a predicament like that these days."

She sounded very cool about it. Perhaps she had already had to deal with a similar problem of her own. I wouldn't be surprised, since—judging by the way St George got around—these girls weren't shy about sharing their favors, and when you do, sometimes there are consequences.

However, something else about Olivia's assertion had caught my attention, and I hoped that it had caught Aunt Roz's, too.

And right on schedule, she asked, "Did the father of the baby not want to take responsibility?"

There was a beat. I imagined Olivia and Violet exchanging a glance.

"We don't know," Olivia said eventually.

"She didn't confide in you?"

"She told us when she first suspected," Violet said. "But she didn't say anything about who she might be involved with."

Aunt Roz hesitated. I could feel as well as hear the pause. "My nephew..."

"Oh, no," Violet denied immediately, while Olivia added, firmly, "That's ancient history."

"At least six months old," Violet added.

"Dead and buried," Olivia said.

Ancient history, indeed. Although it was the same thing that Crispin had told me—February—so I suppose it was nice to have it confirmed.

Aunt Roz didn't say anything, but I could sense her relief. "Who else, then?"

"We thought it might have been Reggie," Olivia said, "but now I'm not so sure."

"The Honorable Mr. Fish?" Aunt Roz clarified. "I'm afraid I'm not familiar with the gentleman."

"The Fishes came here from Normandy almost a thousand years ago," Olivia said. "Reggie's family is from Lincolnshire."

"And he knew Miss Fletcher?"

Olivia's voice turned snappish. "Of course they knew one another. But I spent all of last evening with him, and he didn't have a chance to do anything to her. He was never near her drink to put anything in it, and after he went to his room, he didn't come back out."

"You kept watch?"

"For a bit," Olivia said, "until I fell asleep."

She must have fallen asleep before Cecily stumbled out of bed and into the lavatory, then, I assumed, or she would have come out of her room to see what was going on, as any caring friend would.

"What do you think, Lady Violet?" Aunt Roz wanted to know.

"I spent last evening with Lord Geoffrey," Violet said. "If Ceci's problem was his fault, he didn't act like it."

Which probably meant that he hadn't been too distracted to put moves on Violet when the opportunity came along.

"Are you..." Aunt Roz hesitated, "involved with Lord Geoffrey, Lady Violet?"

Violet laughed. Harshly. "Good Lord, no. We all know better than that. It was just some fun last night."

The silence that followed rang with something more than just the absence of sound, but I was outside the door and couldn't tell what it was. It's hard to make determinations based solely on the sound of someone's voice and no cues beyond that.

"You both knew Miss Fletcher well," Aunt Roz said. They both made confirmatory noises. "Why do you suppose she didn't tell you who was responsible for her predicament?"

There was a beat.

"She didn't know?" Violet suggested blandly.

"Is that likely?" Aunt Roz wanted to know. She was still soft-spoken and courteous. Had it been me in the family way without knowing who was responsible, her reaction certainly would have been a lot more shrill, but then she had no emotional attachment to Cecily Fletcher.

"No," Olivia said, with—I guessed—a scowl at Violet. "She knew."

"How do you know that?"

"She told us," Olivia said.

"She told you who—?"

"No," Olivia said. "She didn't tell us his name. But she said he was someone she couldn't marry."

"Someone she couldn't marry? Or someone who couldn't—or wouldn't—marry her?"

"It's the same thing," Olivia said.

It most certainly wasn't. Bilge couldn't marry Cecily because he was already married to Serena, and Cecily couldn't marry Bilge for the same reason. But that's very different from not being able to marry Geoffrey because he was a cad or Dominic Rivers because he was—or had been—a dope dealer.

Crispin could have proposed to the girl he claims to be in love with at any point these last few months, as there was nothing actually stopping him from doing so, at least until he got engaged to Laetitia. The reason he hasn't done, is because his father would disown him, and then he and his lady-love would have to crawl off to the Continent to live in squalor, and he doesn't want to do that. He calls it that he can't marry her, but in truth, he could if he wanted to. It's the consequences that have kept him from proposing.

And now, of course, there was Laetitia.

But at any rate, there are lots of degrees between can and can't, and Aunt Roz was absolutely correct in inquiring into which one this was.

Not that Olivia seemed inclined to acquiesce. "I told you both," she said. "I don't know who it is. She wouldn't tell me. Just that they couldn't be together."

And there was yet another permutation of the same excuse. Couldn't be together because he was married to someone else, or engaged to someone else, or in love with someone else, or because she was in love with someone else, or attached to someone else, or because her family would disown her, or his family would disown him, or because she couldn't face the consequences of shacking up—in the literal sense—with Dominic Rivers somewhere in the squalor of—never mind the Continent—South London?

"Thank you for your time, girls," Aunt Roz's voice said from inside the room. Her footsteps were approaching the door, and I quick-stepped backwards, until I was standing outside my own door instead of outside Violet's. By the time Aunt Roz stepped out into the hallway, I had my hand on the knob and the door halfway open, and was on my way in, innocently as you please.

CHAPTER SIXTEEN

"YOU DIRTY LITTLE SNEAK," Aunt Roz said, with no heat whatsoever, as she sat down on my bed and watched me peel out of my skirt and blouse. (Aunt Roz raised me, at least from the time I was eleven years old, so dressing and undressing in front of her is old hat.)

"I wanted to change anyway," I answered, and let the skirt drop so I could step out of it. "I've worn these clothes all day."

"It's a bit early for an evening gown, isn't it?"

"I thought I'd put on an afternoon frock for a few hours. Just to wear something different."

Aunt Roz shrugged. "So how much did you hear while you were pressing your ear to the door?"

"The first thing I heard was Violet saying she couldn't believe it. That Cecily would kill herself, I suppose. Or that she would take an overdose of pennyroyal on purpose."

I dropped the peachy-pink frock over my head and yanked it down around my hips. It settled with a final shimmy. The current fashions are quite easy to manage. Nothing at all like the laced corsets and elaborate hairstyles of a few decades ago.

Aunt Roz nodded. "They both agreed on that. She wasn't the type to take her own life. Nor did they get the impression that she planned to do anything drastic."

I shot her a look. "She must have had some form of plan, then. If she couldn't, for whatever reason, marry the baby's father."

"Or she simply planned to brazen it out," Aunt Roz said. "The problem, of course, is that it's difficult to know who to believe."

"Of the two of them, do you mean?" I leaned towards the mirror to fluff my hair. "Do you think one of them lied?"

"I wouldn't be surprised if they both did," Aunt Roz said. "Olivia seems sweet on young Reggie Fish, and determined to hide it from Lady Violet. She believes that he wasn't responsible for Miss Fletcher's predicament, but that could be untrue. She might not be willing to believe it of him, or she might know better, but refuse to admit it. And if he was responsible, that would give both of them a reason to want Miss Fletcher gone."

"Unless he wanted her and the baby," I said, "and then it would be Olivia who had the motive."

Aunt Roz nodded. "Or perhaps young Mr. Fish wasn't responsible, but he was in love with Miss Fletcher, and when she couldn't—or wouldn't—marry whoever the baby's father was, Mr. Fish offered to step up instead."

That was something Christopher might have suggested doing for me, had I gotten myself in the family way by some cad who wouldn't marry me. Not because he's in love with me, of course, but because we're best friends, and the next thing to siblings, and he won't ever be able to marry someone he loves anyway, so the situation would benefit him, too. He'd end up with an heir he wasn't likely to get any other way, and a wife who would be happy to let him live his life the way he wanted.

Reggie hadn't struck me as being queer, or for that matter

in love with Cecily, but I knew better than to discount any possible explanation.

"What about Violet?" I inquired.

"I don't trust Lady Violet," Aunt Roz said. "Olivia at least seemed sincere in her appreciation for young Reggie. Violet seems to me more of a dark horse."

"She spent the evening with Geoffrey Marsden," I said as I sat down on the bed next to her and folded my hands in my lap, "and he's about as dark as they come. Although he's a catch, of course. Wealthy and titled and handsome."

Aunt Roz nodded. "Awful reputation, though."

Indubitably. "And when Cecily said that she couldn't marry the baby's father—if indeed she said it, and it wasn't just something Olivia made up—she could have referred to that. If I had—" I shuddered, "ugh, what an awful thought, but if I had got myself in the family way by Geoffrey Marsden, I wouldn't feel like I could marry him, either. Shackling myself to someone like that would be the utmost in stupidity. It would amount to a lifetime of watching my husband poking other women."

Aunt Roz nodded. "So if it was between marriage to Geoffrey Marsden and a dose of pennyroyal, you might choose the latter."

"I..." I hesitated. It wasn't a choice I ever wanted to be in a position to have to make, frankly. "If the dose of pennyroyal was to fix the problem of the pregnancy, then perhaps. I wouldn't choose to take enough of it to kill myself."

Marrying Christopher as well as raising the baby on my own would both be preferable solutions. I could brazen out an illegitimate baby. Besides, I could always marry Geoffrey and then divorce him again if I didn't like what he was doing. Being a divorced woman with a child—especially when your husband is a known bastard—is marginally better than being an unmarried woman with one. At least it shows that someone was willing to marry you.

"But you don't think she did that," Aunt Roz said, yanking the conversation back on course.

I shook my head. "I don't think she set out to kill herself on purpose, no. When I saw her last night, she didn't seem suicidal. Miserably sick, yes, but not resigned, like it was something she had done to herself. And I can't imagine why, if she wanted to get rid of the baby, she would have chosen someone else's home and engagement party to do it."

Aunt Roz pursed her lips. "You're absolutely certain that this isn't Crispin's doing?"

"He said it wasn't," I said. "He could have been lying, of course. Although I don't see why it would make much of a difference to him whether he marries Laetitia or Cecily. Neither of them is who he wants."

"No," Aunt Roz agreed. "But it would explain why she might decide to do it here this weekend. The event of the season. The home of the woman he chose instead of her."

I supposed it might. And although it pained me to admit, I added, reluctantly, "It would also explain why he looked so shaken when he came out of her room last night. If she had told him about the pregnancy, and then informed him that she had taken steps to deal with it and that it was too late for him to do anything to stop it, of course he would be upset."

But Aunt Roz shook her head. "He wouldn't have left her alone if that were the case, Pippa. He isn't the type to shirk responsibility in that way. If he were responsible, he would have insisted on staying with her until it was over."

"Laetitia might have been waiting for him," I said, "and he didn't want to make waves."

"No," Aunt Roz said firmly. "Stop playing devil's advocate, Pippa. Cecily may have told him what she was going to do, and ordered him out, but if he went, it was because the baby wasn't his. If it had been, he would have stayed. And at the very least, he would have phoned for the doctor."

Fine. "Geoffrey, then. If she did it herself, and there was a reason to do it here, it had to be because of Geoffrey."

Aunt Roz tilted her head consideringly. "Did she speak to Geoffrey yesterday?"

"They danced once, I think. Although I can't imagine a pregnancy being something that she'd announce in the middle of the ballroom. And he spent the rest of the evening with Violet. In the garden, according to Nellie. Cecily received visitors in her room."

"Visitors, plural?"

"Nellie mentioned Dominic Rivers," I said, "and of course you know about St George. I don't know if there was anyone else."

"But there might have been?"

"I was with Constance in her room," I said. "One floor down. Cecily could have entertained multitudes up here for what I know about it. Rivers and the Honorable Reggie shared the room across the hall. We know she spoke to Rivers, but there is no reason why Reggie couldn't have stopped by her bedchamber, as well. I know Olivia said he didn't, but she might be wrong."

Aunt Roz nodded.

"Or Geoffrey might have done, for that matter. He might have walked Violet to her door, and then popped in next door. And of course Wolfgang was directly across the hall for all of it."

"I'm sure you're not suggesting that the *Graf* von Natterdorff is involved, Pippa."

I shook my head. "No, of course not. He doesn't know any

of these people. Of all the men here, he's surely the least likely to be responsible for Cecily's baby."

Or perhaps not strictly the least likely. Christopher was at the top of that list. He doesn't like women in general. Francis was in second place, because he wouldn't cheat on Constance, and this must have happened in the time since he met her.

I supposed Bilge Fortescue might be in third place, seeing as he was married. Then again, marriage isn't necessarily an impediment to dallying, so perhaps Crispin was in third place and Bilge in fourth. Dominic Rivers in fifth, seeing as he was dead. Although he hadn't been dead when Cecily became with child, so perhaps I shouldn't discount him...

"Tea should be ready soon," Aunt Roz said, derailing my train of thought. "Shall we?"

She pushed to her feet and headed for the door. I slid off the edge of the bed and followed. "We might as well. I had no appetite for lunch—not after everything that happened this morning, and... Oh, hello, Nellie."

"Good afternoon, Miss Darling."

We had reached the landing, and Nellie was on her way across the carpet with a vase of peacock feathers between her hands, obviously a replacement for the one that had been broken over Dominic Rivers's head.

"That looks nice," I said, and Nellie bobbed.

"Thank you, Miss Darling."

"It was good of you to replace the vase for the feathers. The alcove looked a bit bare without anything on the plinth."

"Yes, Miss Darling." She moved past us, and we both pivoted to keep her in sight.

"This is my aunt, Lady Herbert Astley," I said. "This is Nellie, Aunt Roz. She might be the one to take care of your room."

Nellie did a quick dip at the knees. "Lady Herbert."

"It's nice to meet you, Nellie," Aunt Roz said kindly. "Lord Herbert—my husband—and the Duke of Sutherland have also arrived downstairs."

"Yes, Lady Herbert." Nellie ducked into the alcove, still clutching the new vase in both hands.

"A minute of your time, Nellie?" Constable Collins's voice said from the other side of the hallway, and we all turned back in the other direction to look at him. He had opened the door to Dominic Rivers's room soundlessly, and now he was standing in the open doorway watching as Nellie placed the vase carefully on the plinth, then reached out to adjust it minutely. Behind Collins, I could catch a glimpse of the sole of one of Dom's shoes.

"Yes, Constable?" Nellie gave him a look from under her lashes. They were long and curled, and her face was lovely, and I didn't blame Collins at all for the flush that stained his cheekbones.

He cleared his throat self-consciously. "Is it your job to take care of the rooms up here, Nellie?"

"The bedchambers," Nellie said, "yes. The hallway is properly Jenny's job—she's the parlor maid—but I often end up doing it, since I'm the one who works up here. Edna takes care of the family's bedchambers on the first floor."

"That's a lot of work for one maid," I said, "isn't it?"

Nellie flicked a look at me. "It's only a problem when there are a lot of guests, Miss. Usually, when it's only the family and perhaps Lord St George visiting, Edna does Lord Maurice's and Lady Euphemia's suite, along with Miss Laetitia's bedchamber, and I take over the two gentlemen's rooms. It makes it a bit easier. Up here, there's just some light dusting to do when no one's staying over."

That made me feel a little bit better, at any rate. I will admit that I had to hide a smirk at the assertion that she took over the care of Geoffrey's and Crispin's rooms from the missing Edna, though. No doubt this pretty young girl enjoyed taking care of the titled young gentlemen, both of whom no doubt appreciated both her attention and her good looks.

"So you're familiar with the vase that was in the alcove," Collins said, breaking into my cogitation.

Nellie nodded. "Of course I am. Dust it every week, don't I?"

"Do you?"

"Of course I do. I dust the feathers, and then I dust the vase, and then I pick up the vase and dust the pedestal, and then I put the vase back."

Collins nodded. There was a trace of something I wanted to call disappointment on his face, although it didn't come across in his voice. "Thank you, Nellie. That was all I needed."

Nellie nodded and turned on her heel with a flick of her apron. The white bow on the back of her gray dress bounced as she walked away. I expected Constable Collins to withdraw back into Dominic Rivers's room now that he had had his question answered, but he stood where he was and watched until Nellie had disappeared through the baize door at the end of the hall before he seemed to wake up.

"What was that about?" I wanted to know.

The tips of his ears turned hot, and he made an apologetic sort of face. But before he could say anything—because that part of it was simple to guess; he thought Nellie was attractive, and had gotten caught up in looking at her—I added, "Not that. I know what that was. Why did you want to know about the rooms and the dusting?"

"Oh." His face cleared. "Fingerprints on the vase. Small ones, likely from a woman. I found them on other things in Mr. Rivers's room, too. But if they're Nellie's, that explains it. They likely don't have anything to do with his murder."

"Not if she picks up the vase every week," I agreed. "Her fingerprints would be all over it. It's not as if she'd wear gloves to do the dusting."

Collins shook his head. "Another dead end. Pardon the pun."

"No problem." I have a tendency to make dead puns myself, if it comes to that. "You should probably get Nellie's fingerprints anyway, just to compare. But whoever picked up the vase and whacked Rivers with it must have been wearing gloves, don't you think? If you didn't find any fingerprints other than Nellie's."

"I don't know that they're Nellie's yet," Collins said. "They might be Jenny's or Edna's. I'll have to get them all, I suppose."

He sighed.

"All of ours, too," I said, "I suppose?"

He made a face and I added, "There was just the one set of prints on the vase?"

He nodded. "Nothing on the door knob, either. But gloves aren't hard to come by. Several people are still wearing what they wore to ride out this morning."

Yes, indeed. There were gloves in quite a few pockets throughout the house, I imagined. And gloves weren't the only option for keeping fingerprints off surfaces, either. Collins had used a handkerchief, and most men carry one of those. Nellie was wearing a handy apron. I could have used a fold of my skirt, and so could any of the other women in the house—at least the ones who had changed out of their jodhpurs, and that was most of them by now.

While I cogitated, Collins had turned his attention to Aunt Roz.

"I'm sorry," I said, "this is my aunt, Lady Herbert Astley. Constable Collins, Aunt Roz, from the Marsden-on-Crane constabulary. We're old friends. He helped Tom with that unfortunate affair at the Dower House in May."

"Of course." Aunt Roz smiled, a friendly smile, and stuck out a friendly hand. To shake, not to kiss. Collins looked a bit nonplussed—perhaps he had expected Lady Herbert to behave more like Lady Euphemia or Lady Peckham, Constance's late mother—but he took it and shook.

"A pleasure, Lady Herbert. Detective Sergeant Gardiner was a standup chap."

"We've always thought so," Aunt Roz murmured. "He was my son Robbie's best friend, you know."

"Is that so?" It looked like Collins was having a think, before he added, carefully, "I don't think I've had the pleasure, ma'am."

"Cousin Robbie died in France," I said. "It's just Francis and Christopher left now."

"I'm sure you wish he were here," Aunt Roz told Collins. "Thomas, I mean. Two murders in a single day must be a lot to handle."

The constable nodded. "Yes, ma'am, Lady Herbert. But I've got reinforcements coming from the village. We'll get through it."

"We'll let you get back to it," Aunt Roz said graciously. She headed for the end of the hallway and the staircase. I took the time to give Constable Collins a reassuring smile before I followed.

"Thank you, Constable. Let us know when you want those fingerprints."

"You'll be the first," Collins said, and withdrew back into Dominic Rivers's room.

As I followed Aunt Roz down the hallway to the top of the stairs, I reflected that as *au revoirs* go, it was a rather ominous one.

. . .

DOWNSTAIRS IN THE DRAWING ROOM, Uncle Herbert had pulled Francis back inside after their talk, and Constance had joined them. Francis looked a bit better, or at least he looked a bit less likely to go off half-cocked than the last time I had seen him. He held Constance's hand and was talking to her, whilst Uncle Herbert was watching his wife cross the floor towards him.

I waved in their direction, but elected not to add myself to the group. Aunt Roz could tell them what we had talked about, and Wolfgang had been joined by Christopher, who must have taken pity on our beleaguered German friend. I headed that way instead, and took a seat on the opposite side of the small table. "Good afternoon."

Wolfgang ran an experienced eye over me. His mouth curved up, so I assumed he approved of my new outfit. Christopher, on the other hand—

"You horrible chit. How dare you go upstairs and change while I've had to spend all day in these clothes?"

"You were outside with Francis and your father," I said. "You could have chosen to go upstairs instead, to change."

"How would that have looked, if I prioritized my own comfort over my brother's mental stability?" He didn't wait for me to answer, just added, "Tea?"

"If you don't mind."

We don't stand on ceremony in our household: Christopher pours as often as I do. "What's wrong?" he added, as he handed me the cup. "You look perturbed."

"Thank you." I set it down on the table. "I'm not perturbed. Or rather, of course I am. Two people are dead. Three if you count Cecily's baby, although I suppose it might have been a bit early to do so."

Christopher made a face, and I added, "But in case you were worried, no. Nothing else has happened, other than that Constable Collins gave me a rather ominous goodbye upstairs earlier."

"What did he say?"

I told him what Collins had said, and watched the curve of his mouth relax. "I'm sure he meant nothing by it. You're not a suspect."

"I might be a suspect. I was the last one to see her alive, and—"

"We were all there when she died," Christopher interrupted.

"Yes, of course. But I meant last night. I was the last one to see her last night. To someone who doesn't know me and love me, I might have been the one to give her whatever killed her. And I was also the last one to speak to Dominic Rivers this afternoon."

"I would think that that makes you a likely victim rather than a murderess," Christopher said, and then seemed to realize what he was saying, because he added, "No, of course not. There's no reason for anyone to murder you."

"Someone shot at me earlier," I pointed out.

"Coincidence," Christopher said airily.

I shrugged. "I had no reason to want Cecily dead. It wasn't your baby. Crispin says it wasn't his. I know it wasn't Francis's. I don't care about anyone else."

Christopher cleared his throat delicately, and I added, with a bright smile, "Of course that doesn't include you, Wolfgang. But you'd never even met Cecily Fletcher, had you? So there's no reason to think you were involved."

"I didn't know the girl," Wolfgang agreed. "Although it was very sad, what happened to her."

Yes, it had been. And nothing much either Christopher or I could say in response to a statement like that.

"What did Uncle Herbert have to say for himself?" I asked Christopher instead.

He shook his head. "Nothing to the point. What about Aunt Roz?"

"Nothing to the point, either. She had a talk with Lady Violet and Olivia upstairs. I listened outside the door."

Christopher's lips twitched and I remembered, yet again, that Wolfgang was sitting next to me. I probably wasn't making a very good impression on him at this point.

"They don't know what happened," I added, ignoring it. "They didn't know who Cecily had been sharing her bed with, but Olivia said it was someone Cecily had claimed that she couldn't marry. I don't know whether that was because he was married, engaged, or simply a cad."

"Could be any of the above," Christopher agreed. "I wouldn't want to marry most of the people here."

I wouldn't, either. Whether that was actually a possibility or not. In Christopher's, it mostly wasn't.

"Your mother thinks that Olivia is sweet on the Hon Reggie," I said. "I had suspected that anyway, from watching them yesterday. But the way she talked about him seemed to confirm it."

Christopher nodded. "He seems like a decent enough chap. Not as handsy as Geoffrey, nor as belligerent as Bilge, nor as immoral as Rivers."

I flicked him a glance. "Don't you mean that he's not as immoral as your cousin?"

"No," Christopher said. "I said what I meant, and I meant what I said."

"Rivers is dead," I pointed out. "You shouldn't speak about him that way."

"Dead, schmed," Christopher said. "He was a dope dealer. He got Ronnie Blanton hooked on cocaine, and I hold him at least partially responsible for that mess we found ourselves in during Crispin's birthday in June. The fact that he's dead now too, doesn't change what he was."

I supposed it didn't. "Nice company we keep."

He snorted. "Isn't it just?"

"Have you spoken to St George? His father was chewing him out earlier, and I can't imagine that this day has been particularly easy for him, with two of his friends dead."

"I haven't." He flicked me a look. "He's over there, with Laetitia and her parents and Uncle Harold. He looks intact from here, although you could go over and inquire as to his health. I would pay money to see that."

I made a face. "No, thank you. He made that bed. Better let him get used to lying in it."

"Cold," Christopher opined.

I shrugged. "That's going to be his family for the rest of his life. I can't spend the rest of mine trying to rescue him from himself."

Wolfgang had been looking from one to the other of us during this exchange. Now he said, "You spend a lot of time worrying about your cousin."

"He's not my cousin," I said, at the same time as Christopher said, "With good reason."

"Can the young man not take care of himself?"

"Of course he can. But that doesn't mean we don't worry."

"What's to worry about?" Wolfgang wanted to know, eyes on the table where Crispin sat, looking cross, surrounded by his father, his fiancée, and his future parents-in-law. Laetitia was gesticulating with the hand that sported the obscenely opulent Sutherland ring, and it caught the light and flashed it around the room.

"He's engaged to a beautiful woman with a wealthy, titled family," Wolfgang added, "one who is young enough to give him many children and lovely enough to assure that they are attractive..."

Christopher made a face. I did, too, but probably not for the same reason. "We're more concerned with his future happiness than his progeny," Christopher explained.

Wolfgang looked nonplussed. Perhaps he didn't understand why a beautiful wife and lots of pretty children wouldn't be enough for any man to be happy, and if he couldn't, I didn't think I could explain it to him.

But it didn't matter anyway, because before I could say anything further, there was the sound of a motor outside, and a moment later, the long, sleek silhouette of the black mortuary car moved past the windows. It came to a stop at the bottom of the stairs, followed a moment later by a standard police issue Crossley Tender.

CHAPTER SEVENTEEN

I SHOULD HAVE KNOWN WHAT—OR rather who—was coming. Of course I should have. I'm chagrined to say that the idea hadn't even crossed my mind. When Tom appeared in the door to the drawing room, in a natty tweed suit and with his Homburg in hand, my mouth dropped open. Christopher's eyes lit up, and I knew it was only the necessity for proper behavior that kept him in his seat instead of hurtling across the floor.

"Let me guess," I said when I had got my voice back. "This is your doing?"

He removed his eyes from Tom to spare me a glance. "I rang him up, yes."

"Why didn't you tell me? We even discussed how we both wished Tom was here." He didn't answer, and I added, "Was it before or after Cecily died?"

"After," Christopher said. "Although that wasn't why. I simply thought he might want to know that someone had shot at us."

Well, yes, of course he would want to know that. He has

spent months ensuring that nothing bad happens to Christopher, including yanking him bodily out of questionable nightclubs before police raids begin. Police raids Tom only knows about because he's a police officer. I'm certain there's some sort of misconduct associated with that.

Not that I'm about to complain when it keeps Christopher safe, of course.

But yes, when I thought about it, it was not surprising at all that Tom seemed to have dropped whatever he was doing in London on a Saturday morning, to jump in the Crossley and motor to Dorset at breakneck speed. Of course he would do that if it was possible.

His first look once he stepped through the doorway had been for Christopher, of course. Tom's hazel eyes had lingered for long enough to assure himself that nothing was wrong. I got the next look, and so did Wolfgang, surely only because he was sitting on the other side of Christopher.

With that done, Tom shifted his attention to the rest of the room. It was just in time for Perkins, who had been trailing behind, to appear in the doorway and announce, a little breathlessly, "Detective Sergeant Thomas Gardiner, my lord and lady."

There was a moment's silence, and then Aunt Roz flowed to her feet. "Thomas! How lovely to see you!"

It wasn't her job to welcome guests to Marsden Manor, of course, but the entire Marsden family was glued to their seats, in various poses of shock and incredulity—or in justice to them, perhaps simple surprise. Geoffrey, who was sitting with Violet and Olivia and the Honorable Reggie, looked rather more worried than anything else, while Laetitia was staring daggers at Crispin, as if any of this was his fault.

"Come," Aunt Roz added, tucking her hand through Tom's

arm. "Let me introduce you to our hosts, and then you can sit and have tea with Kit and Pippa."

She tugged him across the floor towards the head table. I watched from the other side of the room as Lady Euphemia and her daughter dredged up whatever pleasantries they could —Lord Maurice is always pleasant, while Uncle Harold rarely is—and then Tom exchanged a few words with Crispin (I assume they were congratulations on the engagement, because Crispin looked panicked for a moment before good manners took over) and Aunt Roz brought Tom back around to us.

"I presume this is your doing, Christopher?" she asked sternly as she handed him over.

Christopher nodded. "I'm afraid so, Mum. Hullo, Tom." He smiled politely, but the absolute delight in his eyes gave him away. I'm not sure how many of the others in the room could see it—when I flicked a glance at Wolfgang, he wasn't even looking at Christopher—but I had no illusions about what his mother noticed. Aunt Roz isn't stupid, and she knows her children.

"Behave yourself, Kit," she told him. "We're in public."

He flicked her a glance. "Of course, Mother. When do I not?"

Aunt Roz muttered something, but didn't actually respond. It was probably for the best. I don't think she knows exactly what Christopher gets up to in London, but I also think she has a good idea that he gets up to something.

She took herself off to the table she shared with Uncle Herbert, Francis, and Constance, and I took over the hostess duties. "Good afternoon, Tom. It's good to see you. Won't you have a seat?"

"Don't mind if I do, Pippa." He gave me a broad smile and a wink as he put his hand on the back of the chair next to me, opposite from Christopher. "It's good to see you, too. You as well, Natterdorff."

He nodded politely to Wolfgang as he pulled out the chair and seated himself. Tom was one former soldier who didn't seem to have a problem with Wolfgang's nationality, anyway.

"Detective Sergeant Gardiner," Wolfgang retorted politely. I thought I heard his heels click together under the table, but it could have been my imagination. "A pleasure to see you again. I trust everything is proceeding well with the criminals from last month?"

Tom nodded. "Oh, yes. All taken care of. They're all three of them tucked away in Holloway and Hammersmith. They're not getting out anytime soon."

That was good to know, anyway. Of the murderers we had encountered over the past half a year or so—several of whom were now dead—Myrtle Cavanaugh was the one I would least like to encounter again. She had hated me when she went to prison, and would no doubt hate me whenever she was released. And she was definitely the type to hold a grudge. Hopefully she would be in there for long enough that I wouldn't have to worry about retribution for a few decades, at least.

"I see the chaps from the mortuary finally got here," Tom commented, just as a teacup and saucer, along with a pastry plate, dropped onto the tablecloth in front of him. "Thank you."

He smiled up at Nellie.

"Goodness," I said, "you get around, Nellie, don't you? I didn't think this was your job."

It's not normally the chambermaid's duty to serve tea, and I didn't think Lady Euphemia was the type to dispense with the usual customs.

Nellie dropped a quick curtsey. "Jenny wasn't feeling well, Miss."

I wrinkled my brow. "She's all right, isn't she?" Surely we wouldn't have yet one more death on our hands?

Nellie seemed to sense what I was really asking, because she assured me, "She's fine, Miss. Just tired. I offered to serve tea so she could put her feet up for a few minutes while the family is busy."

Ah. Yes, Lady Euphemia probably wasn't the type to look kindly upon any dilly-dallying of that nature from the staff, either.

"I won't tell them anything," I said, and Nellie beamed.

"Thank you, Miss." She curtsied and withdrew. Wolfgang's eyes lingered on her neat little figure for a moment, and so did Christopher's, albeit with a far less appreciative look. So, for that matter, did Geoffrey's, from across the room. Violet, who was sitting next to him, made a face as she lifted her teacup and took a sip.

I nudged Christopher's ankle with the pointy toe of my shoe under the table, and he flushed and came back to himself. "Right you are." He cleared his throat. "The mortuary van was actually here hours ago. This is the second time today."

Tom's brows arched. "You'd better tell me what's going on, Kit. I seem to have missed some of the details."

He sipped his tea calmly while we told him everything that had happened since last night. Cecily's secret and her appearance in the bathroom, followed by her condition this morning when I went to wake her, and then the gunshot—which Tom already knew about.

After that there was Cecily's death and my conversation with Dominic Rivers, the pennyroyal, poison and plant, and finally Rivers's murder.

Tom's face twisted in something that was half pity and half chagrin. "There goes our case."

Scotland Yard's case against the dope dealer, I assumed. I knew they had been working on one for the past few months, ever since Dominic Rivers landed on their watch list after his involvement in the Frederick Montrose murder case.

"It would be difficult to arrest someone who's dead," I agreed as I lifted my teacup daintily and took a sip.

Tom slanted me a look. "Difficult to get information out of him, too."

Yes, of course. "We assume that his presence here was prompted by someone who wanted a substance that would either kill Cecily outright, or if not that, at least get rid of her problem for her."

Tom nodded. "That makes sense. Abortion is illegal, but not so illegal that someone with the right connections can't get his hands on something to deal with it."

"Not so illegal that someone couldn't walk down the road and pick a handful of pennyroyal, either."

He shook his head. "No, of course not. There are always going to be ways and means." He put his cup in the saucer with a decisive click. "I don't suppose you have any idea who that person, or persons, might be?"

So he had already come to the conclusion, as had I, that there might be more than one of them.

"We have ideas," I said, "of course. Lots of them. But no proof. Nor any real indication of who is actually guilty."

"Tell me what you think," Tom said, and included Christopher in the look he gave me. "You're both smart young people, and you've been through this a few times now. I'd be interested to know what you think."

"Are you going to work with the local constabulary?" I

asked. "I thought you were here because Christopher rang you up."

"I *am* here because Kit rang me up," Tom said. "But as I'm here, I ought to offer my services in an unofficial way, don't you think?"

"I think Constable Collins would be delighted to have you," I told him, "even unofficially. We were just talking about you earlier. You remember Collins, don't you? From the case at the Dower House?"

He nodded. "Of course I do. He was very helpful back in May."

"Well, he's upstairs," I said. "Last time I saw him, he was in Dominic Rivers's room, but now that the doctor and the mortuary van are here to take away the body, I imagine he'll be back to searching the upstairs rooms shortly."

"Searching the rooms?"

It was Wolfgang who asked, and I turned to him. "Yes. They always do, when someone's dead. He went through mine earlier."

Wolfgang looked concerned, and I added, reassuringly, "You have nothing to worry about. We all know that you didn't even know any of these people before you came here yesterday. Did you?"

He shook his head, and I added, "See? Whoever killed them both—and it had to be the same person, don't you think, Tom? Or the same people, at any rate?"

Tom shook his head. "I'm not going to speculate, Pippa."

I nodded. "Well, if someone invited Rivers here so he could bring something with him that would deal with Cecily's pregnancy, that someone had to have known about the pregnancy before yesterday. And had to have known Rivers and what his business was before yesterday, as well. So Wolfgang is out, wouldn't you say?"

Tom eyed Wolfgang in silence for a moment. Not for long enough that the latter began to squirm, but I could tell it was a near thing.

"I would say so," Tom said eventually, after what must have felt to Wolfgang like a small eternity, but which was probably no more than a few seconds. "What happened to Miss Fletcher must have been planned, at least far enough in advance that the substance, whether it came from Mr. Rivers or the ditch down the road, was obtained and, in the case of the leaves, steeped. That might have been done in an hour or two, if whoever went picking had the freedom to come and go as they pleased, but if it was Rivers who procured the substance, that part had to be planned at least a few days in advance."

"Or both," I said. Tom arched his brows at me, and I added, "We have a theory—"

"Hers," Christopher shot in, and Tom's lips twitched. I gave them both a crushing look before I continued.

"—that it might not have been a murder, but an accidental overdose. If Cecily herself took a dose, or someone gave her one, and then someone else came along and gave her another—"

Tom nodded. "It might not have been premeditated murder, you mean. Simply manslaughter."

"Something like that."

"Still an arrestable offense," Tom said and pushed his chair away from the table. "If young Mr. Rivers hadn't already been dead, I would have had to arrest him under the *Offences Against the Person Act*, Section 59, whether Miss Fletcher was alive or not."

I made a face, since I knew exactly what he was talking about. Dominic Rivers had told me about it earlier, before he headed up the stairs to the second floor and his doom.

Tom stood. "As nice as it was to see you both—" His eyes lingered on Christopher for a long second, before his attention flicked over to Wolfgang and he changed it to, "—all three of you, I ought to make myself useful. Collins is upstairs, you said?"

"On the second floor last I saw him," I said. "That's where most of us were sleeping. Christopher was on the first floor with the family—Constance and Francis, too; cousins to the bride and groom respectively, you know—but the rest of us plebeians were on the top floor."

"Miss Fletcher? Rivers?"

I nodded. "Both of them, along with Violet and Olivia, Wolfgang and I, and the Honorable Reginald Fish, who shared with Rivers. He's the chap sitting with Geoffrey Marsden and the two girls."

Tom eyed the Honorable Reggie for a moment before he asked, "Is that Bilge Fortescue over there?"

"Oh." I had forgotten about the Fortescues again. "Yes. They're on the first floor, for some reason. I don't think either of them is related to either Laetitia or Crispin, but the bigger rooms are there, and I suppose they rated one. We're all stuffed into the smaller rooms up above."

"I remember Bilge," Tom said, and of course he did. He had been at Eton two years behind Francis and three above Christopher and Crispin. He would have dealt with William Fortescue for at least a couple of those years.

"I haven't gotten to know him," I answered, "although his wife used her wiles on Christopher earlier."

Tom arched his brows. "Is that so?"

He glanced at Christopher, who shook his head. "Don't be silly, Pippa. She wanted an arm to cling to on her way down the stairs, that's all."

"And to ask you questions about what was going on upstairs," I answered.

Christopher nodded. "That as well, I suppose."

He didn't look at me. He and Tom were sharing some form of silent communication that made Christopher's cheeks turn pink and Tom's lips twitch. When they noticed me notice, they stopped, and Tom cleared his throat. "I'll just be going, then."

"Take care, Tom," Christopher said, and I added, "Let us know if you discover anything exciting, would you? It's boring, sitting here waiting for something to happen."

Tom hid another smile—this one at my expense, I assumed —and a flicker of a look at Wolfgang. I grimaced. I hadn't intended to make it sound like he was boring, but the truth was, I would much rather be upstairs trying to figure out who had killed Cecily Fletcher and Dominic Rivers, than be sitting here at the tea table, behaving like a perfect lady while entertaining a potential suitor.

Tom made his way towards the door, and I turned to Wolfgang, determined to make up for my *faux pas*. "You must think we're all ghouls, with our interest in dead bodies."

"Last month was exciting," Wolfgang said blandly. "I'm happy the perpetrators are behind bars, however. I would hate for anything bad to happen."

Yes, so would I. "I'm mostly worried about Myrtle," I confessed. "Sid isn't a bad bloke, just weak, and I think the same is true for Ruth. She just fell in with the wrong crowd, or more accurately, with Myrtle."

After a second, I added, "Not that they don't deserve to rot in prison for a long time for what they did, of course. But it was Myrtle who came up with the plan and talked Ruth into executing it with her. And she'd execute me too, if she could. Although I don't imagine that she'll get the chance, do you?"

I had been chatting with Wolfgang, but it was Christopher who shook his head. "Not likely, Pippa. There's too much evidence and far too much cold-bloodedness there to let her off.

And after she has served her term at Holloway, she'll be deported back to America, I'd think. They deported Billy Chang after he had served his sentence."

I nodded. "That's what I think, too, but I'm happy to have it confirmed. Having her escorted to the docks and put on a boat instead of being set free to roam after her sentence would be a load off my mind."

"Who is this Chang?" Wolfgang wanted to know, and I turned back to him.

"I suppose you haven't been in England long enough to hear about him, have you? Billy Chang was a dope dealer in Limehouse in the early 1920s. They arrested him in 1924, and kept him in prison until 1925, and then he was deported. Back to China, supposedly, but—"

"—rumor has it that he's running a nightclub on the French Riviera now," Christopher said gleefully. And added, "That's from the American gutter press, however, so I don't know how reliable it is."

Not very, I imagined. "He's not in England anymore, at any rate. Let's hope that the same thing happens to Myrtle Cavanaugh."

"Hear, hear." Christopher raised his teacup. I clinked mine against it. A little belatedly, Wolfgang lifted his cup, too, and I gave that the same treatment. We all took a sip. The tea was getting cold, and I put it down with a grimace. Across the room, Crispin was scowling our way, and I scowled back, until Christopher nudged me. "Keep your attention over here, Pippa. Laetitia doesn't like you any better than Myrtle does, and you don't want to give her any excuse to take a potshot at you."

"Like someone did this morning, do you mean?" I eyed him. "You don't think it was Laetitia, do you?"

"She was out there in the woods," Christopher said, "with a

gun, and she would dearly love to get rid of you. But I imagine that Crispin was attached to her side, and he wouldn't have put up with that, so chances are he would have said something to you had that been the case."

"Unless she threatened him into silence," I said.

"And how would she have managed that, do you suppose?"

"I'm sure I have no idea," I said. I wouldn't have had the first inkling how to go about it, but then I wasn't engaged to Crispin, nor had I ever been intimate with him. "Perhaps she invoked Uncle Harold?"

Christopher snorted. "His Grace might want this marriage to work, certainly above and beyond anyone Crispin wants to marry, but I can't imagine him condoning attempted murder. Can you?"

"I suspected Uncle Harold of Abigail's murder two months ago," I said, "so I suppose I can. Besides, it's me, isn't it? We both know that he doesn't like me. Aunt Charlotte didn't, either."

Christopher murmured something indistinguishable that nonetheless wasn't a denial, and I added, "Although as far as Abigail is concerned, she was obviously much more of a threat to Uncle Harold's plans for Crispin than I am."

Christopher gave me a look, one that lasted a second or two too long, before he told me, "She was no threat to Uncle Harold's plans for Crispin at all. Elizabeth wasn't Crispin's child."

"Of course. But we didn't know that at the time. And for as long as we didn't, Uncle Harold had reason to want her dead. You must admit that little Bess looked enough like both of you to be yours."

Christopher shrugged, but before he could say anything to confirm or deny my assertion—and there was no way he could have denied it: the baby had been a perfect Astley, from her fair hair to her blue eyes and that little cupid's bow mouth—a choked cry came from the other side of the room and stopped all our conversations dead. I looked up in time to see Lady Violet Cummings stumble to her feet, with enough force to knock her chair over backwards.

CHAPTER EIGHTEEN

MY FIRST THOUGHT, if indeed I had the time to think any thoughts at all, was that Geoffrey must have been objectionable. Four months ago, he had had me backed into the corner of a sofa at the Dower House, and had proceeded to shove his hand up under the hem of my skirt. I wouldn't have been surprised at all, had he decided to use the same technique on Violet under the tablecloth.

But then Violet's eyes rolled back in her head and she crumpled into a heap, incidentally knocking the back of her head against the overturned chair on the way down, and possibly giving herself a concussion on top of whatever else was wrong.

For a second, we all sat frozen, wide-eyed and staring. Then Francis jumped up from his seat, and so did Bilge, from opposite sides of the room. As they came together over the body, Crispin too murmured an excuse, and went to join them.

As if those movements had pulled the plug from the dam, chatter started up around the room. I turned to Christopher. "What on earth do you suppose happened?"

"Something in the tea?" Christopher suggested.

I squinted at him. "My first thought was that Geoffrey had molested her under the table."

Christopher's face twisted in distaste, and so did Wolfgang's. "Lord Geoffrey is in the habit of molesting women?" he asked.

"He tried to stick his hand under my hem once," I answered. "I thought he might have done the same thing to Violet."

"That doesn't explain why she fainted," Christopher said.

I turned back to him. "Perhaps she's simply too fine-minded to be able to handle that sort of thing."

He snorted. "Unlike you, do you mean? You didn't exactly handle it well when it happened to you."

No, admittedly I hadn't. I had neither squealed nor fainted —the Dower House sat on Marsden property, and I didn't know Geoffrey well enough then to know that this was his usual modus operandi, and that trying to be polite about it wouldn't work. But I had been out of sorts for the rest of the evening. Christopher had had to lock me in my bedchamber, as a matter of fact, until Constance could come upstairs so I'd have company.

"Besides," Christopher added, "considering her history with Crispin, she's hardly what you'd call maidenly, is she?"

Wolfgang looked shocked. I shook my head. "I suppose she's not, now you mention it. And she spent the evening yesterday with him. Geoffrey, I mean. I can't imagine that there wasn't some kind of hanky-panky going on."

Over on the floor, Francis and Bilge were kneeling on either side of Violet's prone body. One of them had her wrist in a grip, no doubt fumbling for her pulse, while the other was peeling her eyelid back and checking whether her pupil was responding to light. I had seen Francis do both before, both with Cecily earlier this morning and with Christopher back in May, so it must be standard procedure.

When he put his hand under her head and pulled it away again, his fingers came back stained with red. He made a face and reached towards his pocket, but Crispin got there first, dangling a handkerchief in front of Francis's face. "How is she?"

The room was quiet enough, even with the whispers, that the question was easily heard.

"Alive," Bilge said shortly. He let go of Violet's hand and brushed his own fingers against the fabric of his trousers. "Not well."

"Clearly not." Crispin's voice was as dry as the Sahara, or a particularly good gin and tonic. "Can you tell me what's wrong?"

"Something in her tea," Francis said, as he finished wiping his fingers clean. He looked at the handkerchief as if he contemplated handing it back for a moment before he shoved it into his own pocket instead. "Pupils are dilated. Most likely it's more of the same thing."

I shuddered. I couldn't help it. Cecily's eyes had been dilated as well, fixed and staring, and then she had died. I cleared my throat. "The doctor should be upstairs, for the —um…"

…*body*, was what I had meant to say. But it was perhaps not the best word to use right now, so I skipped right past that thorny issue, and simply added, "I'll run upstairs and—"

"I'll go." Crispin took off across the drawing room and through the door. I could hear his rapid footsteps down the hallway and then fading up the stairs.

I made a face. I had wanted an excuse to get out of the room, but he had removed himself faster than I could have got up from the table, so I let him go without demur. He would probably be quicker than me in every other respect, as well, and Violet deserved that. Besides, he was probably more worried about her than I was.

Not that I was indifferent to her plight. Not at all. Nor was I indifferent to my own. A third death on top of the two we had already seen today had to be some sort of record. At least when we'd had to deal with three deaths at Sutherland Hall in April, one of them had been the murderer of the other two. This was getting out of hand.

"Is there anything we can do?" I called out to Francis, who looked up and met my eyes and then shook his head.

"I'm afraid not, Pippa. If the doctor is upstairs, perhaps he can do something. But if it's the same substance again, it'll be the same outcome again as well, I fear."

Yes, I feared the same. Several of the others looked ill at the idea, including Geoffrey. He was likely to be especially affected, poor chap, seeing as he had been sitting right next to her, chatting her up, when this happened.

(Did I feel a touch bad for suspecting Lord Geoffrey's wandering hands of being to blame for Violet's reaction? In light of what had actually happened, perhaps I did, just a bit. I was willing to give him the benefit of the doubt, at any rate, and assign him enough compassion to assume he was bothered by the situation.)

I cleared my throat. "Can't we... I don't know, stick a finger down her throat and make her rid herself of the poison or something?"

Francis gave me a jaundiced look, while several of the others, fine-minded people like Lady Euphemia and her daughter, winced.

"Miss Fletcher rid herself of the poison last night, Pippa," my cousin reminded me. "And it made no difference, did it?"

No, it hadn't. But— "Shouldn't we try, at least? Just in case it would help?"

"We don't know that it wouldn't hurt," Francis said. "If it's not the same thing, but something else instead, it could hurt her throat coming back up. Better to wait for the doctor to have a look. A minute or two won't matter one way or the other."

I made a face, but acquiesced. I wasn't an expert, but Francis was. Or as much of an expert as we had access to right now. And he didn't look as somber as he had upstairs, after first seeing Cecily, so perhaps the situation wasn't as dire.

Holding onto that possibility, I did as I was bid, and resolved myself to wait. It wasn't easy. I am not by nature a patient person, and the circumstances—with Violet's shallow breathing practically rattling through the silent room—made things worse. When he couldn't handle my fidgeting any longer, Christopher reached over and took my hand, and threaded his fingers through mine. I gave him a grateful look, one he returned with a twist of his mouth, but neither of us spoke.

It wasn't actually that long a wait. It felt like a long time, but it was only a few minutes before we heard footsteps coming down the stairs again. There were several sets of them this time: Crispin's, quick and light. Tom's, heavier but no less rapid. Constable Collins, thumping in his regulation boots. And bringing up the rear, the slower steps of an older man.

Bilge had gone back to his wife after ascertaining that there was nothing he could do for Violet. Like me and Christopher, they were sitting hand in hand at their table. Serena looked pale under the makeup. Bilge, with his carroty hair and matching complexion, was always pale, but I thought his freckles might stand out a bit more than usual at the moment.

Crispin popped through the door first, with Tom and Collins on his heels. They all three converged on the body. It was only a moment or two, however, before the doctor made his way through the door and across the floor towards them.

Things moved quickly after that. I hadn't been terribly impressed with the man during Christopher's... let's call it illness, at the Dower House in May. The doctor had looked him over and told us that there was nothing he—or we—could do to help, other than to wait for Christopher to sleep off the overdose of Veronal, and that hopefully he would wake up on his own once he was ready, none the worse for wear. That wasn't what I wanted to hear at the time.

It wasn't what I wanted to hear now either, but again, it was what the doctor told us. "Best get her up to bed where she can be comfortable," he added.

Lady Euphemia cleared her throat. "Wouldn't she be better off under medical care?"

I translated the question to mean, 'shouldn't you take her with you so we don't have to deal with her?' and so did the doctor, it seemed. He grunted, and then said, "There's nothing anyone can do, my lady. She'll either wake up or she won't."

I mouthed the last sentence right along with him, and rolled my eyes when Christopher looked at me. "He said the same thing about you. Word for word."

"Hmm." Christopher glanced at the prone body. "I did wake up. Maybe she will, too."

"You were fed an overdose of Veronal," I said fretfully. "It's not the same scenario."

"Perhaps she was fed an underdose of pennyroyal and it'll be all right." He put his finger to his lips before I could respond. "Just watch, Pippa. We'll talk about it later."

No doubt we would. Although I didn't want to watch, really. It felt ghoulish to stare as Francis scooped Violet up and strode towards the door with her, her head lolling over his forearm and her hand dangling uselessly, tennis bracelet sending sparks of light across the walls and ceiling.

I had expected Tom to take that job, honestly, since he was bigger and stronger than either Crispin or Constable Collins, and he had the official standing that Francis lacked. I was surprised when he nodded to Francis and told him, "You take her, Astley. Do you know where her room is?"

"Top floor," Francis grunted, as he stood with Violet in his arms.

"I'll show you." Collins hurried towards the door ahead of Francis, while the doctor brought up the rear.

"Come back downstairs when you're done," Tom called after them, and then they passed out of sight and were in the hallway, and Tom turned to the rest of us. "Have a seat, St George."

He nodded to Crispin. Once the latter was seated, and once Laetitia had staked her claim with a possessive hand to his arm, Tom added, "In case anyone missed the introduction earlier, I'm Detective Sergeant Thomas Gardiner with Scotland Yard."

There was a quick indrawn breath from somewhere in the room, so it was obvious that someone must not have realized exactly who Tom was. Detective Sergeant, yes. Scotland Yard, perhaps not.

"A crime seems to have been committed in this room during the last hour," Tom continued, "and as such, you'll all be required to stay in your seats until we've had a chance to talk to you all."

Euphemia's eyes narrowed at that, and Tom must have seen it, or sensed it, or perhaps just expected it, from previous experience with her type, because he turned to her with a practiced, professional smile. "Lady Marsden, Lord Marsden—" He gave Maurice a deferential inclination of the head, that none of us were thick enough to believe was actually deferential, "if I may have the use of one of your spare rooms to conduct individual interviews? Perhaps a study or library?"

Maurice cleared his throat. "There's a library next door," he indicated the connecting door, "and a study beyond that, between the library and the outer hall. You're welcome to use either of them. Or anywhere else that suits you."

"Thank you, sir." Tom took us all in. "As soon as the others come back, we'll get started. We'll start with you, Lord Geoffrey, since you were sitting next to Lady Violet."

Geoffrey gulped, but nodded. His mother shot him a worried look before she opened her mouth. "Detective Sergeant?"

Tom inclined his head politely. "Yes, Lady Marsden?"

"The local constabulary is in charge of this investigation, is it not?"

Tom's brows rose, and I didn't blame him. That sounded remarkably like the runup to an objection. His voice, however, was perfectly pleasant when he told her, "Officially that's correct, madam. But with two murders and what appears to be two additional attempts, all within a twenty-four hour period, all in this house, the Chief Constable feels—and I quite agree with him—that the local constabulary can use some help. I was here already, so I offered to step in."

Lady Euphemia looked like she had sunk her teeth directly into a lemon, but she capitulated. I hid a smile, but seemingly not quite well enough, because Laetitia slanted a fulminating look in my direction. Christopher dug an elbow into my ribs. "Stop it, Pippa. You know who'll be paying for that, don't you?"

Crispin would, I assumed, once Laetitia had the chance to properly harangue him without having to moderate her voice. "That's what he gets for shackling himself to her, isn't it?"

"If you didn't want him to propose," Christopher said, "you shouldn't have given him your blessing."

"I'd hardly call it that, Christopher."

Christopher ignored my attempt to debate the situation again, and understandably so, since we'd been over this *ad nauseam* these past couple of weeks. "Just behave," he told me. "We'll be done soon enough."

"If you say so," I answered doubtfully, although I settled in to wait while Constable Collins and Francis came back downstairs, and while Tom took Geoffrey off to the study to apply the thumb screws, and while Laetitia hissed volubly in Crispin's ear.

After Geoffrey it was Olivia's turn, and then the Honorable Reggie. Once the table that Violet had occupied was empty, Tom moved on to anyone else who might have something to contribute, which was the rest of the Marsden family initially. I assumed that he would be asking them questions about Dominic Rivers and who might have invited him to Marsden Manor, and other inquiries of that nature. As soon as they were all away, and only the current Duke of Sutherland and his heir were left at the head table, Uncle Harold began hissing at Crispin quite as vociferously as Laetitia had done.

"Poor chap," Christopher muttered. "He just can't catch a break, can he?"

I sniffed. "It's his own—"

He slanted me a look. "It's not his fault that he was born to Aunt Charlotte and Uncle Harold, Pippa. He couldn't help that."

Well, no. I supposed he couldn't. "I don't like your uncle."

Christopher sighed. "I'm well aware of it."

"I didn't like your aunt, either. She tried to shoot me once."

On the other side of me, Wolfgang's eyes widened.

"She's dead," Christopher pointed out. "I'm afraid you'll have to get over that."

"I'm over it. Mostly. It just comes back at certain times." Such as when I was irritated with Uncle Harold and the way he always tried to beat Crispin into submission, sometimes literally.

But then Tom came back and fetched Crispin, and Uncle Harold was left to sit alone, impotently stewing with no one to berate. I smiled, pleased, and of course he looked over and caught me. I can't imagine that he knew the reason for my happiness, but he scowled at me nonetheless. I pretended that I hadn't seen, because waving would have been rude.

The drawing room emptied out agonizingly slowly. After Crispin was called away to the study, Tom let Uncle Harold wait, and instead pulled in Constance, and then Francis, and then finally Aunt Roz. At that point, Uncle Herbert got up and joined his brother, and the two of them fell into a low-voiced conversation. Too low for me to catch, more's the pity.

After Aunt Roz, there was Bilge and Serena Fortescue's turn, and then finally, Tom came and removed Wolfgang. As soon as he was through the door, Uncle Herbert beckoned. "Come here, Kit."

Christopher sighed, but he pushed his chair back and took my arm. "Come along, Pippa."

"He didn't ask for me," I pointed out, even as I allowed myself to be hauled to my feet.

"Father won't mind," Christopher said.

Uncle Harold certainly would, but before I could say so, Christopher had carried on. "Unless you really want to sit at this table by yourself until Tom comes back?"

I didn't, of course, so I let him propel me across the floor by my elbow. "Father." He inclined his head politely. "Uncle Harold."

"Your Grace." I did a barely-there curtsey. I knew that Uncle Harold was peeved at my presence, and I figured it couldn't hurt to show a bit of respect for the title, if for nothing else. "Uncle Herbert."

Him, I gave a warm smile.

"Kit, Pippa." Uncle Herbert smiled back, while Uncle Harold gave us a cool nod.

"Sit," Uncle Herbert added. He gestured to the vacated chairs on the other side of the table. He was in Laetitia's seat, and I let Christopher take Crispin's, after he had seated me in the empty chair where Aunt Charlotte might have sat, had Crispin's mother been alive. "Roz told me that she'd talked to you earlier."

I nodded, as I arranged my skirt across my knees and my hands in my lap, like a proper young woman. "She had a conversation with the two young ladies upstairs while I eaves-dropped. Then we discussed it."

Uncle Herbert grinned, but merely asked, "Was anything interesting said?"

"Nothing that would explain what happened earlier." I glanced over at the spot on the floor where Lady Violet Cummings had lain. The chair was still there, overturned, waiting for the local constabulary to get around to processing what I assumed would turn out to be a crime scene. "Olivia Barnsley seems to be enamored with Reggie Fish. Violet was lying about something, or so Aunt Roz thinks."

"Violet is the young lady who had the medical incident?"

I nodded. "It's open season on St George's old flames this weekend, it seems."

Uncle Harold inhaled sharply enough that his nostrils flared, but he didn't speak.

"Surely you're not insinuating that Crispin is involved,

Pippa," Uncle Herbert said, while Christopher rolled his eyes expressively.

"Of course not." I smirked. "I just find it interesting that they've both enjoyed St George's favors in the past, and now one is dead and the other unconscious."

Christopher muttered something, and his father cast him a look. "What was that, son?"

"Someone shot at Pippa this morning," Christopher repeated, in what had to be a *non sequitur*, because if it wasn't—

"I'm hardly what you'd call one of St George's old flames, Christopher."

By then, Uncle Herbert was talking over me. "I know, Kit. Francis told me. Although he didn't seem convinced that Pippa was the intended target."

"Of course I wasn't," I said irritably. "If anyone was aiming at me, it wasn't because I'm me. It was most likely because I look a bit like Cecily Fletcher."

All three men looked at me. Uncle Harold looked hostile, Uncle Herbert thoughtful, and Christopher amused.

"It's much more likely that it was simply a stray shot," I added. "No one has admitted to aiming in the direction of the house, and I assume they were told not to, so whoever it was, is probably just trying to hide that they made a mistake."

"Or they won't admit it because it was on purpose," Christopher said.

I shook my head. "You're being silly, Christopher. Even if someone is trying to eliminate all of St George's old girlfriends —and if that's the case, my money is on Laetitia—there'd be no reason to eliminate me. I'm not an old girlfriend, and everyone knows it."

And what would be the purpose in eliminating Crispin's old girlfriends, anyway? He was engaged to her now—assuming

Laetitia was the culprit—and even if she wasn't and someone else was, he was still engaged to her. Laetitia had no reason to want to get rid of people from Crispin's past, and anyone else would be more likely to eliminate Laetitia herself than any of the past dalliances, I assumed.

Unless she was next?

"Someone should tell her to watch out," I said, and all three of the men looked at me.

"Who?"

"Laetitia Marsden. If someone is getting rid of Crispin's old girlfriends, surely his current fiancée is next on the list."

"Would you like to confess, Miss Darling?" Uncle Harold inquired snidely, and I blinked.

"You think *I'm* killing St George's old girlfriends? Why on earth would I do that? I'm the reason he's engaged to Laetitia now. If anything, you should thank me. Not accuse me of attempted murder."

"Now, now, Pippa," Uncle Herbert remonstrated, while Christopher sat back and watched, lips twitching. "No one is accusing you of anything."

I sniffed. "I should hope not. For one thing, I had no idea that Cecily Fletcher would be here until I arrived yesterday evening. For another, I didn't know that she was expecting until Crispin told me last night. I don't think he knew until then, either, at least if the expression on his face was anything to go by. I don't see how I could have brought a fatal dose of pennyroyal with me to do away with her if I didn't know any of those things."

"Is that what happened?" Uncle Herbert inquired.

"So we surmise. There's some question as to whether the pennyroyal came from Dominic Rivers, seeing as he was a known dope dealer—"

Uncle Harold made a face, so perhaps he had heard the

name before. Grimsby the valet might have dug up Crispin's connection to Rivers back in the spring, and it might have been in that dossier I read back then. I had mostly paid attention to the plethora of sexual escapades the valet had detailed, I admit, so I couldn't rightly remember whether that specific detail of Crispin's dope habit had been mentioned or not.

"Now, see," Christopher interrupted, "he's a spanner in the works of your theory, Pippa."

"Dominic Rivers is?" How?

Christopher nodded. "He's certainly no old flame of Crispin's. Not unless my cousin has a bent we don't know about."

He smirked, and looked remarkably like the Viscount St George for a moment.

"Don't be ridiculous," I told him. "St George is relentlessly heterosexual. No one dallies with as many women as he has done unless he likes them."

Christopher opened his mouth to continue the banter, but Uncle Herbert clearing his throat brought him back to himself. He flushed. "Sorry, Father."

"As you should be," Uncle Herbert said mock-sternly. "Although I'm not the one you ought to apologize to, Kit."

"What Crispin doesn't know—" Christopher began cheekily, and then he noticed that Uncle Herbert was indicating the Duke, and he caught on.

"Oh. My mistake." He flushed again, all the way to his ears, and cleared his throat. "My apologies, Uncle Harold. I was merely making sport. Pippa's right. Crispin is definitely not queer."

Uncle Harold nodded, mollified, although he looked a bit uncomfortable even so.

"At any rate," I said, and took Christopher's attention off his uncle, "it's obvious why Dominic Rivers had to die. He brought the pennyroyal. Whoever he gave it to, didn't want him to be able to spill the beans."

"So you think it was Rivers's pennyroyal that killed her?"

"I don't know," I admitted. "It can't be a coincidence that there's pennyroyal for the picking just down the road, too. Or can it?"

Christopher shrugged. "This is above my head, I'm afraid. I'm for letting Tom figure it out. He's the one getting paid for it."

"But it's interesting," I protested. "And we should be able to reason it out for ourselves. It's like an Agatha Christie novel, isn't it? All of us gathered here, and people dropping like flies. It has to be one of us. Someone who was here yesterday; I'm not accusing you, Uncle Herbert, or Aunt Roz—"

Or His Grace, the Duke of Sutherland, but I didn't see the need to point that out.

"Of course not, Pippa," Uncle Herbert rumbled. "I didn't know either of the unfortunate young women, or for that matter the young man."

"In an Agatha Christie novel," Christopher said, "it's always the least likely suspect, isn't it? Who's the least likely suspect here?"

We both thought about it. It only took me a second, because the answer was obvious.

"You, Christopher. It's you."

CHAPTER NINETEEN

"ME?" He looked surprised. "Am I really?"

I nodded. "I think you are. It would have been an elaborate plot to get rid of Crispin, I imagine."

Uncle Harold fidgeted on his chair, as if this line of discussion made him uncomfortable, but he didn't say anything, so I went on, spinning mad webs of intrigue with no basis in reality. If Christopher wanted to know who the least likely suspect was, I'd oblige. It was something to talk about, and more entertaining than going over the actual facts of the case yet again.

"You would have waited until Cecily was ginned to the eyebrows," I said, "I imagine, and then you would have convinced her that you were your cousin, at a time when she was too sozzled to know better. But now that she's with child, you can't have anyone find out what you did, so you had to kill her."

"And how does this get rid of Crispin?"

"You frame him for her murder," I said, "obviously. You contacted Rivers, again pretending to be St George, and invited him here. Then, when he arrived, you went to him as yourself, told him that Crispin had sent you to fetch the stuff and pay for it, since Laetitia wouldn't appreciate Crispin doing it—I don't think Rivers would quibble over that, do you? He knows who you are and that you and St George are close—and then you poured the pennyroyal into one of Cecily's drinks last night and waited for her to die. Perhaps you'd get lucky and it would happen while Crispin was in her room. Wouldn't that be lovely?"

Christopher furrowed his brows. "I think we should all be grateful that you're not with Scotland Yard, Pippa. That's frightfully convincing."

I shook my head. "Don't be silly, Christopher. Tom knows better than to think you'd do any such thing. Besides, what would be the purpose of it? You won't actually gain anything by getting your cousin arrested. In a novel, I could ascribe you some sort of motive—you were pathologically jealous, or you knew some sort of secret that would enable you to inherit if Crispin were out of the way—"

All three of them winced, and I added, "but in real life, you're not next in the succession. You'd have to deal with your father and your brother first, and I know you wouldn't harm either of them. Nor would you harm St George. You love him, mad as that is."

Christopher nodded.

"So who do *you* think the least likely suspect is?" I asked. Everyone looked a bit uncomfortable with the direction of the conversation, and I thought I might change the subject away from the idea that Christopher would do anything to Crispin for the inheritance. Mentioning it, even as a joke, seemed to have bothered all three of them.

"Not you," Christopher said. "You're much too bloodthirsty."

"Oh, yes. I'm probably close to the top of the list, actually.

Or I would be, were this a novel and you could ascribe me motives I don't actually have."

"Anyone who claims to abhor my cousin as often as you do, is certainly worthy of a second look," Christopher nodded, smirking. "The lady doth protest too much, methinks."

Uncle Herbert smothered a chuckle. Uncle Harold gave me a gimlet stare. I rolled my eyes. "Shakespeare, Christopher? Really?"

"I was going to say Wolfgang," Christopher continued without responding to my complaint. "Excepting you, me, and Crispin, he has never met any of these people before. In a novel, he would turn out to be the guilty party for certain."

"Make your case, then," I invited, and Christopher drew a breath.

"He's young, handsome, and titled. He lives in London, or at least he spends a lot of his time there."

I nodded. We had no idea where Wolfgang lived, not really. I thought he had lodgings at the Savoy, since we had seen him there on multiple occasions, not always by design, but I had never actually asked.

"He might have known Cecily and Violet. He might have gotten Cecily with child. He might have known Rivers. They're all based in London. And Rivers gets—or got—his dope from somewhere. Perhaps Wolfgang is engaged in the dope trade. He must be doing something with his time, and I don't know what it is. Do you?"

I didn't. Not specifically. Although— "I don't see why he must be doing something, Christopher. You and I don't. Nor does Crispin or Francis, nor, I'm certain, the Honorable Reggie Fish. Nor Cecily or Violet, if it comes to that." Or Laetitia or Geoffrey or Constance or any number of other young people of our station. We're all lazy layabouts who live off family money. Or in my case, off Christopher's family's money.

"He's in England," Christopher said stubbornly. "He must have a purpose for being here."

"I'm sure he does," I agreed. "Although I don't think it's peddling dope. But for purposes of the imaginary plot, I'll allow it. So Wolfgang is a dope dealer who killed Cecily because of the baby and then he killed Rivers because Rivers knew that Wolfgang would have had access to the dope?"

Christopher shrugged. "Something like that."

"Of course. Well, it's not a bad plot. Although neither of us accounted for the gunshot. Is it your contention that it was Wolfgang, then? Shooting at me because he thought I was Cecily?"

"Or at Francis," Christopher said, "because Francis knew that Wolfgang was in the dope trade."

"Of course." I nodded approvingly. "Francis has been doing business with Wolfgang in the past, and their animosity is really just a cover for the fact that they know one another."

"It's been done before," Christopher said, a bit defensively.

I nodded. "You're right, it has. In *The Mysterious Affair at Styles*, Alfred Inglethorp and his cousin Evelyn pretend to be enemies in order to kill Alfred's wife and inherit the money."

A moment passed, and then I shook my head. "What am I saying? Of course it wasn't Francis. And I'm certain it wasn't Wolfgang, either. It's a good plot—"

"Not as good as the one you made up."

"—but we're just doing this for the amusement of it. I really don't think Wolfgang knew any of these people before he came here. Certainly not Francis. I'm sure their animosity—or Francis's animosity, at least—is entirely unfeigned."

Christopher nodded. "Instead of coming up with mad scenarios, is there anyone you think might have actually done it? Agatha Christie novels is one thing, but in life, the solution is usually much simpler. Take the Margaret Hughes thing, for instance—"

"The what, now?" Uncle Harold interrupted, and we both —all three—looked at him.

Margaret Hughes, of course, was Lady Charlotte's maid at Sutherland Hall. Lydia Morrison's counterpart. After Aunt Charlotte's death in April, Hughes had lingered at Sutherland for a few months, and then she had made her way to Beckwith Place, and from there to Bristol, where she had met her demise in a dark alley sometime last month. She had had one of Tom's business cards in her reticule when she was found, so the Bristol police had called him in for a consultation. Otherwise, I'm sure we would have heard nothing about it.

To Christopher's point: There were a lot of peculiar circumstances surrounding Hughes' last few months of life, circumstances that might point to all sorts of interesting possibilities. There was Aunt Charlotte's death—which of course wasn't a mystery—and Duke Henry's and Grimsby's murders, which weren't either. Then there was the disappearance of Lydia Morrison from the Dower House, and the murder of Abigail Dole at Beckwith Place in July, for which Hughes had been present along with the rest of us. And then there was the thousand pounds Hughes had extorted from Uncle Herbert before leaving Wiltshire, although according to Tom, that money had been safely tucked away in a bank account, so that, at least, was not the reason for the bludgeoning.

"You remember Hughes," Christopher asked, "don't you, Uncle Harold?"

He didn't wait for his uncle to confirm or deny, because of course His Grace remembered Hughes. She had been at Sutherland Hall since Crispin was a newborn, dressing and undressing Aunt Charlotte. Uncle Harold was notoriously uninterested in his wife—it was a miracle that Crispin existed at all, frankly—but he wasn't as oblivious as that. "She was found dead in an alley in Bristol last month," Christopher added. "A mugging gone wrong, Tom said."

Which made Christopher's point rather nicely, since, with all the questions swirling around Hughes and her decamping to Bristol, the official finding was manslaughter by person or persons unknown, presumably for the twenty pounds or so she had had in her purse. Nothing to do with the Astley family or any murder or blackmail at all.

"Dear me," Uncle Harold said faintly. "I had no idea." He glanced at his brother. "Did you, Herbert?"

Uncle Herbert nodded. "Tom stopped by Beckwith Place on his way back from Bristol. Kind of him to let us know."

There was nothing in his voice to indicate that he realized that Tom had made the stop at least in part to check up on Uncle Herbert's and Aunt Roz's alibis. When you allow yourself to be blackmailed, and then your blackmailer dies violently a month or two later, it seems you climb to the top of the suspect list.

Of course, I assumed that Tom's stop at Beckwith was more to make sure that Aunt Roz and Uncle Herbert *had* alibis, since I didn't think he seriously suspected either of them of running off to Bristol to bash Hughes over the head. They could afford the thousand pounds, and neither of them are homicidal by nature.

"Dear me," Uncle Harold said again. "How terrible."

We sat in polite silence for a moment. For me, it was in the past and even back when I first heard about it, it had been hard to muster up much sympathy. I didn't like Hughes, and although it's not right for anyone to be bashed over the head in an alley, she *was* a blackmailer who had extorted money from my uncle. Although of course Uncle Harold was right: it was terrible that someone had killed Hughes, and worse that it was for such a negligible amount of money.

But right now, I was more concerned about the fact that Cecily Fletcher was dead, murdered because she had allowed herself to become pregnant; and Dominic Rivers was dead, murdered because he had let himself get tangled up in it; and Violet was... well, hopefully Violet was not dead, and would come around eventually, but she was as good as dead, and all because—

"Why would anyone want to kill Violet?"

There was a moment of silence while they all, even Uncle Harold, looked at me, and then Christopher said, "I suppose because she knew something about who killed Cecily and Dominic Rivers?"

That was the logical explanation, of course. Aunt Roslyn had believed that Violet was being untruthful about something, and that something might be the reason why. If Cecily was killed because of the baby, and Dominic Rivers was killed because of the dope, then Violet was surely killed—or poisoned, at any rate —because she knew something about whoever had done it.

"She spent the evening with Geoffrey Marsden yesterday," I said.

Christopher nodded, even as Uncle Harold bristled at the implication. I ignored him.

"She came here already knowing that Cecily was with child. She knew Dominic Rivers. If we proceed on the assumption that the pregnancy was the reason for Cecily's murder..."

"By all means," Christopher said.

"Thank you. Why don't we say, for argument's sake, that Geoffrey was responsible for Cecily's predicament."

Christopher nodded. "Let's say that. I can imagine that being true."

I could too, only too easily. "Geoffrey's a philanderer, but he definitely isn't the marrying kind. Having a wife and child at home likely wouldn't stop him from spreading his favors around—I don't know if anything would, to be honest—but it might cut down on his chances, since some girls unaccountably won't get involved with a married man, unreasonable as that is."

Uncle Herbert winced. It was probably the subject matter, and what amounted to his presumably innocent niece discussing it so freely (and sarcastically). I smiled at him. "Sorry, Uncle Herbert. But there's no point in prevaricating, is there? Not if we want to figure this out."

"Of course not, Pippa." He waved a hand. "Carry on."

I nodded. "So if the baby was Geoffrey's, and Violet knew it, and she wanted Geoffrey for herself... would she have allowed him to poison Cecily? Or done it herself? They *were* friends."

"That doesn't always stop someone from committing murder," Christopher said, which of course was true. "Did Violet poison herself, then, after killing Cecily and Dominic Rivers? Tom arrived, and she realized she wouldn't get away with it, so she took the coward's way out? Or did Geoffrey poison Violet in retaliation for Cecily? Or were they in it together?"

"I have no idea," I said. "Between Dom Rivers being here, and the plants down the road, I suspect there were two doses of pennyroyal. One very potent one from Rivers, and one less potent in a cup of tea, that might have been enough in conjunction with the first dose to commit murder."

"So your hypothesis is that Geoffrey brought Rivers to Marsden Manor," Christopher said, "with enough pennyroyal to get rid of Cecily's baby, but Violet figured out what he was doing, and because she wanted Geoffrey for herself, she picked some pennyroyal leaves and gave Cecily another dose in a cup of tea..."

I nodded. "No one would have thought anything of it if Violet had asked Cook or the kitchen maid to brew it up, I think. Both she and Cecily had been here before. And they were close friends. If Violet brought Cecily a cup of tea to help her feel better, I think Cecily might have been grateful, and not suspicious at all."

"But then Cecily dies," Christopher continued, "and suddenly, Geoffrey is a murderer. That makes Rivers a liability, so he bashes him over the head and leaves him for dead. And then he poisons Violet, because..."

He trailed off, and I got the impression that he was waiting for me to complete the sentence.

"She knew," I suggested, "and tried to use it to blackmail him into marrying her? He went from the frying pan to the fire, so to speak? From a pregnant girl he had to marry to a girl who knew he was guilty of murder and who wasn't above black-mailing him?"

"If it isn't one thing, it's another," Christopher said dryly. "Or perhaps you're right and Violet realized she was on the hook for murder, and so she killed herself rather than risk being arrested."

"It's possible. Although so are any number of other scenarios, I think."

Christopher looked doubtful, but he didn't protest. There was no time for it, at any rate, because the door to the hallway opened and Tom came in.

"Thank God," I said. "Is it finally our turn?"

"I'm afraid not, Pippa." Tom turned to his right. "Come along, Nellie."

Nellie?

I looked over my shoulder, and there was the maid, daintily perched on a chair in the far corner of the room.

"How long have you been there?" fell out of my mouth, rather rudely. Uncle Harold looked appalled, and it was difficult to blame him.

"I've been here since tea began, Miss Darling." Nellie skirted tables and chairs on her way towards Tom as she spoke. "Excuse me."

She followed him out the door, which shut behind them.

"Goodness," I said as I turned to Christopher, "did you know that she was there?"

He shook his head. "I had no idea. I thought we were alone."

So had I, or I wouldn't have spoken so freely.

Uncle Harold cleared his throat. "That's the mark of a good servant. To be seen but not heard, and preferably not that, either."

Yes, of course. But still, I'm not usually one to ignore the staff.

"I can't believe she has lasted as long as she has here," I told Christopher. "She said she's been here more than a month, and Geoffrey hasn't bothered her at all yet."

Christopher glanced at the closed door. "That's hard to believe. A pretty, little thing like that. You would think Geoffrey would be all over her."

I nodded. "My thoughts exactly. Although perhaps Cecily's predicament has put a damper on his ardor for the time being."

If it had been his baby, of course. But if it had been, it was quite understandable that he wouldn't want to risk making another one right away.

"It would have dampened mine," Christopher agreed. "At least we didn't talk about her while she was sitting there."

"No, why on earth would we? She's the maid. She had no reason to want Cecily out of the way. Not if she told the truth and Geoffrey hasn't approached her."

Christopher nodded. "A pity, really. It would have been easy for her to poison Violet's tea."

"Easy for her to turn pennyroyal leaves into tea for Cecily, too," I said. "Or easier than for some of us, at any rate."

No one would have batted an eye if Nellie had walked into the kitchen to ask for leaves to be steeped into tea, any more than they might have batted an eye if it were Laetitia or her mother.

"I hope Tom asks her whether she knows anything about any tea leaves," I said. "If she comes and goes below stairs, she might."

Christopher smiled indulgently. "I'm certain he will do, Pippa. He'll talk to all of the servants about it, I'm sure. He's actually quite good at his job, you know."

"Of course he is, Christopher." I patted his hand. After a second, I added, "At least she isn't in here to hear me make a case against the lady of the manor."

Uncle Herbert looked intrigued. "The Countess Marsden, do you mean? You have a case against her, too? Or do you mean her daughter?"

"I can make a case against either," I said expansively. "Of course, it's mostly the same case. The same motive and means. They may even be in on it together."

Uncle Harold looked deeply offended by the idea, but when Uncle Herbert said, "Let's hear it," and his brother gave him a judgmental look, probably for encouraging me to disparage my betters further, Uncle Herbert merely added, "Don't be a stick in the mud, Harold. We've got to do something while we're sitting here, and I'm entertained by the outlandishness of the theories."

"Well, this one isn't really very outlandish," I said, while I assiduously avoided looking at the grumbling Duke of Sutherland, because he wasn't going to like any of this. "Nor is it complicated at all. In this scenario, Crispin is the father of the baby."

Uncle Harold opened his mouth, outraged, and I added, "Or Laetitia and her mother think he is, at any rate. I know he isn't. He assured me of it. Repeatedly."

That, for some reason, did not make Uncle Harold any happier. I ignored him and his scowling, and carried on. "Laetitia and Lady Euphemia don't want to give up the Sutherland title and money to Cecily—or to give Laetitia her due, perhaps she simply doesn't want to give up St George—so separately, they decide to take matters into their own hands. Laetitia invites Dominic Rivers to her engagement party, and pays him to bring a quantity of pennyroyal, enough to induce a miscarriage in Cecily. Lady Euphemia, meanwhile, wanders down the road and picks enough pennyroyal to accomplish the same thing. Neither of them knows what the other is doing."

"I like it so far," Christopher said.

I did, too, as a matter of fact. "It explains what Rivers was doing here. Crispin wouldn't have invited him, and it would be very rude of anyone else to do so. Anyone who wasn't a member of the household, I mean."

"So they each dose the young lady," Uncle Herbert said, "but independently of one another."

I nodded. "One dose in one of her drinks after dinner last night, and one in the cup of tea she had in her room later, supposedly to settle her stomach from the first dose. It would have been easy for either of them to bring her a cup of tea to make her feel better, or to ask one of the maids to do it."

"Then she dies," Christopher said, "and Laetitia kills Rivers to keep it quiet about her share of the pennyroyal—"

Uncle Harold winced, but he didn't complain. I nodded. "And in this scenario, I suppose she then goes on to kill Violet, as well."

"Why would she do that?" Uncle Herbert wanted to know. Unlike his brother, he didn't seem bothered by the conjecture, merely interested in where the story might go.

I exchanged a glance with Christopher. "I suppose because Violet, too, at one time dallied with St George. If she's willing to do away with one rival, she might as well get rid of the other."

"Or a third," Christopher said. When I turned to him—which third?—he added, "this would explain what happened on the lawn, you realize? Laetitia was out in the woods with the hunting party. There was nothing to keep her from taking a shot at you when she saw you standing there."

"Why would she—? Oh." I flushed. "I assure you, Christopher, I'm no impediment to her happiness with St George. We've talked about this before. I wouldn't have him giftwrapped with a bow around his neck, and the feeling is mutual."

Uncle Herbert muttered something. Uncle Harold merely looked stony. He didn't like me, I knew that for a fact, but perhaps my cavalier dismissal of his son and heir rankled, even so.

"The same scenario would go for Bilge and Serena," I added. "If the baby was Bilge's, he and his wife could have done away with Cecily in the same way. Violet might have lied about not knowing who the baby's father was, so they killed her, too."

"Or Reggie Fish," Christopher nodded. "He actually brought Rivers here. Physically brought him, I mean. And you said Olivia Barnsley is sweet on him, didn't you?"

I nodded. "In that scenario, I suppose she was the one who

walked down the road and picked the second dose of penny-royal? Much harder for her or Serena to get that steeped into tea and into Cecily's hands, I'd say, than for Laetitia or Lady Marsden. They couldn't exactly walk into the kitchen and do it themselves."

Although anyone could take the pennyroyal leaves to the kitchen and ask for them to be steeped, I imagined, and then brought up to them, and from there, it would be a fairly easy task to pass the cup on to Cecily with caring concern. Any of her girlfriends could have done that without raising her suspicions.

Christopher groaned. "My head is spinning. I cannot wait until Tom is done in the study and we get to leave this room."

I nodded. I felt the same way. We had spent entirely too much time here. "Hopefully it won't be long now. It's just the four of us left, and I can't imagine either of the uncles know anything about this mess."

"Not aside from what you've just told us," Uncle Herbert said cheerfully. "We arrived much too late to have anything to do with what happened last night or this morning, so I imagine we're off the hook for this one."

"Must be nice," Christopher said.

I chuckled, but before I could say anything, Uncle Herbert told him, "I imagine you're off the hook too, Kit. I doubt Tom is likely to think you—either of you..." he glanced at me, "guilty of this."

"He's not stupid," I agreed, "so I don't imagine he does. If anything, I assume he's keeping us for last so he can check everything everyone else has told him against what we know. We have no reason to lie."

"Give the lady a prize," Tom's voice said from behind me, and I looked over my shoulder in time to see him close the hallway door behind him. "Got it in one, Pippa; well done."

He started across the floor towards us, skirting the other tables and chairs. "We'll just stay in here for this one. I sent Collins back upstairs to continue the search. I'll take my own notes."

He dropped into the chair between me and Uncle Harold with a little noise. It sounded like pleasure. Perhaps the chairs were more comfortable in here than where he'd been, or perhaps he was simply tired. He had driven here from London and then gone straight into a long line of interviews, so small wonder if he were.

He pulled his notebook and pencil out of his pocket and put them in front of him, and then he addressed the uncles. "Your Grace. Lord Herbert."

"Tom," Uncle Herbert said pleasantly, while Uncle Harold inclined his head in a barely polite nod.

"I don't suppose either of you know anything about this?"

"Nothing you haven't already heard from other people," Uncle Herbert said. "We arrived too late for any of the excitement last night or this morning. Roz has spoken with a few people since we arrived, but I've really only spent time with my own family."

"We saw that unfortunate young lady collapse," Uncle Harold added, distantly, "but I didn't notice anything untoward before that."

"You didn't see anyone put anything in her tea?"

Herbert shook his head. When Tom glanced over at him, the Duke did the same. "No, Detective Sergeant."

"And you didn't hear anyone say anything that might be germane to the situation?"

They both shook their heads again. I wouldn't have put any money on Uncle Harold telling the truth—he had been sitting with the Marsden family and with Crispin, and he had every incentive to support the status quo as far as his son and heir was concerned, so if anyone at that table had said anything incriminating, Uncle Harold would keep it to himself—but unless I was right in my outlandish suggestion that Laetitia and her mother were to blame, Uncle Harold wasn't likely to have heard anything interesting anyway. Certainly nothing worthy of lying about. They had probably been making wedding plans. And of course Uncle Herbert had been sitting with Aunt Roz, Francis, and Constance, and neither of them was likely to know anything, either. Nothing they wouldn't have told Tom already, at any rate. I'm sure Aunt Roz had shared every word Olivia and Violet had said upstairs.

Tom seemed to come to the same conclusion, because he nodded. "Very well. You can go."

Uncle Herbert didn't need to be told twice. "Come on, Harold." He jumped up from his chair and waited for his brother to rise, with a bit more dignity, before he added, "I'm going to go find my wife. It was good to see you, Tom, even under the circumstances. Go easy on my children."

"Have fun, Uncle Herbert," I told him, even as I felt a warm sort of glow inside at being included among the children in question. Christopher, meanwhile, rolled his eyes at the idea that Tom would be anything but perfectly pleasant.

The two of them headed for the door, and Tom waited for it to shut behind them with a decisive click before he turned to us. "So."

CHAPTER TWENTY

"SO," Christopher echoed. "Here we are."

Tom nodded. And then neither of them said anything else for a few seconds while they stared at one another.

I cleared my throat. "It was good of you to come, Tom." If I didn't speak up at some point, I thought we were likely to sit here for rather a long time.

"Of course, Pippa." If I had interrupted anything important, he gave no sign of it. It was Christopher who looked pink and flustered. "I can't have people taking potshots at the two of you and not come down to have a look around."

"And we appreciate it," I said. "So what have you found out?"

He chuckled. "You realize that this is supposed to be me interviewing you, don't you?"

"Of course I do. But it's not as if you suspect us of anything, so you might as well just tell us what you've learned, and we'll fill in as much as we can, with anything we know that you don't."

Tom nodded, and flipped the notebook open. "Let's start from the beginning, then. Miss Cecily Fletcher died."

"From what we think was an overdose of pennyroyal," I confirmed. "Although I don't know if the doctor has had a chance to confirm that."

"He has. I saw him upstairs. He had time to get started on the post mortem before the next body dropped."

"An overdose of pennyroyal, then. We think it might have been administered by two different people—one during after-dinner cocktails, and the other in a cup of what she thought was peppermint tea that she drank later."

"She told you this?"

"She intimated it," I said. "She had an upset stomach, and she mentioned, specifically, that it was peppermint tea. But when I smelled it, it smelled more like spearmint, which was why I thought of pennyroyal."

"But that was later," Tom said, and I nodded.

"Yes. She was sick in the lavatory, and I helped her into her room, and saw the cup of tea. After she died, I remembered it and realized that it might have been pennyroyal. At the time, I didn't think anything of it, other than that she must have misspoken."

Tom nodded and made a note. "Between Miss Peckham and Francis, I think I have information on everything that happened before and after she died. You already told me about the gunshot, Kit..."

Christopher nodded.

"Is there anything you'd like to add about it, Pippa?"

"I don't think there's anything more I can add," I said. "It was over very quickly. One second we were standing there talking, the next a shot came from the woods. It passed between me and Francis. Christopher was a bit farther away, although of course it's possible that someone simply has atrociously bad aim..."

Tom's lips twitched. "But if you had to choose, you'd say it's more likely that you or Francis was the intended victim?"

"If it was intended for anyone, yes. More likely, it was simply someone shooting off a rifle without aiming at anything at all, and accidentally coming close to us. But if I had to choose, I'd say it was meant for me. Or rather for Cecily Fletcher, since we looked a bit alike and since someone pretty obviously wanted her out of the way."

Tom nodded. "Other than the four of you, and Miss Fletcher, and the elder Marsdens, and of course the staff, everyone else was in the woods. No one admits to shooting at the house or to seeing anyone else do so."

No, of course they didn't. "I don't think it's worth speculating over," I said. "If—when—you figure out who actually killed Cecily, you can ask him or her whether he or she shot at me, but until then, let's just chalk it up to an accident and move on."

"As you wish." Tom consulted his notes. "You went into the house—"

I nodded. If Christopher hadn't mentioned us crawling across the grass on our hands and knees, I wasn't going to.

"—and upstairs to Miss Fletcher's room, and you stayed there until she died."

"We did, yes. Constance was still there when we came upstairs, but she ran down to phone the doctor. Francis said there wouldn't be anything he could do, but we thought we ought to anyway."

Tom nodded. "At that point, did you suspect foul play?"

Christopher snorted. "Pippa always suspects foul play. You should know that by now, Tom."

"I remembered the tea," I said, "so I suspected that it wasn't natural causes. It was later, after Crispin said that Cecily wouldn't have done it to herself, that I began to wonder whether someone else had done it."

"Someone specific?"

Christopher snorted. "We have lots of theories. Just wait."

I kicked at his ankle under the table, and told Tom, "My preference would be for you to arrest Lady Laetitia Marsden. But unfortunately, I don't think it's St George's baby, so we can't get rid of her that way."

"We thought perhaps Lord Geoffrey?" Christopher said. "He's a known womanizer, as you know, and—"

Between us, we went through the entire scenario we had built earlier, featuring Geoffrey, Dominic Rivers, and Violet. Afterwards, for good measure, we also went through the same scenario again, featuring the Honorable Reggie Fish in Geoffrey's role and Olivia Barnsley in Violet's, with the exception that of course it was Violet who had been poisoned, not Olivia.

"But perhaps Olivia did it," I suggested, "because Violet suspected Olivia of killing Cecily. Cecily and Violet were best friends."

"Is that so? Even though Cecily hadn't told her best friend who her boyfriend was?"

"That's what Violet said. Although I suppose she might have been lying. Aunt Roz thought she was prevaricating about something. It might have been that."

Tom nodded. "Then there are the Fortescues."

Of course there were. We hadn't really given much thought to them, although the same scenario worked for them as had worked for the Honorable Reggie and Miss Barnsley.

"They've been married for a few years now," Tom said pensively, "and Lady Serena hasn't provided an heir yet. If there's a problem there, and Bilge went elsewhere, and then Cecily conceived, Lady Serena would have additional incentive for wanting her rival out of the way. Bilge might leave her and marry the mother of his child instead."

Yes, of course he might, the bastard. "She lost a baby," I said. "It came up over lunch. So that might make it sting more. And of course she made a point of pumping Christopher for information earlier, about what was going on upstairs."

Christopher winced. "I don't know that I'd call it pumping —a bit crude, that; thanks ever so, Pippa—but she did make a point of getting me on my own to ask about what Collins was up to."

"She was clinging to your arm on her way down the stairs, too. Perhaps she's enceinte again, and just hasn't told anyone about it."

"Neither of them mentioned any of this earlier," Tom said and made a note. "Lady Serena would have known Mr. Rivers too, I assume?"

"They danced together last night," I said, "while Bilge danced with Cecily."

"Did anyone else dance with anyone in particular?"

"I mostly danced with Wolfgang," I said, "because I didn't think anyone else would do so. Francis was extremely rude, and so, frankly, was Bilge Fortescue. Christopher spent his time trying to talk Francis out of his sulk, and I don't think he and Constance danced at all..."

Christopher shook his head. "Connie didn't drink, either. Nellie brought her a cup of tea."

"That's right." I nodded. "I saw that. Although Francis more than made up for it."

He made a face. "And how. At any rate, I was forced into service at one point. Francis didn't dance, Wolfgang only danced with Pippa, Crispin only danced with Laetitia—there was a dearth of partners on the floor."

"Who did Lord Geoffrey dance with?"

Christopher and I exchanged a look. "Not me," I said, "although I think he danced with everyone else. Cecily looked particularly uncomfortable about it, I noticed."

We contemplated that thought in silence for a moment, before Tom said, "So that was last night. Nothing else happened of note?"

Christopher and I looked at one another. "Not aside from Natterdorff's presence making a stir," Christopher said, "and the ill-will that followed."

Tom nodded. "It's understandable. And as long as it wasn't Natterdorff who died, it likely doesn't have anything to do with anything."

Likely not.

"You already know about Cecily and the cup of tea," I said. "I don't know who visited her room other than Dominic Rivers and St George. I saw Crispin leave her bedchamber, so I know that he was in there, but I can't actually confirm that Rivers was."

"Nellie said he was," Tom said, "although there's only Nellie's word for that, of course. His roommate, Mr. Fish, was out with Miss Barnsley. They alibi one another. Not that anyone needs one, really."

No, not for last night.

"What about this afternoon, when Rivers was killed? Can anyone alibi anyone else for that time?"

"You two were with Constable Collins and St George on the lawn," Tom recited. "Francis and Constance were together. The Earl and Countess of Marsden were together. Lady Laetitia was sulking in her room—"

Because Crispin had escaped her, no doubt. "Surely she didn't say that?"

"Of course not. It was my own interpretation." Tom flipped a page. "The Fortescues were together in their room."

"And could be lying for one another. They're married, so they might lie if one of them had committed murder."

Unless Serena saw a chance to land Bilge with the murder and send him to prison while she kept the title and money, perhaps. If he had cheated on her with Cecily, she might consider it poetic justice.

"Bilge spent some time in France," Tom said, "so he, at least, is no stranger to violence."

"He called his wife coldblooded in the breakfast room this morning," I answered.

Christopher nodded. "He said she was a crack shot, as well."

"It isn't likely to have been either of them in the woods, then. A crack shot wouldn't have missed."

Tom made a notation. "To continue, Geoffrey says he was with Violet this afternoon, but of course she can't confirm that. Olivia Barnsley and Reginald Fish were together again."

"But might be lying. Olivia, at least, would lie for Reggie."

Tom nodded. "And that's everyone."

"Nellie was moving around the house during that time, making beds and tidying the rooms. I don't suppose she saw anyone?"

"She says that she saw Mr. Rivers go past her and up the stairs to the second floor when she came out of Lord Geoffrey's room," Tom said. "Then she went into the suite at the end of the hall to prepare it for your mother and father's arrival—" He glanced at Christopher, "and she didn't notice anyone else going past while she was in there."

"And when she got upstairs?"

"She didn't," Tom said. "Collins came tearing down the stairs after you found Rivers's body, and told her on his way past what had happened, and for her to not touch the upstairs rooms. So she didn't venture up to the second floor."

I nodded. That was fine as far as it went. "She must have been up there at some point, though."

Tom tilted his head. "What makes you say that?"

"Well, I saw her," I said. "After all this had happened, of course. Aunt Roz and Uncle Herbert arrived, with His Grace, and Aunt Roslyn and I spoke, and then she went upstairs to look in on Olivia and Violet."

Tom nodded. "And?"

"I eavesdropped on their conversation, and then Aunt Roz and I went into my room so I could change my clothes. I'd been wearing the same skirt and blouse all day."

"Yes," Tom said patiently. "And?"

"Well, when we came back out in the hallway, Nellie was replacing the vase in the alcove. Collins stuck his head out of Rivers's room to ask her whether anyone else took care of the upstairs rooms—I think he had found fingerprints on the shards of the vase that had been used to bash Rivers over the head—and he wanted to know whether they were Nellie's or someone else's."

"He'd have to take her fingerprints to make sure of that," Tom said with a frown, and I nodded.

"And he planned to do, later. But he was alone at the time. The reinforcements from the village hadn't arrived yet. It was just him, going through Dominic Rivers's room and speculating."

"And what did Nellie say?" Tom wanted to know.

"That there are two chambermaids and one parlor maid here at Marsden Manor. Jenny is the parlor maid—the one who was feeling unwell and had to put her feet up so Nellie served tea—and then there's Edna, who takes care of the family's bedchambers while Nellie takes care of the guests'."

"The fingerprints on the vase are Nellie's," Tom said.

"Collins told me. He must have had time to check them in the time since he asked the question."

"Well, there doesn't seem to be anything sinister about that. She probably dusted that vase every few days. Picked it up, put it on the floor, dusted the plinth, and put it back."

"I imagine so," Tom said, and we sat in silence for a few moments before Christopher cleared his throat.

"How did Nellie know that the vase needed to be replaced?"

"The vase with the peacock feathers?"

He nodded. "Did you see that the vase was missing when you were upstairs?"

"Twice, as a matter of fact. The first time was just after Rivers's murder—I remember thinking that I hadn't noticed it the first time we walked past, but I did look at it when we walked back down again, and I saw the feathers lying on the plinth. And the second time was when I followed Aunt Roz upstairs and tiptoed down the hall to listen at Violet Cumming's door. I glanced into the alcove on my way past, and saw that the feathers were gone."

"And then, a few minutes later, Nellie brought up a new vase."

"It was more than a few minutes," I said. "Perhaps ten or so. But yes, she did."

"So sometime between Rivers's murder and when she did that, she must have realized that the vase had been broken. Or she wouldn't have known to replace it."

"Perhaps Collins told her?" I suggested. "If he told her not to go upstairs because there had been another murder, and she asked what had happened, might he have told her what the murder weapon was?"

"He's not supposed to," Tom said. "That's the sort of information that we can use to trip someone up. Or to determine how much they know about what happened. It's not supposed to be shared with the public until we're ready."

"He's a bit sweet on her, though," I said indulgently. "She's very pretty, you know, and he gets a bit flustered when he talks to her. If she asked, he might have tried to impress her."

"That's not how a copper is supposed to behave," Tom said crossly. "Personal feelings aren't supposed to interfere with the job."

"Of course not." I smiled sweetly. "But we all know that they do, don't we? I don't want to bring up nightclub raids, but—"

"Yes, yes." Tom waved this reminder away with a flap of his hand, but his cheekbones were flushed. "I take your point, Pippa. Say no more."

I sniggered. "Don't get me wrong, Tom. I'm appreciative. I'm probably more appreciative than Christopher." Because I certainly hadn't forgotten that low-voiced quarrel I had once overheard in our foyer in the London flat, in which Christopher had hissed that he hadn't needed Tom's help, and Tom had told him that well, that was just too bad, wasn't it? "But it's easy to get carried away when it's personal."

I thought about tacking an 'isn't it?' onto that last sentence, but decided to hold it back. There was no sense in making things worse, after all. They were both as pink as piglets as it was, and avoiding each other's eyes.

"At any rate," I added, "he probably wouldn't think of her as a suspect. Do you?"

"As far as I'm concerned," Tom said, rallying now that the conversation had moved on from the personal back to business, "everyone is a suspect until I have proven that they're not."

"So you're looking at the staff as well as the guests?"

"We've checked alibis for all of them, yes. None of the staff could have shot at you, of course—" He dared a glance at

Christopher now, "as they were busy inside the house at the time of the shoot. The maids stayed on the first floor or below. None of them made it upstairs."

"Except for Nellie."

"So it seems. No one knew anything about the cup of tea for Miss Fletcher. Nellie said she took a cup of tea to Miss Peckham in the earlier part of the evening—"

I nodded. "Different cup of tea, though. And it was hours before we went upstairs. Cecily was dancing at that point."

"I didn't think it was the same cup," Tom said. "Just that that was the only cup of tea anyone mentioned."

"The kitchen staff was probably done for the day by the time the second cup of tea was made. It was late. And if the kitchen was empty, anyone could have gone in there and made it."

"The Fortescues and the Marsdens, elder and younger, all deny having been on the second floor at any point today. Geoffrey admits to walking Violet to her door last night. Lord St George, of course, was up there, as well."

"But not when Dominic Rivers was killed," I said. "He was on the lawn with us and with Constable Collins when we think that happened."

Tom nodded. "Yes, Pippa. No one thinks Lord St George is guilty of either of these murders."

It was my turn to flush. "My apologies."

Tom smirked. "No matter. It's easy to get carried away when it's personal, isn't it?"

"You tosser," I told him. "That's the last time I hold back when speaking to you."

Christopher sniggered. "Turnabout is fair play, Pippa. And you can't say that he doesn't have the right."

Of course not. "Moving on, then. What else can we tell you, Tom? Any other plot holes that need filling in?"

Tom looked down at his notebook, but before he had the chance to say anything, there was a quick rap on the door, which then opened a crack. Constable Collins stuck his nose in. "Pardon me, Sarge?"

"Yes, Collins," Tom said.

Collins pushed the door open far enough that he was able to come through, and then he pushed it shut again behind him.

"We found this in the young lady's room."

He held out a hand. In it was a handkerchief, and inside that was a small glass vial. He placed it on the table, still on top of the handkerchief, and we all leaned in.

The vial was about the size of my thumb, and unmarked. The stopper was still in it, although there was nothing left to stopper, really. A smear of some clear, thick liquid in the bottom, that spread out into a slick as the bottle went horizontal, but not enough of it to reach the opening, even lying flat.

"Which young lady's room?" Tom looked from the bottle up at Collins, who was leaning on the back of my chair with one gloved hand. "The dead one, the poisoned one, or one of the others?"

"The poor young lady who's ill, Detective Sergeant."

Tom nodded. "I was afraid maybe you'd come to tell me that she'd died."

Collins shook his head. "No, sir. Doctor's sitting with her—there's no rush on the post mortem for the young man; we know what killed him—and so far she's holding on."

"But you searched her room?"

"Not to say searched, sir. It was right there on the bedside table. I saw it as soon as I stepped in to see how the young lady was doing."

"Good work," Tom said, eyeing it. "I don't suppose you've had a chance to test it?"

"No, sir. But I'd have to say that I think it's the same thing that killed the other young lady and knocked this one out."

Tom nodded. "I'd have to agree with you. But we still have to test it."

"Of course, sir. The thing I wanted to show you—other than that I found the vial—is that there are no fingerprints on it."

Tom's brows arched. "None?"

Collins shook his head. "No, sir. Not the young lady's, nor anyone else's, either."

"That's interesting," Tom said, "isn't it?"

"Yes, sir."

There was silence in the room while we all stared at the small vial as if waiting for it to come to life.

"Open it, Collins," Tom said.

"Sir?"

"Pick it up—in the handkerchief, if you please—and take the cork out, and smell it."

Collins did as bid. His face twisted into a grimace as he held the open vial up to his nose—perhaps he was afraid that the fumes would knock him out on contact—but it cleared as soon as he took a whiff (and didn't crumple in a heap on the floor). "Mint, sir."

Tom waved a hand. "Let Miss Darling have a sniff, if you don't mind?"

Collins turned towards me and proffered the vial. I leaned in and inhaled. And nodded. "Spearmint. Yes."

"The same thing you smelled in the tea last night?"

"Spearmint is spearmint," I said, "but yes, as far as I can make out, it smells the same."

Tom nodded. "Best go and make sure, Collins. Hand it off to the lab boffins, there's a good chap."

"Yes, sir." Collins corked the vial again and carried it carefully towards the door.

"Good job, Collins," Tom called after him.

"Thank you, sir." Collins looked pleased as he shut the door behind himself.

Tom let the silence sit for a moment before he looked from me to Christopher and back. "You understand what this means?"

"Violet didn't dose herself?" I said. "I didn't think we thought she had done."

"Of course not, Pippa," Christopher said. "Someone dosed her, and then left the vial in her room to make it appear as if she were the one who killed Cecily. Is that right, Tom?"

"Very good, Kit," Tom nodded.

"So..." I thought about it. "Not Aunt Roz, surely?"

"Of course not, Pippa." Tom flipped his notebook shut and stowed it in his pocket along with his pencil. "And not you, either."

He pushed the chair back and got to his feet. "I better go and discuss procedure with the others. See whether I'm authorized to arrest anyone."

He headed for the door, whistling under his breath.

"Don't you dare!" I called after him. "Tom! If you know who did it, tell us!"

He shot me a look over his shoulder. "You have the same information I do, Pippa. I'm sure you can figure it out."

And then he winked at Christopher and disappeared into the hallway before I could say anything else.

CHAPTER TWENTY-ONE

"OLIVIA BARNSLEY?" I asked Christopher as the door shut behind Tom.

He removed his eyes from the now-closed door and smirked at me. "I'm Christopher, Pippa. Surely you know that?"

"Don't toy with me, you prat. St George gets away with that, but you don't."

"And it really ought to be the other way around," Christopher said, "since you say you love me more. Perhaps you ought to give some thought as to why that is, Pippa."

I rolled my eyes. "Don't be difficult, Christopher. He said it wasn't Aunt Roz—as if I thought there was a possibility of that..."

"Obviously not," Christopher said.

I shook my head. "And he said it wasn't me."

"No. Not that anyone thought it was you."

"I'm sure Uncle Harold hoped it was."

He made a face, but it didn't stop him from nodding in semi-reluctant agreement. "Laetitia, too, probably. And her mother. Although they must have known that you wouldn't."

"So Olivia Barnsley, then, do you suppose?" Who else was there, after all? "She was up there in Violet's room with Violet and Aunt Roz, so she could have left the vial. And Cecily wouldn't have been suspicious of a cuppa that Olivia brought her."

Christopher nodded. "Also, she's goofy about Reggie Fish."

Yes, she was. And Reggie might have been the father of Cecily's baby, at least in theory.

"Did he kill Dom Rivers, then, do you suppose?"

"I think she would have done it all," Christopher said. "The second dose of pennyroyal—Reggie was responsible for the first, obviously, obtained from Rivers, although he probably wasn't trying to kill her; that would have been Olivia's idea."

"There would have been no reason for Reggie to bring Dom here, though," I said, "would there? They traveled down together. Reggie could have just obtained the dope from Dom in London. Dom himself wasn't necessary."

Christopher blinked. "I suppose that's true, really. So perhaps Olivia did it all, and Reggie was simply the motive. Perhaps she got the dope from Rivers in the ballroom and put it all in the tea. No need for two doses if she did it all. Unless she wanted to spread it out, I suppose. Or unless she dosed Cecily once, and when it didn't work immediately, she did it again."

"Perhaps."

"Then she shot at you from the woods, thinking you were Cecily, and then she killed Rivers and dosed Violet. They were sitting at the same table for tea. It would have been easy to pour the rest of the pennyroyal into Violet's cup."

"Right under the nose of the Honorable Reggie and Lord Geoffrey?"

"The Honorable Reggie might have looked the other way," Christopher said, "and might also have engaged Geoffrey in conversation to make sure he didn't notice anything going on."

So he might have done if he were involved. "Would that make him an accessory, then?"

"I'm sure I don't know," Christopher said and pushed his chair back. "Shall we go and watch the fireworks?"

He put his hand on the back of my chair.

"I suppose we ought." I let him pull it out and got to my feet. He presented his arm, and I rested my fingers on it.

The hallway directly outside the drawing room was empty, but as soon as we got there, we could hear raised voices coming from the direction of the entrance hall.

"Better hurry," Christopher muttered, "or we'll miss it."

I nodded. I had spent all day racking my brain to try to determine what had happened and who was guilty, and I was not about to miss the big denouement now. "Let's go."

We went, and stood not upon the order of our going. My heels *click-clacked* rapidly down the marble floors of the corridor, past the doors to the library and the study, and into the open foyer.

Most of the others seemed to be gathered there, watching the spectacle that was taking place in the middle of the floor. Uncle Herbert had joined Aunt Roz, Francis, and Constance when Tom had let the uncles go earlier, and now the four of them were standing at the foot of the curving staircase. Aunt Roz seemed interested in the proceedings, her eyes big and bright as they moved from person to person, while Constance looked a bit concerned. She was holding on to Francis's arm, perhaps so he wouldn't be tempted to throw himself into the fray.

I looked around for Wolfgang, and saw him standing by himself on the other side of the foyer beside the front door. No need to worry about their animosity being the cause of any of this, then.

Uncle Harold had joined his future daughter-in-law and

her parents, beside the entrance to the hallway on the opposite side of the foyer from where Christopher and I had emerged. He looked put out but not actively angry, and the Marsdens seemed more confused than anything else. The Earl had a vague sort of smile on his face, while Lady Euphemia was looking from her daughter's betrothed to her son with a worried wrinkle between her brows. Laetitia was watching Crispin with the unblinking stare of a snake trying to hypnotize its prey.

Or perhaps it wasn't Crispin she was trying to hypnotize. Perhaps it was Olivia Barnsley. He was facing off with her in the middle of the foyer floor, and he wasn't the only one. He had his future brother-in-law beside him, while the Honorable Reggie was standing on Geoffrey's other side, wide-eyed and silent. Bilge Fortescue hovered a few steps behind—not quite inside the circle, but not quite outside of it, either—with Lady Serena clinging to his arm.

"—I promise you, Livvy," Crispin said, and his voice was throbbing with sincerity; he was clearly in the middle of an impassioned defense of something or other—himself, as it turned out, "I wouldn't. Not ever."

I suppressed a sneer at the nickname as well as the over-done earnestness, and saw a similar expression cross Laetitia's face. Olivia, on the other hand, didn't seem softened at all.

"It had to be one of you," she shrieked, as she looked from Crispin to Geoffrey to Reggie to Bilge, eyes wild. "Cecily is dead and Violet is dying! It had to be one of you!"

Reggie cleared his throat, and Olivia swung on him. "Don't you dare, Reggie! Don't you tell me it could be someone else!"

"I wasn't going to, Liv." Where her voice had been border-line hysterical, his was calm. Or at least as calm as one's voice is likely to be when one is accused of murder in the middle of a crowd, with the police standing by to arrest the guilty party.

Unless they weren't, of course. I looked around, but could

see none of the local constables. Nor was Tom in sight, although I wouldn't have put it past him to be standing at the top of the stairs listening, ready to swoop down and save the day when this confrontation ended. And I don't mean that in a disparaging way whatsoever. I have hardly the room to complain about anyone else's eavesdropping, do I?

"As St George said," Reggie continued, with the faintest tremor to his voice and a glance in the latter's direction, "I wouldn't. And you know that I didn't, Liv. I couldn't have. You've been with me practically every second since I arrived yesterday."

Yes, she had been. And Violet had tracked Geoffrey quite closely, as well. I couldn't believe I hadn't noticed that until now.

Or rather, that I hadn't considered what it meant.

"We wanted to make certain that you couldn't get to her!" Olivia shouted, her face blotchy with rage. "We planned it before we came here! She wouldn't tell us who it was—"

Her eyes flicked from one man to the other again, and ended up back on Reggie, "—but we knew it had to be one of you!"

"Doesn't sound like she's ready to confess to murder," I whispered to Christopher out of the corner of my mouth, "does it?"

He shook his head. "Clearly not."

But if not Olivia, then who?

Olivia seemed to be thinking the same thing—*if not Reggie, then who?*—because she assessed Geoffrey before pinning Bilge, who was hovering uncertainly in the background, with a fulminating glare. "I haven't forgotten you, you know!"

"Don't, Livvy," Serena said. Her hand was tight on her husband's sleeve, but her voice was even. "He didn't do it. I've been with him all day. I was with him all last night, as well. I know we talked about the possibility—"

Bilge turned his head and fixed his wife with an appalled look. "You thought that *I*—?"

"Not now, Bilge," Serena said, but I could see her fingers flex as she squeezed his arm. She added, calmly, "We weren't even at your table for tea, Livvy. Neither of us had the opportunity to put anything in Violet's cup. The only ones who did—"

She didn't finish the sentence. She didn't have to, because Olivia's head swung back to Reggie and to Geoffrey, the only two of them who had been at her and Violet's table. I could practically see her tongue flick out to taste-test their guilt.

Reggie raised his hands. "I promise, Liv. I didn't do it. I would never hurt Violet, and I never had anything to do with Cecily."

Olivia stared at him, so intently that she appeared to be trying to look inside him. Whatever she found there, seemed to be enough to allow her to dismiss him after a final probing glance. Reggie deflated a bit, or at least his shoulders sank a millimeter or two once her attention was off him.

"You," she said to Geoffrey, vicious as a viper.

He shook his head even as he gave her the sort of fatuous smile one might give to something very young and quite cute, not to be taken seriously. The equivalent of a patronizing pat on the head. "Now, Livvy..."

Olivia puffed up like an angry budgerigar, and her voice approached the range that only dogs can hear. "Don't you 'now, Livvy' me, you bastard! You killed my best friend!"

Lady Euphemia winced, whether at the accusation, the epithet, or both.

Geoffrey shook his head. "No, I didn't. Nobody killed Violet, Livvy. Violet isn't dead."

Olivia stomped her foot on the floor. It made quite a satisfying sound, I had to say. "Not Violet, you pillock. *Cecily!* You dosed Cecily with pennyroyal, and you bashed Dom over the head, and you put poison in Violet's tea so she couldn't tell on you!"

Lady Euphemia gasped and Laetitia paled, but Geoffrey merely shook his head. "No, I didn't."

Olivia looked ready to kill him, and I sympathized. I wanted to grab his shoulders and shake him until something useful came out, too.

"Well, if you didn't," she hissed, "who did?"

Yes, that was the question, wasn't it? If it truly had been someone at their table, then it was either Geoffrey or the Honorable Reggie, Olivia or Violet herself.

Was it possible that Violet had dosed her own tea? If she had killed Cecily and Dominic Rivers, once Tom arrived and she realized that she wasn't likely to avoid going to prison for it, could she have decided to take that way out?

But if so, who had put the empty vial in her nightstand? The pennyroyal would have been in it, I assumed, until it was in the cup of tea, and she would have had to have had it at the table, and she hadn't, as far as I could recall, left the table during the time we had sat there...

"Let me try, Livvy," Crispin's voice said, and when I looked over, he had put a hand on Olivia's arm and was tugging her away.

Laetitia's eyes narrowed, and so did Olivia's—probably for different reasons—but she stepped back. "I suppose of all of us, you speak his language," she said viciously.

Crispin, who would have taken offence had I said the same thing to him, merely gave Olivia's arm a little pat—"I suppose I do, old bean,"—before he turned to his future brother-in-law. "Geoffrey, old chap."

Geoffrey beamed back at him. "St George. There you are."

"Yes," Crispin said, "here I am," as if he hadn't been standing right next to Geoffrey this whole time. "Tell me, Geoffrey, do you remember the last weekend in April? The Jungman sisters were having a Black and White party, and we played Nebuchadnezzar charades?"

Geoffrey nodded. "Of course I do, old chap. That was when you had to do the banana dance on top of the coffee table, wasn't it? Jolly good bash."

"Yes, it was," Crispin agreed dryly, even as the top of his cheekbones burned. I snorted—Josephine Baker's *Danse Sauvage* was a bit of a joke between us, and I would rather have liked to have seen the coffee table performance—and he flicked a glance my way before turning back to Geoffrey. "You went home with Cecily at the end of the night, didn't you?"

Geoffrey opened his mouth, and then closed it again. "Did I?"

"You did, old bean." Crispin sounded almost apologetic. "She was a bit unsteady on her feet, you know, and needed some help, and you said you'd get her home."

Geoffrey chewed on his lip, while on the other side of the foyer, his mother gave a horrified bleat.

"Did Cecily tell you that she was expecting?" Crispin asked gently.

Geoffrey shook his head. "She didn't, old chap."

"Did someone else tell you?"

Geoffrey's eyes flicked to Olivia, and then away again. "Violet mentioned something about it last night. I asked her why Cecily looked like a wrung out dishrag, and she said it was because she was having a baby."

Olivia shifted on her feet, clearly offended on Cecily's behalf, but she didn't say anything.

"Cecily did look ill last night," Crispin agreed, diplomatically. "But you didn't know about it before then?"

Geoffrey hesitated. After a moment, he admitted, "I may have heard something. Not from Cecily."

"From whom?"

"Letty," Geoffrey said, with a glance at his sister. Laetitia looked thunderstruck for a moment, but then she tossed her head. The ends of her black bob swayed, and so did the ornate diamond earrings weighing down her lobes. They matched the Sutherland engagement ring, so Crispin must have handed over the ostentatious Sutherland parure in its entirety.

"It wasn't a secret," she said shrilly. "Nobody said I couldn't talk about it."

"I was merely curious why you hadn't mentioned it to me," Crispin told her, although none of us needed an answer to that, as the reason was obvious: Laetitia had been worried that Crispin was the father of Cecily's baby, and if so, that she wouldn't get to keep him.

And it seemed as if she had decided to keep him, as well as herself, in ignorance, rather than face the issue head on.

"I didn't go near Cecily last night, old chap," Geoffrey offered. "We danced one dance, but that was it, and it was in front of everybody. Violet hung on my arm the rest of the time. She even stood at her door and watched me walk to the top of the stairs when I took her upstairs at the end of the night. It would have been as much as my life's worth to make a detour, I reckon."

He smirked.

"So we heard," Crispin said, with a flicker of a look at Olivia. She stared back, belligerent.

"I told you. We knew that one of you was responsible, and we were worried that something would happen. Cecily said that the chap, whoever he was, wouldn't be happy."

The glare she leveled at the four men was fulminating.

"Not it," Reggie said again, his hands up in the universal

signal of surrender. "You know I'm not, Livvy. I was with you all night. I couldn't have done anything to Cecily."

"But you brought Dom," Olivia said bitterly. "Him and his paraphernalia."

Reggie shook his head. "I only motored down with him, Liv. It wasn't me who invited him. That was St George's doing."

"I may have made the suggestion," Crispin said, "but the formal invitation came from someone else. And I certainly didn't ask him to bring anything for Cecily."

He waited a moment before he added, "I spent the evening with Laetitia. All of you watched me. The only time I spoke to Cecily was when she made her felicitations when she and Violet arrived. I did make it to her room by the end of the night, but that was the first I heard about the pregnancy."

In the silence that followed that pronouncement, we could hear Laetitia whimper softly while her mother cooed and shot daggers at Crispin.

"Bilge was with me all night," Serena said. "He danced with Cecily once, but unless she died of trampled toes, he's not to blame." She smirked, and then added, more seriously, "Neither of us went near the kitchen for any cup of tea."

"Whoever did that," Bilge added, showing a modicum of intelligence for the first time this weekend, "must have done Violet, too. That couldn't have been us, either. We weren't at her table for tea."

And thus we were back to Reggie, Olivia, and Geoffrey. The three people who had shared Violet's table and who had had access to Violet's teacup.

"It was him," Olivia said, indicating Geoffrey. "It had to be. It wasn't me, and I'll swear that it wasn't Reggie. I watched him all night last night. And besides, if Crispin is right and Geoffrey took Cecily home after the Jungman sisters' bash..."

Then he was almost certainly the father of her baby. The timing worked, and who was responsible for this weekend's tragedy, if not the man who had taken her to bed?

"Violet watched me last night," Geoffrey said again, stubbornly. "And we sat at the same table for tea today, Livvy. Did you see me put anything in Violet's cup?"

She hadn't, of course. She couldn't admit it, so she didn't shake her head, but she sank her teeth into her bottom lip and refused to look at him, or at anyone else. Her anger about it was practically palpable.

And that was that. We had reached an impasse. It was clear that Olivia thought Geoffrey was guilty, or at least that she wanted him to be. But even if he had seduced Cecily, or had taken advantage of her when she was sozzled, and even if her predicament had been his fault, if we couldn't put the pennyroyal in Geoffrey's hand, and if no one had seen that hand hovering over Cecily's or Violet's tea, there was no way to pin it on him.

Besides, it was still possible that Olivia was the guilty party, the way Christopher and I had posited in the drawing room, and she was simply very good at shifting suspicion away from herself.

"What we need," I said, "is someone who had access to the tea this afternoon, and to Violet's room, and who knew where the pennyroyal grew, and who could come and go in the kitchen, and who could give Cecily a cup of tea without raising suspicion; someone who wasn't under scrutiny last night..."

As I spoke, everyone's attention shifted onto Olivia. It took her a second to realize it, and then her eyes widened. She shook her head frantically. "No! I wouldn't. They're my best friends. I've lost both of my best friends today. I wouldn't!"

"I wasn't talking about you," I said.

Olivia opened her mouth to ask me who I had been talking

about, but before she could, footsteps on the stairs made us all turn in that direction. And at that point the question answered itself.

"Well done, Miss Darling," Tom told me, as he descended the staircase from the first floor, with his hand wrapped around Nellie's upper arm. Collins walked on the other side of her, his face impassive. "Means and opportunity before motive."

"Motive still matters, though," I answered, with my eyes on the maid. She looked as put-together and lovely as always, with not a hair out of place under her cap. "I know she could have done it. She's the maid, and nobody ever pays attention to the maid. What I want to know, is why."

"Lord Geoffrey," Tom said, as the threesome stepped off the staircase and onto the foyer floor. Perhaps he thought that that cleared it up, or perhaps he simply wanted Geoffrey's attention. If so, he didn't get it. Geoffrey was staring at Nellie, his eyes wide and his mouth open. I was pretty certain I could see fear flickering in his eyes.

"But I asked you," Constance burst out. "I asked you whether Geoffrey had been a bother."

"And I told you," Nellie said, with her head held high, "that he hadn't. Geoffrey has never been a bother."

She sent a saucy wink Geoffrey's way. Geoffrey's mother moaned, and Geoffrey's jaw clenched. "You... but you..."

I met Constance's eyes across the foyer and knew she was thinking the same thing I was. I had always found it strange that Nellie had been here as long as she had without running afoul Lord Geoffrey and his attempts at seduction. I knew from before that Mrs. Frobisher had a problem keeping female staff for longer than a month because of Geoffrey's proclivities. It didn't make sense that Nellie hadn't been targeted. But now it turned out that all along it had simply been a matter of semantics, and of Nellie twisting the meaning of the words to make us think something that wasn't true.

Yes, of course Geoffrey would have pursued Nellie immediately. She was young and pretty and available, right under his nose. Precisely his type.

"You got the vial from Mr. Rivers before supper," Tom told Geoffrey, "and you passed it on to Nellie. She used it on Miss Fletcher last night, and then put what was left in Lady Violet's cup during tea this afternoon."

Yes, of course. It wasn't just the people at Violet's table who could have put something in Violet's tea. It was the person who filled the cup, too. I should have realized that much sooner than I did. I had been looking at all the guests with suspicion, but had ignored the maid flitting about. I had even mentioned to Christopher earlier how easy it would have been for Nellie to do it all, but without seriously considering that she might have done.

I had watched her bring Constance a cup of tea in the ballroom last night, and still hadn't put two and two together.

"But why?" I asked. "I understand about Cecily, I suppose. Geoffrey wanted the baby gone, and procured the pennyroyal, and then asked you to put it in her drink or food that night..."

Nellie smirked. "It was easy. She was tired and out of sorts after the dancing. I offered to make her a cuppa to settle her stomach and help her sleep. Geoffrey—" She glanced at him from under her lashes, as lovely a sight as one could wish for, "—only wanted to get rid of the baby. But I thought it would be better to get rid of the girl, too."

The obvious conclusion—*less competition for me*—was left unsaid, but I think we all heard it. Lady Euphemia made a sound like something that was trodden on: not a squeal, but a gentle sigh, as if all the air left her body.

"And then you killed Dominic Rivers," I said, "I suppose because he was the one who sold Geoffrey the pennyroyal?"

"That," Nellie said, "and he saw Geoffrey come out of my room late last night." She gave him a look from under her lashes. "I thought it would be better if he didn't have a chance to tell anyone."

That explained Rivers's smirk when he had caught Crispin coming out of my room, anyway. What was it that he had said? *People popping out of rooms all over the place,* wasn't it?

"That's how you knew that the vase was broken," I said. "You weren't supposed to have been up on the second floor, but you knew to come upstairs with a replacement."

This time it was Tom who nodded. "Thank you for pointing that out earlier, Miss Darling. Without that bit of evidence, this might have taken a lot longer."

"Her fingerprints were on it," I said. "Constable Collins asked about them."

"Yes. But as she pointed out, she dusted that vase every week. Of course her fingerprints would be on it."

"But not on the vial."

Tom shook his head. "She had to wipe Lord Geoffrey's fingerprints off that. And of course make sure that her own didn't get on it. Everyone knows about fingerprints these days. But she wasn't able to get Violet's prints onto the vial. She had to take it upstairs while Violet was still at table."

He flicked a glance at Nellie, who made a face, before turning back to me. "Any other questions?"

"Just one," I said. "Whatever did Violet do to be sentenced to death? She wasn't expecting anyone's baby, and she didn't know about the affair or the pennyroyal or Dominic Rivers or anything. Why kill her?"

"She wouldn't leave him alone," Nellie said before anyone

else could answer, her eyes possessive on Geoffrey's face. "I watched her last night, clinging to his arm and making eyes at him. She had to go, too."

I stared at her, appalled. "She was simply trying to protect her friend, you nitwit. She wasn't interested in Lord Geoffrey!"

And he wasn't interested in Nellie, as anything other than a convenient shag. Just the way he had gone through all the other Marsden Manor maids.

I didn't have it in me to explain it to her, though. Not now, and not in front of everyone. The reality of it would catch up to her soon enough, I reckoned. Probably when Geoffrey started to shift as much of the blame as he could off himself and onto her.

Any moment now, most likely.

Tom ignored the exchange. He had already turned away from me. "Lord Geoffrey? Perhaps you wouldn't mind accompanying us down to the village? We have a few questions we would like to ask in a more formal setting."

It was phrased as a question, and sounded reasonably polite. It was, in fact, an order, and non-negotiable. Geoffrey paled. "But I didn't do anything. It was all her!"

"As it turns out," Tom said, "that's not entirely true. She'll certainly spend the rest of her life behind bars for murder. But there's a separate charge for procuring drugs or other means to cause an abortion, and by Nellie's statement, you're guilty of it."

He let that hang for a moment while Geoffrey opened and closed his mouth, apparently speechless. When nothing came forth, Tom added, "It comes with a prison term of three years. After you, Lord Geoffrey."

He gestured Geoffrey towards the front door. Collins preceded them, with Nellie's arm still in a tight grip—the bow at the back of her uniform still swayed invitingly with every step—and Tom brought up the rear.

The moment the door shut behind them, Lady Euphemia turned to her husband with a wail. "Maury...!"

Lord Maurice nodded and patted her hand. "I'll go ring up Eustace, shall I?"

"Please, Maury. We have to get him out of there, the poor boy."

I rolled my eyes. Lord Maurice headed across the foyer towards the study and the telephone. "Pardon me," he muttered as he skirted us and kept going.

Christopher arched his brows. "Barrister?"

I shrugged. "I assume so. Or the Chief Constable, perhaps. Someone who can do something to get Geoffrey out of the police station in one piece."

"Can anyone get Geoffrey out of the police station in one piece, do you suppose?"

"I have no idea," I said. "He didn't plan to kill anyone, so he shouldn't have to worry about a murder charge, but there's still the Section 59 issue."

On the other side of the room, Laetitia sniffed, offended, and put out a hand. "Darling?"

"Yes," I said, eyeing it.

Crispin smirked. He was standing a few feet away from us, and had been since the showdown began. "I imagine she means me, Darling."

"Yes, of course she does. Don't let me keep you."

I flapped a hand at him. He inclined his head and started across the floor. As soon as he was within reach, Laetitia latched onto him. Olivia, meanwhile, had allowed Reggie to take hold of her. When he steered her away from the rest of us towards the hallway to the study and drawing room, it became a sign for everyone else too, and the rest of the gathering broke up into small, chattering groups. His Grace the Duke of Sutherland patted Lady Euphemia's hand sympathetically, and Laetitia kept a tight hold on Crispin as she pulled him over next to them.

"Shall we?" Christopher inquired, eyes on his parents, and on Francis and Constance next to them.

I nodded, but before I could take more than a single step, Wolfgang stepped up next to me.

"Philippa." He clicked his heels together. "May I have a word?"

I smiled. "Of course you may. Go on, Christopher. I'll catch up in a moment."

Christopher nodded and let go of my hand, but not without a look back over his shoulder. I waited until he was outside the range of hearing before I added, "What can I do for you, *Graf* von Natterdorff?"

Wolfgang smirked, but didn't comment on my use of his title. "That was very impressive, *Freulein* Schatz."

"Thank you," I said, "but I didn't do much. It was just a matter of putting the information together at the last moment, and—"

He shook his head. "You are an impressive girl, Philippa."

"Thank you," I said again, "but—"

He reached out and put a finger across my mouth. "The kind of girl any man would be proud to call his own."

That managed to shut me up, anyway. My eyes widened, and while I still thought the words—*Thank you, but*—I couldn't utter them, not with his finger holding my mouth shut.

And then he took what remained of my breath when he added, "I would be honored if you would consent to be my wife, Philippa Marie Schatz."

For a second, it felt as if the world stopped. Behind me, someone squealed. I couldn't tell whether it was Christopher, Constance, or Aunt Roz, or perhaps someone else entirely. All I could do was stare deeply into Wolfgang's eyes while he stared deeply into mine, and while the words echoed in my head.

FROM THE AUTHOR

Dear Reader,

As always, the requisite note about the language. This book is a mish-mash of British and American English. Pippa is British; or mostly. I'm not, and the British English I learned as a child has mostly worn off after almost 40 years in the US, although over the course of writing these books I have found myself reverting to some of the Britishisms of my youth. I told my husband it was too early to knock up our son the other morning.

At any rate, this book spells words like color and honor in the American way, without the u, because that's what I deal with in my daily life. At the same time, I try to stick to the British words for things instead of the American ones, and as a result, we also have words like budgerigars instead of parakeets, plasters instead of Band-Aids, and frocks instead of dresses. Marsden Manor has three floors: ground, first, and second. Pippa's guestroom is on the second, or top, floor, but to an American, it would be the third. I'm sorry if it's confusing.

Now, for the other references:

Rodolfo Pietro Filiberto Raffaello Guglielmi di Valentina d'Antonguella, better known by his stage name of Rudolph Valentino, died unexpectedly on August 23rd, 1926, a few weeks before the beginning of this book. The Latin Lover, star of silent movies like *The Sheikh*, *Son of the Sheikh*, and *Blood and Sand*, was only a few months past his 31st birthday when he succumbed to peritonitis. His death would have been recent, and fresh on Pippa's mind when she mentions him.

The word 'fan' is likely a shortened form of the word 'fanatic,' which comes from the Latin word *fanaticus*, which means 'insanely but divinely inspired.' It sounds modern, but dates back to around 1647. The word was first used in US baseball circles in the 1880s, so also well ahead of Pippa's use of it in the fall of 1926.

The Chinese do, indeed, mourn in white. I know this for a funny reason: When I got married, eons ago, in New York City, my future husband suggested that I might wear a white Chinese dress. I have no idea why, as neither of us have any Chinese in our backgrounds, but perhaps he thought I'd look good in it. And of course I wanted to make him happy, so off I went to Chinatown, where there were no white dresses on display. When I asked, they told me it was because white is for mourning and it's bad luck to have a white dress made up ahead of time. I ended up getting married in pink. In western tradition, of course, white is for weddings. Yes, Christopher did have an ulterior motive for decking Pippa out in ivory at Crispin and Laetitia's engagement party, although the mourning works too, in a way.

The verb 'to puke' may sound modern, but it dates back to the 1600s. Shakespeare is sometimes credited with inventing it, but its first use predates the Bard, to the book *Hawking, Hunting and Fishing*, which was published in Britain in 1586.

Pirandello is a variation of the game charades, one that was popular in London in the 1920s. Instead of acting out the title of a book, movie, or song, as in the modern version, the task was to act out a personality. Nebuchadnezzar charades was also popular at the time, and the goal in that version was to guess the name of a famous person while each player in turn depicted a well-known character whose initial letter formed part of the final word. Crispin, I assume, would have been going for J.

The plant pennyroyal has been used as a natural abortifacient for thousands of years (and still is, by people who want a natural substitute for the medical intervention). It is currently protected in England as a species of 'principal importance for the purpose of conserving biodiversity,' and as such, is illegal to pick or uproot. It is also illegal to collect pennyroyal seeds. In high doses, pennyroyal is extremely toxic. A tablespoon of pennyroyal oil is enough to kill an adult, and once taken, there is no cure. Smaller doses, even ones as small as steeping the leaves for tea, can kill infants and children.

Beecham's Pills were a laxative first patented in England in 1842 by Thomas Beecham. Among the things they treated, according to the box, was 'female ailments.' They consisted mainly of a mixture of ginger, aloe, and soap. SmithKline Beecham produced them until 1998. The more discreetly marketed Dr. Vandenburgh's Female Renovating Pills, as well as the rather aptly named French Periodical Pills, are also no longer in production, but they were available through mail-order in the mid- to late-1800s, during Lady Roslyn's salad days.

Abortion was, at this time, illegal in England. In the Middle Ages, common law held that life began at 'quickening'—when the unborn child was able to stir in the womb—and up until that point, it was not illegal to induce an abortion. But in 1803, abortion was codified in statute law through the *Malicious*

Shooting or Stabbing Act, which imposed penalties up to death for causing the miscarriage of a woman 'quick with child' as well as penalties up to penal transportation for causing the miscarriage of any woman 'not being, or not being proved to be, quick with child'. After that, the *Offenses Against the Person Act* of 1861 detailed two offences as related to abortion: the first being 'the administering of drugs or using instruments to procure an abortion', a crime which allowed for a sentence of life imprisonment, and secondly, 'the procuring of drugs or any other means to cause abortion', which had a potential sentence of three years' imprisonment. It was not until 1967, and the *Abortion Act*, that abortion in England became legal in some, but not all, cases.

————

ABOUT THE AUTHOR

New York Times and *USA Today* bestselling author Jenna Bennett has written more than fifty books, most of them in the genres of mystery and suspense. The Pippa Darling historical cozy mysteries is her most recent project.

For more information, please visit her website,
www.jennabennett.com